THE POLLENSA CONNECTION

Pete Davies

Ebook AISN: B0977PDSQ1
Paperback ISBN-13: 979-8515059392
Hardcover ISBN-13: 979-8516762093

Cover design by: Brian Tarr
(brian-tarr.pixels.com)

*To my dear wife, for her everlasting love,
together with her support and help with my writing*

THE 3R INTERNATIONAL SERIES

This is the second book in the 3R International series.

It isn't necessary to read The Mallorcan Bookseller first, however, it obviously provides the back stories to the main 3R characters, so for that reason, some readers may prefer to read the books in order.

1

"Is Anna in?"

The same three words that had been the start of a new life for him just a few weeks ago.

He looked at her and remembered her face.

"It's Mrs Green isn't it? I'm Sam, Anna's son."

She went to answer, but the tears started again and she almost stumbled.

"Here, sit down and I'll get some tea on. Mum will be in soon."

He grabbed a chair and helped her to sit down.

"He told me not to come. My husband I mean, but I don't know what to do. I'm so worried. I've been to the police, but they say it's too early to do anything and that she's a grown woman anyway."

"Here, have some tea and tell me what's happened," said Sam.

"It's my granddaughter, Lily. She's not been home for two days."

*****

Lily recovered consciousness. She wasn't sure where she was for a moment. Then she remembered.

'Oh my God, no!'

Her mind flashed back to cycling along the road into

town, into Puerto Pollensa. They'd taken her just after she'd set off to meet Mateo.

She tried to think.

'How long have I been here?'

It was like she was in a dream. But it wasn't a dream, it was a nightmare! It had been Wednesday lunchtime, but God knows what day it was now.

She felt her arm and looked down to see the needle marks. How many times had they given her some drug or other? And what the hell was it?

'Oh please don't make me a junkie!'

She looked around the room. It had a single bed in it. The room was small, with one window that was shuttered up. There was no other furniture, except for a bowl on the floor. She squirmed, as she remembered his words.

"Use that if you need a crap in the night. Good luck with the smell."

Even when she did ask to go to the toilet, he stood there with the door open and watched her, enjoying her embarrassment. But whilst she'd accepted that she might need to pee in the bowl at night, so far, thank God, she'd at least been able to control her bowels so as to not need to go until the morning.

It was hard to think, but there was a little bit of sunlight coming through the wooden shutters, so she thought it might be two nights she'd been there.

Hard to think? Not surprising, given her body was full of drugs. She felt tears welling up again. Now she was shaking.

'Why me? What do they want with me?'

*****

Sam handed Helen Green a mug of tea and sat down opposite her and waited until she was ready.

"You're the policeman aren't you?" she asked.

"Well yes, you're partly right Mrs Green," said Sam

Martínez with a smile. "I was in the police, at least up until a few weeks ago, but I'm not any longer. I'm now back home to help Mum run the business."

Again, he waited. He could see she was calmer now. Her breathing was easier and the tears had stopped.

"But you know about people going missing don't you? You were some sort of detective?"

"I was and yes, I do know something about people going missing, so tell me what's happened with Lily. She's your granddaughter?"

"Yes, she's been out with us for.....it must be six or seven months now, after she finished her Masters."

"And you say she's not been home for two days?" said Sam.

"No, she went to work on Wednesday and I haven't seen her since. I'm worried sick that something has happened to her."

"Yes, of course, you must be. Now, first things first. You've got a fairly typical response from the police the world over. They won't look to get involved for the first few days, not unless there's something about the person who has gone missing that brings in another consideration. You know, maybe if someone had seen her being taken against her will, or if she was worrying about something. Now, I'm assuming you'd have told me if someone had seen her being taken, but was she worrying about anything?"

"No, I don't think so," said Mrs Green.

"What about how she's been acting? Any change in her behaviour at all?"

"Not that I've really noticed. She's pretty much been on cloud nine for the past month or so, after she met Mateo. She's been spending a lot of time with him, so we haven't actually seen that much of her."

"Do you know where Mateo lives?" said Sam gently.

"Oh, you don't think he's involved in this do you?"

Her voice had gone tight and she'd sat bolt upright.

"I'm just working through what we know at the moment Mrs Green. Now in a lot of cases, people just turn up back at home, having just needed some space. So let's keep looking at what might have led to Lily not coming home. That's why I asked about Mateo, presumably this is a boyfriend?"

Mrs Green nodded.

"Well maybe she's just spending some time with him and her mobile's gone flat."

"Okay, right, yes, I understand. I'm sorry Sam, my mind's just running away with me. And please, it's Helen, call me Helen."

At that moment, the doorbell over the entrance to Sa Petita Llibreria, 'the Little Bookshop', rang. He looked up to see his mother coming in. She looked at him quizzically when she saw her friend sitting next to him.

"Helen, how lovely to see you," said Anna Martínez.

"Anna, I'm so sorry to bother you, it's......."

The words stopped and the tears flowed down Helen Green's cheeks again.

"Helen's granddaughter, Lily, hasn't been home for two days," said Sam quietly.

Anna looked quickly at Sam for any indication as to what he thought and he just gently raised his hands to signify he didn't have much to go on at the moment.

"Have you told Susan and Keith?" said Anna.

"Yes, I didn't know if we should, because I knew it would only worry them. But when she didn't come home yesterday, I rang and told them. They're in Australia you see Sam, they moved there two years ago with Susan's job."

"It was best to tell them," said Sam. "Do you know if they are going to come here?"

"They've got a flight booked tomorrow lunchtime."

"Let's get back to looking at what Lily had been doing last week shall we?" said Sam. "Do you know where this Mateo lives, or do you possibly have a mobile number for him?"

"It's somewhere in Palma, but I don't know where and I've no idea about a phone number. Whenever I ring Lily's, it just goes to voicemail and…."

Sam saw Helen had started rambling again and he let her settle again before continuing.

"When was the last time you, or your husband saw Lily."

"It was Wednesday morning, when she went to work," said Helen.

"Where does she work?"

"I'm not sure of the name, Global something or other. She cycles to work. It's about two or three miles away from where we live. It's some sort of research place, out on the road to Pollensa."

Sam looked at Anna.

"Helen lives just outside Puerto Pollensa."

"Have you managed to speak to her work?" said Sam.

"Well, I tried and they were most unhelpful. They did say that as far as they knew she had left the office as usual on Wednesday."

"And they weren't worried about her not turning up at work on Thursday?" said Sam.

"Oh, I don't know, I didn't think to ask them that. How could I not ask such a basic question? Oh, Anna, I'm falling apart. How can I explain to Susan we've lost her? She must be worried sick."

Anna gently took her hands. Helen was getting herself more and more worked up.

"It's okay Helen. We can help now. But we need to look at where to start, so we've got to go through these questions," said Anna.

Helen took a few deep breaths and forced a smile.

"I know. I'm glad I've got you two to help."

Sam gently asked another question.

"Now, what about a car? Does either Lily or Mateo have one?"

"Well Mateo came to the house one day in a very flashy sports car. It was yellow and very loud, but that's all I can tell you. Lily uses our car when she needs to, but most of the time she cycles everywhere," said Helen.

"Is her bike at home at the moment?" said Sam.

"No, well not the one she uses for work, but she's also got another one, a racing type – that's still at home."

"What about other friends Helen? Who else does she know out here?" said Anna.

"There's probably quite a few friends, because she's been coming out to see us since she was knee high. But as regards close friends," she paused, "I think that would be Katie and Bertie. Both their parents have houses in Puerto Pollensa and Lily would play with them when she was out here on holiday with us. I know that since she's been back she's seen Katie, although I'm not so sure about Bertie, but I think they both work on the island."

"Let's just do one more question and then I can start making some phone calls Helen. Do you know how she got this job at Global whatever they are called?"

"It was through a friend of Keith's, her dad. Keith will be able to tell you, but what's that got to do with anything, shouldn't we just be out there looking for her?"

Once again, the strain had pushed her emotions to the limit and the tears were flowing again. Anna gently held her.

"Sam knows what he's doing Helen. We can't just go

out blindly looking can we? But what we can do is start with the basics, okay?" said Anna.

"Mum's right Helen. We're going to follow you back to your home and I'll have a look around Lily's room and I'd like you and Mum to start walking towards the research place where she works. Make sure you keep to the right hand side of the road where she would've been cycling and then once there, turn around and come back the other way."

He knew giving Helen something to think about was a good way of keeping her occupied, to take her mind off constantly worrying about Lily.

"Now where's your husband at the moment? At home?" said Sam.

"Yes, Geoffrey stayed there, just in case she came back," said Helen.

"Good thinking," said Sam. "Right, come on, let's get going. Helen, you set off and we'll catch you up. Mum, I'll get the car, if you can lock up the shop. I don't suppose we'll miss many customers today, seeing as we haven't had one since Wednesday," he winked at his mother, who just pulled a face at him.

2

Groom's phone rang.

"So are we in trouble?" said Sir Charles Groom.

"We may have a problem, but at the moment I think we can put a lid on it," said Stephen Rawlings, his Head of Security.

"Putting a lid on it is not enough, not nearly enough Stephen."

"I meant to say….,"

Sir Charles Groom interrupted him before he could finish.

"Just see to it Stephen. You've had her for two days now. What's taking so bloody long?"

"I understand your impatience Sir Charles, but…"

"Well I bloody hope you do Stephen."

"If I can explain….," said Rawlings.

"Save your explanation until you've got something positive to tell me. Now, I've got a Board meeting in ten minutes and I don't need to remind you that the Board cannot get to hear about this."

The phone went dead and Rawlings looked at it.

'Of course I bloody understand, what do you think you pay me for?' he thought, but why waste his breath saying anything. He made a good living from Groom, so

why rock the boat when the old man occasionally blew a gasket. This latest issue was, to be fair, more complex than usual and had a whole lot more things riding on it, but it wasn't anything he couldn't handle. Marsden was managing the risk strategy well and bit by bit, he was working through the plan they had put together.

Yes, it was taking longer than he thought. But he had a good feeling about this and the promised bonus from Groom was looking a good bet.

*****

Tom Marsden looked at her. He had done this sort of thing a good few times before and he could see she still had some fight in her, even after two days. So far she'd given up the information Marsden thought she had, but Rawlings wanted to make absolutely sure that she had nothing else to give, even if she wasn't aware of the importance of whatever that might be.

He put his balaclava back on and shook her. Lily stirred.

She couldn't help but flinch when she saw him above her. It was him again. Even with a balaclava on, she could see his eyes. Cold, cruel eyes. She hated being left alone with him. The other one, the older one, the one with a posher voice, at least gave her some sense that when he was there, the cold-eyed one wouldn't do anything other than asking questions and occasionally slapping her across the face.

A thought suddenly occurred to her. He only ever seemed to slap her. Yes, it was a hard slap, but she hadn't actually been really hurt by it.

And the questions? It took her a time, because they went around the houses asking who she knew and who her boyfriend was, before she'd realised that this was something to do with work. Then she'd told them all she knew, but she couldn't tell if they believed her.

"Come on, get up!" said Marsden, his voice rough

9

and harsh.

Lily stood up and tried to stand still, her legs still unsteady.

He put the cloth sack over her head again.

Even though he was wearing a balaclava, she had to wear this sack every time he moved her from the room, even to go to the toilet. Was it because she might see something out of a window? Or maybe it was so she couldn't describe anything about where she was being held? She'd seen enough TV and films to know that if you didn't see their faces, then there was maybe, just maybe, a chance they would let you go. She clung to that thought, as the alternative was, well just something she couldn't handle.

She felt Marsden take hold of her right elbow and she then followed his lead. They went first into some sort of hallway and then turned left into the 'other' room, the 'questions' room. She felt the door frame brush against her shoulder and she felt the tiles again on her bare feet, as she came off a carpet or a rug. The tiles were cold, so probably porcelain or ceramic maybe?

'Am I some sort of finca?'

He guided her to the chair. She sat down and waited. Same as before. He tied her to the arms and legs of the chair with some sort of tape. Then she felt a pin prick in her arm.

"Now Lily, let's just check a few things should we?"

She just looked forwards, towards the sound of the voice, the same one as before. Not the posh one, but the one who had kept hitting her.

"I hope you can tell that I've tried not to hurt you?" said Marsden.

She didn't answer. She was trying to work out whether being filled full of drugs and occasionally slapped constituted being hurt.

"Have I?" he said again, but louder and she flinched as she sensed him taking a step forward.

Marsden saw the hood move as she nodded her head and made a sound that he took for '*Yes*'.

He took the hood off her head and saw her squinting as her eyes tried to quickly adapt to the sunlight.

"Now just at this moment in time Lily, you have something in your body called sodium thiopental. Do you know what that is?"

She looked down at the syringe in her arm and thought for a moment. She tried to get her mind to focus. '*Sodium thiopental. Come on, you're a chemist, what the hell is it?*'

Marsden saw her face suddenly change.

"Ah, you've got it, haven't you Lily. It's a truth drug, or at least that's what they call it in the movies. Now you and I know that this isn't guaranteed for you to tell me only the truth, but let's see how we get on shall we?"

He didn't wait for an answer.

"Now we do need to get you in to that twilight zone, just before you drift into unconsciousness. So we'll wait a few moments and I'll speak to you again in a minute," said Marsden.

She went to scream. She'd had enough. She'd fight it this time, but the drug was already flowing into her arm. She tried to fight it. Holding her head still, with her shoulders down, she tried to lift herself up. But then she felt a gentle pressure on her shoulders, not much, but just enough to stop her lifting her body up. Then she heard his voice again.

"Okay, there's no need to fight it. I think we're about there now aren't we Lily," he paused. "Are you feeling okay?"

She said, "No, I'm scared."

"Right answer."

He knew the effect of the drug was to make her

more inclined to talk. The drug affects the cortex, the decision-making area of the brain and lying isn't usually something that can be controlled. The brain doesn't think to lie, but it will strive to answer whatever question is put to it.

Marsden had used this often enough to know the potential for people to tell you what they think you want to hear. So how he phrased the questions was really important to avoid any sort of auto-suggestion.

He looked down at her. She was ready.

"Tell me again Lily, what is your job at Global Aggregates?"

"I'm a Chemical Investigator at the Research Centre in Mallorca," said Lily.

No hesitation from her there.

"How long have you worked there?"

"Nearly nine months."

"What are you currently working on?"

"We're investigating the Witterings Shopping Centre collapse," said Lily.

"Who were you working with?"

"Ian, Ian Parsons, my boss."

"What were you tasked to look at?"

"The Director, Paul Brooks, wanted to rule out any suggestion that GA had reduced the concrete cover level in the build."

He nodded. Basic questions, but she was compliant. He decided to go straight to it.

"Where did you find the file on Ultra-Fast-Dry30?"

There was a slight frown in her face.

'This again. Is this what this is all about?' she thought. Then she answered the question.

"It was in a document in a file from back in the mid-2000s."

"Where was this document?" said Marsden.

"There was a copy in a set of papers."

"What did it say?"

Lily thought for a moment.

"They outlined the projects undertaken during 2004 to 2006," said Lily. Her eyes flickered and she moved her head.

'*She's thinking,*' thought Marsden and he wondered about increasing the dose, but she'd had a fair bit already and he didn't want her going under, not yet at any rate.

"What server were these documents on Lily?"

"I found it first of all in the main GA server, but then I found a link to the secure server at the Research Centre, but I couldn't get in to that one."

"Why couldn't you get in to it?"

He knew the answer, but wanted to hear it from her.

"It's limited access only."

"Does Ian have access to this secure server?"

"Yes," said Lily.

"Who else?"

"I don't know."

Marsden frowned. Rawlings was not going to like this, not like it at all.

She probably didn't know who else had access, but he knew it would be Brooks, the Director of the Centre, but Parsons? He'd need to check that out and find out what he knew.

He looked down at her. If he'd had time he would have liked to have done more with this one. She was young and quite pretty. He felt his body stirring, the excitement, the control. He ran his hands up and down the side of her body. Even in her semi-conscious state she could feel his hands and he saw her eyes pop wide open as she sensed and realised what was happening.

"Maybe later Lily, maybe later."

She felt her body shudder again.

"Now who else did you tell about this file?" said

Marsden.

Her eyes were wide and staring, right at him. She could see the fear in her eyes, but she was fighting it though, fighting the drug.

"Now listen to me Lily Green. There is one reason and one reason only that you are not dead, do you know what that is?"

"No."

He took his phone out of his pocket and showed her a picture.

"Your grandparents Lily."

Fear in her eyes again. She could see them getting into their car at their house.

"Now you don't want anything to happen to them, do you?"

"No!"

Almost a scream, but her voice wouldn't let the noise come out. The drugs were letting her talk, in a low mumble, but when she tried to scream, nothing really happened, because it came out more like a slightly louder grunt.

"Okay, so now you understand. This little chat just needs to remain a secret between us, alright? If you tell anyone and I mean anyone, then you know we can take you at any time and therefore we can take your grandparents and if it comes to it, your parents too. Now do you think that is true?"

"Yes," she said slowly.

"I'm sorry, what did you say Lily?"

"Yes, yes! Please don't hurt them. I won't tell anyone. Just tell me what to do," said Lily.

'Fear,' thought Marsden. 'Such a powerful persuader.'

She saw his lips form a smile through the hole in the balaclava and felt a shockwave run through her body.

"I promise I won't tell anyone."

"That's good Lily."

He saw her head moving around again. The drug must be wearing off, as her senses were coming back. Time for a break before he had another go at her.

She felt a sharp prick. Another syringe in the arm.

"Sleep now, just sleep now Lily."

His voice sounded almost kind, she started to smile..., *'But he's not bloody kind! Somebody please help me!'* Again, she tried to scream, but the drug was kicking in again quickly and her head slipped, first to one side and then the other, before she quickly lost consciousness.

3

As he approached his car, Sam saw someone come from around the corner and start walking towards him. He didn't immediately recognise him, but when the young man looked up, their eyes locked on each other. It was one of the two guys who had tried to mug him a few weeks before.

Sam stared at him and the young man didn't hang about, but turned around and quickly ducked down the side alley he had just come from.

He thought back to what had happened with the two muggers. He'd lost his rag. Self-control had gone out the window and that wasn't good. He knew things were improving with how he was managing the PTSD, but, he still had a way to go and he still hadn't done anything about getting any sort of specialist help.

'*Why is that?*' he thought.

He'd told his mum he was going to do it. In fact he'd told pretty much everyone the same thing, which made it that much harder to understand. He'd been getting on great with Carmen, although as time went on he sensed they both seemed to be getting the same feeling that, whilst things between them were good, really good, her job search was very likely going to take her off the island.

He could see her face now, when they'd talked about it.

"So do you want to end this then?" she'd asked him outright.

"No, I'm just trying to help, to make sure…."

"Help? How is breaking up helping me Sam? I'm trying my best to understand and be there for you, but my God, you aren't making it easy."

"I was just trying to say that you shouldn't hold back from taking a job away from the island if…."

Again, she'd interrupted.

"If what Sam? If what? If it means more to me than you? I know we've only been together a few weeks, but don't forget how long we've known each other and I loved you then," said Carmen.

"But you were ten!" said Sam.

"But I loved you then and I love you now, so don't make it feel like you're pushing me away."

He reached his car and got in and sat for a moment. He hadn't wanted it to sound like he was giving her the brush-off, far from it, but he knew he screwed it up. Couple that with the fact that he'd found himself also questioning, whether he did actually want a relationship at the moment, and it left him confused and unsure where he was with Carmen.

'God, I'm such a messed up sod.'

After a couple of tries, he heard the distinctive sound of his VW fire up. The spark plugs needed looking at, again! He'd bought himself the VW Beetle a couple of weeks ago. It was all a bit rushed, but he'd been looking around and a friend of Miquel's rang him and told him about one going in Port d'Andratx. But he needed to act quickly if he wanted it, otherwise the guy was going to take it to the mainland where he had a buyer lined up there.

It was the classic light blue VW colour, but when

Sam had looked under the bonnet, he'd found the original colour was a metallic grey. It was a 1987 limited edition, a Europa 2, made by VW in Mexico and exported to Europe. Yes, it was getting on a bit in years, but Sam had always been pretty handy when it came to cars and he much preferred something he could work on himself, even if it meant getting his hands dirty.

It was burning a little bit of oil, so the plugs kept fouling up and every now and then, the starter motor needed a bit of attention to help get it started, but other than that it drove well. *'Other than that,'* he smiled to himself at the list of faults, but at least the rest of the electrics all worked okay.

The bookshop was only a minute or so away and he slowed, as he saw his mother waiting at the kerbside. She was on the phone as she got in next to him. Then as he pulled back into the line of traffic, she put her phone back into her handbag.

"That was Martin Carruthers."

"How is he?" asked Sam.

"He's good. He's been moved from Asia Pacific back to the London Office. A promotion he says, partly on the back of the success of recovering the money from the scam. He's delighted of course, except for the prospect of having to pay London prices for somewhere to live."

"Tell him he can have my place if he wants," joked Sam. "I can't seem to shift it for love nor money at the moment."

"He's coming across to see me. He's got a flight out tomorrow," said Anna.

"Hmm, wonder what that's about, but hey, it's secret squirrel stuff, so if you told me, you'd….."

"Have to shoot you, yes I know," said Anna, smiling. "Now, why have you jumped on this thing about Lily going missing Sam?"

"Good question. I don't know Mum. Just a hunch maybe. Something doesn't feel right. Helen is clearly beside herself too, so why not do some digging? If only to give her something to think about, rather than just sitting at home worrying."

"So do you think the boyfriend may be involved? Helen seems to think he's a nice young man."

"Who knows? But golden rule is always start with the basics. Find out what we know and what we don't know, then figure out what we need to do to fill in the gaps. Lily clearly knows her way around the island, especially if she's been coming here since she was a kid, so she's not likely to have just wandered off somewhere."

"I'm going to ask you something and you can tell me I'm barking up the wrong tree. But are you missing being in the police?" said Anna.

He looked ahead as he drove, but his mind was digesting the question and he realised he wasn't sure how to answer it.

"I'll be honest, I don't know. I don't think it's got anything to do with it, but maybe the job we did with Greg and Terri got the adrenalin juices flowing and since then, it's been a bit....."

"Too quiet?" Anna finished his sentence.

"Yes, I suppose so. Look, I'm not an adrenaline junkie, but I'd forgotten the high level of stress, and I suppose the excitement that I had when I was back in London. I am keen to get my teeth in to the business you and Dad have been managing and I've got some ideas I want to discuss with you about expanding certain elements of it. But yes, it's a big change from what I've been used to."

"I understand, so you must tell me if this doesn't work out for you. We can get someone in to manage the business, or just get Alfonso to do it full time, I'm sure he wouldn't mind."

"I'm fine Mum, honestly. Just give me a little bit of time to get myself sorted."

"Okay," said Anna. "And Sam?"

He looked across at her as he drove.

"Don't forget to get some help. You still haven't done anything about that, have you?"

He didn't answer, but kept looking straight ahead at the road as he branched off onto the Ma-13 for Alcúdia.

He knew she wanted to hear that he was going to get help. But that was the problem, he didn't feel ready to bare his soul, or at least that was how it felt, to some therapist. He felt he'd made some progress when he was at least able to talk about some of this stuff with Miguel and then Carmen, but he seemed to have hit a bit of a brick wall since then.

She let him drive on in silence for a while before she tried again.

"Sam?"

"Sorry Mum, I went off on one then," said Sam. "I thought I was making some progress…"

Anna went to interrupt, but he gently held up his hand.

"No, it's okay Mum, I've got to talk about this. I was making progress, much better than when I was back in London, but it's still in there, like a bloody ton weight hanging on my shoulders. But it is better. It comes and goes now and you, Carmen, Miquel and all the 3R guys have really helped, so I promise I'll do it. I'll get some help."

She smiled, nodded and patted his leg. She knew things were improving, but she also knew from experience that he had a way to go.

As she turned back, she saw the Honda Jazz ahead of them.

"That's Helen's car," said Anna, "the blue Honda."

He flashed his headlights and he saw Helen wave a hand in acknowledgement.

They were just pulling out of Alcúdia, so he followed Helen around the coast road towards Puerto Pollensa, or Port de Pollença, as the Mallorquins call it.

Sam looked across to his right, as the bay opened up and took in the scene of the wind-surfers and para-gliders catching the warm winds that blew hard across this part of the bay.

"Ever fancied that Mum? Para-gliding?"

"Not since I had a parachute fail on me one time."

"What?"

"It wasn't a great experience…," she tailed off.

"Bloody hell Mum, just how many stories have you got?"

She smiled at him, "Probably the same number as you, but let's talk about them another day shall we? Okay, we're almost here. Presumably you want to have a good look at Lily's room, so I'll keep Helen and Geoffrey busy."

"Good plan Mum."

4

Rawlings listened as Marsden briefed him on what Lily had given up in the latest line of questioning.

"Okay, but we need to be sure if there's anything else she knows and in particular, if she's told anyone else. What's your next move?"

"She's pretty dosed up at the moment, so I don't want to risk giving her anything else, so I think I'll go for a bit of shock treatment," said Marsden.

"That doesn't mean...." Rawlings started.

"No, boss, I know your rules well enough by now. No bruises, no bodies, no police," said Marsden.

"Good, so get to it and I'll come and join you in a bit. We can't keep her out of circulation for very much longer before the grandparents get very twitchy and the police get their hands forced to start looking and asking questions."

*****

'Time to take it to the next level,' thought Marsden, as he took the cloth sack off her head.

"Take your clothes off."

She knew it wasn't a request. He was barking an order at her.

Lily's head started to spin and she went to speak.

Marsden held up his finger to his lips.

She understood that sign. Shut up or get slapped.

"Good. Now either you take them off, or I will. Your choice. I know which I'd rather you chose, but I think you'll prefer option one. Got it?" sneered Marsden.

She didn't wait. She unzipped her skirt and let it fall to the floor, followed by her top. She hadn't looked at him, but she knew he was staring at her. She felt his eyes boring into her. It felt like he was looking over every inch of her body. Was this what she'd been dreading?

She hesitated for a moment, standing there in her underwear, just a plain white bra and pants. She saw him start to move towards her, so she quickly took them off and stood with her knees together and her hands down in front of her, trying to cover herself. She felt the tears streaming down her face.

"See, that was easy, wasn't it? Now put the sack on and let's go and play twenty questions again shall we?" said Marsden.

"Look, please listen to me. I don't know how I can help you if I don't know what you're looking for," said Lily.

"Sit down and put the sack on," he growled.

She took it off him, sat down on and pulled it over her head. She could still see shapes, but they were blurred and hard to make out.

"Now Lily, you've hit the nail on the head. You see, my boss thinks you do know what this is all about and I'll tell you something for free, you do not want to piss him off, okay?"

The chair was the same one as before. It was like a dining room chair, a big heavy wooden thing with arms, but without her clothes on, it felt hard and uncomfortable, so she tried to shift her position.

"Sit still."

Another order. She felt him put her hands onto the arms of the chair and then he bound them around with some sort of sticky tape, just as he'd done previously. He then ran his hand down the side of her thigh towards her ankle. She shuddered and tried to cross her legs, but he slapped her hard across her leg, before he grabbed her right ankle and secured that to the chair leg, before doing the same to her left.

He then left her there. She couldn't tell how long she waited. He hadn't done this before. Was it five, ten minutes, maybe more? She wanted to call out, to get him to ask her questions, but then again, she didn't know this time what else he might do.

He waited just a few steps behind her. He took his balaclava off and stood watching. Seeing how she reacted to this change in the process. Get them used to something and then disorientate them. Classic interrogation technique.

He could see her head and body twisting and turning, as she worked through in her head what might happen next. She was a pretty little thing he thought. But this was not the time to be thinking about that. Rawlings was getting impatient and wanted confirmation that she had nothing else to give up. He'd give her another ten minutes sitting there, before he started on her again. He smiled. He enjoyed this part of his job and he was good at it. Bloody good at it.

Lily sat back. She didn't know if he was there or not. She couldn't hear anything, but it was like she could sense he, or at least someone else, was in the room. Her mind started racing again. It was like she was watching a film running through her head - she was back on the road, where it had happened.

There had been a white van parked up along the side of the road, but she hadn't taken much notice of it. The road had been fairly quiet and she was enjoying the bike ride into town to see Mateo.

It had been so quiet and she'd heard some birds singing nearby. There had only been a few other cars on the road and....that was it! That was the last thing she'd heard. The white van suddenly came up behind her and had swerved right in front of her! She had nowhere to go, because of the ditch at the side of the road.

She had started to yell something at the driver, when the side opening door flew open. Two men jumped out, dressed in black and wearing balaclavas, and one of them grabbed her. They had a gag around her mouth before she'd had time to react and she was bundled into the van.

'Why had they taken her?'

She'd looked at them in vain, trying to understand what was happening.

'His eyes, oh my God, it was his eyes!'

Even with the balaclava on, the man who'd grabbed her..., he had such cold eyes. *'No, they're weren't cold,'* she shuddered, *'they were cruel'.*

*****

She suddenly came to, as Marsden shook her chair from behind.

She flinched.

She felt her nakedness and fear, yes fear. It was growing now. She could feel her body tensing and her feet and hands were getting colder and it wasn't just because she had no clothes on. No, this was different.

'Who was behind her?'

She heard his voice, the cruel one.

She went rigid and screamed as she felt his fingers running across the back of her shoulders.

"Please don't hurt me, please don't hurt me."

"Let's see how we get on this time shall we Lily?"

Marsden put his balaclava back on and walked around in front of her and took the sack off her head.

25

"You work for Global Aggregates don't you?" said Marsden.

She was distracted for a moment as her eyes reacted to the light. Then she thought about home.

'Oh my God, Gran must be going spare.'

But then he grabbed her chin and looked straight into her eyes.

"I asked you a question Lily."

She shuddered.

Marsden looked down at her. He'd pumped her full of drugs over the last two days, so she was as ready as she was going to be to give everything up, whether she thought it was relevant or not.

"Yes, yes, I've told you all of this, but I'm just a researcher," said Lily, tears starting to well up again.

She really didn't know where to go with this now, as she had no idea if this was what they wanted to know.

"I was just told to look at the level of concrete cover they used in the Witterings build."

"What does that mean Lily?"

"It's the amount or depth of concrete they use to cover the rebar, that's the steel reinforcement grids that gives concrete its strength," said Lily.

"What about it?"

"Brooks said it was to help the Health and Safety Executive. He wanted to be able to disprove any suggestion that the company had reduced the amount of cover in the GA reinforced concrete products."

"And what did you find?"

"They hadn't changed anything with the concrete cover."

"Good, so Brooks was happy?"

"Yes, except..."

"Except what Lily?" said Marsden.

She was trying not to cry, but she was scared now, very scared of this man.

"Do you…..do you mean the Ultra-Fast-Dry file?" said Lily.

"Yes my dear, tell us about that," said Stephen Rawlings, who'd quietly entered the room.

A different voice. Coming from behind her. He sounded friendly and gentle. She felt herself breathing more easily. She could answer this and then she hoped she could get out of here and get on with her life again.

"It was just something I found in the notes, the development notes, about the way UFD, I mean, the Ultra-Fast-Dry was made back in the 2000s. They tried a new formula, called UFD30."

"Go on."

"Well, seeing as we were looking in to what may have caused the collapse at the Witterings Shopping Centre earlier this year," she paused, "I just wanted to see if the new UFD30 formula might be connected."

This was the problem in one. Brooks had set Parsons and this girl off on a spurious task and it had backfired. It was supposed to show GA was trying to help the Health and Safety investigation, by checking they hadn't reduced the concrete cover, when Brooks knew all along they hadn't, but then the Green girl had found out about the change to the concrete formula.

"That's good Lily, very helpful."

He saw her almost smile as she reacted to the gentle tone in his voice.

Rawlings nodded at Marsden. They were finally getting somewhere with the girl. The truth drug worked well sometimes, but it also created its own problems since the person might only answer specific questions, rather than offering things up, as Lily was now doing. Marsden had done well. He'd broken her. Getting her stripped naked had taken the last vestige of fight from her.

"Now listen to me carefully. Who have you talked to

about the UFD30 file?"

"Well, Ian obviously."

He knew that, because it was Ian Parsons who had raised the issue with Brooks.

Rawlings caught Marsden looking at him.

He nodded back, then put his hand back down on Lily's shoulder, again making her flinch.

"Now Lily, if only you had told us this before, we could have avoided all this unpleasantness. I think we can take off these bindings now. There's really no need for Lily to be tied up like this and let's get your clothes back on, shall we?"

She still couldn't see who was talking, but she was relieved to be getting her clothes back.

"Now Lily, just a few more things as you get dressed, but please keep the sack on your head my dear."

As Marsden untied Lily from the chair, she felt the blood start to flow back into her arms and legs. He grabbed her hands and pushed her pants and bra into them. She didn't bother with the bra, but quickly put her pants on, then the top he handed her, followed by her skirt.

"What exactly did you see that caused you to raise this as an issue?" said Rawlings.

"It was the test results on the drying time. There were some concerns of the effect of heat, you know climate, the sun. There was something in there about more testing being needed, for possible degradation in the short term."

"That's good, thank you."

Again, the voice was gentle.

'He's thanking me?'

"Now, who else did you tell?"

She heard the question, but a thought flashed through her head.

'Am I out of my mind?' she thought. They dragged me

into the back of a van and tied me up! Why would they let me go? She felt her shoulders drop. She knew she was still in trouble, serious trouble and she couldn't see any way out.

Rawlings saw her body language. *'She's not stupid. Marsden had better make sure she knows she can't talk to anyone.'*

"Now, come now Lily, no need to worry, you'll be home with your grandparents before you know it. Who did you tell? You said Ian?"

She tried to focus, to concentrate. *'Was he really going to let me go?'*

"Yes, I told Ian, and he'll be wondering where I am? What if he's told the police?"

She was starting to wander, so he steered her back to the question.

"He hasn't done that, so don't worry. Now other than Ian, is there anyone else?"

"Why wouldn't he have told the police? Does he know you've got me?"

"He knows you're helping us, yes, so come now. Is there anyone else?" He spoke a little firmer this time and he saw her body tighten, just a little.

"So are you with Global Aggregates?" said Lily, slowly.

"You don't need to be concerned with that Lily. Who else?"

She heard the change of tone in his voice. He was getting impatient with her.

"Well, I didn't tell anyone else.....but...."

"But what, Lily?" said Rawlings.

"I thought I'd ask Kevin Cox. He's at one of our sites in Canada. He's a construction specialist. I haven't actually spoken to him, I just sent him an email on Tuesday," said Lily.

"Damn."

She heard Rawlings and then felt a sudden sharp pain in her arm, as a needle went in and she saw the outline of Marsden's face right in front of her, close up to her nose.

She shuddered, but then fell unconscious as the drugs took effect once again.

Rawlings watched as Marsden picked her up and took her back to her room. From what she'd said, it looked like she hadn't found any specific evidence that proved beyond doubt, that there was a direct connection between the shopping centre collapse and Groom's decision to change the reinforced concrete formula.

However, there was likely to be enough in the papers to suggest to either the Health and Safety Executive, or the Coroner's Court, or both, that the new formula was a significant and likely contributory factor to the tragic death of five people.

'That's why he's offered the additional bonus to get this sorted. Because this will take him down if it gets out,' thought Rawlings.

5

Terri Anderson didn't usually mind flying. Just as well, as she was getting a lot of air miles at the moment with the travel she was having to do with her job. This time she was on a flight from Melbourne to Singapore.

As Operations Director for 3R, her father's security consultancy, she ran the day to day affairs of the business. She leaned back in her seat and thought about how it had grown, even in the short time she had been there since retiring from the Australian Army.

3R, Risk Reduction and Resolution, was expanding fast. New enquiries were coming in all the time and after a quick stopover in Singapore to see yet another new client, she was meeting up with her dad, Greg Chambers, in India to look at what they needed to be doing to manage the business as things moved forward.

Going back to Australia had been great too, she thought. She got to see her mum and step-dad for a few days, as well as some friends from her army days. One of them, Sally, worked as cabin crew for Quantas and it turned out she was working on the flight Terri was on.

She was in Economy and her legs were zinging. She hadn't found too many disadvantages with being tall and leggy, but this was certainly one of them. She wished she'd bumped herself up to Premium. The business could afford it, but she'd rather her team got the benefit of the upgrades on long haul flights. That said, she was now regretting it and was badly in need of a leg stretch.

It also didn't help that a few seats back, she could hear a guy who seemed to be constantly moaning about something. She'd seen her friend Sally going to speak to him on a couple of occasions, presumably after he'd pushed the service button.

As she walked past them on her way to the galley, Terri looked at the couple. He was big, overweight and sat with his legs wide apart as he tried to fit a body that was about half a size too big into the economy seat. The woman, who she presumed was his wife, given she was wearing a wedding ring, was wearing dark sunglasses and a long sleeved cardigan and seemed to be sitting very still, almost rigid.

The same man saw a tall, blonde, very attractive woman look at him and he pushed himself up in his seat and smiled at her as she walked past. Terri ignored the smile and looked again at the woman. Nothing. No facial contact, no connection. She just stared ahead.

As Terri reached the galley she saw Sally preparing some food trays.

"Not the easiest job Sal?" said Terri.

"No, but hey, I still get to see bits of the world and no one's shooting at me either," winked Sally.

She'd been one of Terri's team when they were doing patrols in and around Kabul. Brave, tough and great with the locals. Sally's smile could break down a hundred doors of mistrust. Terri had spoken to her about joining 3R, but she'd said she just wanted a job without thrills and spills, at least for a while, so Terri had put the offer on hold until Sally was ready.

Just then the woman with the sunglasses walked by and stood waiting near to the toilets. Terri motioned to Sally with a questioning look. Sally gave her a, *'I know'* look. She too had picked up on something.

Terri slowly walked up to the woman, who didn't move or react.

"Look, is there anything I can do to help?" said Terri quietly.

The woman shook her head.

Terri went to say something else, when the woman continued.

"Nobody can help. So please don't try. People have tried before and it just makes it worse for me."

"What's your name?"

"Don't get involved. He'll hurt you too. Besides, once we land, I'll never see you again will I?"

"You might, you might not," said Terri, "it depends on you. So let's start with my name shall we? I'm Terri. That's Sally, we served together. She lives in Melbourne. Is that where you live?"

"Yes," the woman looked back at Sally and smiled.

A positive, thought Terri and smiled at her and waited.

"I'm Linda." Another half-smile.

"Let me show you a photo," said Terri, who got her phone and started flicking through some of the photos she'd taken with her ex-army friends a couple of days ago.

"I can't be long. He'll come and find me. He never lets me alone," said Linda and Terri saw her starting to physically shake.

Terri gently placed a hand on her arm. Then when she felt the shaking ease, Terri showed her a photo on her phone.

"This is Gerry. We used to call him 'Breaker'. He lives in Melbourne and so does Sally. So now you have two friends you can call on at any time and if I said I don't know which one I'd rather take on in a fight, well I wouldn't be lying, as I've seen both in action Linda and your old man? Well, let's just say, he'd end up as mincemeat against either of them."

"But.....," said Linda.

"But what?" interrupted Terri. "Have you ever tried to leave him before?"

"Yes, but he found me and he....," she stopped, as tears streamed down her face. "He hurt me, hurt me bad."

"You don't have to answer this now Linda, but if I gave you a magic wand, would you like to leave him?"

"Oh, God yes!" she blurted it out.

"Why are you going to Singapore?"

"We're going on holiday, if you can call it a holiday. Andy will spend all his time at the bar and then I'll try and keep out of his way, when he gets back to the hotel room," said Linda.

"What if I could get you a lift straight back to Melbourne? Would you take it?" said Sally.

Linda looked at them both.

"I don't know....., I don't know if I could do that. He'd stop me, I know he would. He'd....."

"He wouldn't Linda, believe me, not after I've spoken to him," said Terri.

Linda took off her sunglasses for the first time. One eye was almost fully closed and the other showed the signs of constant beatings.

"Could I?"

There was hope in her face. She wanted to believe this could happen.

"I can't go on like this much longer. My daughter says I can go there, but I don't want to lose my house. It's the only thing I feel is mine," said Linda.

"I don't see why you need to move out Linda. As I

said, I'm sure your Andy will see sense and realise it's time for you both to move on. By the way, is Andy right or left handed?"

"Right," she answered instinctively, "but why do you need to know that?"

Just at that moment, the toilet door opened and a man came out with a brief apology.

"Let's talk about this in a minute when you come back out and Terri watched as Linda went in the toilet cubicle and closed the door behind her.

"Can I have a cup of hot, very hot coffee please Sal?"

Sally gave her friend a quizzical look.

"You said, very hot coffee? Do you want it black or with milk?"

"Black will be great," said Terri and watched as her friend poured the coffee into a cup.

"Thanks, now can you keep Linda here until I push the service button?"

"Terri?" Sally asked slowly. "What are you planning on doing?"

"Well, I could call it an advance manoeuvre to look at the potential for a quick incursion into enemy territory...., or, just say I'm going for a little chat with Andy, take your pick," said Terri, as she set off back towards where Andy was sitting before Sally could respond.

"Hi! I've brought you some coffee," said Terri, looking down at the man.

"I didn't ask for any damn coffee," the man started to say, before he looked up and saw it was the attractive blonde he'd seen and smiled at before.

"Well, maybe I will, thanks," he said as he took the coffee from her.

"It's Andy isn't it," said Terri.

He was immediately suspicious.

"How do you know my name? Has she been talking?

She's lying, whatever she's been telling you. She fell over."

"Ooops," said Terri, as she leant down hard on his right shoulder, causing his arm to involuntarily shake and tip the cup, spilling the boiling hot coffee over his groin.

"You, you stupid….."

But before he got any more words out, Terri rocked hard backwards with her elbow and smashed into his nose. She heard it break, before he squealed as he dropped the cup completely this time. And then she turned and saw the blood streaming down his face.

"Mate, did you just squeal? That's got to be embarrassing."

He was trying to stand up but she was pushing hard down on his right shoulder again. He looked like he was pretty strong, so she didn't want him getting up to get any sort of advantage. He tried to put his hands down on the seat arms to give him some leverage, so she released his shoulder and at the same time aimed a short hard punch at his groin.

She felt the wetness of the coffee on his trousers as the punch landed and she heard him groan. With his body rising upwards out of his seat after Terri had released his shoulder, he'd actually increased the full force of the punch as her fist struck his groin.

He fell back down like a sack of potatoes into his seat. She waited in case he tried to get up again, but then saw beads of sweat appearing across his head. He was trying to speak, but couldn't get the words out.

Terri heard a few murmurs of appreciation coming from the passengers around them.

She leant forward and spoke quietly into his ear.

"Now, you listen to me Andy and listen good. Linda will not be staying with you when you land at Singapore, do you hear me?"

He started to squirm, so she hand-palmed him, hard, against the side of his head.

"You're not listening to me Andy. Let's try again. She's not coming with you and as of now, you do not live at your current address back in Melbourne."

"You can't do this," he wheezed through the blood in his mouth and nose.

"Oh, but I can and you see this guy here?" She showed him her phone and the picture of Gerry. "He lives in Melbourne, not far from you. You need to keep a very good lookout for Gerry here. He's a very good mate of mine and as of this moment, he's a very good friend of Linda's."

He was trying to speak again, through the blood and gunge in his nose.

"Listen, this is just a misunderstanding, I love her and she loves me," said Andy.

"Too little, too late mate," said Terri before lowering her voice to almost a whisper. "Now, please believe me when I say that Gerry's bite is a damn sight worse than his bark. He'll hurt you a lot more than I will, so best you do the right thing and agree to the divorce Sally will be petitioning as soon as she's back home. Do you get me?"

"You can't make me do this!" Andy's voice was rising in pitch.

"There you go again, you're squealing Andy. You are just a bully aren't you? And when it comes down to it, you haven't got any balls have you?"

"I'll bust your face, you interfering ...."

He didn't get another word out.

As he tried to force his way up out of his seat, Terri launched an arcing right hook and caught his head side on, knocking him straight back into the seat, where he lost consciousness.

This time there was some gentle applause and even

a few *'Good on you'* comments. She smiled at the people around her as she walked back to the galley, where Linda and Sally were waiting.

"I've got another seat for you to use until we land and then I'll sort out the flight back for you, okay?" said Sally.

"I can't believe this is happening. How can I…?"

"It's okay Linda. Now, here's my card and look this is Sally's number and Gerry's. He works with me and he'll make contact with you when you land. Now, I don't like bullies, but let me tell you, Gerry really doesn't like them, so he'll keep you safe, I can promise you that. Plus, you'll like him," she smiled. "Now go and get some rest."

Linda just mouthed *'thank you'*, to them both as Sally took her to a seat close to where Terri was seated.

As Sally came back, she stopped by Terri's seat and squatted beside her.

"Breaker? What was that all about with Gerry?"

Terri smiled, "Just a little bit of artistic licence, but he really doesn't like bullies does he, so he'd be bound to break something on that shit's body."

Sally smiled. Terri had been her boss out in Iraq. She was tough, spoke no-nonsense, but had a heart of gold when it came to people.

"No, you're right there. So, is marriage guidance counselling, some new part of 3R's portfolio then?" smiled Sally.

"No, but hey, I just don't like seeing bullies making someone's life a misery."

"I get you girl. So, seeing as you're now operating all over the globe now, I reckon you should tell your dad that you should rebrand as 3R International!"

Terri looked back at her and smiled.

"Now, that Sal, is not a bad idea at all!"

*****

Greg Chambers was sitting in the 3R office in Mumbai, unaware that his company was now, at least in his daughter Terri's mind, going through a rebrand.

He'd just seen a text from Anna.

'Martin C wants to talk. Can you come back via here? He's coming tomorrow.'

As he texted a quick response, he wondered what it might be about. Martin Carruthers had made no secret of the fact, that he wanted Anna to return to 'standby' operational status within the Secret Intelligence Service. Greg also knew that Anna was flattered to be asked and it had come at a good time for her, with her losing Luis to cancer six months or so ago.

She'd already been to London in the last two weeks to sit in on a Covert Ops training meeting and when he spoke to her afterwards, she'd been buzzing. He smiled. He hadn't seen her for, what? Well, it must thirty five, no, thirty six years, because Sam was thirty five, but she was still so full of life.

Finding out he had a son was a hell of a shock, but he couldn't believe it had been so easy to engage with the boy. No, Sam wasn't a boy, far from it. He was his own man, that was for sure and he liked that.

'Maybe he gets a little bit of that from me,' he mused.

He looked up as Eschaan Achari walked into the office.

"Sorry Boss, am I interrupting you?"

"Not at all Eschaan, good morning to you. Look, it's been good to see you and the team over the last few days, especially as I wanted to say thank you for all your help last time we were out here," said Greg.

"Thanks Boss, we really appreciate that. So where are you off to from here? Back to London?"

"Well, it was to be London, but I need to change my flight and I'll fly back to Mallorca with Terri tomorrow. Can I grab a car later? I'll go and pick her up."

"Sure, take this one," passing him the keys to his SUV.

Eschaan was the In-Country Manager for 3R in India. Greg knew he was good, really good at his job. Terri had chosen well when she realised they needed someone to handle the fast expanding business in India.

"You know I said Terri had agreed that I can take on more people? Well I've got three new people lined up. This will really help, as we were getting a bit stretched on occasions."

"That's great. Tell me about them?" said Greg.

"Well, we're way too top heavy with guys and we had a couple of situations a few months ago, where the guys just stood out like sore thumbs, so I wanted to bring some women in, to get a better balance in the team. We interviewed six and the three I've chosen should fit in really well."

"Who are they?" said Greg.

"Two are local, born and schooled in Mumbai. One trained and worked as a journalist and the other is a bit of an IT wiz who wants to get out from behind a desk and do something different. Number three is an ex-pat Brit, whose parents moved to England back in the 80's. She's a former police officer who wanted a change of lifestyle and career, so she came back out here two years ago."

"They sound impressive. Can't wait to meet them. Did you go for the one with the IT skills as a result of the job we did recently?"

"Yes, Boss. The guy you mentioned, the one who got in behind the scenes of the IT scammers? He really opened up everything for you, didn't he? So I reckoned we could maybe do with someone who had those sort of skills too."

"That's great, I like your thinking Eschaan," said

Greg.

He looked around the office and smiled.

"So presumably this means 3R will need to look for more office space out here."

6

This was different. Something had changed. He hadn't stuck a needle in her arm this time. Lily had been taken out of her bedroom, still with a sack on her head, but she'd been taken to a shower room.

There was shower gel, shampoo and towels, and they were nice, fresh towels too. He hadn't said anything, just waved his hand at the shower. She thought he'd stay there and leer at her as she undressed, but he didn't, he stood to one side.

After she'd showered, she still had to put the sack on her head, but when she got back to her room he took it off her. Lily saw a set of shopping bags on the bed. She opened them. New clothes. A smart summer dress, shoes and fresh underwear.

She turned and looked at Marsden.

"You're wondering how I knew your size?" he smirked.

Lily ignored his jibe.

"Does this mean you're letting me go?"

"Yes, of course Lily," he said smiling. "But you will remember what I said won't you?"

The smile left his face. He was still wearing the balaclava with the cut outs for his eyes and mouth, so she could see the look in his eyes once again.

"I, er, I won't say anything, I promise," stammered Lily.

"In some ways I hope you don't get to keep your promise Lily Green, because you know what that will mean don't you?"

He had moved forward right next to her and she could smell him, smell his eau de cologne, feel his breath.

She tried to pull away, but he grabbed her by both arms and held her tight.

"Just think about it Lily, me and you. Think what I'd do to you and then your grandparents. I'd make them watch me. Watch me with you. Would you like that Lily? Would you like that?"

She was quivering. She could see the excitement in his eyes, even with the balaclava on his head.

'Oh my God,' she thought.

Then in an instant, he turned.

"But of course Lily, we need none of that unpleasantness do we? Just keep this little conversation between us shall we? Tell no-one else and everything will be fine."

She saw what looked like a smile appear beneath his mask again.

"Now come on, get dressed. What was your boyfriend's name, Mateo you said, didn't you? Let's get you back to him and maybe he can get you home all safe and sound. How does that sound?" said Marsden.

She couldn't believe the change in him. Now he was talking about Mateo and getting home 'safe and sound'. 'Was he mad?' she thought.

"Lily? I said did you want to get home safe and sound?" Again, his voice dropped into the menacing tone from before and the chill in her returned.

She had no fight left in her. She stared at him.

"Yes please," she said quietly. "I'd like that."

He smiled, but not to her.

He could report she was under complete control.

*****

Sam went up the stairs of the Greens' villa and found Lily's room. Anna stayed downstairs with Helen and Geoffrey Green and quietly chatted with them, getting some more background on their granddaughter.

He stood in the doorway and took it all in. The room was about three metres by four. There was a window on the far wall, with a radiator underneath the sill. It was a tidy room, but still decorated in the style of a teenager, with a single bed on the left hand side and a chest of drawers and stand-alone wardrobe on the right. No desk, presumably because she only originally came for holidays.

He had a pair of synthetic gloves on, which he had just in case he needed to get under the bonnet of the VW. He worked methodically, starting at the door frame and then moving left to right around the room. There was nothing to suggest she had anything secreted away, but experience told him that too much was often missed in a search when assumptions were made.

He ran his hands carefully along the doorframe. It was unlikely to be the sort of things he'd come across in his Met Police days, when drug dealers would leave razor blades inserted in door frames, protecting secret cavities. But old habits die hard and a good job too he thought.

'*Think of the space as an area.*' An area in this case with six sides. Four walls, a floor and a ceiling, so always remember to look up – one of the first lessons he was given by his training officer and he remembered his words like it was yesterday.

44

"We tend to look forward and down and not so much up. So Sam, you need to spend as much time looking up on a search as you do looking down."

'Okay, there's nothing to suggest Lily is any sort of drug dealer, but don't make any assumptions,' he thought.

Even before he'd started the search, he'd asked Helen who cleaned Lily's room. He was trying to determine whether Helen had free access to the room, or did Lily keep it locked?

"Oh she cleans it. She's very good, but I usually go in and change the bed for her when she's at work."

That meant that Lily might not keep anything personal out in the open. After all, she was a young woman now, so she may not want her Gran seeing anything like contraceptive pills, or something to do with her boyfriend, Mateo.

He checked the skirting boards as he moved around the room, for any sign of loose panels. The bed was clear, as was the window, inside and outside and the radiator.

He found her contraceptive pills in a small bag inside her chest of drawers. She was up to date and had taken the last one on the Wednesday she went missing. In the second drawer down was what was obviously her 'going out' underwear, rather than her day to day stuff that was in another drawer.

Again, he smiled back to his days at Police Training School, when they'd find all sorts of things in the search exercises designed to cause maximum embarrassment, or awkwardness, for the trainee officers. Far better to get that feeling understood and sorted in training, so that it didn't distract you when you'd need to have your wits about you, when you were out doing the job for real.

He took each drawer of the chest out and turned it upside down. Nothing. He wasn't looking for anything specifically, so he just kept working his way around, to see if anything looked out of place, or unusual, or may give some sort of clue as to why she was missing.

He found her diary in the wardrobe, on the top shelf under some cycling shorts and tops, full-on Lycra gear. Hidden? Yes, but maybe just because it contained her private thoughts. He put it to one side. Better to finish the search completely, before going off on a tangent with the diary.

He finished the search just as Anna appeared in the doorway.

"Anything?"

"Just her diary, with a payslip from Global Aggregates, the people she must work for, tucked inside it. It was under some cycling gear in her cupboard, so out of sight, rather than hidden."

"Well I found the racing bike in the garage, the one Helen mentioned before, but there's nothing else down there," said Anna.

"Right, so let's see what she's got down for last Wednesday?" said Sam.

He flicked through the pages and came to the date two days ago.

"Lunch with Mateo. Okay, so that gives us a start. We really need to find this Mateo. Did they say if they've had any contact with him?"

"Yes, he came to the house. He didn't have their number. No reason why he would really, as he'd be ringing Lily on her mobile. They said he seemed a nice young man. He's got a very smart sports car, so they think he must be doing alright for himself," said Anna.

"Had they seen him before he came to see them about Lily?"

"No, well, only to see him in the car when he came to pick her up, but they hadn't spoken to him. He left his mobile number, so they could ring him if she turned up. She said he looked really worried."

"Okay, maybe he's an innocent, but…"

"But, you're right, we can't rule him out until we're sure," said Anna. "Let's set up a meet with him. Now, I've decided we're better off not taking Helen out for a drive about. I can see she's getting very anxious now, so better she stays here with Geoffrey and we go out on our own."

"Good call Mum. Let's go and have a drive about and pay a visit to where she works. I'll also ring this Mateo," said Sam, taking out his phone.

*****

Mateo Álvarez didn't recognise the number on his phone.

"Hola?"

Sam spoke in Spanish.

"Mateo? You don't know me, but my name's Sam Martínez, I'm a friend of Lily's grandparents," said Sam.

"How did you get my number?" said Mateo.

"You gave it to her grandparents? Remember?"

"Of course, of course, I'm sorry, but I'm worried sick. She's been missing two days now. It was Wednesday I was supposed to see her. We were meeting for lunch."

"Yes, I know you must be. I'm just trying to help, seeing as we can't seem to get the police involved yet."

"No, they're not interested. They say she's a grown woman and…"

"Have you spoken to the police then?" said Sam. "I thought it was just Lily's grandparents who'd done that?"

"Yes, I rang someone I know as well, to see if they'd help, but it's their standard procedure apparently."

"Okay, so do you know any reason why she might be missing?" said Sam.

"No, none at all. Look, we've only known each other a few weeks, but she's a really sweet girl."

"So, no upsets between the two of you?"

"Look, if you're suggesting I have something to do with this..." started Mateo.

"No, not at all, I'm just starting with the basics," said Sam.

"Okay, I'm sorry, I'm jumpy. But those questions you're asking? Are you some sort of cop or something?"

"I'm an ex-cop, from London, but I'm just helping a friend of my family here, is that okay?"

"Yes, of course. What can I do? I've been driving around Puerto Pollensa for the last two days trying to find her. She was due to meet me in town, but she never showed up."

"Right, let's start there Mateo. Where were you meeting for lunch?" said Sam.

"Bar Coral Restaurante, we'd been meeting there every Wednesday for the last few weeks. She loved it there. Shit, what am I saying? I mean she loves it there," said Mateo.

"It's okay. Let's just see what pans out Mateo. No need to start thinking the worst, but...."

Sam didn't finish his sentence when he heard Mateo shout out.

"I can see her! Sam, I can see her!"

"Where? Where is she?" said Sam.

"I'm going downstairs now, so I might lose you in the stairwell, but she's outside my apartment by the front door, hang on!"

Sam waited on the phone. He heard noises, presumably Mateo opening the apartment door, then voices, in English.

"Lily, oh my God, where have you been? Are you alright? I've been so worried and your grandparents...."

Another voice, a young woman's.

"Mateo, I'm fine, I'm fine. I'm sorry, I should have told you, I just needed some time away, but everything's good now."

Sam listened. The woman, presumably Lily, sounded okay, in control and she didn't sound upset. He tried calling out.

"Mateo, Mateo, are you there?"

Mateo came back on the phone.

"Yes, I'm here Sam. Look, I don't know what's happened, but she says she's fine. She says she just wants to just get back home to her grandparents, so I'll grab my keys and bring her back now, okay?"

"Yes, that's great. I'll let her grandparents know and we'll see you back here soon."

"You're there with them?" said Mateo.

"Yes."

"Good, good," said Mateo. "We'll be there as quick as I can."

Anna had heard the conversation Sam had been having with Mateo.

"Good news then?" said Anna.

"Yes! I wish a lot of the 'mispers', sorry, missing persons I dealt with, were resolved as easily as this. The boyfriend is bringing her home, so let's go and tell Helen and Geoffrey the good news."

*****

An hour later they heard and then saw the yellow Porsche as it pulled up on the driveway. Helen ran forward to the car door.

"Someone's doing well for himself," said Sam quietly to his mother.

They watched as they saw a young woman get out of the car. Anna had met Lily a few times over the years, but Sam had never seen her before.

He took in what he was seeing before him. An attractive young woman, aged around twenty four, twenty five, dressed in a bright yellow summer dress with matching shoes.

Helen was firing questions at her granddaughter, who was now out of the car and looking at the two other people on the driveway. She recognised Anna as a friend of her Gran and assumed the guy must be Sam, who Mateo had told her about on the way up.

She had already had Mateo asking masses of questions as they drove up and she just kept telling him there was nothing to worry about and that she was fine.

Of course, she wasn't fine and she kept looking around to see if he was there. The one with the eyes. She knew she'd recognise him again, with or without a balaclava.

Now she had Gran to deal with, plus these other two. What were they doing here? They can't be here!

"Oh, Lily, we were so worried! And where's your bike?" said Helen.

"Look, Gran, I'm fine. I'm tired, I just need to lie down, so if you'll all please give me some space, I just want to go to my room."

"But your bike?"

"I'll sort it, but later, I just need to lie down." With that Lily hugged her grandmother again and went up the stairs to her room.

Helen looked at Anna and then Sam. Sam gently shook his head. Letting her go was the best thing for her to do. He saw something in her behaviour, but he couldn't put his finger on it.

"Thank you for helping us and I'm sorry it was a wild goose chase. I don't know what's happened with our darling girl, but she seems fine and so I don't want to make a fuss around her," said Helen.

"Something's not right," said Sam, almost to himself, but Helen heard him.

"What do you mean Sam? Something's not right. She's fine. You saw her!" said Helen.

Anna spoke, "I'm inclined to agree with Sam, Helen. She's wearing different clothes to what she went out in for a start. And where's her bike? The one she uses for work? And what's she been doing for these past few days that she doesn't want to talk about?"

"No, no, she's fine," said Helen, although her voice was faltering, with a dawning realisation that something may well be wrong and that she could not start to contemplate what that might be.

Anna gently took her hand.

"Look, let's let her get some sleep. That will give us some time to think about what we can do to best help her," said Anna, who looked across at Sam, who was looking out of the window.

He'd seen Mateo was on the phone. As Sam went out to see him, Mateo looked up and seemed to quickly cut the call short.

"Sorry, I wasn't interrupting anything was I?" said Sam.

"No, no, it was just some business. Is she okay?"

"Yes, but she just wants some sleep. Thank you for bringing her back Mateo, but are you okay? You must have been worried sick too?" said Sam.

"I'm good now, thank you amigo. I don't know what's happened, or why it's happened, but at least she's back home safe now." Mateo paused for a moment, "What are you going to do now?"

"Good question. To be honest, unless Lily tells us what happened, we can't really get anywhere. Maybe she needed some time to herself? Maybe..."

"Yes, perhaps that's it," interrupted Mateo. "I don't know why though, but as long as she's okay now, then I can stop worrying."

Sam was listening to what he said. It seemed genuine, but like with Lily, something wasn't sounding right.

"So, are you not interested in finding out what's happened? Maybe she has someone else? Another guy? Or has she had problems at work?"

"No, no! There is no other guy," Mateo fired back at Sam.

"Okay," said Sam slowly. "Let's see what happens and thanks again for bringing her back."

But Mateo was already back in his car and reversing out at speed, leaving Sam watching as the car sped off.

He felt his mother by his side.

"Problem?" said Anna.

"I don't know Mum, but it's another feeling I don't like. And that makes two now. Right, let's leave things here now and go and pay Global Aggregates a visit shall we?"

7

I t had been three months ago. The day the problem Sir Charles Groom had thought he'd buried, resurrected itself.

It had all started well enough. A nice, clear spring morning as he'd driven into work, with the sun shining.

He had left his Bentley in his underground parking space, of the smart offices Global Aggregates occupied in London's Canary Wharf, before he entered the lift and pushed the button for the 34th floor.

Prior to the 2008 banking crash, Groom had built a formidable reputation, first as a Trader and then as the CEO of Global Aggregates, a FTSE quoted company. He was one of the big players on the London Stock Exchange, until the banking crisis hit.

Although GA survived, it was only by the skin of its teeth, when Groom accepted the rescue package offered by OBCR, the Overseas Banking Corporation of Russia and their majority shareholder, Oleg Makarovich.

Groom's company had been about to go under, devoid of cash and creditors literally lining up at the door, so he'd jumped at the opportunity offered by Makarovich and his partners.

He'd been in business long enough to suspect the

funds coming into the GA accounts were of dubious origin. However, beggars can't be choosers and despite the gossip within the financial world, the newly returned to private ownership company was soon in the merger and acquisition market, as Makarovich's funds opened doors for GA to start an aggressive expansion programme across the world.

Cash rich Global Aggregates advanced their position as market leader in reinforced concrete, before Groom widened their portfolio still further, buying up construction companies of his own. Once again, he was the darling of the Stock Exchange and a knighthood followed in 2013.

So, three months ago, when he left the lift, he'd greeted his front of office reception team with his usual cheery smile and greeting before striding into his glass panelled office.

Moments later, the smile on his face had vanished, when he saw the note on his desk.

Media News Release
FIVE DEAD, DOZENS INJURED

"The collapse of a side of the multi-storey carpark at the Witterings Shopping Centre in London SW4 has left five people dead and thirty five injured.

The Witterings is managed by WSC (London) Ltd, a subsidiary of the original developer, 127DevCo, who built the site in 2005. A Health and Safety Executive investigation has commenced."

It stopped him in his tracks.

"Shit!"

Both the name of the shopping centre and 127DevCo rang immediate alarm bells with him.

Roger Wall.

Groom walked across to the full length plate glass

window, where he looked out on to the London skyline.

He had a fine memory for detail and he remembered Wall had been one of his clients back in the mid 2000's. An awkward bugger then and he hadn't mellowed much with age.

Groom had been trying to buy the site back off Wall since 2010 and now it looked like it was too late. A problem that Groom had been trying to tidy up and hide was now dangerously out in the open.

This was the last of the four sites when, back in 2007, he'd been pushed to the edge of bankruptcy, he'd leaned hard on his building team. He'd pushed them to make some key changes in the construction process, thereby reducing costs and enabling him to win these four contracts.

Groom had desperately needed these contracts, as they came with interim payment schedules that were vital to sustain his cash flow. He'd submitted ridiculously low tenders to win them, even knowing he would be operating at a loss on the builds.

It had worked, at least for a time. He'd kept the business going, and the problem, which only he and Paul Brooks knew about, remained hidden. But now it looked like it had come back to bite him!

The problem shouldn't have been a problem. At least not according Brooks, who was one of his product designers at the time. The tests back then had initially delivered positive results on Brooks' new improved Ultra-Fast-Dry30 cement, the key component used in GA's reinforced concrete construction.

Their basic product, UFD10, was already hailed as an industry leader in fast drying concrete, providing significant opportunities for faster construction time. This in turn led to significant cost reductions in terms of labour, not to mention rental time for scaffolding, cherry pickers and all the other equipment associated with a major construction development.

Groom had been confident that the new improved UFD30 would give another 20% saving in drying time and more cost reductions and this was what he used in the four sites Global Aggregates worked on in 2007.

But Brooks had become anxious. Some of the test results started to show a potential weakness to heat exposure and Brooks wanted an extension to the test programme before they started to use the product.

He remembered the heated discussions at the time.

"Listen Brooks, we don't have time for this!" said Groom, who was exasperated at the delays. "You're talking about temperatures here that we don't see in the UK, so sign it off for God's sake and let me keep everyone in a job! Unless you want to tell everyone that it was you who caused Global Aggregates to go down the pan?"

Brooks shuffled from side to side. Groom was not an easy man to deal with. He'd seen many of his colleagues turfed out of their jobs because they didn't agree, or worse still, they tried to argue the point with Charles Groom.

"It's just that….," Brooks tried to put into words that he couldn't guarantee the product for the usual life expectancy of reinforced concrete of seventy to a hundred years.

"I'm not asking you to guarantee it forever Paul," said Groom.

'He called me Paul,' thought Brooks. *'This is it. The sack.'*

"We all know that the London skyline is changing massively. These four sites are highly unlikely to be here in ten, let alone twenty years, are they?"

Brooks nodded. Groom had a point.

"Now I'm really grateful for your work here and just to show you how much I think of you, what about this as a plan? You sign it off and we bring in a review process, which you can monitor from your new position as Head of Research."

Paul Brooks had been waiting for Groom to tell him to clear his office. Had he misheard?

"I'm sorry Boss? Did you say....?"

"Head of Research, Paul. Of course, it comes with some disadvantages I'm afraid," said Groom and he watched Brooks to see if he'd take the bait.

"Disadvantages?"

"Yes. I know you have two young children with your dear wife, don't you?"

Brooks nodded.

"Because of course, the R&D Centre is in Mallorca, so you'd have to move there. We'd pay for your house rental, car, your kids' schooling. All the usual things and they do have a magnificent international school over there. But then again, you might just want to send them to a local school, your choice, but you will still get the relevant fees grant, whichever way you choose to go," said Groom, as he watched Brooks closely for his response.

Brooks had gone from being resigned to losing his job and having to explain to his wife what had happened and wondering how he'd cope getting another job in the industry in difficult times, to the prospect of an all-expenses paid move abroad to Mallorca.

"Well, come on Paul, we haven't got all day. What do you say? Are you the man for this?"

"Er, yes, I mean, I can't believe it Boss, it's a fantastic offer and I'd love the opportunity. I won't let you down," said Brooks.

"Good man and I know you won't, so just get those papers signed off on the product confirmation of UFD30, there's a good chap and then you can go and tell your wife the good news."

Brooks knew what had happened. He'd been seduced by the offer of promotion, a move to Mallorca and everything paid for. He forced a weak smile at Groom.

"Yes, I'll get them signed straight away Boss."

'Got him,' thought Groom. 'Hook, line and sinker.'

*****

That had been then, thought Groom. Problem solved. Everything actually went to plan in the short term. They had completed the sites on time and the interim payments had helped keep the business afloat, at least until he got bailed out by Makarovich.

Brooks had kept an eye on the four sites, watching for any unusual degradation. Three of the site owners were happy with GA's apparently excellent follow-up customer service, but Roger Wall for some reason, took exception to it and stopped Brooks from going.

'Cantankerous old sod!'

Neither Makarovich, nor his partners showed any interest in the day to day running of GA and this meant Groom was free to tidy up the loose ends. Groom quickly offered over the odds prices for three of the sites. Brooks had tested them again and thankfully they still hadn't shown anything to cause concern, so the owners suspected nothing and didn't turn down Groom's gift horse of an offer. Then, to be on the safe side, Groom demolished and re-developed the three sites, to get rid of the problem forever.

That left Wall and the Witterings Shopping Centre. Despite a number of generous offers, Wall wouldn't sell, even though his company, 127DevCo, was operating at a loss every year. He got it into his head that Groom must know something about the site and that it must be worth ten, fifty, maybe a hundred times more than whatever Groom was offering.

Groom thought back and wondered if he'd just told the silly old bugger......, *'Look, I built your Shopping Centre with some innovative new concrete that turns out not to work if exposed to extreme sunshine and so it's likely to collapse, but don't worry, I'll buy it back off you and you'll still make a profit'......* Would he have taken the offer then? Probably like a shot!

But it was too late for that now.

He closed his eyes. The Health and Safety Exec bods would be all over it when they inspected the concrete.

'God help me,' thought Groom, *'unless Rawlings can sort out the HSE report.'*

A construction company with a known faulty product that the CEO left standing? He'd face corporate manslaughter charges, multi-million pound litigation for damages and penalty fines, not to mention those within the market, who would happily look to go for his throat and ruin him.

It never occurred to him, even for a moment, to consider the dead and injured. His entire focus was now on damage limitation, to him personally and Global Aggregates.

But there was another issue, Oleg Makarovich. Groom remembered the only question Oleg Makarovich had asked him at the takeover talks in 2008.

"Do you have any skeletons I need to know about?"

Of course he'd told him there weren't. He couldn't afford for the deal not to go through, but he now knew enough about Makarovich to know that he couldn't find out that he'd been lied to.

Just at that moment his phone rang.

"We've got a problem Sir Charles."

Stephen Rawlings, Head of Security for Global Aggregates.

Groom listened and then cursed himself for

agreeing to Brooks' idea to demonstrate GA's support of the HSE investigation. It was supposed to have been a smokescreen, about whether or not they had reduced the concrete cover, rather than anything to do with the use of the UFD30 formula. The GA Research team would prove the company had not reduced the concrete cover level, whilst Rawlings would take care of making sure the Health and Safety Executive report was inconclusive.

"Damn that girl for finding that bloody UFD30 file and damn Brooks too!"

Rawlings waited.

"Right Stephen, you need to get to Wall. This needs sorting and quickly. You need to take the kid gloves off this time."

Rawlings expected this response.

"I understand. I'll update you later today."

Groom looked out once again across the City below him and took a deep breath.

'No, I will not allow this to take me down.'

8

Martin Carruthers was waiting outside of the office of the Deputy Director of the Secret Intelligence Services, otherwise called MI6, at Vauxhall Cross in London.

It had been a sudden move back to London from his post as Head of Asia Pacific, but one he'd been pinpointed for because of his understanding of overseas financial affairs.

"Come in Martin, come in. So glad you've made it back to London," said Henry Greenfield.

"Glad to be back Henry, but it all seems to have been on the hurry up?" said Carruthers.

"Yes, yes, sorry about that. Look, I've brought you back Martin because you're good at this stuff, but also because you've made some damn good connections recently with a couple of our old friends."

Martin Carruthers smiled. Deniability, he needs something doing with no comeback on the Service. So that's why he's looking for me to use Greg Chambers and his 3R outfit.

Carruthers was long enough in the tooth to know when things needed to be spoken or unspoken and for the right things to be heard and understood.

"Yes, Henry, I understand, so tell me, what is it you

need looking into?"

Greenfield smiled. Carruthers was good. He knew what was required and could be relied upon to know what he was being asked to do, without it being spelt out for him.

"Oleg Makarovich. Russian oligarch, with an estimated fortune of somewhere between three and five billion pounds, with houses here and well, pretty much all over really. Back in 2008..."

"During the banking crisis?" said Carruthers.

"Yes, although it didn't affect Makarovich. Anyway, he used his investment bank, OBCR, the Overseas Banking Corporation of Russia, to front up the negotiations to buy into a failing concrete construction company called Global Aggregates, headed up by Sir Charles....."

"Groom," finished Carruthers.

"Know him Martin?" said Greenfield.

"Heard of him. Charming, persuasive, successful, arrogant, bully and ruthless."

"Yes, that's him. Knighted too, in 2013, when he pulled off some high profile construction work in the Middle East that by way of a quid pro quo, allowed HMG to sign off an agreement with the government concerned, meaning we could moor a couple of frigates there whenever we need to."

"So the knighthood was a bit of a thank you?" said Carruthers.

"Exactly. You scratch our back and we'll scratch yours."

"So if Groom's so helpful, what's the problem?" said Carruthers.

"Well to put it bluntly, we've known Makarovich has been laundering money through Global Aggregates pretty much since they started their little collaboration. Part of the deal meant that GA, which had been a PLC, a public limited company quoted on the stock exchange, was taken back into private ownership."

"Presumably because a PLC has to have Annual General Meetings with their shareholders, where difficult questions can be put to the Board?" said Carruthers.

"Yes, whereas, the opportunity to ask anything of a private company is greatly reduced," said Greenfield, "especially when the owners are Groom, Makarovich, his son and three other Russians."

"I'm assuming we have someone very close to Makarovich who is helping us on all of this?"

"Yes Martin, you can. They have been with him for a good many years, so you'll understand if I don't even share their details with you at this time."

"Of course."

It was always the way with anyone who was so deep undercover. It was imperative that knowledge of them was kept to an absolute minimum, which suggested that Henry Greenfield could well have been the original handler and probably still was.

"Okay, so what would be a good outcome if I can get someone to take a look at Makarovich?" asked Carruthers.

"Best outcome would be to block off Global Aggregates as a means of him laundering dirty money into the UK. Next best would be to slow it down, but Martin, Makarovich is no mug. He's ex-Russian Intelligence and he's not afraid to use his muscle. Mostly through his boy who is, how can I put this? A sadistic bastard," said Greenfield.

"Point taken," said Carruthers, who paused.

"Problem Martin?"

"Well I know Chambers may feel he owes us something, for helping out with the logistics when he was looking into the murder of John MacDonald's wife, but what makes you think he'll be interested in helping us with this?"

"This may be a way-in, but we don't know for sure," Greenfield passed across a file that Carruthers opened up and saw a press release relating to the collapse of the Witterings Shopping Centre."

He gave Carruthers a moment to look through the file.

"We've done a bit of a digging and it seems that Groom is leaning on Roger Wall, the owner of the Witterings Shopping Centre, to sell up for a fraction of the market price," said Greenfield.

"And Wall is?"

"An old friend, a very old friend of John MacDonald....," said Greenfield.

"Greg Chambers' oldest and most important client," said Carruthers.

"I'm assuming this isn't a formal action?" said Carruthers.

"Correct, but it's still bloody important that we try to correct the balance on how much Russian money, or more to the point, dirty Russian money, is coming into the country. Now, one last thing. Tell Chambers to be careful. Groom has an old friend of his working for him. Well maybe not so much a friend, but a former colleague, Stephen Rawlings, who's now running his personal security team."

Carruthers looked at Greenfield.

"Now that might just put a different complexion on things Henry."

"Thought so," said Greenfield, as he walked him towards his office door. "But I'm sure it's nothing he can't handle. Keep me posted."

With that Carruthers found himself outside the door, holding the file and wondering if the link to John

MacDonald would be enough to get Greg Chambers interested in taking this job on.

9

After an uneventful flight from Singapore to Mumbai, Terri had walked through Arrivals to see her dad, Greg Chambers, waiting for her.

"How was your trip my girl?"

"This bit was easy. Managed to get my head down with no dickheads kicking up a fuss at the back of the plane," said Terri.

Greg smiled. His daughter was bright, intelligent and articulate and could converse with the best, but when she needed to, she could still bring out her pure Aussie soldier-talk when she needed to get her point home.

"Someone annoy you on the way?"

"Not me, but he'd sure as hell been messing up his wife's life for way too long. But not anymore I'm pleased to say, because she's getting a divorce," said Terri.

"I have no idea what you're talking about Terri, but it sounds like you might have had a say in helping things along, so good for you," said Greg.

"Yep, if all this goes wrong, I reckon we can get a good recommendation if we want to start up a marriage guidance outfit. Now, how's your trip been Dad? Eschaan been looking after you?"

"Yes, it's been good, really good and he's been telling me about three new additions to the team."

"Ah, yes, my three girls. They look bloody good and I want one of them to be our version of Rob," said Terri. "Ah and something else I've been mulling over. Actually it was Sal, one of my old team, who suggested it. What do you think to a rebrand? 3R International."

He thought for a moment. Was it a bit grandiose? But then again, they were getting a lot of work in new countries.

"I like it. It fits with all the new work we're getting, so let's go with it! Now, come on, let's get to the hotel, change and get out for some dinner," said Greg.

As they walked out of the terminal and headed to the carpark, neither of them noticed the man standing thirty yards away, who seeing them leave, pushed a speed dial number on his phone.

*****

Sam stopped the car at the main entrance gate of the Global Aggregates R&D Centre. The intercom crackled and he heard a voice in Spanish asking what he wanted.

"I'm here to speak to your Head of Centre about a member of your staff, Lily Green," said Sam.

"Can I take your name please Señor?"

"Martínez, Sam Martínez."

"Un momento," the voice replied.

They waited for a few minutes.

"What do you think they do here?" asked Anna, "and don't say 'research and development,' or I'll throttle you."

Sam was looking them up on his phone.

"Well, this says the company has a suggested value of well over £1 billion. But that's estimated, because they're a privately owned company who keep their cards pretty close to their chest," said Sam. "They started off providing reinforced concrete to the construction industry, but after nearly going bankrupt in 2008 - that was the banking crash wasn't it?"

Anna nodded and Sam carried on.

"They went back into private ownership, since when they seem to have massively expanded, buying up their own construction companies along the way."

Just then, another crackle and the voice came back.

"I'm sorry there is no one to see you today."

With that the intercom went quiet.

"Well, I suppose that was maybe to be expected. We'll just have to wait till Lily wakes up and see if she wants to talk. Perhaps she did just need to get away?" said Sam.

"Maybe, but I wouldn't give up on your instincts just yet Sam, because something just doesn't feel right."

*****

Paul Brooks put the phone down to his reception team and then looked at his desktop screen as the images came through.

A light blue VW Beetle with two people in it. The intercom camera got a good view of the driver, a guy in his 30's, tanned complexion and it looked like a woman with fair, or at least light coloured hair next to him, but that was about all he could see of her.

'Who the hell are they and what do they want?'

He dialled a number on his mobile.

"Rawlings."

"Stephen, it's Paul, we've had someone called Sam Martínez at the front gate asking about Lily Green."

"And?"

"We didn't let them in."

"Good. What else?"

"He was driving a light blue Beetle, oh, and he had a woman in the passenger seat?"

"The grandmother?" said Rawlings.

"Don't know. Possibly. I've got the pictures on

screen, so at a guess, I'd say possibly, but can't say for certain."

"Okay, send me the pictures please Paul. And Paul, I can hear some concern in your voice. There is nothing to worry about. Lily will be back into work on Monday."

Brooks was worried, but he hadn't realised his voice was giving him away.

"I'm fine Stephen, fine. I take it everything is all sorted with Lily?"

"Yes it is, but we have a couple of loose ends. Now you haven't mentioned anything to Ian Parsons have you?"

"No, of course not, but I have removed his access to the stand alone server. In fact I've told everyone that we're doing some emergency maintenance, so no one can get into it at the moment," said Brooks.

"Good idea. What can you tell me about a Kevin Cox?" said Rawlings.

"Why, what's he got to do....," Brooks paused, he knew better than to start asking Rawlings questions. "He's one of our concrete experts over in Canada. He's in the Nova Scotia office."

Brooks thought he might have been cut off, as the phone had gone silent.

"Stephen?"

"Yes, I'm still here. Was he involved in anything to do with UFD10 or 30? Or any of the four sites back in 2007 for that matter?"

"No, definitely not. He only joined us in 2012, when we took over the Canadian company he was working for. Do you think he knows something about all of this?" said Brooks.

"He might do, but it's another loose end I could well do without. Listen Paul, you need to bolt this all down at your end, do you hear me? Groom is not happy that your smokescreen idea has now caused the UFD30 issue to come to the surface. If people start making a connection between that shopping centre collapsing in London and what this Lily Green found on that stand-alone server, then we'll all be screwed and you my friend, will be joining Sir Charles Groom in the dock on a corporate manslaughter charge."

Brooks felt himself shaking.

"But I can't be, I can't be held responsible for what Groom did?"

"No need to plead your case with me old boy, it's the judge and jury you'll need to convince."

Rawlings ended the call.

This was getting messy. The Green girl was one thing, but he could rely on Marsden to scare the living shit out of her. She'd never talk to anyone, and he was pretty sure Marsden would do his thing again to sort out her boss, Parsons. But these people in the Beetle and the other guy in Nova Scotia? Yes, it was messy, and that was even before he could sort out the HSE report.

*****

Eschaan had recommended Trèsind Mumbai, a modern Indian cuisine restaurant in the Bandra Kurla Complex, just south of the J W Marriott, where they were staying. As Greg and Terri left the restaurant after their meal, Greg saw a man standing across the road. He was looking at them. Greg turned back to say something to Terri, when he realised who it was he'd seen.

He immediately touched Terri's arm and they both pulled back into the side of the pavement. Greg watched as the man slowly walked across the road with his hands held out slightly to the side, palms up. A clear sign that he was unarmed and offering no threat.

"Mr Chambers and Miss Anderson."

"Ekam, how's your shoulder?" said Greg, as he looked around for any sign of support who Ekam may have with him.

"It is fine thank you. Will you be in Mumbai for long?"

"Just till tomorrow, but why the interest Ekam?" said Greg.

"This goes against all my loyalties Mr Chambers, but you and Miss Anderson need to be careful. Miss Kaur was very upset by your treatment of her when we last met."

"I'm sure she was Ekam, but at least it was just her money she lost," said Greg.

"I know and I appreciate that you had the option to take her life too, but please listen when I say that she has talked to her father of revenge. That is the word she used, revenge."

"Well thanks for the heads up Ekam, but why are you telling us this?" said Terri.

"I feel indebted to you Mr Chambers. You could have killed me back in Goa, but you didn't and in fact you also made sure I didn't bleed to death. This is my way of repaying that debt," said Ekam.

Greg just nodded at him. This was a proud man standing before him. He'd only been doing his job, protecting Jaz Kaur, and it probably took a lot to go behind his employer's back and come here to warn them.

"Consider the debt, if that's how you see it, repaid. I hope we don't get to meet again Ekam," said Greg.

"I hope so too, but please be aware that Miss Kaur's father, Gurnum Singh, may be the one you should be watching out for." With that Ekam gave a brief nod and turned and melted back into the crowd.

"Do you think we need to be worried?" said Terri.

"Forewarned is forearmed, but worried? I don't know without finding out more about what Kaur's father might offer in terms of a threat. We'll get

Eschaan to monitor things," said Greg. "Right, back to the hotel now for a couple of hours sleep. We've got a flight to catch at 03.00."

*****

Lily woke up in the late afternoon. She had to think for a moment. Where was she and what day was it? It felt like it had all been a bad dream. *'It's got to be Friday afternoon,'* she thought. This was her room, where she'd been sleeping since she started coming out to see her grandparents over twenty years ago.

She felt safe again, under her duvet and in her own bed, but the smile that had been starting to appear, quickly disappeared. Because it hadn't been a dream. That feeling of being safe was just an illusion. He could get her any time, and her grandparents too! And she couldn't bear the thought of anything happening to them.

'Tell no one.' That's what he'd said, over and over again. *'I will know if you tell anyone, so for your grandparents' sake, if not yours, do as I say.'*

She looked down at her arm. He must have used fine needles in the syringes, because there was now hardly a mark on her. No evidence, so who was going to believe her anyway?

She felt like crying, just hiding under the duvet, like she did as a child when something was the matter and maybe everything would be okay. But she knew it wouldn't. He and the other one, the one with the softer voice, had made it clear that they wouldn't harm anyone if she just said nothing.

"So that's it," she said out aloud to herself. "I say nothing and just carry on as if nothing's happened and it will all go away."

Did she believe that? Really? She knew she had no other option if she was to keep herself and her grandparents safe. She hoped to God that she could

72

stop her parents coming over, as she wasn't sure she could hold it back from them.

When she went downstairs she found both of them having a nap in the chair. *'They must have been scared witless,'* she thought, *'although they weren't the only ones.'*

She checked her watch.

'Mateo!'

He'd been so worried too and she hadn't been able to say anything to him and he'd been so kind on the journey up. He hadn't pressed her at all, saying she could tell him when she was ready, but of course, that was never going to happen.

"Lily! How are you? I was so worried," said Mateo as he picked up her call.

"I'm much better, after a good deep sleep. Listen, I'm sorry, but can we just not talk about what happened and where I was Mateo? I just needed some time and space, but I'm better now. Can I come down to you and stay for the weekend?"

"Si, si, mi querida. Yes, yes, my darling, if that's what you want."

"Thank you so much. I'll see you in a couple of hours, around seven."

Lily saw her grandmother stirring and went and made a pot of tea, bringing it back in just as her grandfather was waking up too.

"I'm so sorry I worried you both. Now listen, I'm going to ring Mum and Dad and tell them not to come. I've got some leave due, so I'll go and see them soon, but there's no point dragging them over here, okay?"

"As long as you're sure, then that's fine with us, isn't it Gramps?"

"Yes, yes, of course. Now if you don't want to talk about this, then that's fine. Just promise me and your Gran, that you weren't harmed, or hurt in any way," said her grandfather, who could barely breathe as he waited for Lily to answer.

She looked at both of them and when they saw her smile, they thought she must be alright.

"Oh thank God, Lily. We were so worried. I didn't know what to think," said Helen Green.

Lily even thought she saw a small tear running down her Gramp's face. She smiled again at them.

"No, I'm definitely not hurt. I've not been interfered with, if that's what you're worrying about. I'm fine," said Lily.

She heard the rush of air from both of them, as they both breathed out. *'You guys just do not need to know about any of this,'* she thought. *'I can deal with this and make it all go away.'*

10

Mateo had booked a table at one of their favourite restaurants, Tast Club, in Carrer de San Jaume, where he had first met her. He loved the arched ceilings and even though it was always busy, the staff were great at finding you a table, especially if there was just the two of you.

Lily had seemed okay, if slightly withdrawn when she got to his apartment, but as the evening went on he felt her start to relax. He made a point of not saying anything about what had happened over the past few days, partly because he didn't want to know and partly because he didn't want to stir it all up again for her.

However, he noticed she was quieter than usual when they arrived at the restaurant. He knew this was only to be expected, so he made sure he did most of the talking and he even made her laugh.

Later, when they got back to his apartment, she wanted to be held and held close. He could feel her breathing was laboured as she lay beside him in bed.

"Just sleep my darling, sleep."

Mateo then watched her as she drifted off into a fitful sleep. But they had both only been asleep for a few hours when he awoke, hearing her cry out in her sleep. She was screaming his name!

"Mateo!"

He tried to hold her hand, but Lily pulled it away. She was lying on her back, her body rigid, as though pinned down by some sort of invisible restraint. Sweat was pouring from her and her nightdress was soaked. He tried to gently wake her. But she didn't respond.

*****

She'd gone to sleep, feeling safe in Mateo's arms. But now she was back living the nightmare and Mateo could see her head thrashing from side to side.

Lily was in the finca with him, *'the cruel one with the cold eyes!'*

Naked, rigid, terrified.

'What did he want with her?'

The man was standing in front of her again. He was asking her questions. This was the one who had a posher voice, not the one who hit her. His voice was quiet, but she could feel her body was rigid with fear. She didn't even know if she was responding to the questions.

She was trying desperately to understand what he was saying. She couldn't hear the words clearly enough, but it sounded as though he was talking in English.

'Who was he? Where was she? Where was Mateo?' she thought.

Then the questions stopped and there was another man holding her arm. She flinched as she saw the syringe.

Mateo saw her try to pull her arm away. She was still deep in the dream, no it wasn't a dream. It was a nightmare! Her head was thrashing again and her mouth was moving and she was mumbling again. He moved closer and listened hard.

He saw her trying to scream, but he heard nothing.

'Oh my God, what's happening to me?'

She could feel her mouth trying to form the words, but there was no sound.

She saw the man again. Another question and when she didn't answer him, he hit her. A harder slap this time, across the face.

"Tell me what you know and it will be okay, I promise," said the man into her ear.

She really didn't think it would be alright if she told him anything and anyway, every time the nightmare came it was never alright, because she didn't know what she could tell him. She tried again.

"I don't know what you want me to tell you. I keep telling you, I don't know anything."

Another slap. This time harder. It was like she was floating above and looking down at herself. She was sitting in a chair, with her wrists and ankles tied to the arms and legs of the chair.

Then she remembered being on her bike, seeing the van and nearly being forced off the road as it pulled violently in front of her.

All along, she kept hearing him saying those words over and over and over again.

"Tell anyone and I will cut your grandparents to pieces."

She awoke screaming. Looking at Mateo and grabbing his arms.

"No, no, please, please don't!"

Then she whimpered, "You must believe me, I won't say anything, I won't say anything," and then the nightmare faded once again and she heard a different voice.

"It's me Lily, Mateo. It's me. Honestly you're safe now."

She didn't feel safe, but it wasn't '*him*', not the man, not the cruel one. She focused again and saw it was Mateo.

"Thank God," she said and she slumped against him.

"Oh Lily, what have they done to you?" he whispered.

11

Greg and Terri flew in on the Lufthansa flight to Palma de Mallorca International Airport, landing at 10.55am Mallorca time, on the Saturday morning, after a one hour layoff at Frankfurt.

"So you'll be okay if I go and stay at Anna's?"

"Yes, of course, besides, it'll be easier for you to talk about whatever it is Carruthers is bringing to the table for you," said Terri, "but keep me posted, in case you need any help."

"Yes, of course. Look, I haven't mentioned this before, but will you be seeing Daniel?"

He'd wanted to ask how things were going with Daniel, the pilot. Mainly because she'd not mentioned him at all during yesterday's meal, nor during the whole flight back today. As she hadn't said anything, he thought he'd leave the topic well alone, but he also didn't want to think of her sitting in her apartment in Portixol on her own.

"Dad, it's okay. With me and Daniel I mean, but I think we're better off as friends."

"Oh, okay, as long as you're good with that?" said Greg.

"Yes, I'm cool and don't worry, I've talked it all through with Mum when I saw her back home. I didn't mention it because, well because I didn't want you to worry about me. Plenty more fish and all that," said Terri.

"As long as you're fine, that's all I worry about. So just a quiet weekend for you then?"

"Quiet? What in Palma on a Saturday night? Oh no, Dad, I'll be out tonight. Drinks at Abaco with Sam and then we're off clubbing later."

"Good luck on that then. I reckon once I've had a nice hot bath, I'll be struggling to get out for the meal Anna's planning on having with Martin," said Greg.

The taxi master called them forward as the next taxi rolled up and stopped beside them. After dropping Terri off at her apartment, Greg directed the driver to take him to Anna's villa further down the coast in Illetas.

The traffic was reasonably busy for a Saturday morning, but they made good time. The sun was shining brightly over the bay and he smiled at the thought that it had only been a few months since he'd seen Anna after such a long time.

The driver stopped at the front gate to the villa and he paid the fare, before walking up the drive. Last time he'd been here, the circumstances had been somewhat more dramatic, with Anna being kidnapped by some of Sonny Sargsyan's men. But this time Anna was waiting at the front door for him.

"Hello handsome. How do you still manage to look good after twelve or thirteen hours in the air?" said Anna.

"I put it down to good moisturiser," said Greg, giving her a kiss on both cheeks.

"Well, you'll have to get me some for my birthday, whatever it is."

He followed her in and she handed him a cup of hot espresso.

"Have you rang Lori yet?" said Anna.

"No, but I sent her a text when we landed. She's busy though. No rest for an operational cop, weekend or not. She's somewhere in Malaga investigating some new cartel that's flexing its muscle with the local gangs. There's a few too many bodies flying about, so she's getting flak from the local Tourist Board. Anyway, how's Sam?"

"Yes, all good. Or at least, I say good. I think he's covering up the PTSD again. It's definitely better, but he can't seem to settle. I don't see him and Carmen carrying on much longer, not the way he's being with her. He seems to be pushing her away."

"I've just heard the same thing with Terri. Apparently, she and Daniel are now just friends. What is it about our kids?"

"Well I think I can maybe sit on the higher moral ground a little more than you here Greg. I was with Luis for over thirty years, whereas you....."

"Okay, point taken. Maybe I'm not the best person to pass judgement on relationships," laughed Greg. "So, anyway, when's Martin arriving?"

"He's on the 12.55 BA flight from LHR. Gets in about 16.30, so you've got time to get your head down for a few hours if you like?" said Anna.

"Yes, I didn't sleep much on the plane, but Terri and I had a good catch up on work stuff. By the way, she's come up with a name change! We're now 3R International. Sounds a bit grand for a boy from the Britwell in Slough, but, hey, we're now operating across multiple countries, so why not? It does sell the message after all."

"I like it," said Anna. "Terri's idea?"

"Well her and one of her friends, Sal, who she was in the army with. Okay, so sleep seems like a very good idea. I think I'll go for some shut-eye and catch up with you later. Have we got a….."

"Yes, table booked at Gustar, it's just up past Plaza Mayor. Miquel recommended it to me and it's lovely. Table's booked for nine."

He nodded and smiled. The tiredness was hitting him now, so he followed her up the stairs and into a room she'd made up for him.

"I'll come and get you up for a lunch," said Anna.

He lay down on the bed and he was asleep as his head hit the pillow.

*****

Terri saw Tommy's face appear on her phone screen.

"Where are you mate? Still roughing it at home in Barbados?"

"Yes, tough life, but someone's got to do it," said Tommy. Ex-para, tough as nails, big heart and with a beautiful lilting accent from his home country of Barbados. "Where are you hun?"

"Just landed back in my little bit of paradise. I'm with Greg." She didn't call him 'Dad' at work, it was just easier that way, with clients and the guys she worked with. "He's got a meeting with the spy-master, Martin Carruthers, later today with Anna."

"Do you know what about?" said Tommy.

"No, mate. You know what these spies are like. Keep everything close to their chest. Greg reckons it's something where Carruthers needs a big chunk of deniability, so nothing gets attributed to the politicos in HMG."

"Hmm, interesting. So is this a social call, or are you checking in on me?"

"Both, but as the meeting's later today, I thought I'd get my bearings on where you and the Welshman are."

"Well, I'm here. I've been seeing my kids and grandkids and right at this moment, I'm sitting on the beach with a coffee, looking out to sea, talking through old times with one of my chums."

"Bet that's a nice view then?" said Terri.

"It sure is that. In fact there's a very attractive woman running along the beach as I speak. Very mysterious she is too. I've seen her every day for the past week. Same time, same routine, running on her own."

"Well, don't be shy. Go and introduce yourself!"

"I might just do that. My friend Rico here says she's one of the guests here at the Fairmont. He thinks she's European, or maybe East European. She causes quite a stir on the beach," he laughed. "You can generally see a couple of guys on their beach with their wives and the guys are pretending to read, but they're looking over the top of their books as she runs by. But you know me girl, holiday romances are not my thing. Anyway, what about you and pilot boy? Is that still a thing you've got going?"

"Nope, I don't like holiday romances either," said Terri, who quickly followed it up with, "Okay, well keep your phone on mate and I'll be in touch when I know where we stand with this job."

She rang off and sat for a moment. *'Why hadn't it worked out again with Daniel? Did she just not try hard enough at this stuff?'*

Next was the Welshman, Simon. Ex-Special Forces and if Tommy was tough? Well, Simon was way past that.

"Hello, how are you?" he said.

Very formal, quietly spoken, gentle Welsh accent. *'Butter wouldn't melt.'* Oh, but she knew it would.

"I'm good Simon, good. How about you?"

"I'm fine, Still on the same job, but we're in Birmingham now."

This was a new client. A top-end jeweller, who despite the move by others to on-line sales, was opening a new chain of boutique stores. They had asked for help in risk assessing the routes their drivers would be taking, when travelling to and from the premises.

"Shouldn't be too much longer. We've done the recce of the routes and I'm happy with the RA report and so is the client, especially on the risk strategies I set out for him."

"Good stuff mate," said Terri. "Just so you know, there's a possible new job coming in today from our friend Martin Carruthers. No idea if Greg will take it, but be ready to move if I call."

"Will do."

Her phone went dead. Short and to the point as it always was with Simon. He wasn't a man of many words.

*****

Greg felt refreshed after a sleep and enjoyed the lunch Anna had prepared, just simple bread, cold meats, cheese and olives, washed down with a glass of Albariño.

"John's on the island this week, so I thought I'd pop across and see him this afternoon," said Greg.

"Give him my love. I saw him a couple of days ago. He's still obviously missing Sheila, but I think the horror of it all is easing a little," said Anna.

This was how he had come to meet up again with Anna after so many years. John MacDonald was his oldest client and Greg had come straight away when John's eldest boy, Chris, rang to tell him Sheila had been murdered at their home, here on the island.

An hour or so after finishing lunch, he was at the gate to the MacDonald villa, pushing the intercom button. Consuela, the housekeeper, answered it and let him in.

John was at the front door as Greg brought Anna's

car to a halt.

"No little white van today then?" said John.

Greg smiled. Even John knew about his penchant for white vans then.

"Don't you start on me John, I have enough problems with that daughter of mine."

They shook hands. John's was always a strong grip and today was no different. *'The old boy's starting to get back to his old self,'* thought Greg.

"Drink or tea Greg?"

He went for the tea. It was hot, so a cold beer would have gone down well, but no point in chancing things after the Albariño.

"So you've been in India then?"

Greg gave him a quizzical look.

"Yes, so I'm wondering how you know that. Are you keeping tabs on me John?" he said with a smile.

John laughed. "Ha! You see, none of us can do anything these days without someone knowing what we're up to. Terri has been talking to Chris about some stuff they're working on and she dropped in that she stopped off in India on her way home to pick you up. So what brings you to Mallorca? Other than obviously to see me and Anna?"

"Anna and I have got a meeting about something, it's tonight. No idea what it's about, but I'll no doubt find out later."

John nodded. Greg was being deliberately vague, so he knew better than to push further. He knew Greg was ex-Intelligence Service, so it might well be something to do with that.

"Well I've also got something for you as well, if you don't mind taking a look? It might be something or nothing, but it's for an old friend, Roger Wall, who's hit on some hard times," said John.

12

As they walked into Gustar, Greg and Anna saw Carruthers waiting for them at a table.

Greetings over, they sat and chose from the menu and Fidel, the owner came across and welcomed Anna with a kiss on both cheeks.

"These are my friends Fidel. I've told them how much I like this place," said Anna.

"Well we must not disappoint your friends, amiga. Now try this. It's a wonderful new cava I have found." He opened the bottle and poured them each a glass and stood back.

"Delightful Fidel," said Carruthers.

"Now I will leave you for a few moments to decide on what you might wish to eat this evening."

"Greg, many thanks for diverting here from Mumbai."

Greg looked over his wine glass at him.

"How did you know I was in Mumbai Martin?"

"Oh, I'm sure Anna must have mentioned it."

Anna looked at Greg and shook her head.

"Oh, no matter, but I'm glad you were able to make it," said Carruthers brushing off Greg's questioning look with a wave of the hand.

In between Fidel coming back to take their orders

for tapas and to suggest a bottle of wine, they sat and listened whilst Carruthers took them through the background of Oleg Makarovich and his money laundering activities.

"Martin, did you say he's the main backer of Global Aggregates?" said Anna.

"Yes, he bailed out plain old Charles Groom, as he was back then in 2007, when the crash hit and GA's cash flow finally dried up. But why do you ask?"

"Now this may be a complete coincidence, but Sam and I were up in Puerto Pollensa yesterday helping out a friend whose granddaughter had gone missing for a couple of days, but she's turned up now," said Anna.

"Is she okay?" asked Greg. "And what's the link here Anna?"

"That's the thing that's niggling Sam. I think it's his copper's nose. She says she's okay, but she's not talked about what's happened. She just needed some time and space apparently. But she came home in different clothes and there's no sign of her bicycle that she went to work on."

"Boyfriend trouble?" said Carruthers.

"No, he brought her home. He's from the mainland, but has been out here for a while apparently. He seemed genuinely concerned," said Anna.

"So why would she go missing?" said Greg.

"Well that's where Sam's nose really started to twitch. And you asked what the link is? Well it's where she works, she's an intern at Global Aggregates R&D Centre. It's on the road between Puerto Pollensa and old town Pollensa."

"Go on," said Greg.

"They wouldn't let us in when we asked to speak to someone about Lily…, that's the girl…, about her going missing."

"Interesting, but why would there be any sort

of connection with this young woman, Lily, going missing and Oleg Makarovich?" said Greg.

"To be honest, I don't know if there is, at least not on what we know at the moment. Mind you, that's probably more because Makarovich doesn't get anywhere near the day to day running of GA. It means he's far enough away to avoid having to answer any difficult questions about the money laundering," said Carruthers.

"Martin, you mentioned Makarovich bought in to GA back in 2008. Wasn't that around the time they'd completed the Witterings Shopping Centre complex? The one that collapsed three, or so months ago?" said Anna.

Carruthers was about to speak, when Greg interrupted.

"Hang on a minute Anna. This is getting even more bizarre. Did you say the Witterings Shopping Centre?" said Greg.

"Yes, that's the one," said Anna, she saw the look on his face. "Why?"

"It's owned by Roger Wall?" said Greg.

"Yes," said Carruthers.

"Martin, this is getting way too strange. I saw John MacDonald this afternoon."

Martin nodded.

"He's asked me to look into something for Roger. It seems he's an old chum from way back when. They both ran their own companies, both doing well in the 80's, but then John's business really started to take off, whereas Roger's seems to have stalled a bit," said Greg.

"Did he say what it is Roger wants you to look at?" said Martin, trying not to give anything away.

"Something to do with Wall getting pressured to sell the Shopping Centre at a give-away price. It seems that he's built up a pretty significant debt with GA for building supplies for his current projects and now he's being squeezed to sell to pay off his debts," said Greg, "and it's the way he's being squeezed that has got John's back up. He doesn't like bullies and it seems that Groom has a bit of a reputation of being just that, manipulating his competition into a corner and then applying heavy-handed tactics to get his own way."

"So it looks like we've got a couple of things that could be purely coincidental, or might there be some sort of connection linking Groom and the shopping centre collapse with what happened to Lily over here?" said Anna.

Whether they thought it was a coincidence or not, Carruthers tried not to show any sense of satisfaction that he seemed to have both Anna and Greg engaged in the possibility of getting involved.

"You're right, we don't know, but it might be very useful to find out," said Carruthers. "One thing's for sure. Global Aggregates is now so big in the market that Makarovich can bring in as much dirty cash as he wants. So if he, or Groom, needed to protect GA's reputation to keep the money laundering operation watertight, then who knows to what ends they might go to."

"But Martin, can't you set the Monopolies Commission on them, rather than this cloak and dagger stuff?" said Anna.

"They'd tie them up in knots and meanwhile, the dirty cash would keep coming through. No, this needs another type of intervention, where we can persuade Oleg Makarovich that there's good reason that he should take his money elsewhere."

"What about the impact on the construction market? If we somehow manage to persuade Makarovich to take all his cash out, won't that cause a massive implosion of the building industry?" said

Greg.

"Not if he willingly transfers ownership back into the public domain at a reduced market value," said Carruthers slowly.

"Willingly Martin?" Both Anna and Greg said it together.

"Well yes, that would be the ideal outcome," said Carruthers, "and I'm sure you'll come up with a way to make that happen."

They both looked at him and as Greg went to speak, Carruthers went on, "One final thing. Did I mention Stephen Rawlings?"

Greg looked straight at him.

"No, you didn't. How is he involved?"

Anna looked at Greg.

"I have to declare a bit of self-interest here. I don't like him, but he did save my hide big time back in Bosnia. He's definitely one who rides his luck more than just a bit and he takes things right to the edge. But the bosses loved him. He did used to get results and I was bloody glad he came through the door when he did, back in Sarajevo in the 90's."

"He's been Groom's Head of Security since around the time he went into business with Makarovich. There's some suggestion that Groom is very wary of Makarovich and so wanted someone to watch his back, just in case, so to speak. But Rawlings also seems to be a bit of a fixer too. He's been involved in some of the negotiations when Groom has been acquiring other companies, where the purchase price has sometimes been some way below the estimated market value," said Carruthers.

"A friendly persuader of some sort?" said Anna.

"Not so friendly, I think. He uses a man called Marsden. Ex-army, ex-police and ex-doorman. Someone else, who appears to be a nasty so and so when it comes to negotiating," said Carruthers.

Greg looked at Carruthers and then across to Anna. There was something about this whole thing that didn't quite ring true. Anna broke his line of thought.

"This is sanctioned isn't it Martin?" asked Anna.

"Oh yes, yes, it most certainly is, from almost the very top, from Henry Fielding, he specifically asked me to get you guys involved."

"So, it is sanctioned, officially?" said Anna.

Carruthers paused and that was enough for them to understand.

"Look Martin, I'd rather you just came straight out with it and asked us to do it, if that's what you want. You're saying it's sanctioned, but then you hesitated when Anna asked if it was official. Forgive me, but I've been in this game a long time and if you expect me to believe that this is just a bunch of coincidences? Well, I don't. I think you're spinning me a line. I reckon that somehow you already knew John was going to ask me to look into Roger Wall, so to be honest, at this moment in time, I'm inclined to say 'no', unless you just come out with the truth," said Greg.

Carruthers looked at him and then Anna, and then held his hands up.

"I'm sorry, I wasn't sure if the money laundering on its own would be sufficient to get you interested. But…"

"But the link to John MacDonald from Roger Wall was something you thought I wouldn't want to turn down?" said Greg.

"Well no, not with MacDonald being your oldest client and all that," said Carruthers. "But if I may continue? That was my plan, so I hold my hands up. We have some contacts with Wall's bankers and …"

"A suggestion was worked in to a conversation with Wall?" said Greg. He'd done it himself on numerous occasions. That's why John Mac would have had no idea he was part of a set up to get Greg involved.

"Yes, as I said I put my hands up. Next time I'll just ask you."

"So this thing with Lily may be connected, but to the Witterings collapse, more than the money laundering?" said Anna.

"I didn't know about Lily Green, "said Carruthers.

"Perhaps it is nothing more than a coincidence then?" said Greg.

"Possibly, but Sam has a sense for these things and it doesn't feel right to him, so let's not discount anything," said Anna.

"Okay, I'm with you on that. What's Makarovich doing with the money once it's clean?" said Greg.

"We don't know for sure, but to be honest, it doesn't take much thinking. It will be ending up in the bank accounts of the group he works with, for re-investment later somewhere outside of Russia and more likely than not, in the UK," said Carruthers.

"Gaining Makarovich an even stronger foothold in the UK economy," said Anna.

Greg looked across at Anna, who gave a small nod.

"Okay then, seeing as John MacDonald wants me to take a look at what Groom's up to with his old mate, Roger Wall, then whilst we're doing all that, we might just see where Makarovich fits into all of this. Anna, we'll get Sam and I suggest Terri to see what's going on with Lily Green disappearing off the face of the earth for a couple days," said Greg.

Anna nodded again and Martin Carruthers sat back, job done.

"So we're in, but Martin.....please no more half-truths. Just keep it all level and above board and we'll get on just fine."

Martin Carruthers held his hands up in the air in acknowledgement.

"Right, that's sorted. Ah, perfect timing Fidel!" said Greg. "This looks excellent."

"The grilled octopus, as I suggested and a wonderful bottle of Attis Embaixador, a fantastic Albariño!"

Martin sat back, pleased he'd got their buy-in, but recognising he should maybe have just been upfront with them in the first place. That then left him wondering if he should mention the source close to Makarovich, but he decided that was still very much a need to know.

13

Just a few streets away in the city, in the more tourist focused area for restaurants and bars, Sam had grabbed a table at Abaco as he waited for Terri. It wasn't long before there was a slight murmur from some of the other people at the tables as they saw a tall, very attractive blonde haired woman step in through the big wooden doors.

'*Never fails to make an entrance,*' he thought, standing up to greet his half-sister, Terri.

They ordered drinks, Mallorquin gin in the beautiful, huge goblets they use in Abaco. Sam didn't drink there very often, not at almost €20 a pop, but it was a good fun place for a catch up with Terri, with masses of flowers and fruit in displays around the room and after a couple of strong gins, it wasn't long before they were both grimacing, as they each explained how things were going, or rather not going with their respective partners, Carmen and Daniel.

Sam tried to explain what he'd said to Carmen, realising half way through, that it wouldn't have sounded good to her.

"I'm trying to find the right word for you Sam, but I'm struggling to get beyond 'moron' at the moment mate."

"Presumably that's your polite version Sis?" said Sam.

"Oh yes, I'm sure I'll have adapted it by the end of the night. What the hell were you thinking? Is it too late do you think? I mean, I get the basics of what you were saying to her, you know, that you're okay if she feels she needs to leave the island for her job, but there's so many ways you could have put it better mate," said Terri.

"Oh, how I know that now. Now, enough of me, how are things with you and Daniel?"

"Ah well, I might be able to give out some sound advice Sam, but I stand guilty of not being able to put that same advice into practice."

"Okay, so it looks like we're both in the same boat. What about Greg and what have you been up to in Oz?" But he noticed she didn't seem to be listening and she was half-looking across the room at something.

"Something, or someone, caught your eye?" said Sam.

"Someone. Maybe I'm imagining things, but after we had a heads up about some possible retribution by Jaz Kaur, or her old man, I suppose I've been keeping more of an eye out. There's two guys over, by the staircase."

Sam looked across. It was difficult to get a face-on look of the men, as they were looking down at their drinks.

"Do you want me to go over and find out who they are?"

"No, it's probably nothing," said Terri. "They're not Indian, that's for sure and I can't see Kaur's dad putting a job like this out to a sub-contractor. But hey, I'm tired. We took off at three this morning Indian time, but with the five hour time difference, we landed here at around ten, so maybe it's just lack of sleep catching up."

Just at that moment, the two men got up and walked towards them and then straight past, without looking at them, before disappearing out of the main entrance and back on to the street.

Sam immediately sensed something was up. No guy he'd ever known, straight or gay, would walk by his half-sister and not at least glance at her.

"Come on, let's go and have a word," said Sam and he was up and heading for the door before she could get up out of her chair.

As Sam stepped through the Abaco entrance door, he saw one of them turn to the other.

"I told you not to stare, you idiot. The blonde made us straight away. Now go and get the bloody car!"

Sam saw the other man slope off down the street.

"Maybe your friend should have stared a bit more as he walked past. That probably wouldn't have caught my attention quite so much," said Sam.

"Listen mate. I don't know who you are. I've had a long day, so why don't you just piss off back with your girlfriend and give her a good time," said Tom Marsden.

"Who me?" said Terri, as she stepped out through the doors onto the street. "Oh, I'm not his girlfriend mate, I'm his sister. So that's our introductions done. Now who the hell are you?"

Marsden looked at her. All sorts of thoughts rushing through his head. Terri saw him staring at her and felt the hairs on the back of her neck start to rise. *'Strange,'* she thought.

"Yes, who are you?" said Sam. "And what are you doing watching us?"

Marsden looked back at Sam and then across to Terri. They were at his ten and two o'clock. Was that by chance, or did they know what they were doing? Positioning themselves equidistant within his fighting arc. He could do with some back-up from that idiot who'd gone for the car.

"Look, I'm sorry if I caused you guys any offence," said Marsden, trying to buy some time. "Like I said, I've had a long day. Let's just forget all of this, shall we? Or we could go back inside and I'll buy you both a drink? No hard feelings."

Sam was looking at him. The bloke looked big enough to handle himself and he wasn't intimidated in the slightest by them. *'He's taking the tactical option to withdraw and fight another day,'* he thought.

Just at that moment an Audi Q7 SUV came around the corner and stopped next to Marsden.

"Ah, looks like I'll have to catch you guys next time. But I will look forward to it," said Marsden looking directly at Terri. With that, he was in through the passenger door and the car sped off.

"Did you hear what he said Terri? He'd catch us next time? So who the hell is he? And is looking at me, you or us?"

"I don't know Sam, but one thing's for sure. My internal alarm bell was ringing loud and clear when he looked at me. He, would not be a nice man to be on your own with."

*****

Marsden rang Rawlings to report in.

"Unfortunate Tom, that they should see you," said Rawlings.

"Yes, the muppet I was with couldn't take his eyes off the woman and he blew us out. The woman's Australian, whereas Martínez, the one Finn says is an ex-Met cop, he's definitely got more of a London accent, but she said she's his sister."

"Well enough about the family relationships Tom. I want to know who these people are. Was she the one in the car with him up in Pollensa yesterday?"

"Can't say for sure," said Marsden. "Finn's given us

a good head start with the address off the Beetle's number plate, that's how we found Martínez and tracked him to the bar in the first place. I've got a small team here I can put on them. I'll get the guys out and see if they can't find out where these two go tonight."

"Good. And Lily?"

"Nothing, probably still having nightmares though," said Marsden.

"Okay, at least that's one end we've got tied up. Now I may need you to go to Canada, so get yourself ready and if you take someone, make sure you take someone better than the one you had with you tonight."

Marsden didn't like being admonished by Rawlings, but he had a point.

"I'll be ready."

14

As they sat around the kitchen table the following morning, Anna brought in coffee and home baked ensaïmadas, beautiful sweet pastries, as Greg brought Sam and Terri up to speed on the meeting with Martin Carruthers the night before.

"So do we think Lily's disappearing act is connected in some way with Groom or Makarovich, or the Witterings Shopping Centre for that matter?" said Terri.

"I suppose we can't say for sure either way can we? At least not at the moment," said Sam. "But we had a strange encounter last night, didn't we Terri?"

"Yes, we had two guys eyeing us up in Abaco. Well one of them was anyway. We followed them both outside and saw one getting bawled out by his boss for giving them away. We then had a little chat with his boss outside in the street."

"A little chat?" said Greg.

"Yes, just that. It didn't go beyond a few ruffled feathers, before his dozy mate turned up in an Audi and whisked his boss away."

Greg immediately thought of Rawlings.

"How old was he? The boss?"

"Oh, no more than thirty, thirty five tops," said

Terri. "Why?"

"There's a guy who works for Sir Charles Groom who I used to work with, but he's older than that."

"So your guy, he's ex-Intelligence Service?" said Sam.

"Yes. Do you know him Anna?" said Terri.

"No, I was long gone by the time he'd have been recruited. Do we need to be worried about him Greg? You said he runs close to the edge?"

"Concerned, for sure. He's good at what he does, so if he's running things for Groom he'll be covering his tracks pretty well. Okay, we need a plan. What have we got that we know at the moment?" said Greg.

Sam spoke first.

"We've got Lily, who went missing Wednesday, but turned up again at her boyfriend's after two and a bit days on Friday. No explanation and no apparent injuries. Then we've had the shopping centre collapse with five dead and dozens injured and the centre owner, Roger Wall, is being pressured by Groom to sell up. Wouldn't that actually be a good thing for Wall? To get rid of the problem back to Groom?"

"Well yes, but he'd take a massive hit on the property value, something he might not be able to survive," said Anna, who had been searching the business news on her laptop.

"But if Groom's company, Global Aggregates, provided the reinforced concrete for the original build, won't the responsibility fall on his shoulders if the Health and Safety Exec find that's the cause?" said Sam.

"Good point Sam!" said Greg. "How the hell is Groom going to get around that? He'll be up on a corporate manslaughter charge."

"Can they fix the Health and Safety Exec? That's what Martin said Rawlings' sidekick, Marsden, is good at," said Anna.

"It's a tall order, to influence the report to that

extent I mean, but I guess we need to check it out. Groom's reputation is sky high at the moment, but he still can't chance the outcome of a manslaughter charge. His reputation, and not to mention his business, would crash and burn on a guilty outcome," said Sam.

"Okay," said Greg. "So we look at the Health and Safety team who are investigating this too."

"Sam, Terri. You focus on Lily. See if you can get into her and find out what happened, plus see who this Mateo really is. Anna, you and I will get across to London and make contact with Roger Wall and check the scope of the Health and Safety investigation."

"Sounds like a plan Greg, although I'd be surprised if the H&S investigators have been got at. They go through some very thorough vetting, but who knows, with the money Groom and Makarovich have at their disposal, nothing's a hundred percent safe," said Sam.

"One thing," said Greg, a serious look appearing on his face. "Do not underestimate Rawlings and the people who work for him. He will have picked them with care, so they will be good, very good, so make sure you take care with any interactions, okay?"

Seeing them all taking on board what he'd said, he carried on.

"Right, let's see where this takes us, and Terri, presumably, you've given the boys a call?"

"Yep, in hand and ready to deploy when we call them."

*****

Rawlings and Marsden were sat on the morning flight back to London.

"Tom, I've got one more thing I want you to do before you go to Canada. Go and see this Roger Wall again and get that damned contract signed. But this time, you may need to apply a lot more direct pressure to help him make up his mind, because I want this deal done and dusted to get Groom off my back."

Marsden nodded. He'd seen the pictures of Wall's daughter and her children, his grandchildren, on the file. An idea started to form in his mind as to how Wall might be persuaded to sell.

*****

Three hours later and Rawlings was sitting in Groom's study in his London apartment.

"So have you got this thing in hand now Stephen?" challenged Groom.

"It's never not been in hand Sir Charles," said Rawlings, maintaining his calm, albeit through gritted teeth.

Groom heard the irritation in Rawlings' voice.

'Won't do him any harm to know I want this sorted, and quickly.'

"Good, so when can I expect you to close the deal with Wall?"

"I'd say give it a week. But some good news is that you don't need to worry about the Health and Safety Report. It's due to be announced tomorrow and let's just say it won't show anything adverse for Global Aggregates," said Rawlings.

"Excellent, was that our man on the inside?"

Rawlings nodded.

He'd long ago got his hooks into Tony Wilson, one of the Health and Safety analytics team. Groom had been looking for a weakness in the HSE team, as insurance should he ever need help on a Health and Safety investigation and he'd told Rawlings to find someone.

It didn't take too long for Rawlings to discover Wilson had a very heavy gambling habit, one that he couldn't sustain on his salary as a chemical analyst.

The trap was set when Wilson had an unpleasant visit from Marsden, presenting himself as a particularly nasty debt collector. Groom then had his friendly analyst, ready for whenever he might need him and all for the cost of maintaining Wilson's ever-growing gambling debt, which Rawlings had previously bought off.

"Yes, Wilson's come in very handy," said Rawlings. "He kicked off a bit when I told what we needed him to do, but one suggestion that he'd see Marsden again soon changed his mind. So he's made the switch on the concrete samples the investigators gathered at the Witterings. He won't do the actual analysis himself, but it doesn't matter, in fact it's better that way. Whoever does, will find it's perfectly good UFD10 and not the UFD30. There's nothing wrong with the original UFD10 formula, so there'll be no fault laid at your door Sir Charles."

"So as far as the Health and Safety Exec are concerned, it will just be put down to an unknown reason, an unfortunate and tragic accident?" said Groom.

"Yes, although there's still something I need to perhaps tidy up in Canada, because of that damn girl in Mallorca."

"Lily Green, the intern? I thought you said she wouldn't say anything? That Marsden had firmly shut her up?" said Groom.

"Yes, she shouldn't be a problem, but she sent an email to a Kevin Cox. He's had nothing to do with the work Parsons was doing with Green, but we need to check it out. Just to be sure."

"Bloody hell, an email! Have you got rid of it?" said Groom.

"Yes, we wiped it as soon as we knew about it, but we don't know what Cox has done about it. He's out in Nova Scotia. Marsden will be going out there shortly to find out."

"Good, but there's too many loose ends here Stephen, what with the girl, Parsons, Wall and now Cox. I did say there would be a healthy bonus in this for you, so just make sure you earn it."

"As I said Sir Charles, it is in hand, although I note your concerns. But believe me when I say that Green and Parsons are not a problem. The others we will deal with," said Rawlings.

"Make sure you do. Now I've got to get on and you've no doubt got somewhere to go," said Groom.

Rawlings stood up and let himself out. Sometimes he found Groom the most arrogant of men. Groom had brought him in to provide protection against any potential threat from Makarovich, but the way Groom treated him? Well, he just might not stand in his way if Makarovich chose to take a pop at Groom. A half-smile. There was still the bonus to look forward to and he was confident he had the job in hand to keep Groom's precious reputation safe.

Green and Parsons were pretty air tight. He'd dealt with Parsons himself, reminding him of the school fees GA were paying for his kids, not to mention the photographs they had of him with his girlfriend…..that he wouldn't want his wife to see.

'No, things are under control.'

*****

"So what was it about Lily that didn't seem right Sam?" said Terri, as they drove back up to Puerto Pollensa in Sam's Beetle.

"Gut feel more than anything. Too calm, too collected. Her Gran had said she's a real life and soul of the party girl, always bubbly, full of life. And that's certainly not what she was displaying the other day when Mateo brought her back."

"But you said she didn't look like she'd open to you?"

Sam shook his head.

"So, how about we try the *'befriending thing'*?" said Terri. "See if I can get her to open up, girl to girl. It may take a bit of subterfuge, but if direct questions aren't working then it's maybe all we've got to go on."

"I reckon it's worth a go," said Sam.

"Do we keep the grandparents in the loop?" said Terri.

Sam thought for a moment.

"I don't think we can rely on them keeping shtum. Helen is trying to convince herself that Lily is okay and nothing's the matter. I think Gramps, Geoffrey, may have his suspicions, but he won't move on it for fear of upsetting Lily. Any ideas what you'll do?"

"I think the jilted girlfriend comes to mind. I'll book in somewhere overnight if I can, mind you that may be easier said than done in mid-summer. Popular place, Puerto Pollensa," said Terri.

"Yes, it is, lots of people's idea of their little bit of paradise. Beautiful bay, great place for walking, cycling, swimming. That reminds me, Lily seems to be into her cycling. She's got a nice GIANT road bike in her grandparents' garage," said Sam.

"Well, it seems like an ideal place for my imaginary boyfriend to bring me for a romantic weekend, only to then go and dump me. I'll also bear in mind the cycling angle, if we need to bond on something other than boyfriends."

"Perfect," said Sam, as they pulled into the port and he dropped her off. "I've got a chum who lives nearby, who can put me up in his spare room. But wear the comms. It's all wireless and will bounce off your phone," he passed her the covert ear piece and mic set. "Oh, and Terri?"

"Yes, mate?"

"We need a signal word."

She knew what he meant. In case of danger. She

thought for a moment.

"Anything where I mention Daniel."

"Got it, but let's hope it doesn't come to that."

She was out of the car and walking down the road.

15

"You don't need to go back to work tomorrow Lily. Not if you don't want to," said Mateo, as they drove back up north to Puerto Pollensa.

"Look, Mateo. It's okay. I want to go back to work and just put this behind me."

"But put what behind you Lily? You still haven't told me what happened during those two, three days you were gone!"

She was quiet for a moment. She so wanted to tell him. Wanted to tell someone, anyone. But she couldn't, not without risking what might happen to Gran and Gramps. And besides, she'd only known Mateo for just a few weeks. Did she really know him well enough? To trust him enough to risk her grandparents?

"Where are you now? In your head I mean. You seem to be a million miles away. What are you thinking?" said Mateo.

"Nothing, I was just thinking how lovely you've been, how understanding. Please Mateo, please, just leave this be and let's enjoy the rest of today. Let's go for a drink at Bar Bonys!"

He smiled at her. She was brave, he'd certainly give her that.

"Yes, why not. It's a beautiful afternoon, time for cocktails!"

It wasn't long before he was parking the Porsche in the carpark and they were walking through the town to find a table at Bonys.

She'd been going to Bonys since she was old enough to drink and probably a few years before that as well with her parents, she smiled.

"Hola amigo," she said as she saw José, "Que tal? How's it going?"

"Muy bien Lily! It's good to see you," said José, giving her a warm hug and a kiss to both cheeks. "How about a drink amigos?"

They settled on a bottle of Rosado and sat enjoying the Sunday afternoon ambience, with the sun shining high up in the sky and Lily at last, started to feel she could relax just a little.

*****

Terri had found an Air BnB apartment for a couple of days, just five minutes' walk from the town centre. She was dropping her bag in the room when her phone buzzed. It was a text from Sam. *'Just checked in with Lily's grandparents. She's phoned them. She's back in PP with M. Going for a drink. Try Bonys or Capri.'*

Terri googled both bars and then started walking into town. It was hot, especially because the gentle breeze off the bay wasn't making its way into the town. She was used to the heat, but was still glad when she realised she didn't have far to go when she found Bonys on her maps app.

She never thought too much about how she looked to other people, but she was aware that some people found her very attractive. Therefore, if Lily was in Bonys, then Terri needed her to spot her as she walked in and the best way to do that was to probably get Mateo's attention.

As Terri headed for Plaça Miguel Capllonch, she casually fiddled with her dress, but it was to check her comms mic, that was inside her bra. Satisfied it was all secure, she then flicked at her hair, to adjust her earpiece, as she entered the main square.

"Testing, testing, are you anywhere close by mate?"

"Yes, I can see you," said Sam.

"Copied."

Terri recognised her from the photo Sam had showed her. Lily was sat at one of the tables in Bonys with a young man. Terri took a wide circle around the square, to make sure she came into the bar at such an angle that Mateo would see her. She also needed Lily to be able to see that Mateo was looking at another woman.

Terri wanted to make enough of an entrance to get his attention, but also leave Lily with the thought that something was perhaps troubling the woman she'd just seen walk in the bar.

'Cheap trick,' she thought, 'but it should work.'

And work it did.

Dressed in a pale yellow, thin strapped, floaty dress with white sandals, she made her grand entrance into the bar, with tortoise shell sunglasses and a big sunhat perched on her head. She looked around and sat down at a table not far from Lily and Mateo.

Mateo smiled at Terri. Lily saw him and her look made him quickly look back at her, but then he looked back at Terri, who took her sunglasses off and smiled again. But this time she pulled a bit of a resigned face, as though something was on her mind, together with a forced smile.

She looked at the drinks menu and asked the waiter for a Mojito Clásico. She gave her order for the drink in broken Spanish, although this didn't take too much acting on her part. She then sat quietly, sunglasses back on, as though deep in thought, whilst all the time studying the interaction between Lily and Mateo.

They looked like a happy couple, although he seemed to be trying harder to keep the conversation flowing. But that said, Lily was engaged and seemed comfortable in his company. *'These two get on well, that's for sure,'* thought Terri.

Mateo got up from the table. As he walked past Terri, he glanced at her, but she'd seen enough of how men often looked at her, to know that this was just a look, a glance, but without interest.

'Okay, so you seem to genuinely like her. Will she tell you why she went missing?' she thought, but she was interrupted as Lily suddenly got up and came and sat by her.

"Look, I'm sorry, but I couldn't help thinking something's the matter? Please tell me to mind my own business if you're okay," said Lily.

Terri smiled. She really was a sweet girl, just as Sam had described. Whatever had gone on with her, she'd immediately dropped her own problems to help a complete stranger.

"No, it's okay, I'm fine. Just a rubbish weekend," said Terri.

"Well, I can go with that. I had a rubbish week, but the weekend has been better," said Lily. "Want to talk about it?"

"Oh I don't know. Not sure it will do any good. We came here for a clear the air weekend and…., well we certainly did that. He cleared off!"

"What? He just left you here?" said Lily.

"Yep, but I should have seen it coming. He'd got a bit distant and I didn't maybe ask enough questions to see what the problem was. He says it's not me. Not sure that helps, because that might mean he's got someone else." Terri suddenly realised she was talking about what had happened with Daniel, although she had been the one to end it. She hadn't meant to talk about it. So it was strange that it should come out, just like that.

But Lily had been taken in by Terri's story.

"Do you want him back?" said Lily.

Terri thought for a moment. This was getting way deeper than she ever imagined. She was talking about her and Daniel. But then Anna would say *'a half a truth'* is important to support a good back story.

"I thought I did, look I'm sorry, I'm Terri. You've probably gathered I'm a long way from home."

"You're Australian?"

Terri nodded.

"Well, I'm Lily. Look, here's Mateo, my boyfriend."

"Mateo, this is Terri."

"Encantado, delighted to meet you."

"And you Mateo," said Terri.

"Hun, I know you wanted to get back to Palma early this evening, so why don't you go now? I'm fine now and Terri and I have got things to talk about," said Lily.

Mateo looked at Lily and then Terri.

"So I'm cast off by not one, but two beautiful women. How will I get over this?" He grinned at them. "Terri, it has been a pleasure to meet you. Lily, my love, I'm so glad you are feeling better. Wednesday lunch as usual?"

Lily jumped up and kissed him and whispered *'thank you'* in his ear.

"Can we do Tuesday, or Thursday instead? It's just that...," she tailed off.

"Of course, of course," said Mateo. "Let's do Tuesday."

With that he was off and away, already taking his phone out of his pocket and waving as he went.

*****

Sam had been watching Terri from a distance. More

importantly, he'd been looking around at everyone else who was in the vicinity.

When Mateo left, Sam got up and followed him to a carpark. He recognised the car, the yellow Porsche. Mateo was on his phone for pretty much all the time Sam was watching him.

He took a note of the registration number and then walked back to the square, where Lily and Terri were still at the bar. Bonys, it looked a fun place and Lily had seemed to have got a welcome usually reserved for regular visitors.

He sat down in a different bar this time, still with eyes on Terri. He almost missed it, but just as he sat down, he caught a movement to his right, at about his two o'clock. A man shifting in his chair, as though he had just turned for the briefest of glances at him.

'Who are you then?'

It was difficult for Sam to get much of a look at him. Short dark hair. He looked pretty stocky, with a plain blue, short-sleeved shirt that was just fitting him, intentionally showing off the bulges he had in all the right places.

Sam thought it through. Okay, how to play this? He knows I'm here, but is he here for Lily or Terri, or maybe both? He'd wait to see who the guy might follow, if anyone?

*****

"He seems nice?" said Terri.

"Yes, he's been great, especially this past week," said Lily. "But he's always on his phone! He says it's his business. He's into all sorts of sales or something."

"Look, I didn't want to break you guys up? You seemed to be having a nice time."

"No, honestly it's fine and he really did have to get back. He told me he had something to sort out back down in Palma," said Lily, looking around just as José appeared at the table, with her glass, the bottle of rosado, together with a fresh glass for Terri.

"Terri, say hi to José!"

"Hola José!"

"A pleasure to meet you Terri."

As José moved away to another table, the two women raised their glasses.

"Salud!"

"Mateo seems a lovely guy. Where did you meet him?" said Terri.

"It's funny really. It was just by chance. We were in a bar in Palma," said Lily.

"How long have you known him then?"

"Six or seven weeks now. He's from the mainland, but he's been working over her on some sort of project, a property deal I think."

"So you what? Just bumped in to him?"

"Sort of. I'd had a bit to drink and got dared to chat him up. We were out on an office night out in Palma. We got talking and we swopped numbers."

"He's a pretty good catch Lily! So good for you."

"Yes, he's pretty special. Very caring and he does all the right things. I've got my fingers crossed that it doesn't all go wrong," said Lily.

"Why would that happen?"

"Oh, you know. Don't we all worry when we think we've hooked a good 'un....when it all seems so perfect," said Lily.

Terri thought for a moment. She thinks *'it's all too perfect.'* Hmm, maybe it is.

"Well he looks gorgeous and he seems a really nice guy, so don't worry girl! Anyway, you said you'd had a rubbish week? What was that all about?" said Terri.

Immediately she saw Lily's body language change. She stiffened and her eyes lost the sparkle she'd had when she was talking about Mateo. Terri waited.

"Oh, it's nothing, nothing," said Lily. "Anyway, I don't want to talk about it."

"Look Lily, I'm sorry. I didn't mean to upset you. Let's talk about something else shall we?"

"It's okay. I'm the one who should be sorry. It was just a bad couple of days and...," Lily faltered.

Were those tears she could see in her eyes? Whatever had happened, Lily was still in some sort of shock from it. Terri saw her looking at her watch. Best not push this, as Lily might just close the door on her and she'd get nothing more from her.

"Why don't we call it a day, but I'm still booked in the B&B tonight, so how about a coffee tomorrow?" said Terri.

"Well I'm working, so maybe we could do lunch? Save you sitting here on your own all day?"

"That would be great if you don't mind Lily. It'll certainly help take my mind off things. Where do you work? Is it local?"

"Yes, pretty local. I work for Global Aggregates, at their Research Centre up on the old Pollensa road."

'Tread carefully,' thought Terri.

"What do you do there then?"

She saw Lily once again react, with just a slight twist of her neck. As though her brain was ticking over, thinking, 'Why is this woman asking such a question?'

'Time to back away,' thought Terri.

"Tell you what. Why don't we save all that for tomorrow when we do lunch? Here's my number, drop me a text with time and place to meet, okay?" Terri airdropped her contact details and heard the ping as Lily's phone picked up the message.

"Okay, great idea," said Lily and Terri saw the anxious look lift from her face.

"Till tomorrow then," and Terri stood up and waved as she walked away.

She felt a slight crackle in her ear.

"Keep walking. Don't look for me. Possible tango at your four o'clock."

She kept walking.

16

A moment later and the man was up and following Terri. She was about thirty yards ahead of him.

"He's following you," said Sam.

He started after the man and as he came out of the square and onto the street, Sam moved across onto the opposite pavement, whilst still keeping his distance.

He'd only gone about another ten to fifteen paces, when the man ahead of him suddenly stopped. This had to be a trap. The guy ahead knew he was there. He must do.

"Terri, this looks like a set up, so watch yourself. Okay?"

"I can only see the one guy behind me and he seems to have stopped. Where are you? Ah, I've got you. Are you sure this guy was watching me and Lily?"

Just at that moment a white van approached from the other direction. She missed it, because she was looking at Sam, but she saw the guy suddenly start running towards her. Sam saw it too. They'd been out-manoeuvred She was being cornered. Sam started to run and shout at the same time, to try to attract someone else's attention. Anyone, who might be able to help Terri.

Terri was looking around, for somewhere to try to escape. The van, some sort of VW, was only yards away from her now. She heard a noise. It was the side door starting to slide open. The man who'd been running towards her was still about fifteen paces away.

She saw it at the last moment. A possible get away, unless it was a dead end. A narrow alleyway on the opposite side of the road. This meant that whoever was about to try to get out of the van's side door would now be blocked and they'd have to go around the van to get to her. That just left the guy chasing her. Better odds and maybe Sam could catch up. He better had. She'd seen the size of the guy chasing her and he was big.

Sam saw the VW van, then saw Terri suddenly dart across the road in front of it. *'Good girl! Get away from it.'* He was gaining on the guy who had been chasing her. He hoped to God that the alley wasn't a dead end and that she could put some distance between her and this guy in front of him.

He caught a glance at the driver of the VW. He'd been in Abaco. He was the idiot who'd stared too long at Terri and had been reprimanded by the other one, presumably his boss. Sam heard him shouting something and someone, who had just got out of the side door, was getting back in as the VW's tyres were squealing for grip as the driver started reversing.

Sam got to the alleyway and turned in. He couldn't see Terri, but he could see the man in front. He went to speed up to try to catch him, but the man caught him by surprise, when he suddenly turned and faced him.

"What's your problem mate?"

English accent. Fairly non-distinct, maybe southern.

"You're chasing a woman. So what's your problem?" said Sam.

"Ah, the knight in shining armour are we?"

By this time Sam was only a couple of paces from him. Both had taken up an athletic, side-on stance, left arm half way up, protecting their fighting arc.

Sam had a quick glance behind him in case the men from the van had doubled back. He saw the man in front of him do the same, checking to see if Terri had reappeared.

"Just passing-by, but I don't like to see a woman get into trouble," said Sam.

"I think we both know you aren't just passing-by my friend. So what are you? Ex-forces, a cop?" He was smiling, although he hadn't lowered his guard.

"Ex-cop. Look, we can do this, or maybe you can tell me what the hell you were doing following my friend."

"Well if you want to know, you're going to have to go through me, but what about your girlfriend? Don't you want to see she's safe? What if my friends have already got her?"

He didn't wait for Sam to answer, but threw a lunging right hook towards him. Sam saw it coming late and it partially caught him on the side of the head, knocking his ear piece out and on to the ground.

He taunted Sam, "Out of practice are we?" Before he moved in again, this time with a short left jab that caught Sam on his side, winding him. But he quickly got his breath back and feinted with a left and then threw an arcing right punch that caught the man's jaw.

"Not that much out of practice," said Sam, but he felt the anger rising in him. 'Not now, not now.' He couldn't afford to lose concentration.

"Sam, Sam, come in. What's happening?"

But without the ear piece, he couldn't hear anything Terri was saying and he was too caught up trying to not to lose it, to try to communicate anything to her.

His attacker saw the change in him. It was only slight, but something had happened, he'd seen it in the cop's eyes. What was it? Not fear, that was sure. Loss of control? Yes, but why? Then it dawned on him. *'He's got PTSD. Poor sod. But not my problem.'*

"See you got a touch of PTSD then mate? Something happen to you that's giving you nightmares? Shame you can't handle it. You can back away now if you want? You know, live to fight another day."

He was taunting him. Trying to get a reaction, to get him off guard. Using any advantage he could to make sure he won and this other guy, the cop, lost.

Sam knew what the other guy was doing, or at least trying to do. Problem was, it was working. He was breathing hard, trying his best to stay with it, to stay in control, but he could feel the desire, to just charge the guy, taking over. His head was telling him, *'No!'* but his heart was saying *'Rush him!'*

The heart won, despite his brain still screaming, *'Stop!'* Sam rushed forward. The man easily sidestepped him and swung down hard on his neck with a clenched fist, dropping Sam to his knees, leaving him gasping for air. The man followed it up with a kick towards Sam's head. He saw it coming and the slight move saved him from the full force of the kick. But he was down and he knew he was struggling. Then he heard another voice.

"I think it was me you were after?"

Terri. She'd come back!

Sam saw the man turn back towards the sound of Terri's voice.

"Good of you to come back. Your boyfriend was doing okay, but he's not so hot when you apply a bit of pressure is he? PTSD is a bastard. I feel for him, honestly, but all's fair in love and war, eh?"

"Are you going to keep blabbing, or are you going to see if you're man enough to take me on?" said Terri, who was watching for signs of recovery from

Sam. There was no way she could take this guy head-on. Maybe if she caught him off-guard, but she was far from a position of taking him by surprise.

The guy was good, very good. Terri could see him looking at her and then quickly monitoring Sam. He knows he's only winded him, so he's expecting a short recovery time. She readied herself. He's going to attack at any moment.

And he did, he stepped towards her, with arms out and hands open, ready to try to turn and flip her on her back, but she ducked and caught him across his face with a backhand, drawing some blood from his lip, before withdrawing a good ten paces back.

He wiped his mouth and looked at the blood.

"Oh, you're good, aren't you? So come on then, shall we go again?"

Sam was still winded, but knew he had to try to get his attention. He made to lunge towards the man and it was just enough to distract him and Terri was off, running hard at him.

"Anytime you want," said Terri.

Too late the man saw what she was intending to do. She lunged high into the air, reaching for a pipe that ran across the top of the alleyway. She caught it with both hands, praying it would take her weight. She swung forward on it, hard! Kicking her legs straight out, like she was on a trapeze, catching the man squarely on his chest with the flats of her feet.

The force propelled him back off his feet and down on the ground with a sickening thud, as his head hit the concrete.

She was too long in the tooth, as a combat soldier, to just assume he was down for good. She dropped off the pipe and took up her fighting stance.

"Sam, Sam! Are you with me? I could sure do with some help here."

Sam had seen her run towards him and heard the noise as the guy's head hit the concrete path. He tried to get himself back focused on what was going on. There was a noise in his head, like radio interference, but he could just hear her calling. His eyes cleared and he saw Terri standing over the guy. He was down on the floor. Blood coming from the back of his head.

"Bloody hell Terri! What the hell did you come back for?"

"Or how about, 'thanks Terri for coming back and saving my arse'," said Terri with a grin.

"That's what I meant, I just….," said Sam.

"Never mind that. Just check him. Is he breathing?"

Sam made sure he approached the guy with care, just in case he was feigning injury, although it didn't look like it. He felt for a pulse in his neck. It was faint, but there. He flicked the man's eyelids. Nothing. He was out cold, alive, but he needed a hospital and pretty quickly.

"We'd better be careful that his friends don't come back to see what's happened," said Sam, as he dialled '112.'

"Ambulancia y policía por favor."

*****

"The ambulance will come from Alcúdia, so they're about five, ten minutes away, but the local police could be here sooner, so best you get going," said Sam.

"What?"

"Look, there's a good chance they'll take me in for questioning. No point both of us getting locked up for a few hours. Enough people should have heard me shouting down the street, so I'll tell them I saw this guy following a woman who I don't know, so I'll sort it don't worry."

"You sure? It sounds like a plan, but…."

"No, I'm good, now take this kit and go!" He

scrambled to give her his mic and the ear piece he'd found on the ground.

"One last thing, people might have seen a woman in a yellow sundress," said Terri.

As she spoke, she bent down and picked up the hem of her dress and pulled it up and over her head.

Sam stared. *'Wow, she was stunning.'*

"Stop looking you perv, I'm your sister!" She was trying not to laugh.

"Sorry sis," he smiled, "just never seen you without your clothes on."

"What is it with you guys and bras and knickers? They're no different to a bikini," said Terri, turning her dress inside out and putting it back on, tucking the middle in the elastic waist band of her knickers, making it look like a short white dress.

"Ha! You're right. Good job. That looks so different," said Sam, "but maybe lose the hat too?"

"Yep, good idea. Catch you later." And with that she was off down the alley.

Sam bent down and checked the guy again. He was breathing and he didn't seem to be bleeding any more. He thought about putting him in the recovery position, but with a head injury, he decided against moving him. His breathing was fairly steady and his airway clear, but he was out cold.

He heard the police sirens approaching, so he quickly bent down and went through the guys pockets. No wallet, but a phone, just a basic one. *'A burner,'* thought Sam. One that would get used for a few days or weeks and then dumped. *'Who was this guy working for?'* He flicked a couple of buttons. It was locked. He thought for a moment. The cops would be able to get this unlocked, but no point trying to hide it anywhere here as they'd do a search of the scene, or at least he would, if he was investigating someone with a head injury. No, better to leave it on the guy. Make him the mystery one, the suspect, with him, Sam, being the one who could answer all the questions, the knight in shining armour who came to the rescue of the woman being chased. '*Well fingers crossed it works,*' he thought, as he put the phone back in the man's pocket.

As he waited he took his phone out and pushed a speed dial button. She picked up.

"Mum."

"Sam?"

"I'm fine. Speak to Terri, she'll explain why I'm being arrested."

He then saw the police officers running towards him, shouting to him to stand still.

"Got to go now."

Anna turned to Greg.

"Sam's about to be arrested," she said calmly.

*****

Greg and Anna were at the airport, waiting for a flight out of Palma to London.

"Do you think we need to stay, or at least one of us? And see what we can do for Sam?" said Greg.

"I know you're thinking of me Greg, but realistically, what are we going to do? It isn't like it's Terri, or one of the boys. He knows better than most what the police will be doing, plus he didn't sound fazed and of course, he won't have any language issues," said Anna.

It was Greg's phone that rang this time.

"Terri? Are you okay?"

"Yes, I'm fine Dad, but unless you've heard already, Sam's probably been arrested."

"He's just told Anna, but we don't why. What's happened?"

Terri ran through what had happened and Sam's idea to get her away from the scene.

"It means I can still meet Lily tomorrow. I don't

know if she'll fold, but I might drop this on her and see what happens."

"But what about you? You need to be careful. If they've tried once, they could try again. And just a thought," said Greg, "are you still thinking this is all to do with Lily and not linked in any way to Jaz Kaur?"

"I'm sure it's got to be Lily, Dad. We said before that if Kaur, or her old man were after revenge, then they'd come and do it themselves. One thing's for sure, the guy who we ran into? He was good. He had no qualms at all to take us both on. He had Sam on the floor when I went back and..... well it could have been a lot worse, so is he one of your friend Rawlings' guys?" said Terri.

"Could be. He was always very thorough at who he recruited for local help, so your guy could be Special Forces. I take it he's alive Terri?" he said slowly.

"Yes, sorry, didn't I make that clear? But he's out cold and it's a pretty bad head injury, but he was definitely breathing okay when I left."

Anna was whispering to Greg. "Is Simon, or Tommy free to get over here?"

"Did you get that Terri?" said Greg.

"I think Anna was asking about the boys? Yes, I've spoken to Simon and you should be criss-crossing mid-air with you guys, so I'll have back-up in a few hours," said Terri.

"Good, so in the meantime, please take.....," he didn't finish before she was interrupting him.

"Dad, I will, but remember, I'm a big girl now. I'll keep in touch and make sure you guys take care too. Just so you know, I've got James on standby to meet you at LHR, so just text him your arrival time."

He smiled. Now she was the one making sure her old dad and her new surrogate 'mum' were okay.

"Yes, we'll take care too. Catch up soon....love you," said Greg.

"Love you too Dad."

Anna looked at him with a smile.

"Fill me in as we walk, but I gather your daughter's now more worried about us than herself?" said Anna.

"Yep, and she's got us back-up in London. Probably a good call after what's gone on. This is starting to get a bit serious."

17

Terri had already rang Simon to get him heading to an airport, to get the first flight out to Mallorca, before she'd phoned Greg. Then she'd taken a circuitous route back to her Air BnB. Since leaving Sam, she'd kept a good look out for the white VW van, as well as anything else that didn't feel right.

'*Lily?*' she thought. She rang her.

"Hi Terri, everything okay?"

She sounded bright enough.

"Yes, yes, just checking you were okay too. So you're back to work tomorrow you said?"

"Yes, not really looking forward to it." Lily's voice was quieter.

'*This is definitely connected to work,*' thought Terri.

"Well, push through it as best you can and then I'll treat you to lunch. Where do you fancy going?"

"Oh, let's do Bar Coral! I love the people there," said Lily, her voice lifting once more.

"Bar Coral it is. See you there, at what? One, one-thirty?" said Terri.

"Perfecto amiga," said Lily.

Terri put her phone down and lay down on her bed, thinking about Sam.

"He'll be okay," she said out aloud. But decided

against texting him, in case the police were monitoring his phone.

*****

James, was waiting for them as they walked through Arrivals at Terminal 5, LHR.

"How are you James? Terri tells me you've settled in really well," said Greg. "This is Anna."

"Good afternoon sir, Mrs Martínez, it's a pleasure to meet you," said James, grabbing her overnight bag as they walked towards the carpark.

"That's very kind James, but Anna's fine, honestly."

"Same with me James. We're not in the army now, but thanks, I appreciate your courtesy," said Greg.

James smiled. He'd been invited to an interview by Simon, who had been his mentor in the Regiment. Well, it turned out to be more of a chat than an interview. It seemed that both the boss, Greg and Terri, the Ops Director, put a lot of weight on recommendations from the team, so the chat was more of a formality when he met up with Terri. Since then, he'd worked primarily with Simon and Tommy, the ex-para, after joining the 3R team and he'd just started doing work on his own, now he knew the ropes.

"Simon's on his way across to Mallorca. He's probably landing about now, so should be up with Terri in a couple of hours," said James, opening the driver's door and thus unlocking all the doors on the Jaguar I-Pace.

"Good. How is he?" said Greg.

"Same as always, chilled," said James. "Where to?"

Greg checked his watch. He adjusted his watch, winding it back an hour to British Summer Time.

"Let's go and get something to eat and then rest up and make a start tomorrow morning. I'll ring this Roger Wall and set up a meeting. Okay James, head west on the M4."

Forty minutes later, after chatting about work and how they were finding the all-electric Jaguars, compared to the diesel Range Rovers, James dropped them off at Ruchetta, an Italian restaurant in Wokingham, Berkshire.

"Greg, good to see you," said Angelo. "We haven't seen you for a while. And Signora, welcome to Ruchetta."

"Greg has told me all about his favourite restaurant Angelo and I'm so looking forward to dinner," said Anna.

"Prosecco?" said Angelo.

"That would be wonderful my friend," said Greg, "and yes, it's been a while. Busy, busy, but I couldn't miss seeing you, even though we won't be here very long."

He'd known Angelo for a good many years now and had spent many great evenings at Ruchetta's with friends and even, very occasionally, with a date.

As Angelo showed them to a table for two in the front room, Greg noticed the four people at another table. He nodded, recognising them as regular visitors over the years to the restaurant.

"I used to work with Anna many years ago, Angelo and after meeting up again recently in Mallorca, we're now working together again."

"As I said, Anna, it's a pleasure to have you join us this evening."

"Grazie mille, Angelo," said Anna, in very passable Italian.

As Angelo left them, Greg turned to Anna.

"So your Italian's not too bad either then? Exactly how many languages do you speak?"

"Speak? Three or four, but I can get by in a few more. Bit like you with your Hindi."

She was teasing him about how he'd dropped into

Hindi when they'd been in India sorting out the issue with Jaz Kaur.

"Touché," said Greg, raising his glass.

They spent the rest of the evening talking through the events of the last few days and the options ahead of them.

"It seems that if this is all to do with Groom, Global Aggregates and Oleg Makarovich, then they definitely have the upper hand at the moment, because they know more about us, than we know about them," said Greg.

"Well, to be fair, they know about Sam and Terri, but that's about it so far," said Anna. "I was thinking that maybe they'd have just thought it was friends of the grandparents helping out. But now Terri's put this guy in hospital, they'll know something's definitely up."

Greg nodded.

"What if we go on the offensive? After all Groom is the one trying to protect his reputation and his business. Why not just keep pushing him? See if they make a mistake that brings Makarovich out of the woodwork, because he's the one we're after," said Anna.

Greg thought for a moment.

"I like your thinking. We don't need to hide do we? We can go and front him out, Groom I mean and Rawlings for that matter. It might just work. But they've shown they're not to be underestimated, so I don't want them taking it out on any by-standers, especially not Lily Green or Roger Wall."

"No, so we need to see what we can do to try to prevent anything like that happening," said Anna.

With that, the main courses arrived, along with a special bottle of wine Angelo had chosen, from Calabria.

"To friendship," said Anna.

"Friendship," said Greg.

They stayed at Greg's apartment in Wokingham, getting picked up by James after a quick breakfast. Greg had kept a smart two bedroom apartment here for twenty years or so. It was within a close distance to Heathrow, together with good motorway access to wherever he might need to go in the UK. Although for most of the time, it was empty because of his international travel with 3R.

"We're going back towards London James, Richmond way," as he punched an address into the satnav.

Even leaving when they did, after the Monday morning rush hour, traffic on the M3 was still busy, so it took ten minutes or so longer to get there, as they pulled up outside Roger Wall's house at 10.00am.

'Nice looking house,' thought Greg. *'Typical commuter belt, high value, tree lined road, just across the road from Kew Gardens.'*

He was brought back to focus when James said, "Maybe nothing, but there's a guy sitting on his own in a blue VW SUV, about thirty yards down the road. Looks like he's waiting for someone?"

Greg and Anna knew better than to start looking out of windows towards the VW.

"Let's just wait a moment shall we?" said Greg.

Anna nodded. She was behind the driver's seat and had a clear view of Wall's house that was on the opposite side of the road.

"As we still haven't heard from Sam, I'm assuming he's still with the police," said Anna.

"He'll be fine, but I've got the company solicitor ringing the police this morning, just to hurry them up with releasing him."

His phone buzzed and he studied the text.

"Terri says Simon arrived okay last night and he's

gone out for an early recce of the area. I feel better now she's got back-up again," said Greg.

"From what Simon was telling me, it seems they're pretty brazen with their tactics Boss, sorry Greg," said James.

"Yes, you're right, but two can play at that game. Go and see who that guy is in the car will you James?"

With that James was out of the door and walking up the road towards the VW Touareg SUV. As he got closer, he pretended to look around as though searching for a particular house.

He stopped ten yards from the VW. He was directly facing the driver. He took his phone out and held it up, looking like he was trying to get a signal, whilst all the time taking pictures of the driver and index number of the car. He put his phone back in his pocket, as though it wasn't working, then apparently noticing the driver in the VW, he stepped forward and tapped on the driver's window, as if he was about to ask a question.

The driver ignored him.

"Looks like James has got very good intuition," said Greg.

James tapped gently on the window again, almost apologetically. The driver lowered the window.

"Piss off, I'm ....," said the driver, but he didn't finish. He'd made the mistake of lowering the window all the way. James leant in and grabbed him by the shoulders and pulled him hard towards the window, smashing the driver's head into the top of the window frame.

"What the....," started the driver, but again James had hold of the driver's right arm and just pulled him out of the window and then twisted his arm up and sideways. The driver grunted in pain, but wasn't giving up, but with control of the man's arm, James was able to pivot and swing back hard with his elbow into the driver's face. He heard the crack, as the guy's nose broke, but more importantly, he felt the tension in the man's arm drop, as he lost consciousness.

James pushed the driver back in through the window, then quickly leaned in and opened the door. He took out a nylon plasti-cuff from his pocket and slipped it around the driver's wrists, before finding the button to lower the back down on the seat. He then tucked his right arm under the man's legs and lifted them up and then into a rolling movement to get him up and over the seat and into the back of the car.

He then opened the back door, checked the man was still breathing and added another plasti-cuff to the one on the man's wrists, but this time, he attached to the passenger door handle.

He looked around to see no one was about and then went through the man's pockets, found a wallet and a phone and put them in his own pocket. He then closed the car doors and walked calmly back and got into the Jaguar.

"Impressive James, very impressive. Simon said you were good," said Greg.

"I had a good teacher," said James, with a smile, passing Greg the wallet and the phone.

"Okay, looks like your instincts were right. Chris Walker, Security Executive, Global Aggregates. So who's he waiting for?" said Greg.

"This could be him," said Anna, as she saw a man coming out Roger Wall's house. She had her phone out and was taking pictures, with the man unaware he was being watched.

They saw him stop, just for a moment as he approached the VW, as he realised the driver wasn't where he expected him to be. Then they saw his reaction when he caught sight of the driver tied up in the back of the car. He looked around, by which time, Greg and James were out of the Jaguar and walking towards him. He looked around, saw two men, one white and a younger guy, who was black and taller. Both looked fit and capable. He checked his options - run, fight or talk.

Greg spoke first.

"Yes, your man had a bit of a run-in with us. So presumably you're also from Global Aggregates Security?"

Tom Marsden just looked at Greg. *'Who the hell is this?'* he thought, but his mind was going round at a hundred miles an hour. *'First, there was the guy in the VW Beetle, sniffing around the Research Centre, asking about the Green girl. Then we had one of our guys taken out in Puerto Pollensa, presumably by the same guy in the Beetle and now I've got these two here.'*

"What the hell has it got to do with you? I've got a good mind to call the police and report you lot for assault," said Marsden, looking to bluff it out.

"Oh, be my guest, I'm sure you'll want to answer their questions, especially when we all go inside to see Roger Wall," said Greg.

Marsden didn't like the odds. The younger, taller black guy looked like he could really handle himself and there was something about the older guy, the way he carried himself, even though he looked old enough to be his dad.

"A piece of advice old man," said Marsden. "You don't know what you're getting involved in, so why don't you and your friend here, just back away and leave it?"

"Oh, do you know, I don't think we're going to do that. Now let me give you a piece of advice to take back to Stephen Rawlings."

With the mention of Rawlings' name, Greg saw a very slight twitch from Marsden.

"Yes, I might not know who you are, but I do know

who your boss is. He and I go back some way, so give him my regards."

With that he took a 3R business card from his pocket and tucked it into Marsden's jacket breast pocket, patting him a couple of times on his cheek. The first one was gentle, but the second was with a harder, more stinging action.

Greg saw Marsden was smarting at this. He was goading him on purpose, but also leaving a message that he wasn't afraid of him, or Rawlings.

"You're messing with the wrong people here mate. I won't forget this," said Marsden.

"I sincerely hope you won't," said Greg and with that he put in a short sharp punch to Marsden's stomach, just below the ribs.

Marsden took the blow and stayed firm. It had winded him, but he wasn't about to show it.

"Best you got old man? I'll look forward to us meeting again, when the numbers are a bit more even, unless you can do only do this stuff when you've got your boyfriend by your side?"

Greg's phone buzzed. He quickly checked it. Anna had stayed in the car. They'd decided there was no point giving away all their resources to this guy.

'Abaco guy?' she texted.

Anna had been looking at the photographs she'd taken of the man. She didn't know his name was Marsden, but he certainly fitted the description Sam and Terri had given of the guy they'd encountered in Palma, outside of Abaco.

Greg looked back at the guy and smiled.

"It seems to me that you need to look at your recruiting process and get yourself some better back-up. First the one in Palma blows you out, then you lose one of them up an alley in Puerto Pollensa and now it's your driver. He flicked Walker's wallet back to

Marsden."

Marsden looked at him. If he needed any confirmation that what happened in Palma was linked to this guy, then he'd just got it.

"Like I said, maybe you want to just leave all this. It's an internal matter and I wouldn't want that nice blonde girl ending up going through what young Lily just experienced," said Marsden, a smirk appearing on his face.

Greg flinched, just a slight movement, but he'd felt it and inwardly he cursed himself. Greg forced a smile, as he struggled to maintain his composure.

"Oh, we'll definitely being seeing each other again, be it here, or back in Mallorca. That, I can promise you," said Greg.

With that he turned and walked away, followed by James, who took a few steps backwards to ensure Marsden made no effort to come back at them. Greg stopped short of the front gate to Wall's house. James could see the tension in his face.

"No strings, no ties, no commitments," said Greg quietly.

"Sorry Boss?" said James.

"That was the mantra Anna drilled into me a long time ago James, in my undercover training. This was just a little reminder to me, that this was the reason why she did it. Because whether we like it or not, emotions about people we care for will interfere with our reactions."

"Are you okay now?" said James.

"Yes, he just got to me a bit, you know, when he mentioned Terri."

"Understandable Boss."

"Yes James, in a by-gone age, I'd have ridden that without showing anything, but time can be your enemy when it comes to keeping your emotions in check."

They watched as Marsden sped away in the VW and a moment later Anna joined them.

He smiled at her.

"Lost control. You'd have been bloody furious with me thirty years ago."

She saw the strain in his eyes and gently placed an arm on his arm, realising Marsden must have said something about Terri.

"That was then, this is now," said Anna. She waited a moment before continuing, "Come on, we'd better go and see this Roger Wall. I get the feeling he would have just had a similar experience, so we'd best get in and see how he's doing."

Roger Wall's daughter met them at the front door. There were tears in her eyes.

"You'd better come in."

18

"I'm his daughter, Sandy, Sandy Dorchester. I see you met Marsden. I was looking out of the window. He makes my skin crawl."

Anna looked at Sandy. She'd heard the slight tremble in her voice.

'This man Marsden, has just scared her and scared her badly.'

"What has he said to frighten you Sandy?" said Anna.

Sandy looked at Anna. *'How did she know?'*

"It's okay Sandy, we can help."

"My girls! He threatened my girls! What he'd do to them. He said no one would ever know and they'd never remember enough to be able to give evidence against him, because he'd use some sort of drug or something," she paused. "But they would know. That's what he said. They'd know and they'd relive it in their dreams, over and over, every single night. That's what he said, *'every single night'.*"

Sandy was shaking and Anna guided her gently by the shoulders as they went into the living room, where a man was sitting, slumped in an armchair.

Greg thought back to the man John MacDonald had described to him. *'Tough London boy, hard as nails, doesn't take prisoners.'* Well this looked like Roger Wall had just completely surrendered.

His shoulders were down and he was slowly rubbing one hand over the other, as though he was wiping something off the back of his hands, but there was nothing there.

He looked up them.

"I signed it. I had to, after what he said he'd do to my grandkids. I'm sorry to have wasted your time. Tell John, tell him.., thank you for trying, but I can't go on fighting this," said Roger Wall.

"It's okay Roger, I can call you Roger?" said Greg.

Wall nodded, "Of course."

"Sometimes, we have to make decisions to protect our families, rather than standing up to people. But you've not wasted our time Roger. We're also acting for another client, a young woman, who has also been hurt by this man, by these people, because they're trying to hide something. We think it's the reason behind the collapse of your shopping centre, the Witterings?" said Greg.

He saw Wall's eyes flash.

"I thought there might be something wrong! I just knew it. Was it the concrete, the reinforced concrete Groom used in the build?"

He carried on before Greg could say anything.

"But the Health and Safety Exec report said it was okay, so I just don't understand. He's been trying to buy the site back off me for five years or so now, but I could never figure out why. I thought it was just for the development potential. There was no reason to suspect there was anything wrong with the bloody concrete. If I'd known....," he tailed off.

"You say the HSE report is out?" said Greg.

"Yes, came out this morning and Marsden knew all about it. Nothing conclusive on any of the materials apparently, so as far as the HSE are concerned, it's just an unfortunate accident, with some recommendations on reviewing the rest of the building, but no specific cause," said Wall.

"So no liability to Groom as the original builder then?" said Anna.

"No, and if there was something up with that concrete, then I just don't know how he's got away with it. You can't go buying those Health and Safety guys. Their reports go through too many people, so they'd never be able to buy that many people would they?"

Greg nodded in agreement.

"And now that, that bastard Marsden, has come in here and threatened my darling girl and her babies. I tell you, if I was thirty years younger I'd.....," then tears were falling down his face.

Greg sat down on the sofa, next to where Wall was sitting.

"I know you would Roger and you'd probably have John MacDonald standing side by side with you wouldn't you?"

Wall was wiping the tears away.

"Yes, he'd be there. We had to do it a few times in the early years. It got a bit bloody sometimes, but we sorted it. No police or anything like that, but it got sorted. But not now, we're both too old and besides he's lost Sheila and I've lost my wife Betty too for that matter, but at least she wasn't murdered."

Wall stood up. He was taller than Greg had thought. *'Wouldn't have wanted to face you in your prime Roger Wall,'* he thought.

"You sorted things for John didn't you? With the bastards responsible for murdering Sheila?" said Wall.

"Yes, we did," said Greg quietly.

"I'm not bothered about the Witterings, I mean not bothered that I've given it up, but if those five people died because of something I did, then I'll face up to that. But if it was something to do with Groom...," he stopped, as though searching for the right words. "Then I really want him to get the justice those five people deserve."

Wall turned and looked first at his daughter, Sandy, before he faced Greg and Anna.

"Problem is..., I don't mind telling you, I'm now scared, very scared and the only time I've ever been scared like this before, was at the thought of losing my darling Betty." He took in a deep breath. "Marsden, that's his name, Tom Marsden, has made it absolutely clear what would happen if I didn't sign today, or if I go to the police. So, I don't know if there's anything I can do to help you."

"He had photographs of my girls," said Sandy. "As we were leaving the house and again, when they were coming out of school." She had calmed down a little bit, but she was now trembling again.

"Where do you live Sandy?" said Anna.

"Not far. We're in Twickenham. There's just me and the girls. I'm separated. Their father lives in Germany.

"Suggestion," said Greg. "How many rooms have you got here Roger? Five, six?"

"Six."

"Just for the time-being, I think it might be best if Sandy and the girls come and stay here."

"Yes, but, I'm still not sure I feel....," but Greg interrupted Wall before he could finish.

"Safe? That's the second part of the suggestion Roger. Anna, can you get James to come in? I'd like James to stay with you for the next few days or so, just until we can get some sense of where this is going," said Greg.

He saw them both take a couple of deep breaths.

"That would be good Greg, very good Greg. I can

pay for this. I don't want charity, especially not off my old mate John, I'd never live it down." Almost a smile returned to Wall's face.

"Good, so here's James," said Greg. *'Bit of life springing back into the old boy,'* he thought.

Anna brought James back into the house. He was tall, maybe six foot three, or four and imposing with it. Anna saw Sandy's reaction, relief.

"I'll get the beds sorted and then I'll go and get the girls and bring some stuff back from home," said Sandy.

"I'll come with you Mrs...?" said James.

"It's Sandy and thank you. Dad, I'll be back soon." She turned to Greg and Anna as she walked towards the door, "Thank you doesn't seem enough, but I'll say it anyway."

"Glad to help. James, keep your car and we'll get a cab from here. Now Roger, you don't need to tell me this, but did you get a reasonable deal out of them for the Witterings? I'm just wondering if you want me to try to renegotiate the deal?"

"I'm not worried about that Greg. It's probably thirty percent under market value, but to be honest, it's not the money that's important, it never was. I just wasn't going to sell to a man, no a bully, like Groom."

"What do you know about his financial backers?" said Anna.

"Oh, you mean Oleg Makarovich?"

Anna nodded.

"That's the reason why Groom is so cash rich. He's got an endless supply of Russian money flowing through the Global Aggregates' bank account. Probably all dirty money being laundered, but the FCA, the Financial Conduct Authority, can't seem to get near him. That leaves Groom, or I should say Sir Charles. You know about his knighthood? No doubt paid for in exchange for party political funds. Well, with all that

Russian cash, he's also…, well, pretty much free to plunder the market to add more companies to the GA portfolio whenever he's minded to."

"What do you know of Makarovich?" said Greg.

"Let's put it this way. If I'm scared of a little shit like Marsden, then multiply that by ten, no make it a hundred fold if you're talking about dealing with Makarovich. But of course, there's no evidence to back any of this up. But there's a whole bunch of people who went into business with Makarovich and then subsequently disappeared, and I mean actually disappeared. They'd have mysterious car accidents, or sudden heart attacks, but it's all only suspicion and nothing can apparently be proved," said Wall.

"We'd heard he's got a bit of a past," said Anna.

"Yes, you can say that again, Anna. Russian Intelligence or something like that. I'm quite happy for you to go up against the likes of Marsden and even his boss, Rawlings, the Head of GA Security, but Makarovich? I couldn't ask you to do that," said Wall.

"Don't worry Roger, we'll be careful, but let me just say that we're not doing this completely on our own. But that said, I'll have to ask you to fill in the blanks as to who we're working in conjunction with," said Greg.

Roger Wall looked at them both. He'd heard of Chambers before, from John MacDonald, and knew his background was in the Secret Intelligence Service.

"So be it. I won't presume to ask anything more then, as I'm sure you wouldn't tell me anyway. So looking forward then, thank you again for your help, especially with James. He looks very capable and I can see Sandy already feels better." Wall paused and with a grin asked, "Is he married?"

Greg smiled and looked at him, a bit confused at the question.

"Just thinking of Sandy. He seems like a nice lad,"

said Wall.

Greg laughed, "Ha, no, he's not married."

"Oh well, it was worth asking then. I'll break that good bit of news to her later," Wall laughed.

'More signs of life,' thought Greg. *'Just as well, because he may need it before we get this done.'*

19

Lily hadn't slept well Sunday night. The nightmare had returned and she hoped her grandparents hadn't heard her if she'd been crying out in her sleep.

She got up early, to get out of the house before her grandparents came down for breakfast. She still had no idea what had happened to her bicycle. Whilst she had another bike, a racing bike, it wasn't something she wanted to use for the leisurely ride to work, so she'd asked if she could borrow their car. The keys were on the side and she picked them up and was going out the door, when she heard her grandmother's voice.

"Are you okay Lily?"

"Yes, Gran, all good thanks. And thanks for the car again. See you tonight."

With that, she was out of the door. She hoped her voice sounded okay, because it didn't feel like it inside.

She wanted to get into work early, because she had no idea what people had been told about why she wasn't in on Thursday and Friday.

'Who knows about what happened to me?' she thought. 'Ian Parsons? It sounded like he might be in on it, or was he? Is he maybe just terrified like I am?'

She set off towards the old Pollensa road. She tried

the breathing exercises, like Mateo had told her to do. It seemed to help. Then she remembered she was meeting Terri for lunch. That made her feel better.

'I can do this. I've only got a few months left of this contract and then I'll leave and start afresh somewhere.'

She got to the entrance gates and her card worked on the electronic key slot and the gates opened. She parked the Honda in her usual space and started walking towards the main entrance. She didn't know why, but she glanced across at the cycle racks. There was her bike, the one she used for work, with her cycle helmet on the handlebars. *'They've put it back!'* she thought. *'It's as though nothing's ever happened!'*

She steadied herself and carried on in through the main doors, using her security card.

It felt like everyone was looking at her, when in reality, only one person, Stephen Rawlings, was watching her. He could see her on the CCTV images on his desk top back in London.

He followed her as she went up the stairs and made her way towards her office. She was met by Ian Parsons, her boss. Parsons had already been briefed what to say to Green, so he'd better get it right, otherwise he'd get another visit from Marsden and this time he'd be talking to Parsons' wife as well.

The cameras were good and Rawlings had the audio feed as well, so he heard Parsons when he started to speak.

"Lily, it's so good to see you back and feeling better. We had a message from Security saying you'd been taken ill on Wednesday when you went out for lunch? What was it? Food poisoning?" said Parsons.

"Yes, something like that," said Lily. *'So that's what he's been told is it? Okay, I can go along with that.'*

"Well, I'm so glad you're feeling better. Now, we've had a change of direction on the stuff we were looking at last week Lily."

"What's that then Ian?" said Lily, although she suspected what would be coming next.

"It seems that the HSE's report has come back and there was nothing wrong with either, the concrete cover that we'd been asked to look at, nor the Ultra-Fast-Dry compound they used, you know the UFD30 you mentioned to me as a possible factor?"

Lily nodded to him.

"So the Director has told me that we can drop those lines of investigation now."

"Okay," said Lily slowly. *'How the hell is the Health and Safety Report not showing anything?'*

"So we've got a new sustainability project to work on. I've got the paperwork here for you, but basically it's looking at the possible long-term stress impact of roof gardens."

"I thought there had already been lots done on that?" said Lily.

"Maybe so, but this has come from the top. Seems they want to start introducing roof gardens to all new GA builds," said Parsons.

He watched Lily for a moment. Marsden had told him to report anything about her that suggested she wasn't going to drop the UFD30 investigation. He didn't like Marsden. In fact he was downright scared of him. So he dreaded to think what had happened to the poor girl.

'But what could I do?'

He knew he could have done something, but at what cost? Marsden had made it very clear that it wasn't just him who would suffer if he, or Lily, said anything. He'd shown him pictures of his kids and then he talked about accidents…..it had sent shivers down him.

"Ian? Are you alright?" said Lily.

It was her turn to be concerned about him now.

What had he been threatened with? She knew he had a wife and kids. Marsden! She could sort of understand why Ian hadn't done anything, but submit to whatever he was asked, no, told to do.

"Ian?"

"Yes, yes, I'm fine," said Parsons.

She smiled at him and he smiled back.

'Does she know?' He looked at her again. Was that understanding in her eyes? *'Yes, I think she does, but I'm damned if I'm going to tell Marsden that!'*

He knew they were on CCTV and either Marsden, or Rawlings were probably watching them back in London, so he kept the conversation moving forward.

"Come on, let me show you how far I've got with this new project," said Parsons.

"Okay, I'll grab a couple of coffees and be with you in a moment."

Rawlings turned his screen off. The audio from the cameras was clear enough. Marsden had got those two wrapped up. But what the hell had happened to the guy who had gone after the blonde girl? He'd not reappeared and then his guys had circled back to find the police and then an ambulance turning up.

They'd followed the ambulance back to the hospital at Inca and seen him taken in on a stretcher with an armed police guard.

His phone rang. Marsden.

"Boss, do you know a Greg Chambers?"

Rawlings sat back in his chair for a moment. Long time since he'd heard that name.

"Hello Tom, good morning to you too."

"Yes, sorry, morning," said Marsden.

"Greg Chambers? Haven't heard his name in a while, so yes. Why do you ask?" said Rawlings.

"Because he's the bloody fly in the ointment! He's the one who's causing us all these problems in Mallorca and now at Walls' house!"

"Calm down. Now what do you mean *'and now at Wall's house'*, what the hell happened there?"

"I came out of Wall's house, he's signed by the way, to find Chris, my driver, stuffed up in plasti-cuffs in the back of the car."

"What? And Chambers did that?"

"Maybe not him personally. He had a younger guy with him who looked pretty handy."

"Okay, slow down Tom. First of all, well done on getting Wall to sign the deal. At least that's one good thing we can tell Groom. Now, tell me exactly what was said," said Rawlings.

*****

He came off the phone with Marsden.

Greg Chambers? That was certainly a name from the past. Last he'd heard, Chambers had retired from MI6 and had started up his own security consultancy that was doing pretty well. Why the hell would Chambers be getting involved in something like this?

He wanted some more time to think this through and get some background research on Chambers, but his phone rang.

It was Groom again and he'd already rejected a couple of calls from him that morning.

"Sir Charles, good morning to you."

"Yes, whatever. Has Wall signed yet?"

"Yes, Sir Charles, as I told you he would. Plus the girl is back at work in Pollensa and there's no issues there either."

A pause.

"Oh, well that's better news than last time we spoke Stephen," said Groom, his manner changing in an instant.

'He's back to being charm personified,' thought Rawlings.

"And what with the HSE Report's findings, this matter is all but sorted," said Rawlings.

"I thought it would be all sorted with the Report, so what do you mean, *'all but sorted?'* said Groom.

"Well, I mentioned we might need to go to Canada?"

"Ah yes, you did to be fair, but then that's it?" said Groom.

"Yes, I think…," said Rawlings.

"I don't want you *'thinking'* it's alright Stephen! I pay you enough to make sure you know when you've tidied up a problem. What else is it you haven't put to bed?"

Rawlings was struggling to hold in his frustration at the man. Always blaming other people, when it was his mess that Rawlings was having to tidy up.

"We're continuing to monitor the issue in Mallorca, because we lost one of Marsden's guys yesterday afternoon up in Puerto Pollensa, when a team tried to snatch the blonde girl to find out what she knew."

Groom felt a slight tremor in his right hand. He'd had it before when things weren't going well. An ISI, an involuntary stress indicator was what the quack told him.

'Too bloody right it's involuntary!'

"Stephen, I hope I don't need to remind you that we can't afford to have any police involvement in any of this business?" said Groom.

"No, you don't Sir Charles. My team perfectly understands the need to persuade through any means that doesn't leave any physical marking. And as you know," he paused for a moment so as to not lose his temper, "we have been very successful achieving this over the years, so I don't think this is the time for you to start doubting my team's efforts now."

Groom heard the annoyance in Rawlings' voice, "Yes, quite, quite, but please just see this is done and we can move on and put this all behind us Stephen."

Once again, Groom's suave and engaging charm came through to Rawlings, but he soon dismissed any thoughts of him, because he had something else on his mind. He picked out a name on his phone: Finn O'Neil, his business analyst.

O'Neil answered immediately.

"Find out all you can on a former MI6 officer called Greg Chambers and quickly please Finn."

20

It was lunchtime the following day, Monday, when Sam was released by the police. As they handed his personal belongings back to him, he saw his phone had a raft of messages and missed calls.

The investigating officer, Detective Sofia Delgado, was standing beside him as the custody officer dealt with the documentation.

"So, Señor Martínez, thank you for your help. It's unfortunate that you can't help identify the woman you saw being chased by this man, but," she paused, "you're perhaps the fortunate one, as someone saw the woman being followed by the man and heard you shouting out to them to stop."

"Fortunate Detective? Yes, perhaps, however, he was the one in the wrong, but I can understand why you might not have believed me," said Sam.

"Might not have believed you?"

Her voice went up a notch. This man was infuriating her. She knew damn well that he knew more, but he wasn't giving anything up.

"Well you will know as much as I do Señor, that there are always two sides to a story. With this man still being unconscious, we really only have your version of events as to what happened in the alley, so please let me know if you intend to leave the island for any reason."

"Are you saying I can't leave the island? I didn't appreciate I was on any sort of bail restrictions," said Sam.

"No, you're not, because the witness saw the man following the woman, so it suggests you were, as you'd say, 'a Good Samaritan'. So I can't stop you leaving, but I just want to make sure I know where you are, in case I need to speak to you."

"Well I hope he gains consciousness soon. I don't want this hanging over me for long."

"The doctors say there's no change at the moment, however, it should just be a matter of time before he wakes up. Adios Señor."

Sam shrugged his shoulders. He knew where she was coming from, but it didn't mean he liked it.

As he walked outside of the police station, he was hit by the heat of the day. They weren't quite into August, but it was starting to get very hot in the early afternoon already.

He checked his messages. His mum, Greg, Terri and Carmen had all left voice mails. First things first, he rang Terri.

"Hello," said Terri. "So they let you out eventually?" She mouthed 'Sam' to Simon, who was across the room from her. He nodded and gave her a thumbs up sign.

"Yes, eventually being the word. I think they were waiting for our mystery man to wake up, but apparently he's still sound asleep in the land of nod, after you decked him."

"But you're okay I take it?" said Terri.

"Yes, yes, I'm fine. Are you okay? No further problems?" said Sam.

"Yes, all good. Simon grabbed the first flight across and so I've had my minder here looking after me."

Simon looked up again at the sound of his name and

shook his head at the mention of the word *'minder'*.

"Presumably no sign of the white VW van then?"

"No, but I didn't get the chance to say, I think the driver was the guy in Abaco, the one who kept staring at us, well me rather than you," said Terri.

"So what's been happening?"

"Have you spoken to your mum or Greg?"

"No," said Sam.

"Well, let's start with me seeing Lily in about half an hour. We're having lunch in Puerto Pollensa and before you ask, yes, we've got it covered. Simon's been out and scoped up the site around the place we're meeting up at, Bar Coral."

"Be interesting to see how her morning has gone?" said Sam.

"Yes, I rang her Sunday afternoon, but I didn't mention what had just happened. I just said it was to check in and see she was okay."

"How did she sound?" said Sam.

"Apprehensive is probably the best way to describe her, so it does suggest that this has got something to do with where she works Sam," said Terri.

"And what about her boyfriend, Mateo?"

"I just don't know Sam. Maybe you could try and follow that up?"

"Yes, good plan, I'll call him and arrange a meet. Have you heard from Greg?"

"No, not since early this morning. He was going to meet Roger Wall. Look, we're going off to set up the meet with Lily, so can you ring Greg, or your mum, to see what happened with Wall?" said Terri.

"Okay, speak later."

*****

By the end of the morning Lily was actually feeling reasonably comfortable being back at work. She found Ian's company relaxing and knowing they both seemingly shared an unspoken secret, somehow made things easier to deal with everything that had gone on.

She was glad she was driving back into Puerto Pollensa to see Terri, because she didn't think she was ready to face cycling along the stretch of road where she'd been grabbed.

As she walked towards Gran's car, she rang Mateo who picked up straight away.

"Hello my love, how was it this morning?" said Mateo.

"Okay hun, maybe better than I expected to be fair. Ian, my boss, has been great."

"That's good to hear, especially that you've had such good support from your boss, Ian you said?"

"Yes, he's a good guy and security had apparently rang and told him I would be off for a few days, so he knew where I was," said Lily.

"Sorry, you said, *'he knew where you were?'* So he knew, but you won't tell me Lily?" said Mateo.

She'd messed up. She hadn't meant to tell Mateo that she thought her boss had known where she was, or rather he'd known she'd been kidnapped. She thought on her feet.

"No, I didn't mean he knew where I actually was. He was just aware that I wouldn't be back into work. Look, can we just leave it? I don't want to talk about last week," said Lily.

Mateo paused, hearing the agitation in her voice. "Okay, okay, I just thought this Ian knew something about last week. I'm sorry I brought it up. So you're seeing this Terri again, for lunch? Where are you going?"

"Yes, she rang last night, just to check up on me, it was so sweet of her. We're meeting at Bar Coral, but I haven't got long, so I'll ring you later."

"Okay, enjoy your lunch my love and yes, let's talk

later," said Mateo.

Even though the Honda was a good few years old, the aircon still worked and it was coping well with the midday heat.

Lily made her way along the Pollensa road and parked up in a side street, just at the back of the restaurant. As she walked in, she saw Aina, whose family had owned the restaurant for..., well, it must be three generations now.

"Hola, bon día Lily!" said Aina, greeting her with kisses on both cheeks.

"Oh Aina, it is so good to see you too," said Lily, with a hug, that lasted a little longer than usual.

Aina had known her for many, many years and Lily's greeting, whilst being lovely, was slightly surprising, as though she hadn't seen her for some time, but it was only a week ago. She wondered what might have caused this.

'*Maybe it was work, or boyfriend problems?*' but she was distracted as another woman walked in, smiling.

"Lily," said Terri.

"Aina, this is my new friend, Terri."

"Bon día Terri and welcome to Bar Coral. Come on, let me take you to one of your favourite tables Lily. Número 39, out on the terrace."

As she sat them down, she said, "Now what can I get you ladies to drink?"

"Sadly, I'm still working Aina, so just a zumo de naranja," said Lily, "and a bowl of mussels too please."

"That sounds great, so the same for me please Aina," said Terri. "So how did this morning go? You seemed to be a bit anxious about going back into work? Because of what happened last week?"

Lily looked at her. '*Was she just being supportive or did she know something? Was she being tested?*'

She felt herself withdrawing into her own body,

with her shoulders going down, as though…, as though he was leaning on them again.

Terri had seen what had happened. She'd gone in too soon and too hard.

'*Damn it,*' she thought.

"Oh Lily, I'm so sorry, I didn't mean to drag whatever it is, all back up again. I was hoping your morning had gone okay, that's all."

Lily relaxed, hearing the concern in Terri's voice. She was imagining things. She was just asking if I was okay!

"It was actually better than I thought it might be," said Lily.

"It often is Lily. You know we build these things up into something they aren't, or at least something that we feel can't be overcome, when there's often a way around things."

"You're right. I got a good welcome at work and they've put me on another project, so things should be good for now and anyway, my contract expires in about three months, so I can move on then anyway. Maybe move back to the UK and get a job there."

"Will you stay with…., who is it Global Aggregates?"

Once again, Lily was suspicious, "How do you know I work for them?"

"Er, because you told me!" said Terri. "Look, you don't have to talk about work if you don't want to. We can talk boyfriends or ex-boyfriends in my case, if you prefer?"

Lily managed to laugh.

"I'm sorry Terri, I think I'm getting paranoid. I don't know why. Work is alright now. What happened last week is…., well, it's in the past and I don't need to worry about now, because everything is sorted and as I said, I'm starting on a new project."

"That's great to hear. So boyfriends? I now haven't

got one," Terri pulled a sad face and then laughed, "but you have! You said you sort of bumped into him? Tell me how you managed that, so I can see if it works for me!" said Terri, who just at that moment felt a text come in on her phone with the tell-tale buzz.

She took a quick look. It was a picture shared by Anna on the 3R WhatsApp group. She recognised him straight away as the guy from Abaco, the one she and Sam had talked to. *'So Tom Marsden, you're part of GA Security are you?'*

"Just my mum, checking up on me. She's back in Australia, so she worries about me, but I'm nearly thirty two for God's sake!"

"That's where my folks are too! And you're right, they never stop worrying, do they?" said Lily. "So Mateo? He literally bumped into me when I was in a bar with friends from work one night in Palma. You live there don't you?"

"Yes, so what bar were you in?" said Terri. She wanted to steer Lily away from asking anything about where she lived if she could.

"Oh wow, I'm struggling now. It was an alley, at the end of Passeig del Born, you know at the C&A end?"

"Ah yes, I think we all know where C&A is in Palma, so I think I know the alleyway you're talking about. It's got a couple of great hotels up there, I think it's Carrer de Sant Jaume? There's the Hotel Glòria, or something like that and the Born Hotel too. So what happened?"

"Wow, that's pretty good local knowledge! How long have you lived here?" said Lily.

"Well, off and on, I suppose it's a couple of years now, but work takes me overseas. However, when I'm home, I love spending time in the city, so I've got to know my way around pretty well," said Terri.

"Anyway, enough about me, what about your boyfriend Terri?"

So she wasn't biting on the hook Terri was giving her. This could be hard work if she wasn't going to say anything about what had happened to her. She grimaced, which Lily mistook for something to do with her 'boyfriend'.

"I'm sorry Terri, if you'd rather not talk about it, we can leave it."

Aina started to walk towards them with their food, but saw Lily hold up her hand a moment and held back. Something was the matter. She put the food down and walked quietly up to Lily.

"Are you okay my dear?" Aina had her hand gently on Lily's arm, but she was looking at Terri with a fierce stare.

"I'm fine Aina, gracias, I'm fine. We're talking...., boyfriend troubles. Maybe bring the food in a moment?"

"Si, si, of course my dear." Aina walked away, but kept looking back towards Terri.

"Blimey Lily, looks like your Aina only trusts me as far as she could throw me!"

"Ha! She's known me and my family a long time, so she's just looking out for me. Now, what about you? How are you feeling? Had you been with this guy long?"

"No, not really. It's been an on-off thing for some time, but we got together just a few weeks ago after a...," she paused, "after a work's trip which he helped out on. It was after that. We just sort of got back together again, but I suppose that's the reason it's never gone anywhere before."

Lily looked at her, smiling gently.

"We fell back together because we'd been in each other's company for a while on the trip. So it wasn't like we'd suddenly fallen madly in love or anything, not like what seems to have happened to you and Mateo," said

Terri, who was trying hard to move the conversation back towards Lily.

But Lily wasn't having any of it. She felt good that she was helping her new friend work through her boyfriend troubles and it was also taking her mind of her own problems.

"Are you ready to eat now Terri?"

"Yes, that would be good," said Terri, relieved to see a break in talking about Daniel, which she'd found just a bit too unsettling.

21

ina had been waiting for Lily's signal and she appeared back at the table almost immediately, placing the food before them with a flourish.

"Enjoy!"

Terri was thinking hard about how to take the conversation back to Lily.

"Look, I think it's just one of those things Lily. You've always got to be careful about relationships that start at work don't you? I mean, look at you. Mateo isn't anything to do with your work is he? So you've both got different things to talk about. So, what does he do?"

"Yes, you're right, that does help. But it's funny, I can never really get a straight answer from him. He just seems to be a wheeler dealer of some sort. He buys and sells things. Cars, property, bits of equipment. He's some sort of wholesaler I think."

"Looks like he's doing pretty well for himself with the car he's driving? It's a Porsche isn't it?"

Terri could have kicked herself. She only knew about his car because Sam had told her about it.

"Yes, and he loves it! Typical bloke with fast cars" said Lily.

"And fast women?" grinned Terri, relieved Lily

hadn't picked up on her slip.

"Oh God no, I'm really not on that scale, which is why I was so blown away when he asked me out. I think I'm really punching above my weight with this one," smiled Lily.

"Don't you go putting yourself down girl! He knows he's hooked a good one with you. So did you say he lives here, or on the mainland?"

"He's from the mainland. Around Malaga, but if the deal comes off here, he says he'll be here for some time, or so I'm hoping anyway."

Terri was slowly digging away, to try to get more intel on Mateo. He seemed to stack up as the caring boyfriend, but something was nagging at her. Was it all just a bit too tidy?

"So where's he living here on the island? Palma isn't it?"

Lily shifted her body slightly.

'She's on the defensive again,' thought Terri.

"Yes, he's in Palma, so where does Daniel live?"

"Oh, he's got a place just outside London, but he basically lives on-board his plane, which is another reason I don't think it would ever work. He goes where his work is and so do I, so I don't see how we'd ever get a chance to be with each other."

She saw Lily relax again. She needed to try to take things to a different place, because time for lunch was running out.

"Look, this has been great. I've just got tonight left before I go back to Palma, so how about we do something tonight?"

"Well, yes, we could. I was actually going for a bike ride, if you fancy that?"

"That would be great! Now I need to tell you, I'm more of an off-roader, so where were you thinking of going?"

Lily pointed behind Terri.

Terri pulled a face.

"What? You mean the lighthouse?"

"Yep! If you can do off-road, you'll be fine on the climbs. Anyway, we'll take it slow, I promise," said Lily.

Terri pulled another face.

"Okay, I'm up for a challenge. I'll sort out a bike this afternoon, whilst you're back at work. What time shall I see you?"

"Let's go for a five-thirty start. It'll still be pretty warm, but the breeze will help keep the heat off. And don't worry about any cycling gear. Pop round to my house and you can change into some of my kit."

They finished their lunch and Lily gave Terri her grandparents' address and she made a show of asking where it was, even though she knew full well how to get there.

"That's great. I'll see you at your place at around five-fifteen," said Terri.

*****

"How did it go?" said Simon.

"I need to be careful. I keep slipping into conversation mode and letting the cat out the bag," said Terri.

"What do you mean?"

"Well you know, there's things I know about her, but as far as she knows, I don't know, if that makes sense?"

He nodded.

"I keep having to pinch myself to not say things that will arouse her suspicions."

"Wouldn't it be easier to just tell her the truth?"

"I don't think so. She gets so easily wound up and I see her shutting down whenever I take her anywhere near what happened last week. She's really scared mate, but I don't know why. So I think softly, softly is still our best approach, at least for now. I tell you what though

162

Simon, it makes me look at the whole spy thing that my dad and Anna used to do, in a whole different light."

"Different world to us soldiers, that's for sure."

She smiled at him. *'Yes, a man of few words, but whatever he said, always had a point to it.'*

*****

"Mateo?"

"Si."

"It's Sam, Sam Martínez. I'm just checking in to see how you think Lily is getting on?"

"Good to hear from you Sam. Well, on the face of it, she seems fine. It's as though nothing has happened. But then she's still having these terrible nightmares, so I know something happened, but she just won't talk about it. Do you think it's better to just leave it alone as she keeps saying?"

Sam thought he sounded genuinely concerned. Maybe he was barking up the wrong tree that Mateo was in some way involved?

"It's a tough one Mateo. I have a bit of personal experience of stuff like this and if you leave it buried, well, let's just say it can come back and bite you hard, very hard."

"Oh my God Sam, that makes me feel even worse."

"I'm sorry Mateo, I didn't mean to worry you, but just thought you needed to know, seeing how close you are to her."

There was a pause, before Mateo spoke again.

"Sam, I don't mean to sound ungrateful, but what exactly is your part in all this?"

"Good question. I'm trying to separate being the son of a concerned family friend of Lily's grandparents and my experience as a former cop, when I know something doesn't feel right."

"What do you mean? Doesn't feel right? What do you think has happened to her?"

163

"Well that's just it isn't it? We don't know and she won't tell us, but you saying she's having nightmares? Well that suggests something pretty traumatic has happened. Now, there's no easy way of asking this Mateo, but since she's been back, have the two of you had sex?"

"That's a very personal question Sam."

"I know, but there's the possibility she may have been sexually assaulted and that's why she's trying to block everything out."

"Okay, I understand. Well, as it happens, we haven't, but she's happy with me being very close to her. You know, I can hold her and she's said, *'Just not yet,'* but I think that was because she was so tired from whatever has gone on."

Sam worked through Mateo's response. It was difficult to rule anything out at the moment, however, if she was happy to be held close by Mateo, then that might suggest she hadn't been assaulted, at least not in any sort of sexual way.

"Sam?"

"Sorry, Mateo, I was just thinking. Look, there's no real science in my thinking here, but if she'd been assaulted, she might not want you anywhere near her for a while and that's not the case here. We won't go jumping to any conclusions, but in any case, it doesn't actually help us figure out what else might have happened?"

"Do we go to the police then? She says she doesn't want them involved and they weren't interested before?"

"Well we could, but that could lose us an awful lot of ground in terms of trust from Lily."

"I get that. But what do we do then? Just wait until she decides to say something?"

"We shouldn't push too hard, but we can watch for

opportunities when she may be willing to open up."

"Look Sam," Mateo's tone changed. "Are you doing this for Lily, or is there some other reason? Has this got anything to do with who she works for? Because if it does, then I'm not so sure I'm happy about that."

Sam thought for a moment.

"First and foremost Mateo, it's about Lily, however…."

"Okay, so you've just answered my question Sam! *'First and foremost!'* It's not just about her then is it? You're involved in something else. That's why you want to find out what happened. Are you working for, who is it? Global Aggregates?" Mateo's voice was now challenging and demanding.

"No, not at all. Although, yes, it turns out that by chance or coincidence, the company I work for, 3R, has been retained to look at an incident back in London that is connected to Global Aggregates. Whatever has happened to Lily may be completely unconnected, but it's something I need to check and find out, one way or the other."

Mateo was quiet for a moment.

"I think you've tricked me Sam and more importantly, you've tricked Lily. I'm warning you to leave her alone and if I see you anywhere near her, I will tell her who you're really representing. Is that clear?"

"Mateo, I can appreciate how it looks, but you have to believe me when I say that this all only ever started, when Lily's grandmother came to my mother, to ask for help to find Lily. We knew nothing about Global Aggregates at the time."

"Well I don't believe you. Now stay away, or I will tell her!"

22

Mateo stood for a moment. Then went out on to the balcony and into the bright midday sun. As he stood there, overlooking the Passeig de Maritím and the Palma Marina, he looked for the number on his phone and clicked the dial button.

"Yes?"

"Martínez has been hassling me. He's still digging, but I got it out of him that he's working for someone else and isn't just interested in Lily's welfare."

"Go on."

"I played the pissed off boyfriend and told him that if I see him anywhere near Lily, then I'll tell her that he's not interested in her, but working for someone else, looking into Global Aggregates."

"Good idea. Now has the girl said anything?"

"No, not to me, but she's had lunch with the blonde woman, Terri, today and she seems to be getting closer to Lily, maybe too close. I think Lily's seeing her again later."

"You're supposed to be the bloody boyfriend Mateo. Get up there and sort things out."

"But I think she's already committed to going for a bike ride with this woman later. She's taking her up to the lighthouse at…," said Mateo.

"I know where the bloody lighthouse is!"

Silence.

"Señor?"

"One moment Mateo, I'm thinking."

Stephen Rawlings was used to being in control. As things stood, he wasn't at all sure what was going on. A situation he did not like at all. Chambers was being a damn nuisance, sniffing away at something that didn't concern him and Rawlings could only imagine that these other people, the blonde woman and Martínez, were all connected in some way to Chambers' 3R outfit.

"Mateo," his voice was calmer, more controlled now.

"Si."

"You need to get back up to Puerto Pollensa and sort this Terri out, whoever she is. North is still there, so use him, but you will need to help make this happen."

"But Señor Rawlings, that's not something I do. I...," but Rawlings interjected.

"Mateo, you've been paid very well for what you've done so far in helping us get to Lily. Now's the time you need to protect that investment. We've only got one more loose end to tidy up, but I need a few days for that. After that, well it doesn't matter what happens, because everything will lead to a dead end. Bike rides can be dangerous, especially on that road up to Cap de Formentor. Please see to it with North, that some misfortune happens to this Terri woman. If nothing else, it will be a useful reminder to the Green girl that she needs to keep her mouth shut," said Rawlings, who didn't wait for an answer as he cut the call.

Mateo stood in the sunshine, wondering how he had got himself into this position. This wasn't his normal world. He was a thief. He had been since he was a boy and had to steal food from the markets because his parents were so poor. But he now ran a black market warehouse, buying and selling stolen items – cars, paintings, jewellery, in fact anything of high value that was marketable.

Rawlings had helped him deal with a jealous boyfriend one night in a nightclub in Marbella. It was purely by chance and very fortunate too, when Rawlings stepped in to stop him getting a bad beating.

Things had worked out well since then. Rawlings had recognised his talent for acquiring items that were otherwise difficult to source legitimately and he'd been well rewarded.

This work with the Green girl had been different though. He'd been reluctant at first, but Rawlings had offered him a significant amount of money to get close to the girl. All he had to do was to find out what she knew about some issue about a shopping centre collapsing back in the UK. It wasn't exactly a hardship either, because the girl was as pretty as the photo Rawlings had sent him.

He got on well with Rawlings. A tough, straight talking guy and you knew where you stood with him. The same couldn't be said for Marsden. He didn't like him and certainly didn't trust him. Rawlings had said the girl wouldn't get hurt, but since she'd been back home he'd seen her reliving it all in her nightmares. God knows what Marsden had put her through.

He'd kept telling himself it was just business, but there was something he hadn't bargained for. He'd found himself getting close to the girl.

*****

Stephen Rawlings was back in his office in London, having a similar memory.

He'd been in the nightclub, watching over an important client and as he tracked his client towards the toilets, he'd seen a young man just in front of him, who seemed to be being followed by two men.

He'd been in the security business long enough to

recognise the difference between professional security teams and enforcers, and the two following the man were definitely the latter.

His concern at the time lay not with what might happen to the guy, who he subsequently discovered was Mateo Álvarez, but the fact that his client may inadvertently become caught up in whatever the two men had in mind for Mateo. He followed them into the toilets and saw they had Mateo pinned up against the wall.

He remembered seeing his client at the urinal.

"Sir, we need to leave and quickly."

The client had turned and seen what was happening. Startled, he tried to finish as quickly as he could, however, the sound of the men landing punches also helped him speed up, but then he stopped out of habit to wash his hands.

"Sir, I think we can do that later!" Rawlings voice was more insistent this time and the client responded, looking sheepishly towards his security advisor.

"Yes, sorry, old habits," said the client sheepishly, before walking quickly towards the door, with Rawlings providing a barrier between the two men and his client.

"Nothing to do with you," said one of the men, in an East End London accent.

Up until then, it wasn't. Rawlings only priority had been his client, a young man from a very wealthy Spanish family who had been subject to a number of kidnap attempts in recent years.

Whilst Rawlings was Head of Security at Global Aggregates, it was in practice, merely a title to allow him full access within the GA set up. Groom had recruited him when he went into business with Oleg Makarovich, a Russian billionaire. It was clear from how Groom spoke about his Russian backer that he didn't trust him. Rawlings was only actually responsible for Groom's personal security, however, at Groom's request, he had also set up a small team that included Marsden. Their job was to undertake certain discreet tasks, such as the one they were dealing with regarding the Green girl.

Other than that, Groom was happy for him to run his own personal security business and this particular Spanish client, expected to see Rawlings involved at the business end of what was a very lucrative contract.

The enforcer spoke again.

"I said, it's nothing to do with you, so get the hell out of here if you know what's good for you."

Rawlings looked at the man and then at Mateo, who was pinned up against the wall.

Mateo had looked at him. His eyes told it all.

'Help me.'

Rawlings remembered that he hadn't acknowledged the plea for help, but had continued walking out of the door, before passing his client to one of his team who had been waiting outside.

This was nearly five years ago and he still wasn't entirely sure why he had then stopped. *'Was it a sense of fairness?'* He certainly wasn't thinking of recruiting Mateo into his team at the time, as he didn't know him from Adam. That only came later, when Mateo's talents at acquiring useful resources became apparent.

He'd spoken into his covert comms mic.

"Get the club security over here please Chris."

"Yes, Boss," said Chris Walker. "Everything okay?"

"Yes, just something unconnected. Keep the client safe, whilst I deal with this."

He hadn't waited for the security team to arrive. He just wanted them there to tidy things up. He'd walked back into the toilets. There was another man at the urinals and he motioned to him to get out and quickly.

He heard one of the enforcers, who was holding Mateo as the other hit him, saying, "This is nothing personal amigo, but my boss wants you to understand that he doesn't take kindly to someone hitting on his girlfriend."

With that another punch landed in Mateo's stomach. If it had just been that, a beating, Rawlings may well have just waited and let security deal with it.

But then he'd seen one of them pull something out of his pocket.

A switchblade. The man flicked the button and the knife sprung open.

That changed things.

'Fairness? Good Samaritan?' No, this was now purely practical. If they really did Mateo some serious harm, the police would be called and they would start looking at CCTV. Then they'd be looking possible witnesses and his client was likely to be on camera as he made his way to the toilets. His client was married to a particularly fiery girl and this could potentially lead to questions from her as to why he was in a Marbella nightclub, when he was supposed to be on a business trip.

It wasn't a big issue, but the client certainly wouldn't like the hassle and so it was worth an intervention now.

"Okay, enough guys. I think he's got the message, don't you?"

Rawlings had stepped forward, with his hands open, but standing slightly to his right side, providing a blocking area with the left side of his body.

"I said, it's nothing to do with you," said one of the men.

"Yes, I know you did, but you see it does. And as you just said, *'it's nothing personal,'* but I do need you to put the knife away. By all means give him another couple of punches for good measure, but be quick because the security team are on their way."

He saw confusion from the two men. Mateo was also looking up at him, wondering what on earth was going on. *'Who was this guy and was he actually helping him or not, telling them to hit him again?'*

The two men let Mateo drop to the floor as they turned towards Rawlings. It was two against one. The sort of numbers they liked, but he looked different to the usual type of people they went up against. This guy was tall, fit and looked like he could handle himself. The one with the knife moved forward.

"Put the knife down and we can all walk out of here in one piece and you can tell your boss you've given this guy the message you were sent to deliver."

Just for a moment Rawlings thought they'd seen sense and would do just that. But they were hyped-up with the adrenalin rush from the beating they'd been handing out.

'Knife man' was to his left and the other was a couple of yards away, at about two o'clock to Rawlings.

He was waiting for the signs from them. The slight movement of the hands, the intake of breath, a flex of the muscles. There was generally always something to give it away. He didn't have to wait long. He saw the one without the knife move first, but he was more concerned of the threat from 'knife man'.

The knife was in the man's right hand. Whilst still looking at the one who had moved first, Rawlings actually shifted his weight to the right, as though he intended to move towards the one at two o'clock. But at the last moment, he quickly switched his balance and went for 'knife man'.

He smashed his left forearm up and into the man's right arm, forcing it up high and away from him. He heard, rather than saw the knife clatter to the marble tiled floor. He then followed it up with a hard jab to his stomach. He felt fat, rather than hard muscle, leaving 'knife man' gasping for breath.

The other man had wasted no time in moving in. But it was a sloppy, unprofessional movement and as Rawlings re-positioned himself, he caught the man with an arcing left hook that crashed into his face, crushing his nose, forcing him back.

Rawlings smiled at the memory. These two were just bully boys, with no apparent formal training in the art of fighting. Judging by the fat he'd felt, they weren't too fit either. A miss-match, even with Rawlings probably giving them a twenty year advantage.

Rawlings had feinted again, this time to his left, but then went at 'knife man' again, with another straight right, followed by a kick that took the man's leg away and dropped him to the floor.

"One last chance guys. Walk away now, or you'll leave here with some permanent injuries."

'Knife man' tried to get up.

"Wrong answer," said Rawlings and he kicked him again, this time in the head and hard.

The other one had recovered his balance, but was struggling to see, with blood streaming down his face. Like an outclassed boxer in the ring, blundering towards his opponent, the man walked into another right hook from Rawlings. He stood almost stock still for a moment, but then fell down and didn't get up.

Rawlings heard the door open and two men, dressed in the usual nightclub security suits, rushed in and looked at him and the two men on the floor.

"Can you take it from here please? There's a knife over there on the floor."

Rawlings helped Mateo up.

"Thank you, they would have…"

"Yes, quite possibly my friend, so better be careful next time you go chatting up someone else's girlfriend."

"Si, Señor," said Mateo. "How can I thank you?"

Rawlings knew from experience that sometimes favours could be returned from the most unexpected of places. He spent a few minutes talking with Mateo, before he left to return to his client and in that time Mateo told him about his wholesale business. Rawlings hadn't found out the detail of the business immediately, but later, he'd got his analyst, Finn O'Neil, to take a look into Álvarez's background and it became clear that he might be a useful resource for the future.

'Yes, that was quite a while ago,' thought Rawlings.

23

Terri heard her phone ringing and saw it was Sam.

"How did you get on with Mateo?"

"Not great, to be honest."

"Ah, right. Go on, what happened?"

Sam told her about the call and Mateo's challenge on who Sam was representing.

"He doesn't know about me then?" said Terri.

"No. That is, if we still think he's just the boyfriend, which to be fair, is how he's coming across."

"Do you know what he's going to do next?"

"No, but he says that if he sees me anywhere near her, he'll tell her about 3R investigating GA."

"Well, let's carry on treating him as a friendly, at least for now."

"Agreed. What's your plan today then?" said Sam.

"Lily and I are off on a bike ride later this afternoon. Good job I can at least ride a bike, but I'm wondering how I'll feel by the end of it."

"Where are you going then? Do you know?" said Sam.

"Oh yes, I know mate! We're off up to the lighthouse at Cap de Formentor."

"Bloody hell Terri! That's a fair old ride."

"I know, tell me about it. And my minder? Well he's hired one of these suped-up scooters, so he thinks it's a right laugh," said Terri.

"Brilliant. I like Simon's style," laughed Sam. "Okay, I think I've blown it here with Mateo, so I'll wait to see how you get on later today and then maybe I'll head across to London to give Greg and Anna a hand. I'm just about to call them."

"Sounds like a plan. Now I'm off to the bike hire shop. Catch up later."

*****

Anna was relieved to hear her son's voice.

"Are you okay my boy?"

Sam smiled. What was he - thirty five? And she was still calling him 'my boy'.

"Yes, Mum, I'm fine. It went pretty much as I expected, seeing as they didn't have anything other than a guy with a head injury. But they did find a good witness who said he'd heard me shouting at a guy to stop chasing Terri."

"And you weren't hurt?"

"No, just my pride, seeing as I needed my little sister to come back and stop me getting a real battering off him."

"Lucky you've got such a resourceful sister then," laughed Anna. "Have you spoken to her yet?"

"Yep, I just checked in and she's met Lily for lunch and she's had Simon watching over her. I got hold of the boyfriend, Mateo. He seems to be genuine, but I don't know, there's just something niggling away at me," said Sam. "Now what about you guys? I saw the pic of Marsden you sent through and yes, that was definitely him at Abaco."

"Thought so. It would've been too much of a coincidence. So, we're leaving James here with Roger Wall and his family. They've had a big scare from Marsden. He really is a particularly unpleasant individual."

"That's a very English way of putting things Mum," he laughed. "But you're right, he certainly looked it when Terri and I exchanged words with him. He's got that look about him, maybe he's a psychopath? Anyway, enough about you worrying about me. If James is watching over the Walls, who have you got to keep an eye out for you?" said Sam.

"We're okay. We're not hanging about on street corners. We're going straight from here to meet Martin Carruthers," said Anna.

She heard him breathe out.

"Stop worrying, we're fine," she said.

"I know, *'you've done this before'*, but with them trying to kidnap Terri and the way you say Marsden put the frighteners on an old fighter like Roger Wall, we just need to watch our backs with this lot."

"Yes, good point and we will. Now, the cab's just turned up, so let's catch up later."

After they finished off saying the goodbyes to Wall, Anna and Greg walked out to the waiting cab.

"Sam?" said Greg.

"Yes, he's been released. He's okay, but now he's worrying whether we're taking sufficient care."

"Worried about his old Mum and Dad? That's nice," he grinned. "But I think we got a good reminder after this morning's little episode. So, I heard you say you had an idea about Makarovich?"

"Yes, I'll explain on the way."

*****

"Good morning Anna, Greg," said Martin Carruthers.

"Nice office Martin," said Anna, as she looked out the window on to the Thames.

"Yes, it's nice to be back home. I've been away for

a good few years, so I'm exploring some of my old haunts, well those that haven't been knocked down and redeveloped anyway."

"To get to the point Martin," said Greg, "you got my texts about Terri and the photo Anna sent through?"

"Yes, Tom Marsden, formerly Tom Baker and before that Tom Harris. He's got quite a background, with a number of arrests in the past, but nothing in the last five years since he's been working for Rawlings and GA."

"Looks like he's upped his game under Rawlings then?" said Greg.

"Yes, presumably he's been on a tighter rein under him. That, or Rawlings has just made him a smarter operator, or maybe a bit of both, but certainly nothing has ever stuck with him and he's been arrested for a number of particularly nasty incidents."

"Such as?" said Anna.

"He left the army under a bit of a cloud, something to do with suspected interference with two female recruits, although there's nothing of any substance in the reports.

"He then joined the police, although he didn't make it through his two year probationary period. There were a number of misconduct allegations, including various assaults, including one on a prisoner when he was a probationary police officer.

"After he left the police, there's an arson with intent to endanger life. It was on a former colleague, his tutor constable, that's the officer who would have been working with him out on the police area after his basic training."

"That sounds serious. So the tutor constable, who presumably had a big say in him not getting through his probationary period is subject to an arson after Marsden, or whatever he was called then, leaves the police?" said Anna.

Carruthers nodded.

"Yes, this happened about a year or so after he left the police. Marsden's name is on the file as being of possible interest. However, it's not clear why anyone would suspect him of being involved, since it seems a bit extreme for him to be taking out a revenge attack on his former tutor constable."

"Extreme, but not impossible," said Greg quietly.

"Quite," said Martin. "And finally, he was then questioned, but not arrested, about the circumstances of a serious car accident that resulted in the death of a former colleague from the army and the police."

"A former colleague is killed? Someone who knew Marsden from both the army and the police and nobody could pin it down to him?" said Greg.

"Yes, he was strongly suspected, but not enough it seems to be arrested," said Carruthers. "However, there is a little more to this part of the story."

Greg and Anna looked up at him.

"The former colleague who died was a 'Jim Barnes'...,"

"You said, *'Barnes'*?" interrupted Greg.

Carruthers looked back at him and nodded, "Yes, the brother of one of your guys, Simon Barnes?"

Greg turned and looked at Anna.

"Hmm, might need to have a think about how we approach this. What was he called, I mean Marsden, when he was questioned?"

Carruthers checked his desktop.

"Harris."

"Okay, we'll have to choose our moment to drop this on Simon. But I can't have him going off on a personal crusade to avenge his brother, but then again, I won't lie to him," said Greg.

24

Martin Carruthers broke the silence.

"Anna, you said you had an idea about Makarovich?"

"Yes, but before I get onto that, can you get someone to take a look at this phone? It's a burner, so we're after any numbers that we can try to start cross referencing."

Carruthers took it from her and made a quick call from his office phone. A moment later there was a knock at the door and a young man tentatively came in.

"Ah, Philip, get this burner examined for numbers and then start doing the usual checks on them please."

After the young man had left, Anna resumed.

"I'm thinking we go after him with some bait and then we make him an offer he can't refuse."

"Go on," said Carruthers.

"He's presumably hiding some of his money in offshore accounts and therefore not keeping all his eggs in his Russian bank, so to speak?"

"We think so, yes. We suspect it's in a variety of banks spread across the globe, so the usual suspects in Switzerland and the Cayman Islands. What are you thinking?"

"We want to reduce his influence on the construction industry in the UK, but if he takes everything out in one go, we'll potentially create a significant vacuum in the UK economy that you could well do without," said Anna.

"Yes, very true, so when you say 'make him an offer', are you thinking of buying him out of GA?"

Anna nodded, "I am, but I'm assuming Martin, that obviously you don't have that sort of ready cash to do the buy-out?"

"Er, no, we don't, well certainly not that HM Treasury would be prepared to risk anyway."

"I thought so. Therefore, my plan is that we use his own money to buy himself out."

"Now, I'm interested," said Carruthers.

"Okay, we set up a background history of a bank in the Caymans. Let's call it, I don't know? What about 'Stevens and Co'?"

The others nodded, "Sounds like an old, established, private bank," said Greg.

"So this is a very private bank. The current CEO is Fiona Stevens, granddaughter of Sir Martin Stevens who originally set the bank up. With me so far?" said Anna.

"Yes…, but why haven't we heard of this bank and just how will you persuade Makarovich to invest in it?" said Carruthers.

"You would know the basics about our bank, Stevens and Co, because of the usual banking regulations and disclosures, however, we are very protective of our client base and therefore, we keep very much under the radar of the authorities."

"Okay, go on. This is sounding good so far," said Carruthers, who liked that Anna had slipped into the role of Fiona Stevens, the bank's CEO.

"Stevens and Co specialise in helping clients maintain a high degree of secrecy around their investments."

"But what's to stop a client who declines their services from blabbing to one and all about Stevens and Co?" said Greg.

"Fair question. So to achieve these levels of confidentiality, our bank only approaches those potential clients who have something they, the client themselves, wish to remain hidden well away from the public or their investors' eyes."

"I get that, but how do you find that out?" said Greg.

"Let's just say our bank has a significant intelligence network, built up over many, many years. I'll be telling Makarovich that our network can access all manner of things, such as off-shore account details, transaction data and photographic evidence of account holders visiting their banks in the Caymans. Martin, I take it that you either have some of this available, or can at least get hold of it with regards to Makarovich?"

"Yes," he paused. "We've got a fair bit of this already, but why would Makarovich think this is a secret worth hiding and who from?"

"This is the part that is in fairness, a bit of a gamble Martin. He already owns a bank in Russia doesn't he? The OBCR, Overseas Banking Corporation of Russia?"

"You've done your homework Anna, so yes, although I'm not sure we can necessarily prove he owns it, but, yes, it's definitely his," said Carruthers.

"So you've seen transactions moving around from the OBCR to other accounts in banks across the globe? Switzerland, the Caymans. Bahamas and so on?"

"Yes, true," said Carruthers.

"Good, so we bet on the assumption that he's hiding things from the other business partners in his group in the Kremlin. They're probably all doing it to each other, but the first one to get caught will be likely to have to make a forfeit," said Anna.

"And that could be a pretty permanent forfeit

knowing the way these guys operate," said Greg.

"Yes," said Carruthers quietly. "They'll go after him like a pack of wolves. Then they'll share his portfolio out between themselves."

"Exactly," said Anna.

"Do you think this would all stand up to scrutiny?" said Greg.

"Well let's remember it's just a façade and one that doesn't have to last too long," said Anna. "Makarovich just needs to believe that, if he, as a potential client chooses not to take up the offer from Stevens and Co, then he can't start gossiping about it, because his secret stash will be quickly exposed to his business partners."

"And you think that would work?" said Carruthers.

"Even if Makarovich was to feel it was worth the risk, then I'll be telling him that my bank can call on a number of other clients, even more powerful than he is, to help persuade him of the continued need for privacy," said Anna.

Carruthers made up his mind about telling them about the source.

"I think that might work. Plus, there's something else and I can't tell you anything of the detail, but we do have someone close to him and it seems that he may be under some pressure at the moment from his partners."

Greg and Anna looked at each other, recognising that he was talking about someone who must be deep undercover.

She looked across the table at Carruthers who was studying his glass of wine, deep in thought. Greg looked across and smiled at her and nodded. He thought it could work, particularly given Makarovich's appetite for money, greed and now the apparent pressure to improve performance with the money laundering operation.

"This just needs to work long enough to get him to bite and make a transfer into Stevens and Co," said Carruthers slowly, "but how much were you thinking of skimming him for?"

"He's worth at least £3 billion isn't he Martin?" said Anna.

"Yes, around that sort of figure."

"So £300-400 million isn't going to sound too far out of the ballpark to him, is it?"

Carruthers nodded.

"It seems like an enormous amount, but I agree, to him, it's not an unreasonable amount. That said, GA is supposed to be worth in the region of £1 billion. So why would he be happy with accepting a pay-off of only £300-400 million?"

"Well, clearly he's not going to be happy is he? But with the prospect of the whole business being put under the microscope by the FCA and HM Government freezing all the assets, he may see it as the best solution," said Anna.

"Whilst Anna, or rather Fiona Stevens, will be handling the hook to get him to use Stevens Bank, I'll then move in to persuade him to sell his part of GA, in exchange for not being hounded and persecuted by either of HM's Security Services," said Greg.

"So timing is going to be crucial," said Carruthers quietly.

"Absolutely! Timing and the illusion, but I think Martin, you know some people who can create the smoke and mirrors necessary to make this whole thing look genuine. What do you say?" said Anna.

Carruthers thought for a moment. This was risky, very risky, but he knew she used to be very good, if not the best at what she did. But that was well over thirty years ago. Could she pull this off?

"I can see the cogs in your head spinning Martin. I

might be a few years older, but I can do this. I just need a solid backstory for the bank and Fiona Stevens, so is that something you can deliver?"

Greg was watching her. She might be older, but she was still sharp as a tack and she'd worked this all through as to how it would play out.

"Yes, I think that's very feasible Anna and I like it. The element of secrecy and elitism is what I think will attract a man like Makarovich. I'll get the team on it. Now you'll also need some sort of branding and some marketing blurb. Greg, have you got someone who could look after that, if we do the backstory?" said Carruthers.

"Yes, we've just recruited a young woman in the Mumbai office. We'll make a start on that. Anna, how do you see us making the approach to Makarovich?" said Greg.

"We'll keep it formal, so I'll make direct contact with him and leave a carrot dangling that should be enough for him to take the bait."

"One final thing Martin?" said Greg.

Carruthers looked back at him.

"Apparently the Health and Safety Executive Report is out today?"

"Yes, I haven't been through the whole thing yet, but I suspect you're going to ask if this was the expected outcome?"

"Something like that."

"Well obviously it's not. We don't know how he's done this, Groom I mean. Those HSE guys are usually right at the top end of the integrity ladder, so we have to assume he's got to someone somehow."

"Does that affect things?" said Anna.

Carruthers thought for a moment.

"It doesn't affect the overall objective. By which I mean our intent is to remove Makarovich's ability to launder money through the construction industry."

"What about the victims and their families of the shopping centre collapse?" said Greg quietly.

"Unfortunate, very unfortunate. However, more than one way to skin the proverbial cat. Clearly Groom is desperate to protect his reputation here, because a finding of guilt, or blame, or whatever they call it, could have a significant impact on GA's marketability. More importantly, any fall off in their market share would result in reduced opportunities for Makarovich to launder money," said Carruthers.

"And that presumably is the crux of the matter, at least as far as Groom is concerned? Makarovich will not take kindly to that and he would hold Groom personally to account and I think we all know what that would probably mean," said Greg.

"It doesn't answer the question of giving the families some sort of closure on this though, does it?" said Anna.

"No, however, if your plan goes through, the new Board at GA would have total freedom to make some sort of compensation payment as a goodwill gesture," said Carruthers.

"That sounds a very good option. Now I think this is starting to go quite well. Martin, the backstory? It does need to be absolutely rock-solid if Anna here, is going to go into the proverbial lion's den as Fiona Stevens. If Makarovich smells a rat...," said Greg.

"It will be. We're very good at this sort of stuff now Greg, far better than, dare I say, in your day. The team can create a whole raft of back history and show money in foreign accounts that isn't actually there. Couple that with a type of photoshop software we've developed that will help us produce images of Anna, or rather Fiona, at her desk in the Caymans, that would fool 99% of intel officers around the world, then I'm pretty confident Makarovich won't suspect a thing."

"That all sounds excellent Martin, let's get to it!" said Anna.

'Let's just hope Makarovich hasn't got someone from the one percent working for him,' said Greg under his breath.

25

Rawlings looked at the intel file on his desk. Finn O'Neil had done a good job on Chambers, who looked like he'd done well for himself since leaving the Service and setting up his 3R security consultancy.

There was no record of a wife, but he did have a daughter, Theresa Anderson, who was ex-Australian Army and now Operations Director at 3R.

"Who the hell are you working for Chambers?"

He spoke out aloud to himself, but just at that moment Tom Marsden came through the open door, closing it behind him.

"Well I don't think it's Wall, because I'm pretty sure he'd have said something, or at least shown a bit more fight knowing he had Chambers behind him as back up."

"You could be right there Tom. So it begs the question *'What was Chambers doing at Wall's address?'* if he isn't being engaged by him?"

"I don't know Boss, but you mentioned something about me going to Canada to tie up some loose ends? Is this the Kevin Cox guy?"

"Correct. We're almost there on this job Tom. It doesn't matter that some people know what's happened, as long as they keep their mouths shut."

"Do we know if he's seen Green's message?" said Marsden.

"Yes, we can see he's opened it. Finn has accessed Cox's email, but we don't know if he's done anything about it. That's the loose end."

"What did it say?"

"It was only a two line email from her, asking if he knows anything about UFD 10 and 30, the quick dry concrete formulae."

"I need to be clear here Boss. What exactly is it you need me to do?"

"Have a conversation with this Kevin Cox and establish what he has done and if he intends to do more, then persuade him that it's not a great idea."

"How far do you want me to go to persuade him?"

"Tom, the rules of engagement haven't changed here. We stick with the same thinking of no bruises…"

"No bodies, no police." Marsden finished the sentence. "Okay, but if you ask me, there's a few too many loose ends here Boss and it only needs one of them to talk and this could all collapse around us like a pack of cards."

He realised he'd over stepped the mark. One thing he knew Rawlings couldn't abide was any sense of criticism.

"I appreciate your words of wisdom, but there's a reason why I'm in charge and you're not. We will not have any sort of bloodbath to deal with this. People will react well enough when you apply sufficient threat of retribution. That is all I need from you. Do you understand?"

"Yes Boss, perfectly."

Marsden knew there was little point in arguing the point. In fairness, the work he'd done throughout his time with Rawlings backed up what the man was saying. They had managed to deal with everything before this, without a sniff of the police getting involved. It was just that this time, he'd have quite enjoyed sorting out some of those loose ends. Especially that Green girl, not to mention this new mysterious blonde woman who'd turned up in the picture.

"Good, as long as that's clear. Now here's the file on Cox. Get yourself over to Nova Scotia and have that conversation. Come on Tom, cheer up. This is the final piece of the jigsaw."

Marsden forced a smile and nodded, although he was a long way off agreeing with Rawlings' assessment.

*****

The desk phone rang once. Carruthers saw the extension number was one of his intel officers and grabbed the phone.

"Sir, you asked to be notified of any movements involving Tom Marsden?"

"Yes, what have you got Bob?"

"He's just booked a flight to Halifax, Nova Scotia. T3 at Heathrow, Air Canada, leaving late this afternoon."

As he came off the phone, Carruthers was already reaching for his mobile.

"Greg, I don't know if this is relevant, but Marsden, the guy you had words with outside Roger Wall's place?"

"Yes?"

"He's booked on a flight this afternoon to Nova Scotia. I can partly cover this over there. You know get some photos of him leaving and whether he hires a car or gets picked up, that sort of thing, but that's as far as I can take it really. Can you get someone over there to track him?"

"Yes, of course, no problem. Nova Scotia you say?

That's Halifax International isn't it?"

"That's the one."

"Okay, leave it with me."

*****

Greg was in a coffee shop in Oxford Street. As he came off the phone from Carruthers, he immediately rang his daughter.

"Terri?"

"Dad, how's it going? You all okay?"

"Yes, yes, we're fine. We've a plan coming together. Two things. I'm going to get Sam to head for Nova Scotia. Marsden is flying out there tonight and I want to find out why. Is Tommy anywhere reasonably close? So he can get out there as back up."

"Wonder what he's going there for? But Tommy? Yes, no problem. In fact he's halfway there, as he's back home in Barbados. Just ring him direct Dad and he'll be on his way. Second thing?"

'She was always no-nonsense was Terri,' he thought with a smile.

"Eschaan was telling me you've just recruited three new women and one of them is a bit of an IT guru? I need her to do some background work and create a website that looks like it's been around a while. Do you think she's up for that?"

"Yes, that's Anju. I'm pretty sure she can do all of that sort of stuff. She's a great girl. You'll love her, full of life and brilliant at the IT stuff."

"She sounds ideal. Shall I send the file, with the stuff we need her to work on, direct to Anju?"

"Yes, do that, I'll call Eschaan to give him the heads-up. Now, how's Anna?"

"She's having a great time buying up Oxford Street, getting herself kitted out as the CEO of a private bank in the Caribbean."

"Brilliant! Make sure she gets the accessories, bags

and shoes!"

"Nothing to do with you being a similar size is it?" said Greg.

"No! Of course not, just making sure she looks the part," laughed Terri. "Now whilst I've got you on the phone, I just need to update you on Lily. I'm still making no headway at all. Anytime I get close to thinking she's going to open up, she clams up. We can't keep going on like this, so I'll give the softly, softly, approach one more go this evening and if I still get nothing, I'll do a re-think with the rest of you guys and we can decide how we want to take things forward. Okay with you?"

"Yes, that's fine by me. You take care and yes, I know, you're a big girl and you've got a hunk of an ex-SAS guy watching your back."

She smiled.

"Yes Dad, I'll take care."

She came off the phone and rang Eschaan with the update on what Greg needed Anju to start working on.

"I've got Anju here in the office and she says she'll start building the site now and then she can add the actual content once she's been briefed by Mr Chambers, I mean Greg.

"That's great Eschaan. Keep in touch."

26

S am took the call from Greg about getting to Nova Scotia to track Marsden.

"Do we have any idea why he's going there?"

"No, so I appreciate it could even be a bit of a wild goose chase. I've just got a feeling that it's connected to all of this. Don't ask me why, but I've been to Nova Scotia and it's a lovely place. That's why it doesn't sound like our friend Marsden is going to go for some sort of holiday. Therefore, it makes me think he's going there on business."

"I see where you're coming from. But it's still a pretty big place," said Sam.

"I know, but we've got some help being sorted by Tommy. I forgot to say, he'll meet you out there. He's in Barbados, so he'll be there before you arrive. Anyway, he's got an ex-army chum who does some private detective stuff out there. He's going to call him and one of Martin's mob will also let us know if Marsden gets picked up in a car, or if he rents one. Either way, our friends in MI6 will inform us as soon as they see what he's up to."

"Great, but why can't Martin's outfit follow Marsden?" As soon as he asked the question he realised why they couldn't, or rather, why they wouldn't.

"Scrap that question Greg. They could, but they won't. Right?"

"Yep, spot on. They're keeping their distance for deniability reasons."

"Of course. Okay, I'll sort a flight and get over there. No point in asking Daniel is there?"

"Sadly not. Terri was telling me the other day that he's on a long term commitment, with some new teenage singing sensation who's on tour. Easy for some – huh?"

"Ha! I'll get back to you when I get there," said Sam.

*****

Tommy had been taking in the final couple of hours of sunshine before heading to Barbados International Airport.

He'd enjoyed his time back home, seeing friends and family, but he was pleased when he got the call from Greg.

"Time for me to go back to work my friend."

Charlie St. Clair looked up at him from the beach lounger he was on.

"It's been good to see you again Tommy. Don't leave it so long next time."

"I'll try not to Charlie."

"Hey, and Tommy, did you ever get to talk to that lady you saw on the beach? The one you kept seeing running up and down every morning?"

Tommy smiled. Despite his apparent out-going nature, he was actually quite shy and reserved when it came to talking to women. Charlie on the other hand, wasn't and could sit and chat with anyone.

"Maybe next time my friend, maybe next time. Now, can you give me that lift you promised me?"

Charlie St. Clair raised his eyebrows at his friend. Another potential love interest that looked to have got away from his childhood friend.

Tommy's flight took him first to Montreal and then after a couple of hours stop-over, he was on his way on the short flight to Halifax, Nova Scotia. During the stop-over he had got hold of his friend, Billy Jarvis, another ex-para, who'd emigrated to Canada after he got out of the army.

"What's this all about Tommy?"

"Bit of a long story chum, but I'll get some pictures sent across to you. I'm also sending you the contact details of Sam Martínez and Greg Chambers. Sam will be joining me out there. Okay?"

Billy waited for the contact message to arrive.

"Yes, got them."

"We'll be told if the target, a guy called Marsden, gets picked up, or if he hires a car. He's on a late afternoon flight from the UK. If I'm still in the air, my boss, Greg, will message you direct. I need to know where Marsden ends up. But Billy, we haven't got clear cut evidence, but we reckon he's a bit of a handful, so don't take any chances, right? I'd rather lose him, than you."

"Understood. Do you think Marsden is likely to be carrying?" said Billy.

"He's flying in on a scheduled flight with Air Canada, so he won't be bringing anything in with him, but he's part of an organisation called Global Aggregates. Heard of them?"

"Yes, they've got a site north of the city. Reckon he'll aim for there?" said Billy.

"Possibly as a base. He's part of their security team, so if they have access to weapons, he'll obviously be able to pick one up."

"Well let's work on the basis that he can get hold of a firearm then. I've got a couple of guns that are licensed to me that you're welcome to use Tommy, but if you get caught with them they'll have my PI licence off me in a flash. So maybe it's best if I ride along with you, if that's okay?"

"I was going to ask if you could anyway Billy. And at your top day rate, because these people pay well mate."

"Job's a good 'un then chum, count me in."

*****

Tom Marsden was sat on the Air Canada flight to Halifax. He had the file Finn O'Neil had prepared on Kevin Cox resting on his knee.

He'd been through it once as a quick read through and then a second time, to focus in on the details Finn had included on the potential weak links in Cox's life.

Cox was married with two young children, aged eight and ten. That was enough for Marsden. Rarely had anyone given him anything more than a half-hearted challenge, especially when he had used their children as leverage, so he didn't see why this should be any different.

He packed the file away in his bag and settled back in his seat, cursing Rawlings that he wouldn't let him go anything other than cattle class. But after a couple of whiskeys, shortly after take-off, they weren't in the air long before he was asleep.

*****

Whilst the Air Canada flight to Nova Scotia was making headway, Sam Martínez was waiting at Palma de Mallorca for his flight to London Heathrow. He'd been looking at the various messages from Tommy, including contact details for Billy Jarvis.

'Hi Billy, just confirming you've got my details? Sam'.

'Confirmed Sam. See you soon. Billy'

He remembered he was supposed to tell the police he was leaving the island. He rang the number she'd given him.

"Detective Delgado? Sam Martínez," he spoke in Spanish.

"Si, good afternoon Señor Martínez. Why are you at the airport Señor?"

He smiled. Whoever was following him was good, because he hadn't seen them. He turned around in his chair. He was used to operating in surveillance teams, but clearly he wasn't so skilled in counter surveillance.

Nobody was standing out. He looked again, turning more slowly this time. Still he didn't immediately see her, not until she took off her summer hat and stopped walking and looked directly at him.

"Detective, what a pleasant surprise," he laughed out loud as he put his phone down and waited as she joined him.

"I wondered if you'd spotted me, which was why you called me?" said Delgado.

"No, nothing as devious as that I'm afraid. I did just remember that you'd asked me to tell you if I was leaving the island and that's what I'm doing, calling you as requested."

"Honestly?" She looked at him.

"Yep, honestly. I'm going to London and then onto Nova Scotia. It's a business trip."

She looked at him again.

"I don't know what to make of you Señor Sam Martínez. Do I trust you or not?"

He smiled at her. She was just doing her job and besides, he quite liked her.

"Well why don't you start with trusting me until you find out something that changes your mind?"

"That sounds as though I might find something out Señor?"

"I suppose it does, but I can tell you that it won't be anything to do with the case you're investigating, I promise."

"Now things are getting mysterious. So you're saying I might find something out that I don't like about you? Is that it?"

She was smiling at him, until she saw his expression change. *'What was that?'* she thought. *'Guilt or something else?'*

He half-smiled again.

"I don't mean to be mysterious, detective, but secrets? Yes, I suppose I have a few."

"Something to do with why you left the Met, your home force?"

He was starting to feel uncomfortable with where this was going now. This was when he knew he started getting defensive. He'd tried his best with Carmen. It had gone well to start with, but then he'd messed that up, getting moody again and just being difficult to be with. He had no idea if she was asking as a cop, or for some other reason, but he could feel the angst rising inside him.

'Damn this PTSD!'

She could see he was fighting something. He was tensing up, his whole body seemed to be shrinking as he closed in on himself.

"Look, you don't need to answer that Señor Martínez," she said quietly.

"It's Sam, just call me Sam and no, it's okay. I'm making this all sound way too dramatic. There are no secrets, Detective. I was involved in a police shooting back in London and I'm struggling to deal with it, that's it."

"¿Es TEPT?" and she repeated it, but this time in English, "Is it PTSD? Sam."

"Your English is very good, Detective."

"It's Sofi, call me Sofi."

"Does this mean you're going to trust me then Sofi?"

"Let's just say someone gave me a call and said you were one of the good guys."

"Lori?"

"That's Detective Inspectora Garcia to me, but yes, she called me this afternoon. One thing. Did you ask her to?"

"No, I think we probably both know what it's like when a colleague's friend, or member of their family gets arrested for something, innocent or not, and the colleague starts asking questions about the investigation. It can get, well, difficult, yes?"

"It can, but to be fair, she made some good friends over here when she was working on the Armenian OCG murders. Apparently one of them saw your name and tipped her off. She was great about it. Very professional and didn't ask anything about the case. She just gave me the heads up who you were."

"So you've been stringing me along then?" He looked at her in mock outrage.

She laughed.

"Yes, of course!"

"Okay, so you're cool with me leaving the island?"

"Yes, but is this trip anything to do with the incident up in Puerto Pollensa?"

He paused.

"Okay, that's enough of an answer Sam, don't say anymore unless you're going to tell me the whole story."

"I don't think I can do that Sofi."

He saw the look on her face as he said it. She'd lost the soft gentle look and back was the almost cold, direct and intense look she'd had when she'd been interviewing him at the police station.

He tried to explain.

"It's because we may be chasing shadows with all of this. We just don't know at the moment. The guy in Canada may be completely unconnected, but it's possible he may know something that links the incident here, with something that's going on in

London."

"I told you not to tell me anything. You're making it worse Sam!"

But at least the expression on her face had softened.

"I'm telling you this because I think it's the right thing to do. If anything comes out of Canada that has a bearing on anything here, I promise, I'll let you know."

"You'll let me know huh? I think you'll let me know when you're good and ready, but hey, I've already been given the heads up on that too."

Sam looked at her, before he twigged.

"Lori again?"

"Yes, who else. She also said to give you her love? So am I missing something here?"

Sam was smiling. He couldn't blame Lori for what she'd said to Sofi. He didn't think he should labour the point that it was more about what Greg had told Lori, or rather not told her, during the thing with Sonny Sargsyan, the Armenian OCG boss, which was the issue here.

"No, you're not missing anything regarding me and Lori, Sofi. The closest thing she might be at some stage in the future is my biological step-mother."

"I don't know why you're smiling Sam Martínez and I haven't the slightest idea what you're going on about regarding a biological step-mother. But just remember, when our mystery guy in hospital wakes up, well, I may just need to speak to you again….and I mean, in a professional capacity."

'Was she getting embarrassed?' He wasn't sure.

"I understand Sofi, although I suspect that your man may be an unwilling witness."

"Possibly, but we'll have to wait and see. Now this looks like it may be your flight."

"Ah, so you didn't follow me here? You got a tip off I was booked on this flight," said Sam.

"Yes, so you don't need to worry that your counter surveillance skills are slipping." Once again, there was a smile on her face.

He nodded to her with a grin, grabbed his overnight bag and turned and made his way towards Gate A19.

27

Terri had picked up her hire bike a few minutes before she got to Lily's grandparents' house. It was 4.45pm when she knocked at the door and the Honda Jazz wasn't on the driveway.

"Mrs Green? I'm Terri. Did Lily tell you I'd be coming around to borrow some of her cycling clothes? She's dragging me off up to Cap de Formentor."

"Yes, Terri. Lily's on her way, so should just be a few minutes. Come in, come in."

Simon watched from a hundred yards or so away, sat astride his scooter. He'd also seen the Honda wasn't there, so he'd eased himself and the scooter in between a couple of vans, so that Lily wouldn't see him as she drove past.

Terri was getting Lily's life history from her grandmother, albeit without the events of the previous week. It just went to reinforce Terri's thinking that this was a life-loving, out-going girl with masses of energy and personality who didn't compare with the girl Terri had first met at Bonys Bar and then Bar Coral.

Terri could still see a caring young woman, someone who'd been willing to talk to a complete stranger who she thought had boyfriend issues. However, it was also pretty clear that Lily had changed in the space of just a few days. She was now someone who could be up one minute and down the next, becoming withdrawn, even distant, with some fairly dramatic mood swings if the conversation ventured anywhere near what had happened to her.

It was only about five minutes later when Lily came in through the door and her eyes lit up when she saw Terri.

"I wondered if you might chicken out," said Lily.

"Don't forget you're talking to an Australian here young lady," teased Terri. "I've got my bike and I'm set to go. I tried to go with a hybrid, because it's what I'm used to riding and I didn't fancy those thin race tyres on the road bikes, but the guy at the shop was adamant that I needed a road bike for the climbs, so that's what I've got."

"That was a good call, but it still doesn't mean you'll be able to keep up with me."

"Don't be too sure about that!"

"Ha! Right, let's get you sorted with some clothes. Gran, we'll be gone a good few hours. Depends how our Aussie chum gets on negotiating the climbs, so keep an eye on the phone in case we need Gramps to come and rescue us."

'It was good to see her laughing,' thought Terri and it looked like her grandmother was thinking the same thing.

"What about food? Will you want anything?"

"Thanks Gran, but I think we might grab some food out in town. It's Terri's last night here."

"Okay, now I know you'll tell me I'm silly, but please be careful. That can be a dangerous road up to the lighthouse."

"I'll be sure to take it steady and keep us both safe Gran," said Lily.

They went upstairs and Terri changed into the Lycra

top and shorts Lily offered her.

"Lime green?" She laughed.

"Yes, thought it might be useful to keep an eye on you if you lag behind!" said Lily with a grin.

'At least Simon won't lose me,' thought Terri as she smiled back at her.

*****

The ride up to the Cap de Formentor lighthouse started easily enough. Terri wasn't too concerned, even at the prospect of a couple of hours, or more, bike ride, as she rode a lot whenever, and wherever, she could.

Nevertheless, Lily had made sure they went through a series of warm up exercises before they set off.

"Okay, you're sure you're up for this?" said Lily.

"Let's do it!" said Terri, muttering under her breath, *'The things I do for 3R International.'*

Terri had checked the route on the internet beforehand and had seen the climbs and noted which ones were likely to be the most demanding.

The first three, or four kilometres, weren't too bad. They were climbing about 200 metres and although the gradients were 7%, the stunning views over Puerto Pollensa definitely helped take her mind off how her legs were feeling already.

She occasionally looked around and thought she could see Simon on his scooter. *'Next time, he can ride the bloody bike!'*

"You're doing just great Terri. Nice easy rhythm going up those hills. You're looking good."

Terri grinned back at her. She was actually enjoying it, both the ride and Lily's company. It was good to see she was enjoying herself.

"Okay, this is where things start to hot up a bit. We've got fast descent coming up. It's the other side of Col de sa Creueta, followed by about 10K of a mix of climbs and almost straights."

"Almost straights! Can't wait!" said Terri.

"Ha! Come on slowcoach, it's 3K downhill, then we go back up through a tunnel and after that, you'll get your first look at the lighthouse – it's awesome."

Lily was relaxed and really was enjoying herself, probably for the first time since she'd been kidnapped. Terri also saw Lily had barely broken into a sweat, whereas despite her own good level of fitness, she was starting to feel the effects of the climbs kicking in.

The good thing was that it wasn't so hot as to be unbearable. With a little bit of sea breeze as well, it was making it a fairly comfortable ride, especially as they had the occasional stretch of trees to take shade from as well.

The long three kilometre descent definitely helped Terri recharge her batteries, before they went up a short climb and into a 300 metre tunnel.

"Wow!" said Terri.

"Pretty impressive isn't it?" said Lily. "It used to be unlit and you couldn't see your hand in front of your face."

She waved up above her head, to the central strip of lighting that ran the length of the tunnel.

"These lights are an absolute godsend. It was pretty dangerous before, as the cars, not to mention the coaches, just couldn't see you."

Terri heard the sound of a car coming up fast behind them. *'Bloody good job they've got them now,'* she thought, but suddenly the engine noise changed, as it slowed down. Terri was immediately on her guard.

"Lily, keep in!"

But Lily had stopped and was waving.

"It's okay, it's Mateo! Hello my love," she shouted. Then hearing the echo, she shouted again, "Hello Mateo!" and she let her voice carry the note on to pronounce the echo.

"Terri! It is good to see you. So, she's dragged you up the mountain, eh?"

Terri was looking around, on edge. The three of them were stopped inside a tunnel. She turned and saw a solitary headlight behind them. "I hope to God that's you, Simon," she whispered, before she realised even a whisper carried in the tunnel.

"What was that Terri?" said Lily.

"Nothing, I'm just thinking we've still got a bit of a way to go, so we'd better get a move on."

"Yes, you're right. Don't strain yourself my love, you know. Getting up these hills in your flash Porsche," said Lily with a laugh.

"I'll try not to. Hey, I'll grab some cold drinks at the top, hopefully the café will still be open," said Mateo.

"And get some energy gels too, if they've still got any left!" shouted Lily. "Right, time to start shifting Terri. This is the exciting bit."

Lily pushed them hard to get up and out of the tunnel and then along a stretch of road with a mix of trees and then craggy outcrops.

"There, can you see it Terri? On your left, just coming through a gap in the rocks. Isn't it amazing?"

Terri looked across and saw the Cap de Formentor lighthouse as it appeared. She smiled. Lily's enthusiasm was infectious.

"Yes, it certainly is."

"We've not far to go now. So this is where it gets even better," said Lily. "Now we've got another steep descent coming up, so enjoy it whilst you can. You need to conserve your energy too, as the last climb up to the lighthouse is a bit of a killer."

"Oh good," said Terri, as she sat up on her seat, stretching her back and letting the bike freewheel down the slope. "I can't wait."

"You sure you're okay?"

"Okay? I'm loving it, Lily!"

*****

Simon wasn't taking anything for granted. He didn't want to get too near to them, in case Lily recognised the scooter and got twitchy about what might be going on.

He was a bit concerned that they had no comms, but they couldn't risk it. Terri was going to be changing in Lily's house and they couldn't guarantee that Lily would leave the bedroom as Terri was only going to be slipping a top and shorts on.

Instead, they would have to do it the old fashioned way, by line of sight. There was quite a lot of traffic on the road, both other cyclists, but also a whole raft of scooters and motor cyclists, as well as cars and tourist coaches. This was good in some ways, in that it was unlikely anyone could spring a trap with so many people about, but bad in others, because it made it harder to spot any potential danger until the last minute.

He knew they'd passed the halfway mark and Terri was going at a good rate. It didn't surprise him, as they occasionally went for a run together and she was fit and strong and he often struggled to keep up with her when they went for anything more than a 10k run.

It was a stunning piece of scenery, but he kept his eyes firmly on the job in hand. There was no point thinking the guy in the VW van would necessarily still be in the same vehicle, so he was watching for anything that looked out of the ordinary.

When he saw the two women enter the tunnel, he held back a little. Traffic had eased and so he felt he could afford to hang back. He cut the engine, so the noise didn't carry into the tunnel and listened. He could hear their voices and laughter. He smiled, but then was back on his guard, as he suddenly heard the noise of a car coming up behind him.

It had a tell-tale growl to the exhaust. *'Porsche?'* he thought to himself. The 911 was so distinctive. Then he saw a car approaching, so he tucked in a little behind one of the signs before the tunnel, as though he was on the phone.

He recognised the car before he saw the driver. A bright yellow Porsche, then he saw the driver, Mateo Álvarez, Lily's boyfriend.

'What are you doing up here?'

Simon watched as the car slowed and then he could hear Lily's voice, even above the bumbling exhaust note. Then the engine noise increased as Álvarez blipped the accelerator and the Porsche took off.

*****

As he came out of the tunnel, Mateo Álvarez was wondering if he could go through with this. All he had to do was keep the two women occupied and North would do the rest. He knew North had swopped the VW van for a scooter and by now he should already be up at the lighthouse.

The plan was that North would get himself acquainted with the layout around the lighthouse. He'd then be ready for when Álvarez arrived and pointed out where the women were going to leave their bikes.

*****

North saw Álvarez arrive. He couldn't miss him, not with the bright yellow car and the bellowing exhaust note, especially as he revved it up as he was parking.

'Flash car for someone who's just a pimped up stolen goods merchant,' he thought.

He was sat astride the scooter he'd stolen in Alcúdia earlier that day. He knew he needed to be careful of getting too close to the blonde. She had seen him twice now and was likely to easily recognise him, even with the cap and sunglasses he was wearing.

Álvarez nodded to him as he walked past and

up towards the café. He wasn't gone long before he returned and North saw he had some bottles of water and what looked like energy gel sachets, the sort cyclists use to restore salts and minerals in their body.

He watched Álvarez sit on the front wing of the Porsche.

'What a poser! But hey, who's the one with the Porsche?' he thought. He needed to get this right. He had fouled up in Abaco when he'd got distracted by the blonde. She'd caught him staring at her and then they'd also missed her when they went to grab her as she left Bonys in Puerto Pollensa. He couldn't afford to make a mistake this time, otherwise he'd be out on his ear according to Marsden.

*****

"Almost there Terri. God, you're a bloody good cyclist for someone who doesn't get out much girl."

"Why thank you. That's praise indeed coming from someone who has to keep stopping to let me catch up!"

"No, I mean it Terri. This is an incredibly demanding climb, even for really experienced riders, so suck it up, well done."

They pushed hard up the last section and were both breathing heavily as they came to a stop in the carpark. "Okay, let's chain the bikes together and there he is, sitting on his Porsche. He's such a show off, but he's so sweet too."

Terri looked across at Mateo, who waved back at her. He was smiling and looked genuinely pleased to see them.

She watched as Lily strapped the lock through the bikes and then they walked off to join Mateo, before carrying on up to the lighthouse café.

Simon had stopped a little way below where they had left their bikes. As he saw them walking up towards the café, he moved forward and into the carpark. After parking up, he went to check the site around the café.

He saw someone walking down towards him and he nodded as they went by. The guy was wearing a cap and sunglasses and was carrying a bottle of water. Nothing unusual in that given the temperature it still was.

Simon walked further around and saw Mateo and the two women. They were sat at a table overlooking the bay. Even at this time of the evening there was still a good few people about, so he took his time as he completed his circuit of the carpark and café.

He had a feeling something wasn't right, but he couldn't put his finger on it. It was just a sense, and he'd had these before and more often than not, they were proved to be right. But what was it? There was nothing standing out to him.

He walked back to his scooter and put his helmet back on and it was just a couple of minutes later that the women reappeared with Mateo.

Terri even looked across at him and smiled, although she couldn't see his face and wouldn't have seen the frown.

"I'll see you down in the town," said Mateo and he was already in the car and starting the engine.

"Make sure you get a move on as I won't be hanging around," shouted Lily, as he blipped the throttle of the Porsche.

He reversed out of his space and Terri saw Lily watching him as he disappeared down the road.

'She really does like him,' she thought.

"Now come on, tell me. Is it easier going back or worse?" said Terri.

"Well...., you know that great descent we came down just before we got here. That's a 90 metre drop in about a kilometre. And what goes down...," said Lily.

"Must go up," finished Terri. "Tough start then!"

"Yes, but after that it's a doddle. All downhill, with some very fast sweeping bends where you've got to keep your nerve and grab a big chunk of brake when you need to. But you'll love it. Just watch out for the sheer drops!"

"What!" laughed Terri, "Now, you tell me!"

28

O leg Makarovich was sat at his desk in the office of his town house in Eaton Square, Belgravia. He had bought the house in 2008, at the same time he acquired the majority shareholding in Global Aggregates.

The house purchase was part of the Tier 1 Investment Scheme established by the then UK Prime Minister, Gordon Brown. The £10 million investment granted him temporary residence status for two years, during which time he could apply for permanent residence. Such was the influx of Russian money into the country during this scheme, Eaton Square became known as Red Square.

Penny Hastings had worked for Oleg Makarovich for over ten years as his PA and knew when, and when not to interrupt him.

"Yes, Penny?"

"I have a Fiona Stevens, CEO of Stevens Bank on the line, asking if you're free to take her call?"

"Never heard of her, or the bank."

"She said you might say that sir. Apparently they operate out of the Caymans."

The mention of the Cayman Islands sparked his interest.

"What does she want?"

"She mentioned an investment opportunity that might appeal to you."

"How the hell did she get the number for here?"

Penny Hastings didn't answer. He often spoke out aloud when he was thinking and this wasn't one of those times when he was looking for any sort of response from her.

"As I had her on hold, I ran Stevens Bank through various internet checks and nothing much came up. Then when I went back to her for more information, Miss Stevens did tell me that if I had been checking on the internet, I wouldn't have found very much of interest. She says they are a very private bank, with just a few elite customers."

Penny paused to allow the words to sink in.

"She's still on the line. Would you like me to put her through?"

Makarovich thought for a moment. He already had a number of bank accounts in the Caribbean. However, he'd never heard of these people, Stevens Bank. But then again, how had she got his private number?

He knew something about the world of private banking with his ownership of the OBCR Bank. The level of highly discreet and confidential services, demanded by private customers at the top end of the exclusive banking market, was way beyond that of even many of the renowned Swiss banks, let alone the High Street banks.

"Put this Miss Stevens through will you please Penny. Let's see what she has to say."

There was a pause before the line clicked.

"Mr Makarovich? Fiona Stevens, thank you for taking my call." Anna spoke softly, but with confidence. She wasn't taking any risks with accents, as she had enough to focus and concentrate on, but she was accentuating her 'private school' voice just a little.

"Miss Stevens, let me start off by saying that I don't usually take cold calls, but I'm intrigued to know how you got my personal number?"

Anna had been expecting this question. She'd walked through the scenario with Martin Carruthers when he'd given her Makarovich's phone number. She didn't need to know exactly how Martin's intel team had actually got the number. But she definitely needed an answer that would satisfy Makarovich.

"We're a very private bank Mr Makarovich, established nearly one hundred years ago, by my grandfather. During that time we have built up a network of contacts and sources that I can confidently say is perhaps second only, to the very best intelligence services."

"That doesn't answer my question."

"It answers it as far as I'm concerned Mr Makarovich," said Anna firmly, before she continued in a lighter tone. "We tend to find out a great many things of interest through our contacts and this in turn helps maintain the relationships we have with our clients."

"Go on."

"Since our clients know that we know many of their key secrets, it helps to ensure that few people ever feel the need to talk about our specialised banking operations."

"That sounds like you blackmail your clients Miss Stevens?"

"Not at all Mr Makarovich, but in the same way that they like to protect their privacy, well, so do we. Knowing that we may share their secrets helps to maintain what is perhaps best called the 'status quo'."

"In other words, you expect me to keep our dealings entirely under wraps, otherwise you will…"

She interrupted him quickly. He'd got the point, but

she didn't want to labour it. Instead she wanted him to start seeing the positives of what she could offer him.

"As I said, by us both maintaining a high level of confidentiality Mr Makarovich, I can assure you that no one will know anything about the monies you are transferring into and out of Stevens & Co."

He didn't say anything for a moment. She was right. The fact that he'd never heard of them was testament to the level of secrecy under which they operated.

"I can see how such a degree of trust could be beneficial to both sides Miss Stevens."

She couldn't help but smile.

"Oh good, I'm so pleased you feel that way. Now if I may, I'd like to get straight to the point. I'm in London for just a few days and you are someone I think would be a good fit for our very exclusive client base. Can I assume that this is a secure line?"

"Yes, you may." He had his office line checked every hour by his security team, to ensure no one could track his calls.

"Thank you. I am in a position where I can offer you some extremely attractive investment opportunities. The sort that will remain far away from prying eyes of any of the authorities, but also," she paused for effect, "from any of your friends and business associates."

"Tread carefully here Miss Stevens. If you have done your homework on me, as you seem to have, you will know I am not a man to trifle with, so please do not infer that I may be involved in any sort of mis-management of funds regarding my associates."

"I wouldn't dream of it Mr Makarovich. Perhaps we can meet to talk more about how I might be able to offer some additional services to those already provided by your banks in the Virgin Islands, Nassau, China and…."

He couldn't contain himself.

"How the hell do you know about my personal bank

accounts?"

She waited for a moment. She'd hooked him with the information Carruthers had sent her. Whilst it wasn't completely up to date, she only needed enough to convince Makarovich to believe that she had access to the sort of information that he definitely wouldn't want his business associates to see.

"As you said, I've done my homework. Now perhaps we could continue this conversation over dinner, or perhaps lunch would suit you better?"

He wasn't used to being caught off guard. He'd never heard of this woman, or her bank, but she clearly knew something about him.

When he answered, Anna noticed he'd regained the composure in his voice.

"I think I can make lunch tomorrow Miss Stevens. Where would you like to meet?"

"Why not at Kasper's? I'm staying here at The Savoy anyway, so I should be able to get a table."

"Yes, I like it there. Give them my name if you get any problems, it usually helps."

"Thank you and I look forward to seeing you tomorrow Mr Makarovich."

*****

Anna came off the phone. Greg was with her in her room at The Savoy. She felt a slight tremble in her right hand. Nerves? She'd been out of the game for so many years and this man was dangerous, even if she was meeting him in the heart of London. She couldn't afford to make any mistakes.

Greg looked at her. She'd seemed calmness personified when she'd been speaking to Makarovich on the phone, but he'd seen the tremble.

"Are you alright Anna? You don't have to do this you know."

She forced a half smile. She'd always been in control

of things when she'd been working in the field. It was never bravado, nor false confidence. She was good, really good at doing this type of thing, but she knew she couldn't pull the wool over Greg's eyes either.

"Yes, I'm okay, but you saw the slight shake? Now I don't think I've got anything physically going on with me, as I went for a thorough medical when Luis fell ill. He made me do it, to make sure I'd be okay after he'd gone, bless him."

"Maybe just first night nerves so to speak? I mean you didn't have any of this when you fronted up Sergei Grigoryan, when we were in Yerevan."

"No, you might be right. Perhaps I just hadn't fully got into role. I'll be fine tomorrow, when I'm in front of him."

"Yes, you'll be more than fine. Now, I need to skidaddle, before your new friend Oleg gets someone across here to check you out."

"Skidaddle? Haven't heard that in a long while!" She grinned.

"And Anna?"

She looked back across the room at him.

"You were the best, the very best in fact. And I've got no doubt that you've still got all your skills, particularly when you're going to be dressed for the part as well, so you really will be fine," said Greg, "especially wearing this."

He held up the wig she had bought. He couldn't believe how much it was, but he had to admit that it definitely changed her look with the way the hair wrapped around her face.

She smiled back at him.

"Thank you," and she kissed him on the cheek.

As he left the room, he just hoped they weren't biting off more than they could chew with Makarovich, who was a much tougher nut to crack than an

Armenian OCG boss.

*****

As soon as he came off the phone, Makarovich was yelling out of his office door.

"Penny! Get this place swept again immediately and when they've done it once, I want them to do it all again and that includes the cars too!"

"I'll get on to it immediately sir."

"Thank you Penny. And Penny? I'm sorry, I didn't mean to shout."

"Thank you sir."

He'd quickly regained control. She knew that he could sometimes lose his temper, but he'd never raised his voice towards her. He was clearly thrown by how this Stevens woman had got his number and what she'd said to him.

He picked up his phone.

His son answered.

"Papa?"

"Mikhail, I need you to do some digging for me on a woman called Fiona Stevens, CEO of Stevens Bank in the Caymans. She says she's staying at The Savoy so start off by checking her out there."

"Urgent Papa?"

"Yes my boy, I'm having lunch with her tomorrow and she knows far too much about me and I know nothing about her."

As he was putting his phone down, he saw an email appear on his laptop:

From: Fiona Stevens, Stevens Bank, Cayman Islands.
Dear Mr Makarovich, it was a pleasure to speak to you this afternoon. I have booked a table at Kasper's for 12.30 tomorrow.....and yes, when I mentioned your name, it certainly helped, regards, Fiona Stevens.

How had this woman got hold of his email address?

'*Was this a trap?*' Either her intel sources were very, very good, or this was indeed some sort of trap. He wondered if he should ask any of his colleagues back in the Kremlin, or maybe Groom, as he might know something about them.

The problem was that if he told anyone, then he immediately lost the confidentiality that she was promising. Worse still, he didn't know what secrets of his that she might then leak.

'*Maybe if he looked at this from a different perspective?*' he thought. After all, she may well have something of benefit to him, so why not meet her? He sent a brief response, saying he'd see her at Kasper's tomorrow.

*****

Anna saw his response. She wondered quite how Makarovich had reacted to some of her comments. She got the sense that she'd rattled him. This was good in some ways, but it also meant she needed to be careful. As much as he tried to come across as the cultured and suave benefactor of many charities, Martin Carruthers had told them enough of his background, for them to know Makarovich was a dangerous man.

She looked around her room. It was a Luxury King size with a view over the Thames. '*Definitely befitting a Cayman Islands banker. I must do this more often,*' she thought with a grin.

She then took a bath and changed into some of the beautiful and very expensive clothes she'd bought in Oxford Street during the day.

'*Well you've got to look the part. And I get to keep them,*' she thought to herself, a smile appearing as she felt the silky material against her skin.

29

Anna took the lift downstairs and out into the lobby of The Savoy. She stood for a moment. It brought back memories of a life before Luis and Sam.

She'd enjoyed her life back then, really enjoyed it. The risk, even the danger, had given her a thrill. But did she miss it? She thought for a moment. *'No, that was then.'* But she was brought back to the present with a jolt when she saw a young man come in through the swing doors at the front of the hotel.

He walked straight past her without looking and went to the reception desk. Her old skills and senses were coming back and quickly! He looked East European, so he might be something to do with Makarovich, sent here to check up on her.

The reception desk at The Savoy in London is set into an alcove on the right as guests come through the main entrance to the hotel.

Anna knew she couldn't risk getting too close to the desk, partly because she didn't want him to see her, but also because the standard of service at The Fairmont Savoy was excellent, so there was a good chance one of the team might greet her by the name she was using, Fiona Stevens.

She slowly moved forward to get as close as she could, to see if she could hear what the young man was saying, whilst still not being seen.

He spoke with an East European accent. She was good with accents, both recognising them and mimicking them. He was Russian. Good English, no actually, very good English, maybe educated over here at some stage?

"Hello, I represent a client of Miss Fiona Stevens, who we believe is staying here? She's having dinner with him in Kaspar's tomorrow. Please could you get a message to her that he will be delayed by fifteen minutes?" said Mikhail Makarovich.

The receptionist nodded and smiled and made no comment as to why this person couldn't just ring Miss Stevens themselves. They knew enough about how the rich operated to know that simple wasn't always in their vocabulary.

"Of course sir. I'm afraid I can't tell you her number though."

"That's totally understandable and I wouldn't dream of asking, but could I just wait whilst you pass the message? My boss would not be happy if I couldn't confirm Miss Stevens had received the message," he smiled as he spoke.

He'd manoeuvred himself to a position where he could just see the desk phone. He watched as she pushed the numbers on the unit, an internal number for room numbers, followed by the room number, 334.

"I'm sorry, there's no reply. Shall I leave a message?"

"No, please don't. My boss only likes us to leave personal messages. I'll find another way. Thanks for your help."

With that he smiled and walked away, by which time, Anna had already moved from where she was standing and was heading up the short flight of stairs to the American Bar.

She heard his footsteps behind her, but kept her pace as she approached the bar entrance, where she was met by one of the meet and greet team.

The young woman looked at Anna and recognised the look: the hair, possibly a wig, but a very expensive one. Plus her clothes, accessories and demeanour of a woman with money and influence.

"Madam, I think you're a guest with us, yes?"

'Good guess,' thought Anna and a useful tactic no doubt employed by all the staff. Better to get a negative response, than have to ask outright and potentially cause offence to some guests.

"Yes, I am. Room 334." She said it loud enough for him to hear behind her.

The Savoy software brought up her details.

"Ah, of course, Miss Stevens, please come with me."

She heard a slight exhale of breath from behind her. He'd heard and probably couldn't believe his luck, not knowing she'd set him up and he'd swallowed the bait.

She followed the young woman to a table and turned and looked at the young man who had been asking about her. He was tall, about six foot, athletic and stocky, with short dark hair. She took her phone out and went as though to look at some messages whilst taking a couple of photos as best as she could from where she was.

"Got you!" she said.

"Madam? I'm sorry?" said one of the cocktail waiters who had appeared by her side.

"Oh, it's nothing, just a message I was waiting for. Now what can you recommend for me?" She took the cocktail menu from the waiter whilst looking towards Mikhail Makarovich, as he turned and went back down the stairs, presumably, she thought, to try to get into her room to try to find out more about who she was.

"I think Madam may like a 'Sun, sun, sun.'"

"As in the George Harrison song?"

"Exactly Madam, all twenty cocktails in our Savoy Songbook menu are inspired by songs that have been played in the bar."

"Then I shall gladly go with your recommendation. Thank you."

When he returned he could see she was concentrating on her phone, but Anna looked up and smiled at him.

"Thank you, you're very kind."

He smiled back.

"It was my pleasure."

Anna returned to her phone and checked the text she was sending Greg and then pushed the *'return'* key.

A text bounced back almost immediately.

'Contact made then. Good going. Are you sure you don't want me to send someone to keep an eye on you?'

He'd asked before he left, but she'd said *'No,'* but he wanted to check, especially now she'd had confirmation that Makarovich's son was indeed checking up on her.

'No, too risky. He won't do anything until he's seen what I have to offer tomorrow,' texted Anna.

'Fair point. What are you doing now? Cocktails in the American Bar, or are you in the Beaufort?'

'The American....I needed to make it easy for him to find me! Now leave me in peace to enjoy my cocktail!' She added a smiley emoji for good measure.

'Ha! Enjoy.'

She looked around the bar. There was no sign of anyone she'd regard as being out of place, or just a little too interested in their drink or placemat to be of concern to her.

She assumed the young man would check her room, so hoped the back story material Martin Carruthers and Greg had given her would be enough.

She sat back and sipped her drink.

'Well, I'm here, so I might as enjoy my surroundings.'

*****

Penny Hastings nodded as Mikhail Makarovich walked past her and into his father's office. He didn't acknowledge her, but he rarely did. They were like chalk and cheese these two. The father had the ability to turn on the charm as and when he liked, but it always seemed a lot more forced with Mikhail.

"Good work Mikhail, but you say there was nothing suspicious in her room?"

She just caught the first few words before Mikhail closed the door behind him.

"No Papa, she's got a very nice set of clothes, plus a small top case, like a pilot case?"

"Yes, yes, go on."

"She's got a main case and I found a couple of flight luggage tabs inside that."

"Did you check those?"

"Of course Papa. They were from her flight from the Caymans to the UK. She came Business with BA, arrived here Sunday."

"No laptop?"

"Yes, but it was left out on the side, so I'm assuming she'll have everything on a stick, or in the Cloud, so nothing likely to be on the hard drive, so I didn't even bother trying."

"Yes, good thinking. What about...."

He didn't finish. His son was good at this stuff, so he shouldn't be interrogating him. He'd been going to ask about a room safe, but Mikhail would have easily accessed that with a key code device, so he knew he shouldn't be even asking the question.

Mikhail could see his father was deep in thought.

"Papa? Who is this woman? Why are you so

interested in her?"

"I'll tell you in a moment. But one question. Was it too perfect?"

"Are you thinking it's a trap?" said Mikhail.

"Possibly, just possibly. This woman has appeared out of nowhere and we can find nothing on her. I want to check all possibilities, that's all."

Mikhail thought for a moment. It had all looked very normal. There was a mix of tidy and clutter in the way the things were sitting in the room, so if it was a set-up, it was a damn good one.

"If I had to make a call on this Papa, I'd say no, it's not got any signs of a set-up."

"Okay, right, so this woman. Sit down and I'll tell you the little I know about this Fiona Stevens."

*****

Greg knew she'd turn him down about having someone watch her. But she was right. Makarovich wouldn't be doing anything other than checking her out at the moment. The risk would go up after she met him tomorrow at Kasper's.

It was just as well. 3R had a lot of work on and their resources were already pretty stretched, so he had no other teams readily available. This left Terri and Simon in Mallorca, him with Anna here in London and James looking after the Wall family and finally, Sam and Tommy, who were on their way to Nova Scotia.

'There's not a lot of backup immediately available should we need it.'

His phone rang. He smiled. He needed this distraction.

"Just the person I wanted to talk to," he said.

"Buenas tardes my darling. I hope you're staying out of trouble?" said Lori Garcia.

"Of course."

"Well I hope you are. Now what's Sam getting

involved in on the island? Is this the same case you're working on in London?"

She didn't ask a lot about his work, the same as he didn't ask her. It helped to keep their work separate from their lives, but it also prevented any sense of hiding things from each other. But as she was asking, there must be a reason.

"Do you mean about Sam being arrested?"

"Yes, Greg, what else do you think I meant?"

He loved her Spanish temperament. Sometimes fiery, always passionate and yet, also so gentle and loving. But he sensed this was fiery Lori, who wanted some straight answers.

"We don't know is the simple answer. If I was to put money on it, I'd say, yes, they're connected, otherwise it's just too much of a coincidence."

"Well, I have a young detective getting more than a bit annoyed at what she thinks is a distinct lack of cooperation."

"Ah yes, Detective Delgado. Sam likes her."

He heard her voice soften. Less fiery now.

"He does, does he? Hmm, interesting, I got a similar sense from my conversation with her. But before we go match-making, what about Carmen, is that all over?"

"Oh, who knows Lori? He thinks he's blown it with her, but maybe not? It's because he said he'd go for therapy. But he didn't and things got a bit heated when she quite rightly challenged him."

"Well, as long as he doesn't go two-timing these two girls, or he'll have me to answer to!"

He smiled. The passion and her sense of right and wrong was coming out.

"I'm sure he won't Lori and I think you know that too."

"Yes, yes, I do. I just want him to be able to deal with the PTSD and settle down."

"I think that's exactly what Anna wants too, so let's try to get him to deal with the PTSD first shall we?"

"Okay, you're right. So, getting back to this mysterious man, the one in hospital in Inca. Who is he?"

"Depends if you're you asking officially, or unofficially. Officially, we don't know. He's just a random who was following a pretty girl into an alleyway and Sam was the shining knight who came to her rescue. Except in reality he didn't."

"He didn't?" said Lori.

"No, in fact he was getting his butt kicked when Terri came back and rescued Sam! Then as the guy fell to the floor, he hit his head and it seems he hasn't come around since."

"So unofficially, you think he's connected with what happened to the young girl, Lily Green?"

"Yes, and the driver of the VW van who tried to corner Terri, before she ducked into the alley? He was the guy I told you about before. The one she'd seen in Abaco with Marsden."

"Look, you'd better stop there because you're starting to draw me into something that officially, I'm better off not knowing anything about. But Greg, Delgado is a good detective, so bring her into the story when you can. I think she'll be more of a help than a hindrance."

"Okay, I get you."

She smiled. She wasn't sure if he did, at least not going by what happened with the MacDonald murder a few weeks before.

"I hope you do my darling, but no doubt you'll do things when you're good and ready."

It was his turn to smile to himself this time.

"I think you're beginning to know me a little too well Lori Garcia."

"Good night my love."
"Good night to you Señora."

30

T erri was breathing hard over the first kilometre back up from the lighthouse. Lily had said it was a tough climb and she was feeling the strain on her calf muscles already.

"You weren't kidding about this first bit then?"

"No, it's ninety metres straight up in less than a kilometre."

Lily turned to look at her, but saw Terri was grinning at her.

"So you're not done yet then!"

"Not by a long stretch, in fact I'm just getting warmed up," said Terri, who really wasn't feeling like she was warming up at all, but she was damn sure she was going to show this young whippersnapper how she really felt.

"Okay then, let's get going!" and with that Lily was back up out of her seat and pushing hard for the top of the climb.

Terri grimaced at the sudden increase in pace from Lily.

'Why did I open my big mouth?' she thought, before she braced herself, dropped a couple of gears and took off after Lily.

She thought Lily must have slowed a little as she

caught up with her sooner than expected. Then it wasn't long before they were back negotiating the tunnel, but it was downhill this time and Lily was shouting again.

"Last one out the tunnel's a ....."

But Terri didn't hear the last few words of what Lily said because she'd heard a noise from her bike.

She might have missed it, except for the echo effect from the tunnel. It was just enough for her to catch the *'twang'*, as one of the strands on her front brake cable snapped.

She was already flying down the tunnel and checking what her front brake cable looked like wasn't going to be easy, especially in the reduced light inside the tunnel.

"Lily! Lily!"

But Lily was ahead of her and Terri realised Lily probably just thought she was just playing *'bounce your voice off the tunnel'*.

"Problem, Problem!"

With that, Lily must have heard her, because she started to slow. But then she had to speed up as Terri flew by her. Lily could see Terri was trying to gently apply her back brake and knew she couldn't risk being too hard on it, otherwise she'd spin the bike and she'd be off up over the handlebars and at the speed she was going, that was not a great plan.

Terri carefully pulled on the front brake again.

She heard it snap again and suddenly felt the front brake handle lose all resistance in her hand. Nothing!

"Shit, shit, shit!" yelled Terri.

She started trying to turn to look for Simon, hoping by some miracle that he was close by, but he wasn't, he was still hanging back as they'd agreed he would.

"Lily," she shouted. "What's at the bottom of the tunnel?"

She saw the worried look on Lily's face.

"There's a pretty sharp right and then a left and then we're into another fast descent."

It wasn't far to go. Terri estimated she must be doing well over 75kph, if not more. She tried the back brake again. It was working, but without the balance of the front brake she was having to be so careful, but even then she thought she could smell the brake pads burning up.

"Lily, you need to try to help me," she shouted.

She didn't know if Lily could hear everything she was saying, but she saw her manoeuvring her bike, so she must have got the message.

"Lean on me as we go through the bends. It's an 'S' bend, but it's pretty smooth, so we should make it."

"Should!" yelled Terri.

"Will, we will make it. Trust me Terri!"

Lily had no idea if she could make this work, but she'd ridden this stretch of road often enough to know what was waiting for Terri if she couldn't help her get through the 'S' bend.

"Okay, I'm braking too now, so gently does it with your back brake Terri."

Simon was easing down the tunnel behind them. He'd wondered what was going on, when he saw Lily first drop back and then move forward and close in next to Terri's bike. He could hear their raised voices and thought they were just having fun.

Then he saw Lily hadn't moved her position.

"Bloody hell, she's in trouble."

*****

He grabbed the scooter throttle and accelerated hard as he took off after the bikes. He could see what Lily was trying to do, to give Terri something to lean against as they prepared to go through the 'S' bend at the bottom of the tunnel.

He was cursing hard and not under his breath. He knew something hadn't been right, but he hadn't spotted it. It must have been the guy on that scooter.

"He must have screwed with her brakes, the bastard!"

He was closer now, but he wasn't sure what he could do, because the two bikes were almost on the 'S' bend.

Lily had moved out into the middle of the road, with Terri by her side. She was going to chance that nothing was coming the other way. That was pretty much the least of their worries, compared to a rock face and a sheer drop.

Terri was fighting hard to stay with her and Simon saw the space for him to ease up on Terri's left side. He could see she was focusing only on what was in front of her. He didn't want to startle her by calling out, but knew she'd know that if he'd seen something, he'd act.

The bend was getting closer and he could hear Lily shouting instructions in a clear and calm voice.

'She's one hell of a cool cookie, that's for sure,' thought Simon.

Terri caught a movement to her back left. She couldn't look, but she knew it must be him. Her Welsh dragon.

He flipped up his visor, so she could see him and he smiled.

"Need a bit of help?"

She nodded and tried to grin, but he could see the strain on her face and then he glanced across at Lily and gave her a thumbs up.

"Let's get through this bend and then see what we can do," shouted Simon and Terri gave a nod, followed by Lily.

He looked down at his speedo. Almost 80kph, too fast, way too fast to safely make these bends in a normal situation, let alone with two bikes and a scooter riding three abreast.

'God help us if there's a TUI coach coming the other way', thought Simon.

31

Simon realised too late that he was on the wrong side of her. He couldn't try to hold onto Terri, because the throttle and his front brake was on his right handlebar grip, which he obviously needed to operate to try to stop them gaining even more speed.

'*You stupid bloody idiot.*'

He thought about trying to get her to grab hold of him as he braked hard on the scooter, to try to slow her down. But by now they were going too fast and she was more likely to lose her balance and fall, so all he could do was apply the scooter brakes in gentle bursts.

That said, what he could do was give her something solid to lean against as they went through the bends. He pushed his body across on to the right side of the seat, giving Terri as much of a solid mass as he could, as they careered down the slope.

"We'll make this, so stick as close to me as you can!"

She looked across at Simon and nodded.

"Lily, you know this road. Count us through the bend. Okay?" said Simon.

Lily nodded, but her face was wracked with confusion.

They were almost on it. With Lily and Simon carefully applying their brakes, they had knocked some speed off, but it was still going to be close, very close.

Lily shouted again.

"We start on five and we'll be safe by one."

They nodded back to her and waited.

"Five…..   Four…."

Simon couldn't do much else as they went into the first right hand bend. He felt Terri leaning harder and harder against him, as they went through the bend. She was holding on well, but then he felt her starting to slide away.

He quickly took his hand off the throttle and grabbed her seat, just as he saw her starting to fall into Lily. The muscles in his right arm felt like they were on fire, but he clung tightly to her seat and she stabilised again.

"Three…." he heard Lily shout.

They were still going way too fast for this section, especially three abreast. 'Three' took them into the start of the left hand bend and Simon needed to let go of Terri and try to apply his brakes again. But at least now she could really tuck her left shoulder in against him.

Feeling his body against hers and his rock solid strength, Terri saw a chance and took her left hand off her handlebar and took hold of his shoulder for support.

"Hang on Terri, you too Lily! Let's get through this…." But his words tailed off as the thing he'd half joked about suddenly appeared in front of them, a tourist coach!

The driver was staring in disbelief and already had his hand on the horn, as though they needed any warning!

If Lily hadn't have reacted as quickly as she did in grabbing her brakes, she would have hit the coach head-on. But she got enough traction on her brakes and it made her look like she was suddenly going in reverse, before she tucked safely back in behind Terri.

After the coach had passed, she drew up alongside Terri again.

"Close one!"

"Stop enjoying this will you!" yelled Terri, "We're not done yet."

Lily gave a sheepish grin and then moved to one side as Terri got in as close as she could to Simon's scooter. She'd seen it done often enough on the televised cycling events like the Tour de France, but she'd certainly never attempted it and even though they'd manage to slow to about 60-70kph, this wasn't a great speed to start practising.

"Just grab hold of me and swing across. Okay?"

Terri looked at him and heard Lily still counting them down.

"Two…"

She saw his face was calm and it was like watching someone in slow motion. Every movement was measured and precise and this was helping slow everything down in her mind as well.

She had felt the wind rushing past, but now she seemed to enter a zone, like she was in a film being shown at half speed.

She looked back across at him, then at Lily and nodded to her to ease back, to make sure she wasn't hit by Terri's bike once she stepped off it.

Simon called out one last instruction.

"Slowly and with intent. When you're ready, just step off the bike and let it go."

She nodded, took a deep breath and as she slowly exhaled she stood up out of the saddle and carefully hooked her right leg back over the seat and paused for a moment, getting her balance as she stood cross legged, with her right leg behind her left. Then she leaned in against Simon and deftly placed her right foot on the scooter's passenger footrest, so she was now straddling the bike and his scooter.

"Ready?" she called to Simon.

"Ready."

She took hold of his shoulder and put all of her weight on her right leg. Simon adjusted his weight further left, to compensate for the change in balance. He then felt the scooter shift again, as she pushed away from the bike and he caught sight of it in his mirror, as it bounced back down the road.

Terri stood for just a moment, balancing precariously on her right leg, almost sideways on to Simon, before she slowly swung her left leg over the scooter seat and sat down behind him.

He felt her breathing slowly and deeply. No panic, just controlled and rhythmic, just as she'd been trained as a sniper in the army.

"Thank you," and she hugged him around his waist.

He patted her hands and then held them tight, for just a moment. It had been close. Too close.

"One.....," yelled Lily. "One, One, One, we did it!"

*****

Simon slowed to a halt and Lily caught up with them. She got off her bike and ran to Terri and hugged her.

"I thought, I thought...."

"Lily, it's okay, we got out of it in one piece."

Terri could see the tears on her cheeks and then she felt her own, just like it had sometimes been back in Afghanistan, after an engagement with the enemy, when the relief came that you'd survived, or sometimes when others hadn't.

"But what happened? Why did your brakes fail?"

Simon had walked back and had carried the bent and twisted bike to them.

"They didn't fail Lily. They were deliberately tampered with," said Simon. "Look you can see where the first part of the wire has been cleanly cut through, whilst the last few strands have just given way under braking."

"But that's ridiculous! Who would do something like that? You could have been killed if it wasn't for...." She suddenly stopped speaking, realising she had no idea who this man was, but that he somehow knew her name.

"Who are you by the way? And how the hell do you know my name?"

"I heard her call you Lily," Simon said, pointing to Terri.

"I don't believe you! Who are you?" Lily's voice was getting more agitated now.

She started backing away.

Simon looked at Terri for some sort of guidance. This was not going to be easy for Lily to hear.

"What? Hang on. You two know each other? Please God, don't tell me you're something to do with it?"

"Do with what Lily?" said Terri gently.

"Oh, I think you know damn well what I'm talking about. Are you part of that bastard's outfit? The one who kidnapped me and, and, and....."

Lily collapsed on the ground, tears streaming down her face.

"No, no, no. I trusted you, but you're one of them. You've just been checking on me all of this time. I said I wouldn't say anything and I haven't, please don't hurt my grandparents," the words poured out of her.

'So that was it,' thought Terri. 'They've been threatening her that they'll harm her grandparents. But why? What does she know?'

"Lily, look at me. Please. I'm not one of them, whoever, they are, but yes, I'm sorry, I haven't told you all of the truth about who I am," said Terri gently. "I need you to believe me when I say that everything I've done," she looked at Simon, "everything we've done, has been to try to help you."

"But who are you? And who's he?"

"Well, you know Sam and Anna who were at your grandparents' home when Mateo brought you home?"

"Yes," Lily said quietly.

"Sam's my half-brother, and Anna and Simon all work for the same outfit as me."

"But don't you understand, this was a warning to me, to injure, or even kill you! If I say anything to you, they'll hurt my grandparents, my parents and then me."

With that she shuddered at the prospect of meeting Marsden again, especially after the promises of what he said he'd do to her.

Terri went towards her. She wanted to hold her, protect her, but Lily shied away. Terri tried to explain again.

"Look, this wasn't the way I wanted you to find out Lily, but the fact is, you seem to be tied up in something that has cost the lives of five people, plus countless injuries to others back in London. There's also more at stake here, but I can't tell you about that."

Lily had gone very quiet.

"I don't understand what you mean. What else can't you tell me about? I just know you lied to me Terri. So was it all made up? The boyfriend? Pretending to be a friend?"

"No, it wasn't Lily. The boyfriend wasn't why I was up here, but it was actually true. I had broken up with him and I was feeling pretty miserable about it and you really helped me talk it through."

Simon stepped forward and took Lily's hands and pulled her to her feet.

"We haven't been introduced Lily, but my name's Simon and without you and your courage and strength today, well it doesn't bear thinking about what might have happened to Terri here."

He waited for her to take in what he'd just said before he continued.

"Can I suggest that we get back down to the town and carry on this conversation there?"

Lily felt the strength in his arms and hands as he pulled her up as though there was nothing of her. She'd felt so alone dealing with everything that had happened. She looked at him again. He was big and strong and maybe, just maybe, things might be alright with him, and Terri, on her side.

"Okay, let's do that. And Simon?"

He nodded.

"It's nice to meet you too and I'm glad you came along when you did."

He smiled back at her and just as they set off in convoy back down to the town, he heard Terri whisper, "Charmer."

She had her hands around his waist again, and once more, he patted them with his hand.

'Was it her imagination, or maybe the shock was kicking in, or had he left his hand there just a little longer this time?'

32

North had watched the two women fly past him and start the steep descent inside the tunnel from a position, where he was hidden from view from the road.

At the speed they going he had expected things to happen sometime around now, particularly because the blonde would have been using her front brake over the last couple of kilometres, so it shouldn't be long before it gave way completely.

He was about to return to his scooter, to follow them into the tunnel and wait for the inevitable crash once her front brake failed, when he saw another scooter approaching from the lighthouse. It was the speed that struck him as odd. It seemed to be hanging back. He ducked back down again and watched the rider go past.

It was the guy he'd walked passed in the carpark!

'Now who are you?' thought North.

He started to hear voices from inside the tunnel. Maybe they were just calling out? Then he heard the scooter accelerating. Something was definitely happening. He ran to his scooter and started it up and followed slowly down into the tunnel.

There was no traffic about. A bonus. No witnesses.

He was freewheeling down the tunnel and he could still hear raised voices from further on down the tunnel.

'Were they three abreast?'

He lost sight of them as they hit the first right hander. A horn sounded, followed by air brakes being squeezed hard. Then he saw a tourist coach coming back up the slope, with a very agitated driver.

Surely she hadn't survived that? It wasn't that he wanted the blonde woman dead. No, but Mateo had said he needed 'an accident' and it was hardly his fault if that meant she went off the side of the road.

He sped up until he reached the bottom of the tunnel. If the guy on the scooter was connected to the two women, then he needed to be ready for him if, as he hoped, he ran into a scene of some sort of carnage.

But as he came out of the tunnel there was nothing, at least not for another seventy five metres or so, when he saw one of the bikes, a crumpled mass of metal, at the side of the road, but no sign of the others.

"Shit!"

'How had they got out of that?'

A whole raft of things went through his head, from a possible police investigation and the guy had seen him, to what Rawlings would say to him. He'd told him it was his last chance after the cock-up in Puerto Pollensa, when he'd tried to grab the blonde, but she'd got away and one of his guys had ended up in hospital. If he didn't do something quickly, he was pretty certain he'd be out on his ear from what was a good, well paid little number with Rawlings' outfit.

North accelerated quickly and was travelling a lot quicker than Simon, who was taking it easy going back down to the town, so it wasn't long before he saw them a couple of hundred metres ahead.

Simon was still watching the road, ahead and

behind, watching out for the guy he thought was responsible for tampering with Terri's brakes.

He caught a flash in his wing mirror.

"Possible problem."

Terri heard him and turned her head.

"Scooter?"

"Yep. I think he did your brakes."

"Maybe he's coming to try to finish the job?"

"Or try to."

She heard the edge in his voice, then felt the scooter accelerate and they caught up with Lily.

"We need to get a bit of a shift on," said Simon.

"Okay. What's up, someone need the loo?"

"Something like that," he smiled at her.

He didn't want to worry her. She'd shown she could cope with pressure really well, but he didn't want to test it again on a high speed cycle dash downhill in to the town.

The scooter had felt reasonably quick, when it had just been him, and although Terri was light and fit, her weight was still enough to slow it down.

"This isn't good. We won't outrun him. We need to grab the advantage."

"What are you thinking?" yelled Terri.

"We stop and face him."

"Okay, two on one, sounds like a plan."

He moved up alongside Lily. He needed to be sure scooter guy wouldn't take off after Lily, so they all needed to stop.

"Lily, when I say 'Stop', we stop okay?"

She looked a bit puzzled, but nodded.

He pushed the pace until they had moved around a bend and were temporarily out of scooter guy's view.

"Stop!"

Lily heard him and braked hard.

"Okay, off your bike and lay it across the road."

Lily just followed the instruction, as Simon parked the scooter next to her bike.

'Why is he blocking the road?'

She looked at Terri, who just nodded, but her face was looking tense.

'Not the time to ask questions,' she thought.

She didn't have long to wait to find out what was happening. The scooter came around the corner at speed. North had to brake hard to avoid running into the barricade they'd set up across the road.

It was a stand-off. North was sat across the scooter with his visor still down, whilst Simon, Terri and Lily were stood in the middle of the road.

Simon half-turned to Terri.

"Terri," he said quietly. "I want you to take the scooter and Lily to get on her bike and get clear of here."

"I'm not going to do that Simon. We can take him, there's two of us."

"You're not listening. She's had enough to deal with without seeing what's going to happen here. Please," he paused, "please do this for her. Get her away from here and down to safety."

"But what about....?"

"No *'buts'* Terri, just do it. You know it's the right thing to do."

She did. She could see the look on Lily's face. She was going into *'freeze'* mode and it was going to get harder by the second if she didn't get Lily moving quickly.

"Sure?"

Simon looked at her and nodded. He had the same look on his face as she'd seen when they'd been ambushed in Egypt. He was breathing slowly and there was almost a ripple of energy passing through him, across his shoulders, as she watched his body prepare for what was likely to follow.

"Come on Lily, time to go. Get your bike."

Lily stood motionless.

"Lily," she spoke louder this time and with more urgency. "Time to go. Now!"

33

Lily looked at Terri, eyes wide open, the strain showing on her face.

"It's okay Lily. Get on your bike, we're going and Simon will deal with this," said Terri.

North had heard them talking and realised what they were going to do. *'No matter, I just need one of you and you'll do just fine big man.'* He pulled the scooter up on its stand and waited. Then watched as Terri got on Simon's scooter and followed Lily off down the hill, before taking his helmet off.

"Special forces?" he called to Simon.

"Yes. You?"

"Marine. Shall we move off the road? Don't want to give everyone a free show do we?"

"Suits me," said Simon.

The two men kept their distance as they moved across the road and out of sight, behind a small outcrop of rock.

"This isn't personal mate," said North. "But I do need to take something back to show my boss and after you cocked up my plan for a little accident for your girlfriend there, then it may as well be you."

"She's not my girlfriend, but after what you did? This is personal."

Simon was happy to talk whilst he weighed up the guy in front of him. Marines were tough, very tough in fact. They were both about equal height and physique. He knew this would come down to fight tactics and probably more to the point, *'Which of us is the dirtiest street fighter?'*

"She looked like she was your girlfriend to me mate, especially the way she was looking at you."

Simon ignored him, but North thought he'd seen a chink in the shining knight's armour and he was determined to try to play on it.

"So, you've never told her? Why's that tough guy, afraid she'll laugh at you?"

Simon smiled, but it wasn't a pleasant smile.

"Keep going Marine and I'll take even more pleasure in breaking your neck."

"My, my, you are touchy aren't you?" and with that North suddenly pounced forward and threw a stinging right hook.

Simon saw it coming late and only just moved his head in time to avoid the full force of the punch, but it still caught him a glancing blow.

"Slowing up a bit since we left the forces?" said North. "No wonder, you think your girly would say *'No'*. By the look of it, she needs a Marine looking after her."

Simon knew what the Marine was trying to do and he intended to use it as a double bluff, but not yet. He needed to find out first what this guy knew about Lily.

"So, what's the score with you and this outfit then Marine? You into kidnapping young girls for kicks then?"

With that it was his turn to try to catch North out. He feigned one way and then the other and then let loose a left jab that caught North on his right cheek, drawing blood and making him take a step back.

North spat a mouthful of blood out.

"Not bad, not bad," said North, who then used his momentum going backwards, to suddenly rock forward and launch himself towards Simon, with his arms held out wide. He crashed into Simon, like a crunching rugby tackle that took him to the ground and then started pummelling him with kidney punches.

Simon was desperately trying to bring his arms down to protect his kidneys. He tucked his body in as tight as he could, before he pulled his head in and down and then he flipped it up as hard as he could in the direction of North's face.

He heard a crack. Contact. He'd probably broken North's jaw, but more importantly North had stopped punching him, as he tried to recover.

North tried to say something, but the broken jaw made it come out like a mumble.

"What's the matter Marine boy? Cat your tongue?"

"Bastard!" said North. It was a bit muffled, but still clear enough for Simon to understand what he'd said.

"Ah, you've got it back then, must just be a hairline? You okay to carry on?"

He was goading North now, but he still wanted to see if he knew anything useful.

"So tell me, where's Marsden now?"

He saw the recognition of the name on North's face.

"Yes, we know about him and one of your other mates, Walker is it? My mate took care of him back in London, not to mention the guy in the alley, back down in Puerto Pollensa."

North was reacting badly to what he was hearing.

'How did this guy know about Marsden, let alone Walker?'

"What? You're wondering how we know about you guys?"

North didn't wait for Simon to say anything more,

attacking again, with a vicious right side kick, catching Simon on his left leg, causing him to momentarily lose his balance. It wasn't by much, but it was enough to allow North time to throw another punch, this time a hard left jab into Simon's face, connecting with his nose.

'He's tough, I'll give him that,' thought Simon.

"So what's the deal with all of this?"

"That suggests you don't know what's going on," said North, who was focusing on lining up another attack. "So are you as clueless about this, as you are about your girlfriend, soldier boy?"

North was back trying to wind him up. So Simon gave him what he was expecting, followed by something he wasn't expecting.

Simon starting shouting, "Just shut up about her, will you! One more word and I'll...."

"You'll what soldier boy? You'll what?"

North thought he had him lined up for a sucker punch, when Simon suddenly pulled back, changed the balance on to his other leg and literally threw himself through a pivoting spin, coming out the other side with a flying kick aimed at North's head.

North missed the sudden change of direction and was off balance as the kick came in hard. It caught him square on the side of the head, throwing him sideways and in a moment, Simon was on him, pinning him down in a headlock.

"Two choices mate, talk and you might just get to walk out of here in one piece."

"And the other?" gasped North, trying to catch his breath.

"Best you focus on the first."

"Or else what? What are you going do hard man? Really? You can't prove I did anything to your girlfriend's bike. There's no cameras up there, no witnesses. You've got nothing! And to think I nearly got away with blue murder. Ha!"

It was the last thing North said.

"Wrong choice," said Simon and with a sudden violent twist of his arms, he heard a crack and North's head and body slumped.

"I wish to high heaven she was my girlfriend, but it matters not, she was still the wrong woman to pick on."

*****

He hadn't said where they should go, because he knew Terri would decide where was best. He started with the obvious place, her grandparents' home and as he approached, he saw the scooter and Lily's bike.

He was parking up North's scooter when they came out to meet him.

He smiled at them both, as though he was just back from getting the shopping. The look Terri had recognised from the ambush in Egypt was gone. He smiled at her again and Terri ran and hugged him.

"Are you okay? Except for your face that is, that's a bit of a mess," she grinned.

"Simon, oh my God, oh my God," Lily was shouting.

By now Helen and Geoffrey Green had joined them. Lily had now told them who Terri really was, but it was a bit of a shock to see this man in front of them, with dry blood around his nose.

"Do we need to call the police Terri?" said Helen.

"Er, no, perhaps best not to," said Terri gently.

"But what happened? Where's the other guy?" said Lily.

Terri looked at Simon.

"He's gone and won't be bothering anyone again," said Simon.

"But he could have killed Terri! You can't let him get away with it," said Lily.

This was getting awkward. Terri had a pretty good idea that the guy wouldn't be coming back and in all likelihood, he wouldn't be found any time soon either.

"I assume you had a little chat with our friend and he saw the error of his ways Simon?"

She was looking at him, with her eyes doing some sort of rolling motion.

"Yes, yes, that was it. I left him walking down the road. I decided there wouldn't be enough evidence to get the police involved, so we were better off just letting him go and focusing on what we need to be doing next," said Simon.

This seemed to satisfy Helen and Lily, although Terri caught Geoffrey looking at Simon in a way that suggested he was a lot less believing of the story he'd just been given.

"Yes, good plan Simon. Helen, would it be okay if I slept here tonight? I don't mind going on the sofa, but it's been a bit of a day."

"Of course, that's fine Terri. What about you Simon? Will you be staying too?"

He wasn't sure if it was a genuine invitation, or whether it really was because she had no more room.

"No, I'm fine thanks Mrs Green. I can kip down at Terri's Air BnB, it's just around the corner."

He saw the relief on her face, so it may have just been because she was perhaps more than just a bit worried about who this man with the bloody nose actually was.

"I am one of the good guys Mrs Green."

"I know, I know, it's just that…"

"It's okay, honestly."

He couldn't help but smile and when she saw his face soften, she grinned back at him.

34

The two of them were sat in Lily's room.

"Let's change and go and grab some supper in the town," said Terri.

"But aren't you worried they might try something again?"

"No, I reckon we'll be fine. Besides I think they must be running out of resources at the rate we're knocking them off."

"That's not funny Terri and what about that guy from this afternoon? What if he comes back?"

Terri realised that Lily still hadn't twigged that he wouldn't be coming back, ever.

"No, he'll be long gone now, you can bet on that. So where can we go? Oh, and I hope your Gran wasn't expecting us to eat in? It's just that I think we should have a little chat, don't you?"

Lily went quiet for a moment.

"Yes, I think maybe you're right, but to answer your first couple of questions, if it's okay, I'd like to go back to Bar Coral? I love it there and I need to be somewhere I feel at home."

"Good for me, I loved the lunch we had there. What about your Gran?"

"Oh, she'll be fine. She long gave up on expecting me

to be home for meals, but don't worry, I'll let her know anyway."

Lily went to get up, but stopped.

"Will Simon be about tonight?"

"Hey, you've got Mateo! Simon's mine," laughed Terri.

Lily looked at her.

"What really? I thought you'd only just broken up with Daniel?"

"I'm joking Lily. We're just colleagues, that's all."

Lily looked back at her.

"That wasn't what it looked like to me. Not the way he held you after you'd got safely off the bike."

"No Lily, you're barking up the wrong tree there. We've worked together for over three years now and he's just like a big brother to me, that's all."

Whilst she tried not to show it, she thought back to him leaving his hand on hers. 'Was it just a little while longer than maybe just a friend would?'

"Okay, whatever you say, but I can see what you're thinking," said Lily with a flash of a smile. "Right, you shower and I'll go and tell Gran we're out on the town tonight."

*****

Before he let himself back into the apartment, Simon had scouted around the location looking for any sign of either the white VW van, or anyone else who might be connected with the Marsden's team.

As he came out of the shower, he sat down on his bed and scrolled his phone for messages. He saw one from James.

'Call when you can. NU.'

"What's not urgent then?" said Simon, as James picked up his call.

"Simon, good to hear you buddy. Just with Mr Wall's daughter at the moment. Give me a couple of seconds."

"Okay chum."

James motioned to Sandy that he needed to take the call and she nodded and waved him away.

"Yes, all good here. We've had a bit of fun this morning, with a guy called Tom Marsden and one of his team."

"Yes, I got the pic of Marsden. So presumably we think he's the one who's been doing the *'persuading'* do we?"

"Yes, he's a nasty bastard by all accounts. Scared the shit out of Roger Wall that's for sure and he looks like he was a tough old boy in his day."

"So you're doing a bit of watching over the family?"

"Yes, I moved Sandy and her kids into her father's house, just for the time being."

"Okay, now remember, keep it professional. As much as they might like you and want you to start having meals with them and the like, just politely decline, but explain why. Sorry mate, I'm sounding like you don't know what you're doing," said Simon.

James smiled. Ever since joining the Regiment, Simon had taken him under his wing and he hadn't stopped after nearly five years' service together, or since joining 3R for that matter. It didn't mean that Simon hadn't given him a hard time when he needed it, especially in the early days of his SAS service, but he'd learned fast and learned well.

"It's okay," he laughed, "I'm used to you bloody lecturing me all the time! But you make a good point. Sandy, I mean Mrs Dorchester, is on her own with two young girls. That's who Marsden's threatened. So she is very jumpy at the moment. I'll be mindful of your advice chum, so no worries on that score. But I actually wanted your advice on something else."

"As long as it's work and not your love life mate, then I'm your man," said Simon.

"It's work, as you're hopeless with your own love life."

"Fair play, go on, what is it then?"

"I'm just thinking that when I go on the school run, I'll be leaving the old man, Mr Wall, on his own. I guess the boss would have got me a partner if he thought it necessary to cover Mr Wall at home?"

"Listen, Greg is always happy to take questions James, but unless he's said otherwise, he'll have decided that Wall is big enough to look after himself and it's just the daughter with her girls who needs a watch over. So my advice is, stick with them as your primary focus. Okay?"

"Yes, that's sound mate, cheers."

"So what happened this morning James?"

"We saw a guy waiting in a vehicle close by to Wall's house. He didn't look right, so I went and had a chat."

"Had a chat, hey? I bet he's now got a couple of bruises here and there then?"

He heard James laugh.

"You could say that, but Simon, these guys aren't clowns. Yes, maybe the driver was sloppy, but neither he, nor Marsden wilted away, so take care."

He'd known James for a while now and he'd recommended him to Terri, when James was looking to finish his career with the army. He knew James was good, very good in fact and in some ways, he was probably better than he was. *'The student will soon become the teacher,'* he smiled.

"Yes, you're right on that score. Well we also had a little incident this afternoon, when things got a bit hairy."

"You okay Simon?"

"Yes, but thanks for asking."

"I take it the other guy isn't so good?"

"Not good at all and he's now officially on their

missing list. Shouldn't be found for a good few years hopefully, especially where I've left him, half way up a mountain. But like your guys, he was no mug and didn't give up."

"Glad you're okay, so one last thing. Do I need to worry about the boss and Mrs Martínez running around London on their own?"

Simon thought for a moment. He'd never questioned any of Greg's calls in the time he'd worked for him, but what happened this afternoon was making him think he at least needed to brief him on an increased risk.

"Good point chum, I'll ring him. Stay safe and keep in touch."

*****

Simon rang Greg straight away.

"Simon, good to hear you buddy. I'm stuck in a 3 star hotel, whilst Anna is up the road in The Savoy. How did that happen?"

"Well I can match that with Terri's one room Air BnB," although he quickly added, "but we're not sharing Boss, she's staying with Lily's grandparents tonight."

Greg missed anything that Simon may have meant, because he'd only picked up on him saying Terri was staying at the grandparents' villa.

"What's happened Simon?"

"We had a bit of an incident on the cycle ride up to Cap de Formentor this afternoon."

"Go on," said Greg, his voice going a tone quieter, something Simon knew Greg always did when he was starting to get concerned about a job.

"Someone tampered with Terri's brakes on her bike."

"Bloody hell! Is she alright?"

"Yes, yes, sorry, I should have said. She's fine and so

is Lily. But what I wanted to say Boss, was that there was some serious intent there. I've dealt with the issue and he won't be bothering us again, but I just wanted to brief you to make sure you and Anna have some proper back up in place."

Greg thought he could make the safe assumption that Simon had permanently negated the problem, as he was not a man to avoid using deadly force if he needed to. "Are you okay Simon?"

'He was always like that,' thought Simon. First things first, he wanted to know if you were okay and then he'd ask about the job, that's why he liked him.

"I'm good thanks Boss. Appreciate you asking. Actually it was the girl, Lily, who was amazing. So calm and controlled during the ....," he tailed off.

"Yes, maybe tell me later about what exactly happened, but I get the picture. So what now?"

"Has Terri rung you?"

"No, we're catching up tonight."

"Well, she may have some news for you. She's taking Lily into town for some supper. I'll be close by, but it looks like Lily may be ready to tell us what has actually happened."

"Excellent and Simon, good point about back-up. I'll get it sorted."

Greg had entrusted his life to Simon on more than one occasion, so he wasn't about to start turning down his advice any time soon.

"Good to know Boss, catch up soon."

Greg smiled. Simon really was a man of few words, but when he spoke, you always wanted to hear what he was saying.

He then made a couple of calls. One to Chris MacDonald who was happy to agree to his request, to temporarily take a team off a job they were doing for Trent MacDonald Engineering.

He then followed this, with a call to Sharon Bridger, who was the team leader on the job.

"We'll be with you by midnight," she said.

35

A ina was there to greet them at Bar Coral. Once
again, Lily got a warm embrace and kisses on
each cheek. Terri stood back, wondering how
Aina would react to her, but this time, Terri got the
same welcome.

"That's a sure sign that Aina trusts you now Terri.
She's known me a long time, so she was only watching
out for me before."

"She's lovely. This is such a great place, no wonder
you love it here. Okay, so drinks? Aina, shall we go with
Cava?"

"Si, Terri, that's the only way to start the evening!"

Once Aina had returned with two glasses and placed
a bottle of Cava in an ice bucket, she left them to
consider the menus.

Terri left it to Lily to choose from her usual
favourites and she settled on the meat filled stuffed
aubergines and suggested the chicken breast with
pepper sauce for Terri.

"So it was a bit hairy this afternoon Lily, up the
mountain?"

"Yes," said Lily. "But I can't quite believe how I held
it together, you know, when the shit was hitting the
proverbial fan!"

"Good way to put it Lily. You did good, bloody good in fact. Simon was seriously impressed and it takes a fair bit to get him to open up."

"I think it was because it all happened so quickly. I just reacted to what was there."

As Terri watched her, she went quiet again. Terri said nothing and let the silence build until Lily was ready to speak.

"I was kidnapped."

Terri could barely hear her voice.

"They kept me in some sort of finca and kept asking me questions. Questions I couldn't answer, because I didn't know what they meant and didn't know what they wanted to know."

Terri didn't want to break the flow, so just nodded her encouragement.

"There were two of them. One was evil. He had such cold eyes." She couldn't stop herself from flinching as she thought about him.

"Did he hurt you," Terri paused, "in any way?"

"No, well, not really. He slapped me around the face a few times, but I thought it was a bit strange, because he always seemed to be holding back. So the slaps weren't like, really hard, but they were just enough to unsettle me."

"So nothing of a sexual nature?" Terri was very careful with how she asked the question. They were in a restaurant, but she thought this might actually help, as this was one of Lily's favourite places, where she had already said she felt safe.

"No, nothing where he actually touched me. At one point he made me take all my clothes off. I just had to sit there whilst he looked at me. He had a mask on and that was when he told me all the things he'd like to do to me."

Terri reached across and took her hand.

"It's okay, I won't let him hurt you, or anyone else in your family. Do you hear me?"

"I know you won't, but you won't be able to stay with me will you? Not for the rest of my life."

"No, which is why I really need to know what this is all about. We've got a pretty good idea, but you might be able to fill in some detail that will help us bring this all to a conclusion, so you can go back to living your life, without having to constantly look over your shoulder."

Aina arrived with the food and after she'd gone, Lily look across at Terri.

"Where do you want me to start?"

"The beginning would be good, from the time you were grabbed. Tell me about that and then what happened afterwards."

*****

Simon was watching from a distance. Close enough to get there in a hurry if the need arose, but far enough way to give them space.

This was one of those situations when three would definitely be too much of a crowd. He could see Terri listening intently, whilst Lily was barely stopping for breath.

He'd been around to check the immediate area a couple of times now and there was nothing looking untoward. He moved into the restaurant and when a waiter appeared, he pointed to a table where he could maintain eye-line on the two women, whilst he could get some food inside him.

*****

"So who is this Kevin Cox?"

Lily had been telling her about emailing someone she'd met, when he'd been across in Mallorca on one of the company secondments.

"He's one of the development managers across in

Canada. He's a really switched on guy, so I thought he might be able to help with what I was finding out about the UFD 10 and 30 variations, sorry, I mean Ultra-Fast-Dry concrete."

"And this was two different types of concrete?" said Terri. "UFD 30 was the developmental formula they were testing back in 2008 and they actually used on the Witterings Shopping centre?"

"Yes, but they only used it on that and I think three, or four other building projects. For some reason, they withdrew it. That's what I was asking him about. Whether he knew why."

"Where is Kevin based?" asked Terri.

"Nova Scotia. He works in the Halifax office."

"Have you spoken to him since you went back to work?"

"No, like I said, Ian, my boss, well he said we'd been taken off the job because the Health and Safety Exec Report was now out and there was no need for any further work."

"Is there anything else about this formula, the UFD30, that you think might be relevant?"

"Just that the guy who came up with it, the designer. He's now the Director of the Research Centre and has been since 2008 or 2009."

"Who's that then?"

"Paul Brooks."

Terri thought through the detail of what Lily had just given her.

Was this what the Global Aggregates security team were trying to protect from getting out into the public domain? She could understood the potential serious impact on the reputation of the company, because that was pretty obvious. But GA was a private company, therefore it wasn't publicly quoted on the stock exchange.

Therefore, it might not be so much about the share price. This was probably more to do with the likelihood that they could lose a whole bunch of significant contracts and that could mean millions of pounds in lost revenue.

Lily was unlikely to know about the owner, Oleg Makarovich, and even less likely to know that a dramatic fall-off in contracts would impact on the opportunity to launder money through the GA books.

"And he's not going to like that one little bit?"

"Who? Paul Brooks?" said Lily.

Terri hadn't realised she spoken out aloud.

"No, I was thinking about Oleg Makarovich."

"Who's he? And what's he got to do with this? With the UFD?"

"Him personally? Nothing," said Terri. "He owns Global Aggregates and what happens to their trading opportunities will significantly affect his other less legitimate operations."

"I thought Sir Charles Groom owned GA?"

"He did, or at least he had a major shareholding, but during the 2008 economic crash GA was going bankrupt and Makarovich shored them up and became the major shareholder."

"Not sure, I entirely understand, but where does that leave me? Do I go back to work now?"

Terri thought for a moment.

"I suggest you don't. We've got to assume that the guy who we ran into this afternoon wouldn't have reported anything back until the job was done. However, someone told him to do this, so whoever that is will now know things didn't go to plan."

"So what do I do? Leave, or ring in sick?"

"Let's go down the sick route, at least for the moment. Things are moving pretty fast Lily, but for the time being I think it might be an idea to get you and your grandparents away from here. Is there somewhere you can go?"

"I don't know."

"Don't worry, I'll make a couple of calls and we might be able to sort something quickly. In the meantime, let's get you back home and tell your grandparents to get a few things packed too." Terri smiled as she spoke. She hoped this would be a really short term solution, but until things started moving in London they just wouldn't know.

"Okay, if you think that's the right thing to do."

"Yes, it won't be for long. But hey, before I forget, you were telling me all about how you met Mateo?"

At the mention of his name, Lily brightened up.

"We could stay with him. His apartment is huge!"

Terri tried not to show anything, but this wasn't where she wanted the conversation to go.

"I think I'd rather you were well away from everyone you know, just for the time being Lily."

"You can't be suggesting that he's involved are you Terri? That's just not possible. No, he can't be. He can't."

Lily's voice was getting tighter as she spoke, as if for the first time she thought that he might, just might, be a party to what had happened.

"I'm sure he's not Lily." Terri needed to get her back in control of her feelings and thoughts. And quickly. "It's just what we usually do, you know as a precaution. It creates what we call a sterile area, where we know that no one knows where you and your grandparents are."

"But he couldn't be, could he?"

Lily was desperate to believe that he wasn't involved in some way. But Terri couldn't give that complete reassurance, because she just didn't know. He looked the genuine article. A caring and concerned boyfriend, but Sam had spoken to him a few times now and she knew that he wasn't completely sure. So until they could rule him out altogether, he'd stay on the *'We don't know which side he's on'* list.

Terri saw Lily was starting to shake. They really had got to this girl. Every time she seemed to be thinking about what had happened, or who might be involved, she seemed to go into some sort of psychosomatic reaction, where her body was responding to the mental turmoil going on in her head.

Lily was close to losing it again and she had tears running down her face as Terri tried to slow things down, to bring Lily's body back under control.

"It's a great idea, about staying with Mateo, I mean. But can we go with my plan, just to start with? Because actually, it's as much about protecting him as you guys. You know? We don't want anybody going after him, do we?"

"No, we don't," said Lily quietly. "Let's go with your plan."

Terri smiled at her, "Now then, come on Lily, you can tell me more about how you met your Mr Wonderful as we walk home."

36

erri settled the bill and they waved to Aina as they left the restaurant. Simon nodded across to Terri, as the two women left and started walking home and he took up a position on the other side of the road, about twenty metres behind.

"Tell me all about it then," said Terri.

She saw the start of a smile begin to appear on Lily's face again.

"It must have been fate I reckon. He walked into the bar we'd been at in Palma, the one with arched ceilings and the seats along the wall on the opposite side to the bar?"

"Sounds like Tast?" said Terri.

"Yes, that's it. Well, we were sitting there, the last ones standing after a pretty heavy night on the town, courtesy of the company. Team building they called it, but it was just a good excuse for a great night out, all expenses paid."

"Sounds great. I must speak to my boss about one of those!"

"Everyone else had gone home, but there were about six or seven of us left and in walked Mateo. Well, as you know, he's pretty good looking and me and a few of the girls, well we'd had a few drinks."

"And?" encouraged Terri grinning.

"I couldn't help but stare at him as he walked to the bar."

"Now it's getting interesting. So who chatted up who?"

"Well it was me actually, but only after Ian, my boss, gave me a shove and I bumped into him, Mateo I mean."

"Ah right, so he didn't bump into you, you bumped, accidently on purpose into poor old unsuspecting Mateo?"

"Well yes," Lily grinned. "I don't know what got into Ian. He doesn't usually come out with us. He's married with kids, but he went out with us that night. He seemed a bit on edge to start with, but to be fair, once he'd had a few drinks he was on it, with the rest of us die-hards, right throughout the night."

"Sounds like you had a great time. I really like Tast too, so who suggested you went there?"

Terri slipped the question into the conversation as smoothly as she could.

"It was Ian. He said he'd got a couple of tables booked through the GA Social Club, courtesy of the bosses, and there they were when we walked in."

"Brilliant!"

"Love it Lily, great story and good job your boss was looking after your love life for you," she joked.

"It was funny, but we hit it off straight away. We found we liked the same things and same type of music. I also liked the fact that he didn't try and get me into bed. Well at least, not straight away...."

"Lily Green, are you blushing?" said Terri, but was already thinking 'set-up!'

*****

Terri made the decision not to say anything to Lily about her concerns over Mateo. It wasn't going to help the situation and she'd at least got Lily around to thinking that by not staying with him, then she'd be protecting him too.

She stopped and waved to Simon to come and join them.

"Change of plan. We're going to go back and get some clothes packed and take everyone away for a few days. I'll ring Anna and see if she can suggest somewhere."

"Okay, I'll go and pack up our stuff from the apartment and I'll be back with the hire car in ten minutes," said Simon.

"We may need a little longer," grinned Terri, "but I'll see you soon."

She'd realised that Lily had gone quiet again, as though suddenly realising the upset this could cause her grandparents.

"It's okay, I'll explain," said Terri.

*****

They took it remarkably well. Helen was calm, whilst Geoffrey asked a few practical questions about how long, and should they take their car.

Terri decided to leave the Green's car and once Simon had brought the other car, she sent him to Sam's friend's place to pick up the Beetle. That gave them two cars and plenty of space, something that turned out to be more of a necessity for the growing amount of luggage that was appearing in the hallway.

"Is this too much dear?" Helen was asking Terri, who just smiled and shook her head.

"No, that's fine Helen, better to be safe than sorry, hey?"

Whilst she was waiting, Terri went outside and rang Anna.

"How's the Ritz then?"

"It's not the Ritz and stop teasing, I'm working."

"Some work you've got then Anna," laughed Terri.

"Look we're taking Lily and her folks back down to Palma. We don't know if they might come looking for her, so I'm opting on the side of caution, even from telling the boyfriend, as I'm still not a hundred percent sure of him."

"Good thinking. You can take them to my place tonight and then decide tomorrow if you want to move them."

"Thanks Anna, that's what I was hoping you'd say. Is the key lock the same?"

"Yes and there's fresh bedding in the cupboards upstairs."

"That's great, thanks Anna. Everything okay with you?"

"Yes, we're set for tomorrow. Your new recruit in India, Anju? She's done a fantastic job on setting up the IT for Stevens Bank. I just need to get Makarovich to bite the bullet now and invest in this wonderful opportunity I'm going to be offering him."

"Good luck with all that, but take care Anna. These guys can be pretty mean, as we found out again this afternoon and they're only the B team when compared to your Russian guy."

"Yes, I heard you'd had another close call, so same applies to you, so take care."

"Yes, absolutely, now I've got to run. I'm driving Sam's Beetle down to Palma, another potentially scary life experience for me!"

Anna laughed, "You don't have to tell me. Watch out for the engine overheating!"

Terri came off the phone laughing, just as they all trooped out of the house with their bags.

Lily went in the VW Beetle with Terri driving, whilst Simon took Helen and Geoffrey in the hire car.

Terri quickly explained where they were going.

"And guys, it's really important you don't tell

anyone where you're going. Not even your closest, most trusted friends. We need a complete wall of secrecy around us."

"Not even Mateo?" said Lily.

"Not even Mateo," smiled Terri, although she was actually thinking, *'definitely not Mateo!'*

*****

Anna had undressed for bed and was looking over the website Anju had set up one more time when Greg rang her.

"Just checking in for a quick review of the day."

"Looks like there's been a lot going on. Terri's just rang me."

"Why is it so hard not to worry about our kids Anna? They're both in their thirties for God's sake!"

"The price of parenthood," laughed Anna, "and it never goes away does it!"

"You're right there, anyway, I just wanted to run a couple of things passed you."

"I'm listening," said Anna.

"The biggest thing is that we're spread a bit too thin for my liking. We're covering things on three fronts. Here, Mallorca and Canada and whilst I think we can manage in the short term, it's not sustainable."

"No, I know where you're coming from, but Tommy and Sam shouldn't be in Canada too long hopefully, as presumably Marsden will be back once he's done whatever it is he's over there for."

"Yes, true. I'm glad Tommy's sorted out his chum, Billy, to help out over there. It's a bloody long way if they need to start calling for back-up."

"They should be fine Greg, so it's my turn to tell you not to worry about them. They're big boys and damn tough with it too."

"I know, I know. So what did Terri ring you about?"

She briefed him on the move of Lily and her

grandparents down to Palma and that they'd stay in her house.

"She's also worried about the boyfriend, Mateo."

"Anything in particular?"

"She's just got a feeling. And if she's got anything like half of your gut feeling, then she's best off taking notice of it, as we are."

"Sam has the same thoughts doesn't he? But we've got nothing to put to him?" said Greg.

"No, nothing, so until he makes a move, if he indeed he will, we can only sit and wait. Plus the fact the girl, Lily, is besotted by him. So that's not helping. Anytime Terri goes anywhere near suggesting he might not be the clean-cut guy he pertains to be, she goes off the deep end."

"Useful catching up Anna. You set for tomorrow? We'll stay away from coming into Kasper's, but Sharon will have people hiding in the shadows, front and back, just in case."

"Yes, I'm good. The fact he's coming means he's half-way hooked. I just need to be patient and not pull the line in too quickly."

"You're loving this aren't you?" said Greg.

She waited a second.

"Yes, but before you go joining the worrying set, I'm focused and ready for tomorrow, together with my bail-out plan."

"Good and Anna, I'm glad, on both counts. Now rest up and speak tomorrow."

"Same to you."

37

Sam's flight into Halifax touched down twenty minutes early after they'd come in with a following wind.

He found the car hire units down on the ground floor. He'd pre-booked a mid-range saloon and as he got to the car hire desk, he was immediately asked if he'd mind an upgrade. Problem was, they were offering a Dodge Charger. A five litre beast of a car that ordinarily he'd have jumped at, as it would have been huge fun, but it was a long way off inconspicuous, in the event of him needing to do any sort of loose-follow surveillance.

"Have you got something other than that?"

The young man looked at Sam as though he was mad, but he looked again at his computer screen.

"I can do you a Ford SUV at the same price?"

"What colour?"

Again, the young man looked at him.

Sam could see his mind working overtime, *'Colour? No one ever asks the colour of a hire car!'*

"Dark blue, or I can do you a white one?"

"Dark blue will be just fine."

As Sam walked out the doors towards the hire car pick up bays, the young man finished the documentation update on his desktop and muttered to himself, *'Those Brits can sure be odd folk.'*

*****

"Tommy? I've landed and I'm mobile in a dark blue Ford SUV. Where are you chum?"

"Hi Sam, good to hear you my friend. We're on speaker phone. Come and find us, we're in a silver grey Hyundai Santa Fe, down at the Holiday Inn, a couple of miles away."

Sam heard the ping on his phone. Checked the maps app and was with them a few minutes later.

"Billy, thanks for your help here," said Sam.

"Pleasure mate." Short, no nonsense response in a strong Geordie accent.

"We got the pics of him picking up a hire car from the spooks at Five, then Billy went and watched him check in at the hotel. He's in Room 256, so that's on the other side of this carpark," said Tommy.

"Nice work Billy. Where are you staying Tommy?"

"Here, with Billy, so we're ready to go if need be. Seeing as you've already met this guy Sam, I suggest you go down the road a bit, so Marsden doesn't get anywhere near you. There's an Alt Hotel not far away. Close enough, but far enough, if you get me?"

"Yep, understood."

"Sam, it's Billy, I've already done a recce of the GA site. It's north from here, near Hantsport, just off Exit 8 on Highway 101, about an hour or so away."

"That's great Billy. Any issues for us keeping an eye on the place?"

"No, not really. I took some pics and I'll airdrop them to you now. There's fencing, but only what you'd expect of an industrial site. There's no guards patrolling, just a guy on the front gate checking the trucks in and out."

"Wish we knew why Marsden was here. This might all just be a wild goose chase, but let's see. Okay, let's go

273

for an early start, to make sure we're ready. On plot at what? 6.00am?" said Sam.

"How about 05.30 Sam? Just to be sure. No point coming all this way and missing him," said Tommy.

"Good call, I'll look forward to that, be just like old times for me, getting up for an early shift!" grinned Sam.

*****

Marsden sensed immediately that Rawlings was in a foul mood when he phoned him after landing at Halifax.

"Boss, I got your texts. What's the problem?"

He stressed 'texts'. Rawlings knew he was in the bloody air, so why had he bothered to keep sending him texts? It wasn't as though he could receive them, let alone answer them.

"About bloody time. Now what the hell's gone on in Mallorca? Mateo's heard nothing from North and he's not answering any calls."

"Boss, I've been on a plane for six hours, so I've no idea. Wait a minute, has Álvarez..," he never liked calling him Mateo, "had any contact with the girl?"

"No, she's missing as well. He got himself clear of the area after he'd had a drink up at the lighthouse café with her and Chambers' daughter. Terri isn't it? But tell me, what exactly was North going to be doing?"

"It was supposed to look like an accident, to give Chambers a distraction. I'd then make sure Green knew it wasn't an accident, to keep the pressure on her to keep her mouth shut after seeing her new friend take a nose-dive on the tarmac on the way back down."

"Which part of 'no bruises, no bodies, no police,' does an accident on the side of a mountain, fall into Marsden?" said Rawlings quietly.

"Boss, you give me a degree of operational freedom and I thought we needed to elevate our response."

"Well next time, talk it through with me before you start engaging on such a course of action. Do I make myself understood?"

"Yes."

Marsden didn't follow it up with any other response. He didn't take kindly to be given a bollocking, because that's what it was. He never had and never would.

"Anyway, I thought you said North was good?"

"Boss, you know he's good, he's been with us for a good few years now and has never let us down."

"Until now! And now he's done it spectacularly well!"

Marsden decided it was best to let his boss have his rant. North was good, so that meant whoever had got one over on him was even better.

Was that just the blonde? She'd looked fit and strong when he'd seen her at Abaco, but it seemed unlikely, although not impossible, that she could take on North. So did that mean she had someone watching over her? Maybe Martínez, the guy who'd been arrested? But Álvarez knew him and he'd have said something if he'd seen him. So it had to be someone else.

"Look Boss, let me sort this thing out here and then I'll get back over there and deal with things properly."

Rawlings didn't answer straight away. He was annoyed, bloody annoyed, but that wouldn't help rectify things and give Groom the answers he was after.

"Right Tom, good point. Get Cox to toe the line and then we can review the issue over in Mallorca."

Marsden heard him call him 'Tom' and knew Rawlings was back in control. But it still didn't mean he appreciated the bollocking.

*****

At 5.30am the next morning, Sam was parked up outside the Holiday Inn when Tommy and Billy emerged out of the front entrance. Although early, the summer sun was already up and the warmth was already starting to come through.

Tommy pointed across to the silver coloured Jeep, the one Sam had seen in the pics Five had sent through of Marsden's hire car. He then handed Sam a takeaway coffee and a bag.

"Breakfast."

"Nice one Tommy. Okay, let's take up positions, I'll head up towards the 102 and wait for you there."

"Roger that and we'll let you know when he's rolling. Sam?"

"Yep?"

"Billy has got some stuff for us, if we need it. Glock 19s, although they're the Canadian spec, so just ten in the mag. Apparently the US version is a prohibited weapon over here. Who knew?"

"Things we learn mate," laughed Sam. "Anyway, that's good to know."

"Only thing is, we'll need to keep them on board with us. They're properly registered and everything to Billy, so he'd get right in the dilly-doo-dahs if you got stopped with one."

"Dilly-doo-dahs? Like that one Tommy."

"Yes, been with the grandchildren, so I've been watching my P's and Q's," he laughed.

"Good one, anyway, hopefully, we won't need anything like that, but much better to be prepared."

With that, Sam fired up the Ford and moved slowly out of the carpark and headed up towards the highway.

*****

As he was pulling out of the Holiday Inn Hotel carpark in Nova Scotia, his mother, Anna Martínez, was just finishing her breakfast at The Savoy in London, where it was 9.30am, four hours ahead of Eastern Time.

She planned on spending the morning walking

around the shops in Oxford Street and Regent Street. It was likely that Makarovich would have someone watching her, so it would give her a chance to see if she was being followed.

Mikhail Makarovich had tasked one of his team to keep watch on Fiona Stevens during the morning. She was ex-GRU, Russian intelligence and highly skilled in surveillance techniques. She had seen the Stevens woman go in for breakfast and now watched from a short distance away from the lobby, as Stevens went to the lift and presumably back to her room.

Anna had seen the faces of the people in the lobby as she walked into breakfast and scanned the lobby again. No one there who'd been there before. But it didn't mean she wasn't being watched.

'Maybe they just know what they're doing.'

As she got back to her room, her mobile rang.

"Good morning Sam, you're up bright and early!"

"Yep, early start. I was telling the guys, it's like being back on early turn in the Met."

"So have you located Marsden?"

"Yes, he's in a Holiday Inn, just outside the airport, so we're sat up in a couple of vehicles ready to see where he goes."

"Good, now Sam, Terri and Lily had a near miss yesterday. Don't worry, they're both okay, but it could have been pretty serious. Someone tampered with her brakes when they were up having drinks at the lighthouse."

"Bloody hell Mum. Are these guys ramping things up? We're pretty stretched to deal with things on three fronts."

"I know and Greg is concerned about that as well, but it is what it is and we've all got some back up."

"I was just about to ask, because last time I mentioned it, you said everything was okay."

"Well things changed after Simon told us about what had happened up at Cap de Formentor and now we've got Sharon down with her team. Greg pulled them off the Trent MacDonald job."

"Is Chris, or more to the point, old man MacDonald okay with that?"

"Less of the old man MacDonald if you don't mind! John's younger than me, and yes, Greg okay'd it with Chris first."

"Well, that's good to hear you've got support there. Are you ready for today?"

"Yes, all prepped and ready to go," said Anna.

"You happy your Fiona Stevens cover will hold up?"

"I've been in dodgier situations with a lot less cover, so this will be fine."

"Good to hear Mum, but I still need to say this – please take care."

"Probably not worth me saying 'don't worry', but yes, I will and you too as well Sam."

"Yes, Mum."

He smiled as he said it. Up until a couple of months ago, he thought his mum had worked in an admin role of some sort in the Foreign and Commonwealth office in Madrid before she had him.

It had been a real shock to find out she was a former MI6 covert field agent and then an even bigger shock to discover Greg Chambers was in fact his biological father.

When he'd then seen her operate in the field, when they worked on finding Sheila MacDonald's murderer just a few short weeks ago, well, he'd been impressed, very impressed.

"Talk later today Mum, for a catch up."

"Yes, look forward to it Sam."

As she put the phone down, she checked her hair. She liked the wig, it was different to her own hair and provided something for her to work on with Fiona's character. The wig was platinum blonde and styled as a 'bob'.

She checked the room. Not too tidy, not too scruffy. She had known someone, probably Mikhail, had been in the room the night before. A couple of things she'd left had been disturbed, almost imperceptible to the eye, but not to Anna's, who could see her case had been moved, as had the laptop.

"Okay, time to get out and about and be seen."

As she left the lift, she smiled at the Reception team, who greeted her.

"Good Morning Miss Stevens."

'Well that should definitely tell them it's me, if nothing else,' she smiled to herself.

38

Marsden came down at 7.00am for an early breakfast and was then soon outside, walking towards the Jeep.

No messages from Rawlings, but equally nothing from North. *'What the hell has happened to him?'* He had to assume North was now history, either having cleared off knowing Rawlings wouldn't be happy, or more likely, he'd somehow been sorted out by Chambers' daughter, or possibly her minder.

Marsden was surveillance savvy, so even though he had no reason to think he might be being followed, he checked the car for any 'lumps', tracker devices, that would give his location details via smart phone, or laptop.

"Good job we didn't put one of those on mate," said Billy.

"Yes, definitely. Keep your distance on this one Billy, I think he knows his stuff."

Tommy rang Sam, keeping his phone out of eyesight, but on speakerphone.

"He's just checked the car for a lump, so keep well back Sam."

"Will do."

Marsden started slowly moving off. He drove a

circuit of the carpark, as Tommy watched from a position right at the back of the carpark, shielded by a motorhome.

"He's off, off, off, Sam, heading towards the highway junction."

"Copied."

Billy kept his distance, as they had to make the assumption, right or wrong, that Marsden would make for the GA offices up near Hantsport.

"Still heading your way, no deviation."

A few minutes later Sam saw the silver Jeep go past and he eased out onto the road, after first letting another car go past.

"I've got him Tommy, with one vehicle for cover."

"Copy that Sam, we'll hang back for the time being."

The Jeep was soon on Highway 102S, heading south towards the city, Halifax. The traffic was thick enough, that made things easier for both Sam and Billy, to keep an eye on the Jeep without fear of standing out.

They followed him around the city by-pass and once Marsden joined Highway 213W, it looked for sure that he was heading for the GA site.

"Guys, it looks like it's Hantsport, but we'll know for certain in ten minutes or so."

"Should we come past and get up there, so you can drop back?" said Tommy.

"He's sticking to the speed limit Tommy, so no point flying past him as you'll only stick out, but if the traffic slows, then yes, get yourself past and head for Hantsport."

Just as they approached Bedford, where the highways converge into the 101, Billy saw an opportunity as the traffic slowed and he eased past both Sam and then Marsden's Jeep.

"Nice one Billy," said Tommy, then he spoke into his phone, "Sam, according to the SatNav we've got about another 60 kilometres, ETA is around 08.45. We'll see you up there."

"Okay guys."

Sam watched them pull slowly away from the Jeep, until they were just a spec in the distance. By now, they had left the outer confines of the city. There wasn't a lot of traffic heading towards Hantsport, but Sam could see the commuter traffic, going the other way down towards the city, was very steady.

He was hoping the Subaru in front of him would stay there all the way, so when it turned off soon after, he got a little concerned with no cover between him and Marsden.

This was always the quandary for surveillance teams. With no cover, did you try to stay where you were, but with the risk that maintaining a constant distance, might arouse suspicion with a surveillance savvy target?

The alternative of dropping back wasn't that much better as an option, since Marsden might then wonder where the car behind had gone.

He checked his speed. He was at the national speed limit, 110kph and he wasn't gaining on Marsden's Jeep. *'Canadians aren't renowned for speeding, so let's stick with this as best current option,'* he thought to himself.

Every now and then he'd call up Tommy on the phone with a *'no change, no change,'* message, but other than that it was an unremarkable trip, although he did have time to look at the immediate scenery and surroundings.

He couldn't get over the gap between the two carriageways. It was much wider than the motorways back in the UK and Southern Europe. It had to be, to deal with the snow drifts, to give the snow ploughs somewhere to push the massive amounts of snowfall off the highway. This was a national route into the city for the northwest of the region, so no doubt it was a priority task when the snow came.

He was busy looking at the trees lining the highway when Tommy's voice brought him back to the present.

"Sam, we're here. No change at the site. One guy on the gate checking traffic in. We've parked up at a coffee shop close by."

"Nice one guys, I'll come and join you once we know he's on the site."

It wasn't long before Sam saw the Junction 8 signs and he turned off onto the Hantsport Connector, the stretch of road leading into the town.

"Just turned off Junction 8, any sign of him?"

"Yep, he's just passed us and is turning into the GA site now. I'll get you a coffee."

*****

Marsden showed his security ID to the man at the gate who swiped the card and saw the 'Executive Access All Areas' message appear.

"Good morning sir, can I help direct you somewhere?"

"No thank you."

The fewer people who heard him mention Kevin Cox's name the better, thought Marsden.

"The executive parking is just over to your right sir, by the front entrance."

Marsden nodded.

The gateman raised the entry bar and Marsden drove in and parked. As he walked through the main entrance he couldn't avoid seeing the smiling portrait of Sir Charles Groom staring down at him.

He shook his head. He'd only met him a couple of times. He was like Rawlings, but worse. Old school, full of bullshit and only ever looking after one person, himself.

Marsden had seen the news about the Witterings

shopping centre collapse. It wasn't as though he had any great empathy with the victims, but it was more that he detested how Groom would dodge any bullets coming his way. *'Then again,'* he thought, *'I'm the bloody tosser who is helping him!'*

The young man at the reception desk smiled at him.

"Mr Marsden? How can I help you this morning?"

The software that had read his ID at the front gate clearly had some sort of link through to the reception desk, as he didn't think the gateman wouldn't have had time to ring through.

"Thank you, can you tell me where Kevin Cox's office is please?"

"Shall I ring him for you?" said the young man helpfully.

"No, just the directions will be fine."

His office was on the first floor. As Marsden turned to leave he caught the young man picking up the phone.

"Please don't ring him. I want to surprise him." Marsden tried to grin, but it failed miserably.

The young man could see the word 'Executive Security Team' against Marsden's name on the system. This probably wasn't someone he should go upsetting, so he quickly replaced the phone.

*****

"It's Kevin isn't it?"

Marsden was standing at the door to Cox's office.

"Yes, I'm sorry, do we know each other?" said Cox, standing up.

Marsden walked into the office and sat down. He didn't shake hands and his face was expressionless.

"No, we don't and sit down Kevin, this is your office after all."

He could see confusion on Cox's face. He was a big, well-built man and wasn't giving any indication that he was in anyway intimidated by Marsden.

"Well you have the advantage over me in that you know my name. So you are?" Cox left the question hanging.

Marsden ignored it, part of his tactics to disorientate Cox.

"Do you live nearby then Kevin?"

Cox was starting to bristle with anger. But there was something about this man's manner that was making him feel uncomfortable.

"I don't know who the hell you are, but if you don't explain yourself immediately, I'll call security."

"Go ahead big man, call them. Oh, but hang on, they won't come to your rescue, because they know I'm with you, so sit down like I told you."

Cox didn't know what to do. He didn't know if he was about to be fired, or... or what? He didn't know."

"Look sir, I ..." stammered Cox.

"Sir, I like that Cox. You never know, maybe we might just get on."

Cox sat down, simply because he didn't know what else to do.

"Good. Now my name is Marsden. You can call me Mr Marsden. I am from the Executive Security Team." He saw a look of recognition on Cox's face. "Ah, so you've heard about the EST?"

Cox nodded, concern showing on his face. The EST had a reputation within GA. He actually had no idea what they did, except that he'd seen them on a couple of occasions, when senior managers had been dismissed and immediately escorted from the building.

'But surely this guy isn't here for me?' thought Cox. He hadn't done anything wrong, not least as far as he was aware.

Marsden always enjoyed this part of the

proceedings. Seeing the worried looks grow, first of all to concern and then sometimes to fear.

"I don't believe I've done anything wrong sir, err, I mean Mr Marsden."

"You don't believe? So perhaps you have Kevin? The question is Kevin, was it deliberate, or an inadvertent error? That may be the difference to keeping your job, or not?"

Marsden let the last two words hang in the air. He could see Cox was starting to go into a spiral of self-guilt, thinking he'd done something wrong, when he suddenly stood up again.

"Hang-on just a minute, I haven't done anything wrong, so before we go on, maybe you should just tell me what the hell you're doing here?"

He was a big, well-built guy, thought Marsden, but he wasn't here to fight him. He was here first and foremost to find out some information.

"Of course Kevin, you're absolutely right, how rude of me."

Cox looked at him. Again confusion on his face. Marsden was keeping him guessing.

"I'm Tom Marsden and I just need to check something out with you, that's all. I'm really sorry if I came across in the wrong way, please put it down to my lack of sleep."

The confusion was still there, but Cox had sat back down.

"Okay, well then Tom, how can I help you?"

"Lily Green? Do you know her?"

"Yes, we met when I was across in Mallorca for a few weeks. I'm sorry, what's this all about?"

"Have you spoken with her recently?"

"No, not at all. In fact not since I came back off my secondment. Why? She's not said anything has she? She's not making any sort of allegation, because I never touched her!"

"Guilty conscience Kevin? Playing away when your wife and kids are at home? You do have kids don't you?"

"Yes, yes, I do, but what's that got to do with anything. Look, she's a lovely girl, but I never did anything to her."

Marsden saw that for some reason Cox was thinking the girl may have made some sort of complaint against him. He wasn't about to disabuse him of this, at least not for the time being, as it might come in useful at some stage.

"Let's leave that for a moment then. You say you've not spoken to her since you returned home," he paused, "to your wife and kids?"

"Yes, but please, don't bring my wife into this. She wasn't happy with me going to Mallorca in the first place."

Marsden had no idea why this guy had such a guilty conscience. Maybe there was something between him and Green, or maybe, he thought, maybe he'd had a fling with someone else? Yes, that must be why he's so touchy.

"What about texts or emails?"

"From Lily?"

"Yes, who else do you think I mean Kevin? Unless you have got some other secrets from your time in Mallorca?"

Cox didn't say anything.

"I'll take your silence as a bit of a giveaway my old mate. Well, what goes on in Vegas, or rather Mallorca, stays in Mallorca."

He saw the relief on Cox's face.

"As long as, that is, you tell me all you know about Lily Green."

Any fight that had been in Kevin Cox had now quickly deserted him. "I haven't spoken to her, but I did get an email a little while ago, but it was just a work thing. She was just asking me about something, that's all."

"So that wasn't too hard was it? Where's the email and what did you do about it?"

Cox clicked his desktop mouse a couple of times.

"Here it is. It's just two lines, asking me about Ultra-Fast-Dry10, that's our quick dry cement compound. But she was asking if I knew anything about UFD30."

"Where's your reply?"

Marsden had come around by Cox's desk, looking over his shoulder at the emails on the screen.

"I just told her I hadn't heard of UFD30, it was before my time with GA. I didn't even know they'd experimented with a different compound, not until I did a bit of digging that is."

That wasn't what Marsden wanted to hear. It would have been a lot simpler if Cox had just said he'd sent a response saying he knew nothing of the UFD30, the compound that was used on the Witterings site.

"Did you send her anything about what you'd found Kevin?" said Marsden quietly.

"No, it wasn't anything really, just some papers deep in the archive and besides I got caught up on a rush job we had here, so it's still in my list of to-do things."

"Good, please show me your response."

Cox was feeling better now that things had moved away from what he might have got up to in Mallorca, which wasn't anything really, just a kiss and cuddle with a woman from Sweden who like him, was on a secondment.

He pulled up the response he had drafted and Marsden read it.

"Have you got any hard notes of this Kevin?"

"Look, why are you asking me all these questions? Is she in some sort of trouble?"

"I'm asking the questions Kevin. Where are your hard notes, please?"

Whilst Cox heard Marsden add in the word 'please', it came out in such a threatening way, that he sat back in his chair.

"I'm not sure I can do this. I think I need to speak to my boss before I give you any more information."

"I tell you what Kevin, I'll ring my boss and he'll ring Sir Charles Groom if you like? Maybe you'd like to speak to him?"

That put Cox on the back foot.

"No, no, that won't be necessary."

"Damn right it won't be necessary. Just tell me if you have any bloody notes will you?"

"Just tell me why!"

"No, you don't need to know any more than you already do. It's for your own good Kevin," said Marsden, before adding, "and for your wife and kids."

"Why do you keep mentioning them? If you go anywhere near them, I'll ..."

"You'll what? Go on tell me. Tell the police? Tell your boss? Do any of those and I'll be telling your wife to check your phone, because I bet you've got something on there that you won't want her to see."

"It's nothing and besides I can explain," said Cox, although with little conviction.

"That's another giveaway Kevin. Now get out of my way."

Cox's chair was on wheels and Marsden pushed him out of the way, before flicking the mouse backwards and forwards across the screen until he saw the notice *Delete permanently* appear.

"You can't do that!" yelled Cox.

"Can't I?" said Marsden as he clicked *'Yes'*.

Cox's indignation returned, together with an ounce or two of confidence.

"You can't just come and in start deleting emails without any sort of written authority! You can sack me if you like, but this is not right and I won't stand for it!"

Marsden was tiring of the sparring match with Cox. He'd at least got rid of the emails with Green, but he really wanted to be sure if Cox had any paper notes.

"Look Kevin, just tell me, one way or the other, do you have any paper notes on what you found on UFD30?"

"No, there isn't. It was all internet searches and I always delete the history at the end of each day – it's company policy."

"Yes, I know. Well that's good to hear Kevin, as long as you're telling me the truth?"

"Of course I am, why would I lie about that?"

Cox was trying hard to get Marsden to believe him. The problem was, Marsden had been in the game of interrogating people for a long time and he knew the signs to look for when someone wasn't telling the truth. But this wasn't the place to try to find out more, especially as people were starting to look in through the office window.

"Good, then I believe you. Thanks Kevin, that's all I needed from you."

He didn't wait to see what Cox might say, but as he turned to leave, he did have a quick glance around the room and saw an open briefcase to one side.

"Oh and please don't say anything to anyone about our little conversation Kevin. We wouldn't want your wife finding out about what you got up to in Mallorca would we?"

"But I didn't…."

"It's not me you need to be explaining things to old fruit."

With that Cox fell silent.

'*Leverage,*' thought Marsden.

39

Marsden rang Rawlings as he was walking towards the company restaurant area.

"How did you get on?"

"Partial success Boss. I've destroyed the emails off his desktop and gone into the archives and removed them from there as well."

"I sense there's an additional problem Tom?"

"Yes, I think he's got some paper notes on the response he was working on. He'd drafted something, but hadn't finished it because of some rush job he was working on out here. That sort of rings true, but it also sounds as though he was doing a lot of digging."

"So you think he's still got some hardcopy notes somewhere?"

"Yes, I'm pretty sure he has. So I'm hanging about here for a while to see if he makes a run for home. Oh, here we go, speak of the devil, I've just seen him going down in the lift."

"Good man Tom, but remember, no bruises…"

"Got to go Boss."

Marsden didn't wait to hear Rawlings' mantra for yet another time, as he set off down the steps and out of the main entrance.

He manoeuvred the Jeep into a position where he

could see the cars coming out of the staff carpark.

Across the road, in the coffee shop, Billy was the first to see Marsden come out of the office building.

*****

"Aye, aye, heads up, we've got movement," said Billy.

He put some cash on the table to cover the bill and the three of them left and got in their vehicles. Sam was leaving the carpark as he phoned Tommy.

"Same routine guys. I'll head for the highway exit."

"Okay Sam, no movement yet. He's moved his vehicle, but looks like he's waiting for something?"

It was less than a couple of minutes later and Tommy saw a blue Audi A3 pull out of the main driveway, followed a short time later by Marsden's silver Jeep.

"I think he's tailing a blue Audi A3 Sam."

"Could that be Kevin Cox?" said Sam.

"Tommy, I'll call a friend. Can't promise anything, but I'll see if I can get the registered owner and address from the index plate."

"Sam, did you hear that? From Billy?"

"Yes, that would be brilliant!"

"Okay, we're heading your way Sam. Marsden's hanging back, so that means we have to as well, so we might not be able to give you that much notice."

"Copied, no problem."

Sam was parked to one side of the Hantsport Connector, the road leading to the highway.

He saw the Audi approaching and confirmed to Tommy that he had *'eyeball'* on the target vehicle.

"Sam, Billy has just got through to his friend. The registered owner is Kevin Cox. Address is 11 Gravenstein Road, Wolfville. That's north of here, so Cox could be looking to turn right onto the 101."

"Okay, Marsden has just passed me too and I can see you now, so let me out guys and I'll take over."

Billy slowed a little and Sam pulled out and accelerated after the two vehicles in front of him.

"Yes, they've gone right, heading to Wolfville."

"We're just letting a couple of cars through to give us some cover Sam."

"Okay Tommy, good thinking. Right, we're settling into a cruising speed now. 110kph, traffic is very light."

*****

Marsden saw Cox driving out in a blue Audi A3. He cursed as he'd seen Cox in the glass sided lift, carrying his briefcase.

"What's in your bloody briefcase Cox?" he said out aloud.

If was going to collect the papers from home, why would he need a briefcase? So did that mean he'd had the damn papers in his office somewhere and he was now taking them home?

He knew where Cox lived from Finn's file, so he guessed he'd be heading northwest, up the 101 to Wolfville.

He was far enough back from Cox's Audi, so as not to cause any alarm and at the speed they were doing, he had time to work through his options.

He didn't like the idea of waiting till they got to Wolfville, because he didn't know who else might be there, maybe someone who could potentially give a lending hand to Cox. Marsden looked about. Traffic was quite light. There was a car some way behind him and a few more behind that, but nothing close and every now and then, when they moved around a bend, or down the other side of a hill, he'd lose sight of the cars following.

Suddenly the Audi was a lot closer to him than before. He checked his speed. No, he hadn't speeded up. Still 110kph showing on the speedo.

"He's slowed down!"

293

Marsden lifted his right foot and immediately started feeling the car slowing. 100kph, 90, 80.

'If he goes any slower, I'll stand out like a sore thumb,' thought Marsden.

The Audi wasn't getting any closer, so he'd stuck at 80kph.

"What are you up to Kevin Cox?"

Behind them, Sam Martínez was having a similar moment, realising the Jeep had slowed down too.

"Guys, he's slowing. We can't all slow down. So just keep going and get by him and then pass Cox too. Head for Wolfville."

"Roger that Sam. What about you?"

"Junction 9 is coming up. I'll slow and nip off there if I find I'm going to get too close to Marsden."

"Okay. We've got the Jeep just in front of us." Tommy paused for a moment. "Right, we've just passed Marsden it and we're closing fast on the Audi. Okay, we're on him now. Cox is looking agitated. I think he's on his phone."

"Keep going guys. I don't like the look of this, but we'll have to see how this plays out."

Marsden could see the Junction 9 Exit approaching. Cars were closing on him from behind now. In fact one, a Santa Fe, had just gone by and another one was slowing. He watched it for a moment, it looked like a Ford. He saw the indicator go on and then it moved to the right exit lane.

He checked his rear view mirror again. Nothing now for a good while. Cox slowing suggested he was getting suspicious, so a plan began to form in Marsden's mind.

He increased his speed back up to 110kph. No cars came on from Junction 9 behind him and they were now going uphill. As they got to the crest he saw a red sandstone headland in the distance and then the signs for Junction 10, Grand Pré, Hortonville and Wolfville.

*****

Marsden closed quickly on the Audi and he was behind it before Cox could react. He watched Cox shifting about in his seat, with a smile slowly appearing on his face.

Too late Cox went to pull away, but the Jeep was now right behind him.

Marsden accelerated again and surged forward into the Audi. Cox felt the impact, like a nudge, on the back of his car. He looked at the driver in his mirror. It was Marsden!

"What's he doing?"

Cox didn't know why he was talking out aloud, but he could feel the beads of sweat on his face.

Marsden pushed the Jeep forward again, another nudge, but harder this time. He'd sort this out once and for all. He started waving at Cox, signalling to him to pull off the road.

Cox felt the Jeep hit him again.

"Bloody maniac! He's trying to kill me!"

He was checking his mirrors, the rear view and driver's wing mirror, to see what Marsden was doing. But the sun was very high in the sky by now and it was catching his driver's mirror, reflecting directly back into his eyes, like a laser.

Marsden could see Cox shifting about in his seat, although he couldn't see what he was doing. He accelerated again and hit the Audi, but this time it was even harder. He'd had enough of trying to gently persuade Cox to pull over. This time he'd make sure he got the message.

But Cox was trying to flick the electric mirror switch, trying to avoid the sun's reflection.

He'd just taken his hand off the steering wheel, to adjust the mirror, when Marsden's Jeep hit him. He grabbed the wheel, but over compensated, losing control almost immediately and the Audi suddenly whipped into a spin and Marsden saw it start to roll.

"Oh shit!" He hadn't meant this to happen.

He watched as the car flipped over and over and then shot across the crash barrier and down a slope.

Marsden hit the brakes and came to a stop, before reversing back up the edge of the road. He got out and looked around. Still nothing behind him, but then as he looked down at the Audi, he saw the driver's door was still closed. He was climbing over the crash barrier, when he saw flames start to appear under the Audi.

He knew about car fires, as he'd set a few himself over the years. Cox would only have seconds now to get out, but there was still no movement from inside the car.

The flames hit the fuel pipes and then the fuel tank moments later and the car exploded. He ran down the slope. Another car had stopped and someone, a woman, was getting out of the car.

Marsden thought fast.

"Quick, call the police, fire brigade – stay back! I'll go and see if I can help."

The woman was just standing there, looking at the car on fire.

"Ring the emergency services for God's sake!" yelled Marsden. He needed to get down there and quickly. He ran down the slope towards the Audi. He had to chance the woman just thinking he was trying to help, but as he got close, there was another explosion as two of the tyres burst.

He saw Cox slumped in the driver's seat. He couldn't care less about him, it was the briefcase he wanted, but he had to make it look like he was trying to save Cox in case the woman was looking. He made as though he was trying to get the door open and was shouting at Cox.

"Get out! Get out Kevin!"

There was no use pretending he didn't know the guy. He just needed a cover story as to why he was following Cox for when the police asked him.

The woman shouted down at him.

"They're on their way and there's another man here now."

Marsden nodded. He needed to get to the other door to get to the briefcase. He could see it on the front passenger seat.

He ran around the other side. The fire was burning hot, so he pushed his hands up into his jacket sleeves to try to protect his hands as he tried to open the passenger door.

It popped open. He kept shouting.

"Kevin! Get out mate! Get out," whilst he grabbed the case and quickly flipped it open and scanned the contents.

He couldn't risk taking a file out with him, so he scattered the papers inside the car and saw them starting to curl as the fire took hold. Now the door was open, the air was helping the fire take hold again.

Cox wasn't moving. Marsden hadn't really looked at him before, but now he saw he was slumped in the seat. He couldn't tell if he was dead, but by now he couldn't reach him anyway, even if he had really been trying to rescue him. He staggered back, creating the look of a man who has valiantly tried to save someone.

The woman on the bank was screaming at him.

"Get back, get back, you can't help him anymore, save yourself!"

He waved an arm at her in acknowledgement, but just as he did, he saw the man she'd said was coming, running down the hill towards him.

Martínez!

'What the hell's he doing here? Bastard must have

followed me. How much had he seen?'

*****

Sam had slowed as he exited at Junction 9 and came to a roundabout at the end of the slip road. He waited for a while, checking the SatNav again for directions for Cox's address,

"Guys, I was getting too close, so I've pulled off at Junction 9. I'll get back on in a minute, but I'm thinking he'll take the next junction anyway."

"That'll be the one Sam," said Billy. "You'll see Cape Blomidon right in front of you as you get to the Junction signs. Can't miss it, it's a huge red sandstone headland, across the Bay of Fundy."

"Got it. So are you parked up?"

"Yep, at Cox's address," this time it was Tommy. "We've got some cover, but we'll see them when they turn up here."

Sam pulled back onto the highway and as he hit the top of the hill, he could see the headland in the distance, Cape Blomidon, but then he saw two cars parked up on the side of the highway and smoke billowing up in the air from below the carriageway on the right.

A sickening thought crossed his mind.

'Where's the Audi?'

As he got nearer, he saw Marsden's Jeep and then a woman standing by the other car. She was waving at him, flagging him down.

He slowed and parked a little way back from her car, thinking she'd probably called the fire service and they'd need access to whatever was going on.

As he got out of his car, the woman was shouting at him.

"Help him, please help him! He's trying to save the driver, but he can't get him out!"

"Have you called the police and fire service?" Sam

298

said calmly.

"Yes, yes, they're coming."

"Well done, now stay here and guide them in when they get here. Okay?"

She nodded. Panic was setting in. Not helped by the smell from the burning fire. He recognised it straight away, as he'd been to enough fatal fires to know it wasn't just the rubber from the car.

"You've done great. I'll go and help him, don't worry."

Sam jumped over the crash barrier and made his way down the slope as fast as he could, taking care not to slip on the grass, baked dry in the hot Nova Scotia summer sun. Last thing he needed to do was break his leg.

He saw Marsden crouching by the passenger door of the Audi.

Sam's mind was fast-tracking through the possibilities. *'What the hell happened? What's he done?'* Then he felt it. Guilt. It was kicking in and hard. He'd turned off the highway and then Marsden must have done something and it looked like it was going to cost Cox his life.

He was starting to freeze and his head was swimming. He could see Marsden looking at him. He was saying something, but he couldn't hear it at first. It was just a fuzzy noise, then slowly the words were becoming clearer.

"Can't you hear me? I said he's gone, he's gone. I tried to help. I couldn't get to him. I was just following him home to get some papers from his house that he wanted to give to me," said Marsden.

Sam saw Marsden had his jacket sleeve held down around his right hand, although he could still see he had burns to his fingers.

'Had Marsden really been trying to save Cox?'

40

Marsden had seen the look on Sam's face. Seen that he'd switched off and wasn't hearing anything, let alone seeing anything.

'What was that all about?' he thought, but then he went back into his pretence that he'd been trying to save Cox. His fingers were bloody painful, but he had to admit, they were a damn good bit of cover for his story, even if he did only burn them as he opened the car door and made sure the papers in Cox's briefcase properly caught fire.

Sam looked at Marsden sitting on the ground, nursing his fingers, then he ran to the car and looked in. The fire was still burning and he could see Cox, or at least what was left of him, still sitting in the driver's seat.

"Is he….," Marsden paused for effect, "dead?"

Sam looked at him. He knew it was a performance, but to the untrained observer, it was a bloody good one.

He caught sight of the woman starting to come down the hill. Guessing by her previous reactions, he gathered she'd never encountered a situation like this before, so this was probably not a good time to start now.

"Just stay there and watch out for the emergency

services please. They'll need to be guided in."

He knew they wouldn't, because they'd see the cars and the smoke, but she wasn't to know that and she needed something to do, to feel useful.

She nodded back at him. Reassured that she was helping. He looked back at Marsden.

"So what are you doing here Martínez?"

The sneer on Marsden's face was back. It had all been an act, just for the benefit of the woman who might have been looking down at them before.

"What? Did you force him off the road then?"

"No actually, I didn't. He lost control for some reason and the car started swerving. I admit I was probably slightly too close, because he braked so hard I couldn't avoid just tapping him, but it wasn't enough to push him off the road, so I don't know what happened. But can't you see?" He held up his injured hand. "I tried to save him officer." He mimicked what his response was going to be to the police.

"You won't get away with this. People saw you with Cox at the GA site."

"Ah, so you followed me there did you? Well, all they'll say is that I said I wanted to surprise him, like an old friend would."

Sam was thinking fast. Marsden was no mug. He'd figured all of this out in the space of time it took for the Audi to flip over the side of the carriageway and burst into flames.

"Admit it Met Boy, I've got you on this one haven't I? And by the way, how's the PTSD, I guess that's what happened earlier? Bit of a flashback was it? You know to letting your partner get shot?"

Sam knew Marsden, or Rawlings, would have done their homework on him, so the Met reference wasn't anything unexpected, but knowing about Jimmy getting shot and his PTSD? He'd no idea how Marsden could have sourced that sort of information.

"All you've done is confirm that there is a cover up as far as Ultra-Fast-Dry30 is concerned."

Sam saw the flicker of recognition on Marsden's face and smiled.

"My turn now Tom. It is Tom isn't it?"

But Marsden didn't respond. The police would be arriving any moment and he wanted to be seen to be helping them, whilst getting ready to leave the scene as quickly as he could.

"I take it, you being the Good Samaritan, you'll hang around for the police and answer any questions they have for you? I wouldn't want you thinking you'll somehow slip away from here," said Sam.

"Of course, besides, I've got nothing to hide. Anything there might have been is now just ashes and dust." Another smirk. "Anyway, can't you see I'm desperately upset?"

With that Marsden started crying. Tears coming down his face. Sam looked at him, at this sudden outbreak of emotion, only to realise that a police officer was on her way down the slope from the road.

"You bastard! You won't get away with this."

"I won't? Just watch me."

*****

The Royal Canadian Mounted Police officer approached them.

"You guys okay? Which one of you was here first? I'm guessing it was you sir?"

She looked at Marsden and nodded towards his injured hand.

"Yes Ma'am," said Marsden.

Another good performance. Just enough deference, without being over the top.

"Wait here please, both of you."

She left them and walked across to the Audi, whilst

giving it a wide enough berth for safety. The driver's door window was now blackened, so she went around to the passenger side. Even from a safe distance she could see the driver was dead.

They saw her tilt her head. She was radioing in. Probably for help to investigate the scene. *'A Traffic Accident Investigator, or whatever they call them out here,'* thought Sam.

"We've got fire and ambulance on their way, so can you hold out okay with your injuries sir?"

Marsden looked suitably pained, but stoic.

"Yes, I'm fine, I just can't believe what happened. It was all so quick. I…, I just wish I could have done more."

Her voice was professional, but empathic.

"It looks like you tried your hardest sir. Sometimes, these things just happen. You were very brave even going near the car when it was on fire."

"I wasn't being brave. I was just trying to save my colleague."

Sam had to give him credit. Tears were welling up in Marsden's eyes as he spoke. He thought about challenging him there and then. But what was the point? Marsden held all the cards. Sam hadn't seen what had happened. Marsden had already told him his 'credible' story as to why there would be paint from the Audi on his Jeep and to top it all, he had the burn injuries of a gallant would-be rescuer.

"Officer, I'm not sure I can be too much help here?" said Sam. "I just stopped when the lady up there waved me down, so if you don't mind I'll just be on my way."

"So you didn't see anything at all?"

Sam watched as Marsden looked directly at him, waiting for his answer.

"Sadly no, I didn't. I wish I had, as I'd have liked to be able to shed some light on what *'actually happened'*."

The RMCP officer didn't pick up on what Sam said and merely nodded, thinking she had one less name to go in the Vehicle Collision Report.

"Yes, of course and thanks for stopping."

The officer turned back to look at the Audi and started to take down some of the details, giving Marsden the chance to look across at Sam. Again, the smirk.

"Better luck next time Met Boy."

*****

As he got to the top of the slope by the crash barrier, Sam saw the Fire Service had arrived and were unravelling water hoses and then the ambulance turned up as well.

He took the opportunity to take a closer look at Marsden's Jeep whilst everyone was distracted. It was open. A quick look inside showed there was nothing instantly visible, but then he found Cox's file tucked in the driver's door. He flicked through it and saw references to Lily Green and the email she had sent to Cox. Other than the address that Billy had already got for them, there was nothing else new for him in there.

He checked the front of the Jeep. Yes, there was the blue paint from the Audi. He took a few pictures on his phone. He didn't know why, but it was worth doing seeing as he was there.

Just then his phone rang. It was Tommy. He closed the door to the Jeep and walked back to his car.

"Tommy."

"Sam, no one's turned up. Where are you?"

"We've had a situation mate. Cox is dead. His car flipped over and off the carriageway and burst into flames, just before Junction 10."

"Bloody hell! Was it Marsden?"

"I don't know. I didn't see it. I think it probably was. He's basically been boasting to me about it, but when the RCMP turned up he was all sweetness and light and he's the knight in shining armour with burns to his hand, as he tried to save the guy."

"You were right when you said he's no mug Sam. So what now? Stand down?"

"I think so Tommy. We can't go blundering in to see his wife, as she's going to be in a right state when she's told about this. Plus the fact Marsden made it abundantly clear that any evidence Cox might have had, has now literally gone up in smoke."

"What made him say that?"

"I could see remnants of an open brief case in the car. I reckon that's how he got the burns on his hand, not trying to save Cox. I don't think he went near the poor bugger. He was just trying to make sure that whatever was in the briefcase was well and truly destroyed."

"Can't they do that thing you see in the movies? You know, where they take fire damaged stuff and patch it together, or look at it under UV light, or something like that?" said Tommy.

"Theoretically, yes, but you're right Tommy. That's generally just for the movies. They won't look to be doing that sort of stuff without very good reason and a straightforward road accident, albeit with a fatality, won't fall into that category by any stretch of the imagination."

*****

"Thanks Mr Marsden, you've been most helpful. You say you'll be going to see Mrs Cox?"

"Yes, it's something we do as company policy, to support them in any way we can. I hate doing it because it's so sad, but it's an important part of the job isn't it?"

"But I bet you're really good at it Mr Marsden, providing such support I mean," she blushed as he smiled back at her.

She was warming to him, just like the others did. He was good at attracting women, often with his slightly downbeat expression and hard luck stories. But sadly, he wouldn't be able to take things further with this one.

"I wish you all the best with the family. Now, the ambulance is here and I'd like them to check your burns over and then I just need you to see the Collision Analyst."

She saw the blank look on his face.

"I'm sorry. We have our own investigators who examine the scene at every fatal collision and then determine the cause."

"Yes, of course," said Marsden, who wondered if his story might actually stand up to scrutiny to an expert.

"Look, I'm feeling a bit tired now. Do you mind if I go and see Kevin's wife first? You've got my details and I can make the car available to you back at my hotel if it helps?"

She thought for a moment. The Collision Analyst would be here for a while examining the Audi. This looked a pretty open and shut case and he had, after all, tried to save the driver, not to mention he was going to see the deceased's wife to break the sad news, so she saw no harm in letting this guy go.

"Yes, that should be fine. Please keep your mobile on and I need to ask you to not leave Canada for the time being. It should only be for a few days."

"Yes, of course, that's no problem at all officer. Happy to help."

She smiled as he walked away.

'*Nice guy,*' she thought.

*****

Marsden sat in his vehicle thinking through the difficult call he needed to make to Stephen Rawlings. He decided to delay the call until he had the complete story to tell him. Instead, he called the GA Security Site Manager.

"Tim Faxton? Good, it's Tom Marsden, from the EST."

Faxton immediately knew who Marsden was. He'd had a call from the Reception Team and had been expecting a visit, or a call, from this EST guy at some stage.

"How can I help Mr Marsden?"

"Tim, please call me Tom. Look there's no easy way to tell you this, but there's been a terrible accident up on the 101. I was following Kevin Cox back home, he was taking me home for some lunch, and his car suddenly went out of control."

"Oh Jeez Tom, is he alright?"

"That's the thing Tim, he's not. In fact I'm really sorry to tell you, but Kevin died at the scene."

"Oh my God, Tom, he's…, he was, such a nice guy."

"I know, I hadn't known him long. I met him across in Mallorca, when he was across on his secondment," lied Marsden.

"Okay, so we've got local protocols around this Tom, do you want me to handle all of that?"

"I'd heard you were a good guy Tim. That's what I was hoping you could do, so thanks. But there's something I'd like to do first and I want you to either get someone up here from HR, or come up yourself. I want to go and see Mrs Cox and break the news myself, because I was right behind him when it happened."

"Wow, Tom, that must have been quite a shock and man, I really respect you for doing that, you know, going to break the news to her. That's not an easy job and even harder because you were there."

"It's only right that I do it Tim, so what do you think is best? Should you come, or a senior HR rep?"

Marsden put the ball firmly in his court. Give him a

sense that he was being trusted, confided in.

"I think the HR route might be best, after all there may be questions around death benefits and the like. It might be too soon, but just in case there's any immediate needs for the family."

"That's great thinking Tim, I'll make sure I mention that in my report."

"Why, thank you Tom, but it's…"

Marsden didn't wait for him to finish. He was done with flattering the guy. He now just needed some cover when he went to the Coxes' house.

"Get them to meet me as soon as possible up in Wolfville. You've got my number Tim, so text me who is coming and give them my number. Quick as you can too mate. This is important we move fast."

"Yes, sure. I'm on it."

Of course it was important, but not for the reasons he was telling Tim Faxton. Marsden had no intention of being in Nova Scotia any longer than he needed to get inside the Cox house and check through any work papers he might have at home.

*****

Sam met up with Tommy and Billy at the Holiday Inn.

"Do you think we can get inside his room Billy?"

"We can give it a go. Most hotels these days have pretty decent security, but then again, most people don't have one of these."

Billy pulled out an electronic key scanner.

"Handy bit of kit. Obviously completely illegal to be carrying around without good cause, so gentlemen, which of you wants to hang on to this?"

Tommy grinned.

"I'll take it. I hear Canadian prisons aren't too bad anyway."

"Let's get this done guys. I want us to be on a flight

back home tonight Tommy."

They took separate lifts up to the second floor. Sam held back, to avoid drawing attention to three men walking down a corridor together, whilst Tommy and Billy moved forward to Room 256.

Within moments of Billy activating the device, there was a click, followed by a green light on the door lock and then he opened the door.

"Blimey Billy, that was too bloody quick! Last time I trust hotel security," said Tommy.

"That's why you should always at least use the safe in the room, or even better, lock your valuables in the hotel safe."

Tommy gave a low whistle and Sam walked quickly along the corridor and into the room.

Sam went through the same procedure as he always did when searching a room, starting with a visual scan of the area, looking at it almost as a 3D image.

"No need to rush this guys and I'd rather he doesn't know we've been here. He may suspect, but let's not give the game away entirely. Tommy, you take the bathroom. Billy, you work clockwise and I'll go anti-clockwise and we'll pass in the middle on the other side of the room and then meet back here, okay?"

"Good for me."

Slow and steady just as he was trained. Sam worked his way around the room. He hadn't got more than half way when he realised it was likely to be clean. As he'd said, Marsden was no mug and he hadn't left anything untoward in the room.

They still took their time and worked methodically through the room.

"Okay guys, it's clear, but it was worth doing. Let's regroup in your room. Billy can we leave you to safely exit from here?"

"Sure thing Sam. Give me two minutes."

They were back in the room Tommy and Billy had used the night before a few moments later.

"Tommy, we need to head back out. Can you sort out flights for tonight if you can? Different routes if you have to, as long as we're back in London early tomorrow morning. Billy, you've been a star and consider yourself an Associate of 3R if that's okay with you? It comes with a retainer, just not a massive one," Sam grinned.

Billy laughed.

"A retainer? I like the sound of that, however small. Sam, it's been a pleasure. Hope to see you guys again soon."

As they were walking back to the car, Tommy came off his phone.

"Flights booked. I'll need to fill in some of the details, but we can do that at the airport."

*****

Marsden got the text five minutes after he'd spoken with his new friend, Tim.

'Jane Watson, Senior HR Manager en route.'

He acknowledged the text and went to find a coffee shop in Wolfville.

41

Anna had been in enough shops around the Oxford Street, Regent Street and Bond Street triangle to satisfy her shopping needs for the next few years.

She hadn't seen the woman immediately, indeed it had been at the fourth shop she went in, that she was finally sure she'd spotted her follower.

She was in New Bond Street, looking in the window of Mikimoto, the jewellery and pearl specialist, when she just caught a passing look of the young woman in the reflection of the shop window.

'Oh, you're good, very good, young lady. But, you just needed to stay a fraction further back with all of this glass about.'

Anna was still smiling as she walked towards the door entrance to the jewellers. The shop assistant looked at the woman at the door and immediately weighed her up as a potential buyer, rather than a 'looker'.

Anna heard the quiet click, as the assistant released the electronic security door to let her in, and she walked in to a warm welcome.

"Madam, how can we help you today?"

"Good morning to you too. I'd like a new string of

pearls for an important lunch date I have today."

*****

Mikhail Makarovich took the call from Anna's tail.

"So she's back at The Savoy?"

"Yes, Boss. She's been to a few shops. High end, luxury retail and bought some clothes and a string of pearls from Mikimoto."

"Good, thank you."

He turned to his father.

"Papa, she's been shopping. Got a new set of pearls from Mikimoto."

"Thanks Mikhail. Okay, let's go and see what this lady has to say."

"Papa?"

"Yes my boy?"

"Be careful."

He looked at his son and smiled.

"I will." He was about to go, when he looked back. "I always am."

*****

Anna saw him as he walked into the restaurant. Oleg Makarovich certainly had presence and by the look of it, the staff recognised him as a regular visitor.

He was tall, maybe a shade over six foot, just like Luis, her husband had been. His hair was thick and wavy and brushed back. Age-wise? Well she knew he was fifty eight, but he looked fit and healthy and could have passed for someone just into their fifties.

She stood up from the table and he walked straight to her.

"Miss Stevens, a pleasure to meet you."

"Likewise Mr Makarovich and please call me Fiona. If we're to do business together I always like to be on amicable terms with my clients."

'Of course he'd recognise her, as her tail would have provided pictures of Fiona Stevens.'

312

"Thank you Fiona. Now, have you been here before? I imagine you have, but how often do you get across to the UK?"

Gentle, conversational questions. But he was checking her out. Anna smiled.

"Yes, but not for a while Mr Makarovich. I'm assuming you come here quite often?"

"Yes, would you like me to order?"

It was less of a question and more of a confirmation of what he intended to do.

She smiled again and nodded.

"That would be lovely. What do you suggest? Oysters and champagne?" said Anna.

It was his turn to smile this time. Was that a lucky guess from her? Or were Russians so predictable?

"Yes, why not?"

He called the waiter across and a moment later the champagne was being poured.

He was about to raise his glass, when Anna got in first.

"A toast Mr Makarovich. To secrets! May they allow us to become the closest of business partners."

Makarovich touched his glass against hers.

"To secrets Fiona. But nothing so important as to die for."

He watched for any sort of reaction from her, but Anna was in total control. She'd felt like that from the moment she'd stepped into the restaurant. This was her arena and she felt the confidence of her years of experience flooding back through her body.

"So let's get down to some business shall we?"

She talked with ease about the services Stevens Bank could offer him and saw him slowly relaxing into the conversation. She was being careful not to push too quickly. The amount of money was still vast, even by a billionaire's standards, so he wasn't about to agree to the first thing she said.

"You mentioned some special services Fiona, reserved for your elite customers?"

'Was this a test? To see her response? Or was he now getting genuinely interested?' If it was a test, it nearly worked as Anna just caught herself from taking a deep breath.

"We work with clients who need to move money around the world, in order to help with clearing the previous history of those funds."

"I think we both know what you're talking about here Fiona."

"I prefer those terms to…"

He finished her sentence, "money laundering."

"Quite," said Anna. "My sources can see how you're using Global Aggregates to enable this process for you. You're presumably using your own bank, OBCR, for part of this process, but I imagine this still leaves you quite stretched with the other companies you use for a similar reason?"

"You are very well informed Fiona. Go on."

He liked her. She was smart, elegant and yes, attractive and good company. He guessed she must now be in her early to mid-sixties, but the way she looked now only went to suggest that she must have been extremely attractive when she was younger.

Anna had been talking for well over an hour by the time they finished their lunch and were being served with coffee. As time had gone on she'd been getting a growing sense of Makarovich being drawn into her net.

She also knew that he'd been studying her. She could feel his eyes watching how she moved. It was a sensation she remembered from way back when, but whereas then it had been part of the job to accept that physical and mental undressing, she was feeling distinctly uneasy about it now.

She didn't want to speed anything up, so as not to alarm him and she was now being increasingly careful to not mention any specific amounts of money, as she wanted that to come from him. However, when he'd made a couple of comments to draw her on more detail, she'd seen them as *'more tests'*, but she'd easily been able to deal with everything he'd raised with her.

When he started to ask about her Bank's reserves, she knew the time was right to move to the next stage. She took out a mini iPad from her bag and opened up the Stevens Bank webpage Anju had created for her.

"Is this accessible on the open web Fiona?"

She'd anticipated he might ask this. It would be too easy to have a dummy site set up on her iPad. So whilst Makarovich thought he was testing her again, in reality, Anna had dropped the hook that would now prove her authenticity, with him using his own device.

"Yes, of course. Have you got your phone here? Oh good. If you search Stevens Bank, you will find a login option. So is it actually fully accessible to a public search? Well, no, not really, as that's how we retain our low profile. However, if you type in the following code," she gave him an eight digit code, "you can now access the site as though you are a full client."

"Presumably this code will now change?"

"It changed the moment you entered it Mr Makarovich. We take security of the Bank and our clients very seriously," Anna smiled. "If you click on menu at the top right hand of your screen, you can see how you would access your personal accounts. I've set up some dummy accounts in your name, so you can see how easy it is to switch accounts, transfer monies, check on current rates and so on."

He worked his way around the menu and so didn't notice Anna checking her watch for the sixty seconds Anju would need for the next phase.

A minute had passed before he closed the site, but Makarovich wasn't finished. He closed the site and then opened it again and tried the same code. Nothing, just a message, *'Access is unfortunately denied, please contact your banking relationship manager.'*

"It's good Fiona."

The hook was digging in deeper. This time she could afford herself a smile.

"I'm so pleased you think so Mr Makarovich."

*****

Anju saw the code number come through from Anna's iPad and watched for the expected second code to appear from Makarovich's phone.

As well as the code Anna had given him, gaining him access to the Stevens Bank website, it also triggered a switch that allowed Anju to access the contents of his phone.

She clicked her mouse a few times and sat back as the data save indicator started moving quickly across the page.

"Got you!"

She then rang the number Eschaan had left for her.

"Mr Chambers? It's Anju. It worked perfectly sir."

"Well done Anju, and Greg is fine, please."

"Thank you Greg, yes, Mrs Martínez managed to keep him looking through the site on his phone more than the sixty seconds we needed, so I had more than enough time to secure the data capture. I'll be able to deliver a summary within the hour and then a more detailed document by the end of the day if that's alright?"

"That will be brilliant Anju and well done again for a great piece of work."

Anju felt her face flush with pride.

*****

Anna was thinking that things couldn't have gone

any better with Makarovich. Whilst he hadn't actually signed up to anything yet, she had seen all the tell-tale signs of someone who had bought the storyline and was about to commit.

Now was the tricky time of securing the deal, whilst not appearing to be too pushy. But then Makarovich threw a spanner in the works.

"I like what I have seen today Fiona. However, I make a point of never signing a deal at the first meeting. I would like you to come to my house tomorrow evening, for dinner. We can complete the arrangements and I can promise, it will be very worthwhile for you and your Bank."

Going to his house was a big step. She'd have no backup, or support. But she couldn't refuse as he'd be likely to smell a rat.

"Oh, Mr Makarovich, that would be lovely. I've seen pictures of your house and it looks delightful."

"Good, that's settled then. I'll send a car at 7pm tomorrow and you'll get a full tour of the house as well," he said with a smile.

She smiled again, but wondered how she'd talk Greg into allowing her to go into the proverbial lion's den.

42

Marsden was sat in Just Us, a coffee shop in Main Street. It turned out that it was in the foyer of the old cinema, where there was also a small coffee museum.

The young woman behind the counter smiled at him and asked him what he wanted. He saw a long, hand written, list of coffees high up on a chalk board and despite a small queue forming behind him, she didn't rush him and spent time telling him about the day's specials.

He accepted her recommendation of the blueberry muffin with an espresso, before taking a seat at the front, by the open windows, looking out on to the main road through Wolfville.

There was a steady flow of people in and out of the coffee shop, a good indicator of its popularity, so it was quite busy inside when he saw a woman in a smart business suit come through the door.

She was clearly looking around for someone and didn't see him at first, as she partially had her back to him.

He guessed she might be from the HR team. He stood up.

"Miss Watson?" he said softly.

She jumped a little, but then smiled when she saw him.

"Mr Marsden?"

"I'm sorry if I startled you. Thank you for coming so quickly."

"No, it's okay, I just didn't see you there. And please, Jane is fine, Mr Marsden."

She'd regained her composure.

"I think Tom is probably best for this situation as well Jane, don't you think?"

"Yes, of course Tom. It's just so awful. Kevin was really well liked. It must have been terrible for you."

She was looking at his hand. He suppressed a smile at the thought at how well things had worked out, when all he'd been trying to do was destroy what was in the briefcase.

"It was Jane. God, I tried my best to save him and I feel such a failure that I couldn't."

She saw tears in his eyes and reached across and took his left hand.

"You mustn't say that. You did your very best, but it was just an awful accident."

He forced a smile back at her.

"Thank you Jane, I appreciate that, I really do."

He looked at her and then down at her left hand. Pretty and no rings. *'Maybe there might be time afterwards...,'* but he caught himself before he wandered too far off the job in hand.

"Now we need to support Mrs Cox and I want to tell her personally, although I'm not sure if the police may already be there. Either way, it's only right the company gets involved and quickly."

She liked his business-like and professional approach to what needed to be done, whilst also managing to retain a level of empathy that she didn't often see in senior managers. She was impressed and she couldn't help but admit, he was charming and handsome with it.

"I can get you a coffee, but I think we should get down there straight away. Can I leave all the detail questions she may have to you?"

"Yes of course and no need for coffee, I grabbed one before I left and had it on the way up."

"Okay, let's go. And Jane, it's Christine Cox isn't it? With two kids, daughters? Rose and Frances?"

"Yes, that's right, it is Christine, although I didn't know his daughters' names."

He'd nearly slipped up. '*Stop trying to be a smart arse.*'

"Oh, Kevin told me about them when we met across in Mallorca."

They took his car down to the Coxes' home. There was no sign of a police vehicle. He assumed they'd either been and gone, or they hadn't got there yet.

"I'll lead if you like Jane? I've done this before."

"I was hoping you'd say that Tom."

He rang the doorbell and a woman came to the door."

"Hi, how can I help you?" She was bright and breezy and clearly the police hadn't seen her yet.

"It's Christine isn't it? I'm Tom Marsden from Global Aggregates and my colleague, Jane Watson. May we come in? I'm afraid I have some difficult news for you."

*****

Marsden looked at Kevin Cox's widow. He'd actually surprised himself at how he'd delivered the news. She was obviously distraught and he'd found himself having an element of sympathy for her. She had no part in anything that had taken place throughout this whole episode and yet, here she was now, left having to cope with two young kids.

This side to him didn't last long. He soon switched back to the real reason for his visit, gently asking if he could check Kevin's office for any GA work materials.

"It's another thing you then don't have to worry about Christine."

She'd nodded in thanks and pointed to where his office was, just along from the kitchen.

He wasn't expecting to find anything, as he was pretty convinced in his own mind that he'd got the story right. Cox had been taking his notes home in the briefcase for safe keeping, not going home to pick anything up.

He was right. Nothing. As he finished the search, he could still hear her crying, even though the HR woman was doing a good job at supporting her. He had one last thing he needed to check on, before he could get out and head back to the airport.

'Did Cox tell her anything about me on the way up?'

"Thank you again Christine, but Kevin was clearly very well organised and there's nothing else here that you will have to worry about."

"Thank you for checking anyway. He told me you were coming, although he didn't say your name. He said someone was coming to the house and that I shouldn't believe anything you were going to tell me. What did he mean by that?"

Marsden saw that Jane Watson was also looking at him. He was searching, desperately for a story to tell. He looked back at first Jane Watson and then as he turned to Christine Cox, he half-smiled with sadness in his eyes.

"I suppose because he hadn't believed it himself Christine."

She looked at him blankly.

"I had just told him that we wanted him to take over a major project, one that's still on the secret list."

"Was it to do with the trip he went on to Mallorca? Because he said you might speak to me about something that went on out there?"

"Yes, that was it. He'd made such a good impression over there. It's such a shame that he won't be able to take up the offer now, but I think we can look at Kevin's benefits package as though he had taken up his new position. Don't you think Jane?"

Jane Watson looked at him. *'What a kind gesture,'* she thought.

"Thank you, that's very kind of you Mr Marsden," said Christine Cox.

Marsden couldn't believe his luck. Cox had clearly been warning his wife that he might talk about whatever he'd got up to whilst on his trip in Mallorca, but now it had fallen into a perfect excuse for him following Cox back to his home address.

Her parents only lived around the corner, so they waited until they arrived before leaving, giving their condolences once again.

Marsden dropped Jane off at her car by the coffee shop, declining her invitation to have another coffee.

'I can do without any more distractions,' he thought, before he set off towards Highway 101.

'And you thought I wouldn't get away with this Martínez? Ha! Think again Met Boy, think again!'

43

Marsden rang Rawlings as he drove back to his hotel. He anticipated it wouldn't be a great reaction, even though he'd done his level best to tidy things up.

"For God's sake man! How the hell did this happen? I'm telling you now that this is on your head if it ever gets out. Is that clear?"

Marsden didn't know why Rawlings was even bothering to say all of this. Of course he knew it was his own bloody fault, so he didn't need preaching at. Not now, not ever.

"Look, I told you Boss. It was an accident. Honestly. I was just trying to get him to slow down and pull over, so we could talk. I don't know what happened, but he must have lost control. It wasn't intentional and yes, I read you loud and clear. You'll drop me like a stone if this ever gets out."

"Marsden, I don't like your tone and let me remind you that you're still employed by me, so watch your tongue."

Marsden thought for a moment.

'*This is how things always turn out. First it was the army, then the police and now with Rawlings and this outfit. Sooner or later, it all goes tits-up and I have to bail* out. *Well this time, I'm going out when I want and how I want.'*

"Marsden? Are you still there?"

"Yes, Boss."

Rawlings was having second thoughts himself. Marsden had worked for him for a fair number of years now and he'd been grateful, on a good many occasions, for some of his more specialist skills. *'Maybe he should give him some leeway?'* He had said it was an accident, so maybe it was.

"Okay, look, Tom. If you say it was an accident, then I'm sure it was, but it just makes things a bit more difficult doesn't it. Do the police want you to stay there until the investigation into the accident is over?"

"Yes, they do. Unfortunately, I got a look at their collision analyst and how he went about his work. He was good, too good for my liking, so I don't think I want to hang about here too long."

"Because?"

"Because there's paint from Cox's Audi all over the front of my hire car. I'd rather get a rap across the knuckles for skipping the country, even though I'm not actually on bail for anything, than risk that analyst finding some reason to doubt my version of events as to how the paint got on there."

"Will you come out on your own passport?" said Rawlings, who knew Marsden had a number of passports in different names.

"Yes, like I said, I'm not on bail, so I can't see how they could put any markers on me, plus the fact it will be better to say I just needed to get back for a family emergency and accept the knuckle rap."

"Good thinking Tom. What about Sam Martínez then? Where is he now?"

"No idea and I've no idea how he knew I was coming here. Gave me a hell of a shock when he wandered down the hill towards me. He knows he's got nothing though. He can't prove anything."

"Even more reason to get back to Mallorca and find out what's been going on with things over there. But Tom, come and see me first, before you fly out there. We need to think this through."

All things considered, the call had actually gone quite well, thought Marsden. An hour later he was checking out of his hotel and on his way to the airport. Traffic was light and he was soon parking up the Jeep in the car hire zone and putting the keys in the drop off box.

He walked into the lounge area of Halifax International Airport, just as the front wheels of the Air Canada flight, with Tommy and Sam on board, lifted off the runaway as it began the journey to London Heathrow.

*****

"You're seriously thinking of going into his house? After what Sam's told us went on in Canada with Kevin Cox?"

Anna had rang Greg to brief him on how the meeting with Makarovich had gone.

"Yes, and before you say anything, I know this has certain elements of risk that we can't cover."

"Certain elements? Hell's teeth Anna! This has a bit more than certain elements. I can't give you any cover in there, even if you call for help, it's not the sort of building we can just barge in to."

She could hear the concern in his voice, but she knew this was the only way she could persuade Makarovich that Fiona Stevens and Stevens Bank were the real thing.

"Greg," she said quietly. "I said, I've worked this through. We have no reason to believe Makarovich is in any way involved in what Rawlings and Marsden do on a day to day basis."

He didn't say anything. She had that voice. The one he'd heard when she had been the one training him in covert operations over thirty years ago.

"That may be so and I'm not saying it's the wrong call Anna, it's just...."

"I know, and it is dangerous, but that's why we were good at doing this sort of thing. And before you say it was over thirty five years ago, I know that too."

She'd made her mind up. He could tell. She'd need a damn good reason to change it, something which he didn't have.

"You'll wear a wire?"

"Yes, I think that's a risk we'll have to go for, plus I can't see Sam, let alone you, letting me go anywhere near his house, without at least knowing you can hear me."

"They're on their way back from Canada, Sam and Tommy, so we'll have them to help manage your support team."

"Greg?"

"Yes?"

"Thank you."

He smiled to himself. She'd known he'd be worried about the plan, but she'd clearly thought it all through. Then again, she always could talk him around to anything and she'd done it again.

*****

Lily was getting bored sitting about Anna's home with nothing to do. It was a beautiful villa and her grandparents seemed quite at home, sitting out in the sunshine, reading.

Terri could sense her frustration and was trying to keep her occupied taking her up in the hills for bike rides, but it wasn't working.

"Terri, I feel like a prisoner!"

"It's only for a few days, just until we see how Sam gets on in Nova Scotia."

"He's gone to see Kevin?"

"Well, more to the point, he's gone to see what the guy who we think kidnapped you is doing over there, but yes, we think that's probably to see Kevin Cox."

"So when will you know?"

"Anytime soon. Just waiting on a call with an update, so please, can you just be patient for a little while longer."

Lily forced a smile. She'd had another nightmare last night and both her grandmother, and Terri, had come running in after hearing her screaming in her sleep. She was missing Mateo and wanted to hear his voice and be held by him.

"What about Mateo? Couldn't I just meet him somewhere, maybe tomorrow? I won't tell him where we're staying?"

"It's just a couple of days Lily. The fewer people who know, including not telling Mateo, the better."

The smile disappeared, replaced by a shrug.

Terri had considered taking her phone from her, but then that really would make her feel like a prisoner, and besides, she felt she could trust her not to do anything stupid.

"Thank you for going along with all of this," she said softly.

Half a smile returned.

"I'm the one who should be thanking you, not being a grumpy cow."

It was Terri's turn to smile now.

*****

A few kilometres down the road in Palma, Mateo Álvarez was sitting in his apartment looking at the tracker on his phone.

He could see Lily's location. She was in Illetas, just

south of the city. He'd uploaded one of those 'Find my Friends' apps the day she came back from Marsden. It seemed the simplest way of keeping an eye on her and she had so many apps on her phone, that there was a good chance she wouldn't notice another one. Even if she did, he could explain it away by saying he'd only been looking out for her.

"She's still there."

"Okay, keep me posted if she moves again, even if it's another bike ride," said Rawlings.

Álvarez sat back in his chair. This really had gone way beyond the original brief he'd been given, which had been to get to know a young girl in a bar.

Whatever Marsden had done to Lily, it had affected her badly and he hated seeing the distress she was in when she had one of her nightmares.

At least Marsden was off the island for the time being. He didn't like him and he didn't trust him. His problem was that he was now in this way too deep and he had no idea where it might be going. Worse still, he knew he'd grown very fond of Lily.

'God, I think I might actually be in love with her!'

Whatever he felt, his feelings for her were torn with saving his own skin, less from the police, but more from Rawlings, who was someone he'd never want to cross. Besides, why would she ever forgive him if she ever found out about his part in all of this?

*****

"Hello Dad, just checking in," said Terri.

"I was just about to ring you," said Greg. "Sam and Tommy are in the air, heading back to London. There's been some developments."

"That sound ominous?"

Greg then brought her up to date on what had happened to Kevin Cox and Anna's plans to go to Makarovich's house the following day.

"Blimey Dad, that raises the ante a bit, doesn't it?"

"Yes, Sam couldn't believe how calculating Marsden was. He had it all worked out, the story he was going to give to the police. Are you all okay there? With Lily and her grandparents?"

"Yes, but she's getting very twitchy. I was just saying we were waiting on news about Canada, but I don't know if I should tell her Cox is dead. It could tip her over the edge even further."

"Maybe don't tell her then, not for now."

"You said Anna's going to see Makarovich again?"

"He wants her to go to his house, Says he never signs anything on a first meeting."

"Can you cover it?"

"We've got Sharon's team and with Sam and Tommy back, I'll have the numbers, but if she calls for help? I just don't know Terri. I suspect his house is like a bloody fortress, so the chances of an SAS team getting in there, let alone us, is probably pretty low."

"Doesn't that mean it should be a non-starter?"

"I think you've known Anna long enough now Terri, to know she's considered all the angles, including the risk against the potential outcomes and it's hard for me to argue against her logic."

"But what was it you said Carruthers mentioned about his son, Mikhail? He sounds like he's a particularly nasty bastard."

"Sums him up quite well."

"So?"

"I've thought about asking her to take someone in with her, I'm thinking of Sam? Anna's still a fine looking woman, but I can't see this being any sort of seduction scene and why would he bother with all of this if it was a trap? In fact, if it was a trap, the chances of him inviting her to his house, rather than a neutral location, are low to negligible."

"Good point Dad. That's a sound idea. I agree, run the *'Sam riding shotgun'* idea past her. He probably doesn't know too many intricacies about the banking system, but he'll know more than enough, about the practicalities of money laundering, to be her expert."

"I like that idea, plus it may be the only way Sam will agree to letting his mum go in there, not that she'd take any notice if he said 'No', anyway."

"You're right. He could huff and puff all day, but she'll go in if that's what she thinks is the best option," said Terri. "Night Dad."

"Good night my girl."

*****

The following morning, when Greg rang Anna to run the idea of taking Sam in with her, he expected some resistance, so was surprised at her response.

"The idea's got some merit Greg," she said slowly, as she thought how it might play out.

"Wow, high praise indeed!"

She laughed, "I'm sorry, that must have sounded so patronising."

"I felt like I was back in the training room."

"No, it was a way better idea than some of the things you used to come up with then!"

"Anyway, if we can move on past my previous feeble tactical suggestions. If you're up for this, we'll get Sam briefed when he gets in. They should have landed by now. Speak later."

She thought for a moment. This did make sense and it was unlikely that Rawlings, or Groom for that matter, would have shared anything with Makarovich about anyone in the 3R team.

"Now for some breakfast."

*****

Greg saw Sam and Tommy as they got out of the black cab at the hotel.

"You two look like you've just come off an overnight flight."

"Very funny," said Sam. "Next time I'll make sure we get extra leg room Tommy, I promise."

Tommy grinned back at him. What with the limited leg room and the screaming baby two rows back, it wasn't the best night's sleep he'd ever had.

"It is what it is. Greg, good to see you."

After a couple of warm embraces, the three of them walked back into the lobby.

"Sam, change of plan for you. You'll be booking in to The Savoy. Tommy, you'll be staying here. The room's booked, so you just need to check in."

Tommy nodded and Sam looked at Greg.

"Let's get you guys some proper breakfast and I'll tell you all about it."

Half an hour later, they were finishing off a not so healthy full English breakfast and Greg had briefed Sam on the plan for going to Makarovich's house.

"It's risky Greg, but I assume you've worked it through with Mum?"

"Yes, plus I got Terri's opinion, to make sure I'm not being overly protective of Anna. There's just a few too many unknowns for me to feel comfortable letting her go in there on her own."

"Presumably one of those unknowns is Mikhail Makarovich?" said Sam.

"Yes, got it in one. We've heard a bit about him, but then again his father didn't get to be a billionaire by being a nice guy."

"Okay, I think it's sound. But if I'm supposed to be the son of a millionaire banker, I'd better go and get some suitable clothes. Is my room booked already?"

"Yes, Anna has put it on her Stevens Bank credit card, the one she got courtesy of Martin Carruthers, so you won't get asked for any credit card. They'll obviously ask for your passport, but you'll have to fob them off and I'll see if Martin can get something done in double quick time."

"Tommy," said Greg.

"Boss?" Old habits died hard with Tommy when it came to calling his boss, Greg.

"Liaise with Sharon and start putting a support plan together for Makarovich's house in Belgravia."

Tommy nodded and he was off and gone. Greg didn't need to tell Tommy what to do. He'd put these things together many times before and knew what Greg would want.

"Sam, if you need help in there, we might not get to you very quickly, so…"

"It's okay Greg, I understand, but like you say, this doesn't have the feel of any being sort of trap," said Sam, although he wasn't a hundred percent convinced with what he was saying.

44

Rawlings was bristling with anger. Groom had given him another unnecessary grilling on what was happening.

'Perhaps it's time I look for some new clients.'

The thought was put to the back of his mind as he saw Tom Marsden appear at the door.

"Tom, welcome back. Come in and Tom? I'm sorry I went off on one before. You know about the accident. I trust your judgement and I shouldn't have given you the sense I'd just abandon you."

Marsden was taken aback. Either Rawlings was going soft, which he knew he wasn't, playing a very cagey game, or, and he was struggling to believe he was even thinking this, Rawlings was genuinely sorry.

"Thanks Boss, I appreciate it and I know you always have my back."

The two men looked at each other for a moment. It was a game of chess, neither quite believing the other had just made such a move.

Rawlings made the next play.

"Groom is hassling me again Tom. I haven't told him about what happened in Nova Scotia. I'll break it to him later, when we're sorted once and for all."

"Once and for all? What are you thinking, Boss?"

"You know I always want us flying well below any police involvement Tom, but circumstances have pushed us into a situation where I feel we need a more permanent solution to the Pollensa side of things."

Marsden wished Rawlings didn't talk in riddles all the bloody time. If he wanted the girl to disappear he should just say so. The room wasn't bugged, at least it wasn't as far as he knew. Maybe it was? Was this another of Rawlings' mind games again? Making him, Tom Marsden the fall guy, when Rawlings could say *'I never gave that instruction'*. Well this time he wouldn't let that happen.

He casually took off his coat, reaching inside his pocket as he turned to put it over the back of his chair, and flicked the microphone switch on.

"Okay, so by permanent Boss, I'm assuming you want me to get rid of the Green girl?"

Rawlings hesitated. This was a big step, but he needed to close the lid on any sort of connection between the Pollensa Research Centre and the Witterings Shopping Centre collapse. Since he'd found out Greg Chambers had got involved, he'd had a constant nagging at the back of his mind that this wasn't going to go away on its own.

"Yes and that includes anyone else from Chambers' team who might get in the way, but quietly and without fuss Tom. I suggest you get yourself back to Mallorca using a different passport, just in case you're being watched over here too."

He saw Marsden smile.

'Was he really some sort of psychopath?'

Marsden knew himself that he probably was a psychopath, but he wasn't smiling at what he'd been asked to do. It was because he felt that just for once he'd got one over on Rawlings. He had him on voice record on his phone. A bargaining tool, should he ever need it.

*****

"Hi Mum, I've seen Greg and I've been shopping and I'm now a very presentable son to the banker, Fiona Stevens."

"Glad you're back in one piece Sam. I'll see you soon."

He made a point of getting a cab, so that it looked like he'd just arrived from the airport.

The Savoy doorman stepped forward as the cab came to a stop. The door opened and Sam stepped out.

"May I take your luggage sir?"

He'd bought a new smart holdall and cabin trolley, abandoning his old one at the shop, much to the confusion of the shop assistant who wondered why he was getting rid of a perfectly adequate trolley for a far more expensive, but not necessarily any better, piece of equipment.

Sam smiled and nodded and breezed in through The Savoy swing doors as though he was a regular there.

"Mr Stevens? Yes, we have your reservation for you. May I take your passport sir?"

"I'm really sorry, but I dropped it somewhere in the airport lounge. I'd gone in for a quick shower and freshen up and a spot of breakfast. I rang them as soon as I knew I'd lost it and amazingly they've found it. I'm having it couriered over. Is that okay?"

The receptionist saw the amount of the bill already sitting on Fiona Stevens' account and smiled back at Sam.

"Yes, that's no problem at all Mr Stevens. We'll get your bags up to your room. I hope you have a pleasant stay."

Sam turned around, looking for his mother, Anna. He couldn't see her, so walked down past The Savoy Tea Shop in the hallway, on the right. A bizarre memory of macaroons struck him, when he'd been there once before, for an afternoon tea.

He saw her sitting on one of the sofas. He had to admit she definitely looked the part of a rich banker.

"Hello dear," she said and gave him a warm hug.

If anyone from her Makarovich follow team was looking, thought Anna, they'd just see a mother welcoming her son, which of course, was exactly what it was.

"Hello Mum, fancy meeting you here!" he grinned at her.

"Let's have some tea and you can fill me on the detail of what happened in Canada."

"Likewise with your lunch here yesterday."

To all intents and purposes, they were a mother and son having afternoon tea in Kasper's, whereas they were far more focused on what they'd be doing later that day at 5 Eaton Square, Belgravia.

They were talking in hushed tones, about how the team could gain access to Eaton Square, given the level of security that protected what's known as *'Billionaire's Row'*, when one of the Reception Team approached them.

"Excuse me Mr Stevens?"

Sam was momentarily caught off guard, before Anna interjected, "Yes, how can we help you?"

"It's Mr Stevens' passport, it's just arrived by courier."

Sam had recovered himself and took the package and opened it and flicked through it.

"Excellent, what a relief. Do you want to take it now? I'll pick it up later."

"Thank you sir, that would be appreciated."

As the member of hotel staff left, Sam couldn't help but laugh.

"First time out and I forget who I'm supposed to be. I think I need re-training Mum!"

"Just as long as you remember tonight!"

He looked at her. She had her 'game face' on and so he wasn't sure she'd seen the funny side.

"I'll be on it."

He decided against saying, *'don't worry',* since she was the professional in these circumstances and he really would need to be on his guard, so as not to let anything slip.

*****

"Martin, thank you for getting that passport through so quickly."

"No problem Greg. It might not get him through passport control, but it should be more than enough for a hotel checking-in process. Now is there anything else I can help you with?"

"As a matter of fact yes, there is. Our player has invited Anna to dinner tonight at his place."

Greg could imagine Martin at the end of the phone, already thinking through the risk strategies of dealing with this scenario.

"I see. Interesting. If I may ask Greg, what are you doing in terms of back up?"

"Sam is going in with her, as her son, an expert of money laundering, rather than banking."

"A very appropriate cover. Do you think he can pull it off?"

"Yes, he knows this stuff from his major crime days and the fact that he doesn't have to play a part with Anna, well, that can only help."

"Yes, good point, very good point."

"I've got something that may help too. We've had some detail through from our source. Apparently our player has been making a number of calls through the day and Anna should expect one more person at the table. We know this person. It's his personal financial advisor. Goes by the name of Artem Ivanov. Aged forty two, been with our man for well over ten years and seemingly trusted with his confidential financial data."

"That is helpful Martin, extremely helpful. But there is one more thing. Can you get us access to Eaton Square?"

He heard Carruthers breathe in.

"It's like Fort Knox in there. I could get you into Buckingham Palace more easily, but leave it with me. One last thing. How many people?"

"Let's say six to be on the safe side."

"Okay, but Greg," said Carruthers slowly, "we can't be having any pitched battles going on in Eaton Square."

"I know. This is just precautionary."

"Good to hear. I'll get on it. Presumably you want this by…, shall we say six o'clock this evening at the latest?"

"Perfect."

*****

"Can we go out somewhere tonight? Maybe go down into Illetas, or what about Portals Nous?" said Lily.

Terri looked at her. She could see she was getting listless again.

"What about if we go for another bike ride?" said Terri.

That wasn't cutting it with Lily. She'd had enough of bike rides. She wanted to go out, not be cooped up in the villa.

"No, it's okay, we won't bother then."

Terri could tell she wasn't happy and tried to placate her with a promise to do something the following morning.

"Yes, whatever."

Lily dismissed the idea and walked away.

*****

"Are we ready Mum?"

He'd finished getting showered and changed and had gone to her room and was waiting as she finished putting her make-up on.

"Yes, done. How do I look?"

He turned his head, then jumped up.

"Mum!"

He was having one of those moments when as a son, you suddenly realise your mum must have been an absolute stunner when she was young.

Her face fell.

"What is it? Too much? Should I change?"

"No! Mum, wow, you look amazing!"

She breathed out.

"You're sure? You're not just saying that? Look, I've been out of practice for a little while."

"Mum, shush, honestly, you're beautiful."

She flushed. It had been a while since anyone had called her beautiful and it sounded even better, hearing it from her son.

"Thank you, that makes me feel ready. You look pretty good yourself Sam Stevens," she grinned.

Sam's phone rang. He switched it to speaker phone.

"Greg, Mum's listening too."

"Okay so we're set. Martin has pulled off a small miracle to get us as close as we can inside Eaton Square," said Greg.

"That's brilliant. Okay, final thing on comms. Any last minute comms checks might be tricky. We'll do it as the car enters the Square and you'll need to tell us if you can hear us. If we can hear your response, Mum will drop her handbag on the floor."

"What if you can't?" said Greg.

"I'll have you lined up on speed dial and if you get the call, we need help, and quickly."

"Got it. Not the best back-up plan, but it'll do. Now here's another thing. We think Makarovich must be biting. The source tells us there will be another person at the table. Artem Ivanov, his personal financial advisor. We think he's the one who looks after his dirty money."

"That sounds promising. Now, the car will be here soon, so let's get this done," said Anna.

Sam heard that tone in his mum's voice again. She was in full operational mode. He could only wonder what she'd been like when she was at the very top of her game.

They took the lift downstairs and one of the doormen approached them.

"Mrs Stevens, Mr Makarovich's car is here."

They walked through the swing doors and saw a Rolls Royce Phantom. The doorman opened the car door for Anna, before moving around to the other side for Sam.

"They're moving off," said Greg, who was watching from across the other side of the road. "Tommy, Sharon, you guys in position?"

"Yes, yes," said Tommy.

"That's a yes from me too," said Sharon. "We've been given emergency access into the Square by the security teams, to deal with a mysterious water leak – I won't even ask how you managed to make that happen."

Greg smiled. Martin had let him in on a little secret. When they realised so many Russians were moving into Belgravia, the Security Services, MI5, set up a number of devices that could cause either gas leaks, electric power failures, or water leaks, all to enable them to get a team close into the Square, under the guise of emergency repair workers.

"How often have they had cause to use this?"

"Actually never, so they're very happy we're testing this, to see if it works. Let's go with the water leak shall we? It's nothing major, I mean it doesn't mean the houses don't have any water, that would cause too much of a furore around there. It's just water seeping across the road from a dummy pipe."

"Sounds good to me."

The traffic was reasonably light, so the journey didn't take long and as the car pulled into Eaton Square, Sam saw two water vans, a work tent and two men in jackets with a water company logo were walking around looking at the stream of water running across the tarmac.

He started talking to his mother about the beautiful summer evening sky. His mother responded and then they heard Tommy's voice.

"Loud and clear. Repeat, loud and clear."

The chauffeur got out and opened the door for Anna and as she stepped out, she dropped her handbag.

"Madam, allow me," said the chauffeur.

"Thank you, that's very kind," said Anna.

"Roger that," said Tommy.

45

As they walked through the front entrance they both tried to maintain a sense of calm. The place looked like a palace.

"So this is what a billionaire's house looks like," whispered Sam.

Anna had to admit, it was impressive and in an elegant, stylish way.

Oleg Makarovich appeared at one of the many sets of double doors in the lobby.

"Welcome to my house Fiona."

He stopped for a moment and looked at Sam, then back at Anna.

"Forgive me if I am making an incorrect assumption, but is this your son?"

"Yes, it is Mr Makarovich. I hope you don't mind me bringing him, he's only just flown in today and he has some particular knowledge around some of the services I think we can be of help to you with."

If he had any suspicion, Makarovich didn't show it. Instead he welcomed Sam with a firm handshake.

"Come through, come through," as he walked them into a lounge area.

"Fiona, you must I think, call me Oleg now. Here, I've got champagne again. Is that alright?"

He lifted the bottle from the ice bucket and as he poured it into some beautiful crystal glasses, Sam caught the name on the bottle, Boërl & Kroff.

'Never heard of them,' he thought. 'So presumably that makes it a very exclusive and very expensive bottle of bubbles!'

"That's perfect Oleg, thank you. Long time since I have had a glass of this," said Anna.

"You know this brand Fiona?"

"I've heard of them, but don't know a lot about them, other than they're two childhood friends aren't they?"

Sam tried to not look astonished at his mother's knowledge of champagne, but it had worked on Makarovich.

"Yes, they are. I met them when they first started back in the nineties and they now keep me well stocked in my homes."

They were on permanent transmit, so Tommy and the team outside could hear everything, as could Greg, who was sat with Martin Carruthers in his office.

"She's still very good, isn't she?" said Carruthers. "We only made a slight mention of preferred wines and champagnes on his file notes and yet, she's obviously dug deep in to that."

Greg nodded in agreement.

"It's certainly very nice Oleg," said Anna.

"Now, I want you to meet a couple of people who you will need to liaise with Fiona, because I've decided to go ahead with your proposal."

"I'm delighted to hear that," said Anna, raising her glass towards him, just as Artem Ivanov entered the room.

Sam looked across at him.

"Mr Ivanov, a pleasure to meet you," said Sam.

Ivanov paused just enough for it to register with

both Sam and Anna that he was surprised that he was known to these two bankers who he'd never heard of before.

"Artem, don't worry. I've got used to the surprises Fiona, and now her son Sam, have thrown at me. It seems they have an extraordinary intelligence network available to them."

Greg nodded to Carruthers. Makarovich really was on the back foot with what Fiona and Sam were able to suggest they knew about his business dealings.

"Please call me Artem. Mrs Stevens, it's a pleasure. Mr Makarovich has told me about the level of confidentiality you provide with Stevens Bank and I'm interested to know more."

Sam saw just a flicker of a look from his mother. Ivanov might be a much harder nut to crack than Makarovich, especially if it came down to the detail. He wasn't likely to fall for the trick she'd played on Makarovich's phone, using Anju and the fake code words.

"I'll be delighted to tell you whatever I can to be of help Artem. Let's just make sure you're not asking me to give up the very secrets that keeps Stevens Bank out of the news and away from even professional financiers like yourself."

Ivanov gave a smile to the very clear put down Fiona Stevens had just given him in front of his boss. If Makarovich now trusted this woman, then why should he risk being made to look even more foolish in front of him?

Nevertheless, he'd keep watching this woman and her son. Something didn't feel quite right, but everything Makarovich had shown him so far seemed to stack up. His boss was also very keen to exploit any new opportunities they could from Stevens. Performance was not good at the moment and they were getting pressure from the other group members to deliver better numbers.

"Come Fiona, I have not one, but actually two more people I want you to meet," said Makarovich.

He called out, *'Mikhail,'* and a smartly dressed young man in his late twenties, with wavy hair like his father, walked in.

"I'm sorry Papa, I was on a call. Mrs Stevens, a pleasure to meet you. I'm Mikhail."

It was the young man who had been at The Savoy.

"Nice to meet you Mikhail," she smiled.

Carruthers had told her to be wary of Makarovich's son. Charming, very engaging when he wanted to be, but with a ruthless streak running straight through him.

"Mikhail, hi, I'm Sam, Fiona's son."

"It's like a family gathering here isn't it. Except of course, for Ivanov," said Mikhail.

Anna and Sam saw Ivanov visibly flinch. Despite his position within Makarovich's trusted inner circle, Mikhail Makarovich had put him well and truly in his place.

The son's charm had disappeared in an instant. He could clearly turn it on, but underneath the veneer, was a coldness they could both feel.

Outside in the vans, Sharon gave a low whistle.

"I do not like the sound of him at all."

Whilst this interaction was playing out, Anna noticed a woman come to the doors and stand there, as though she was waiting to be summoned.

"Ah, Penny, yes, come, come. Fiona, Sam, this is Penny Hastings. My personal secretary for the past.., how long is it Penny?"

She knew Makarovich knew exactly how long it was. He had an eye for detail and he was just playing one of his games with all of this.

"Oh, it's well over ten years sir," said Penny. "Mrs Stevens, it's a pleasure to meet you in person. We spoke on the phone?"

"Yes of course we did Miss Hastings. You did a very good job at holding me at bay from Mr Makarovich, until that is, he was ready to talk to me."

Penny Hastings smiled at her, as she made her exit back out of the door, *'So this is the legend that is Anna Martínez and it looks like her reputation in the Service is well deserved.'*

*****

Greg realised it straight away.

"That's her isn't it Martin? Hastings is the source."

Carruthers didn't know himself, or at least not for sure, but Greenfield had said it was someone very close.

"I honestly don't know Greg, but I think you might be right."

"I don't know if this is a good or bad thing, having so many resources packed into one room. One false move..."

"I know Greg, but she's been with Makarovich for over ten years now. If Anna was the best, then Penny Hastings can't be far behind."

*****

"But this is a lot of money you're suggesting as an initial investment Mrs Stevens. What assurances can you give that you can deliver on your promises?"

The conversation had progressed over dinner and Ivanov had started asking more questions about the validity and credibility of Stevens Bank.

"Ivanov, I think you could perhaps change your tone when addressing Mrs Stevens," said Makarovich, although it seemed to Anna that this was once again, part of the show Makarovich was putting on.

"No, it's fine Oleg. I understand Artem is just looking out for your interests. He has after all, been

346

the one who has been struggling to deliver the type of performance we'd usually expect, particularly with the amount of money you're putting through a cleansing process."

It was a stinging rebuke to Ivanov regarding the profit, or rather lack of it, that he was making from cleansing the 'dirty money' and he was clearly unsettled by it.

"Ivanov, what do you have to say to that? Huh?"

This time it was Mikhail, who was adding pressure to someone who he clearly regarded as being no more than the hired help.

Ivanov tried to regain his footing in the conversation.

"So what percentage do you think you could offer then Mrs Stevens?"

"Perhaps I could answer that Artem. If you're not performing as well as you'd like, then I'd guess you may currently be paying fees of somewhere around 25%, maybe a little higher?" said Sam.

He caught Ivanov's look and knew he had him.

"Oh, so you're paying higher than that?"

Sam was trying not to overact. With Ivanov fidgeting in his seat, Sam let the silence hang in the air.

Mikhail was the first to break it.

"Papa, didn't I tell you? He's incompetent, useless and it's taken these people to come and tell us our business."

Oleg Makarovich looked at Ivanov and then nodded at his son.

"Show Artem out please Mikhail. Shall we hold desert until you come back?"

"No thank you Papa. Fiona, Sam, please excuse us."

Ivanov went to say something, but Mikhail was already at the back of him and had him in a headlock and was lifting him out of the chair. Despite a few futile attempts to resist, it was clear Ivanov wasn't a fighter and Mikhail dragged him out of the room and closed the door behind him.

It was as though nothing untoward had happened. Makarovich toyed with his wine glass whilst Anna looked to Sam.

"I'm sorry Mr Makarovich if I've overstepped the mark here? I didn't mean to imply that Artem wasn't doing his job properly."

"It's okay Sam, we've thought for a while that perhaps something wasn't right. All you did was help speed the process up. So tell me, what do you think you could offer in regard to terms?"

Sam shifted in his chair, warming to the task of getting down to business. He was about to say something when he heard a muffled cry. It sounded like Ivanov's voice. Presumably Mikhail was asking a few initial questions and not getting the responses he wanted.

"We usually operate on a sliding scale Mr Makarovich. The more you invest, the better the terms. That said, we're keen to have your business. That's why my mother asked me to come across, to help with the detail around the negotiations. I'd need to check with you Mother, but could I suggest a three year rolling contract initially? We could start Mr Makarovich on 17.5% for an initial six months, rising to 18% for a further six months as an introductory offer. After that we'd increase it by one percent a year, holding then at 20%."

"Fiona, I imagine you've had this conversation already with Sam? Are you agreeable to what he's suggesting?" said Makarovich.

Anna smiled at Sam and then across to Oleg Makarovich.

"Yes, although for those sort of figures Oleg, I need

to be seeing an initial investment of at least £500 million."

Makarovich blinked.

Anna took that as a sign that it wasn't an unreasonable sum, but that he might want to negotiate.

"Perhaps we might start at say three hundred?"

Anna had to pinch herself. She was talking about sums of money as though it was tens of thousands of pounds, rather than hundreds of millions.

"Let's call it four hundred shall we? How's that for you?"

"I like how you do business Fiona Stevens. I'm assuming you have something for me to sign?"

"Of course, Sam, perhaps you can email the paperwork to Miss Hastings?"

"Of course Mother, I'd be delighted."

"Most satisfactory. Now, please let's eat the desert my chef has prepared," said Makarovich, "and we can sign the papers afterwards."

*****

Outside in the water company vans, Sharon saw movement from the underground car park.

"Vehicle is leaving the target address. Two people inside, driver and front seat passenger."

"Now that might be Artem Ivanov being transported somewhere. He's probably in the boot," said Tommy.

"Yes, copied," said Greg, before he turned and looked at Martin Carruthers who was shaking his head.

"She's done it Greg! And she went for an extra hundred mill more than we talked about."

"She's quite something," said Greg.

"Legend!" said Carruthers.

*****

Makarovich insisted they toast the signing of the

papers with some of his finest Russian vodka.

"That would be most appropriate Oleg. I'll just get a new code for you and we can arrange the transfers," said Anna.

Moments later Anju responded and using an eight digit code, Anna opened up the Stevens Bank website on Makarovich's laptop.

"Presumably this will come from OBCR Oleg?"

"Yes, but in the future, it will come from those other banking regions, the ones you spoke about before."

"That's excellent. I think it's probably best if you make the payments in ten lots. That will help keep things more under the radar of the majority of the interested authorities. We'll put it into a composite account, but to anyone looking, it will look like ten different accounts in different names."

"I'm impressed Fiona. Let's make the toast. To many years of working together!"

"Yes, here's to a successful joint venture," toasted Anna.

With the transfers done, Makarovich called out to Penny Hastings to arrange the car to take Anna and Sam back to The Savoy.

As they said their farewells, Anna saw Penny Hastings looking at her. She wasn't sure, but was that a smile, or a perhaps a nod, that Hastings gave her?

Once back in the car, Sam and Anna made small talk on the way back to the hotel. They could hear the comments coming through on their earpieces and gathered someone from Carruthers' team had arrived, in the same water company clothing, to reinstate the dummy pipe. Then Tommy's voice came up on the comms.

"Stand down, stand down."

There followed five confirmations from the rest of the team, by which time Sam and Anna had finally got back to her hotel room. Sam closed the door behind them and let out a huge sigh.

"Mum! That was so bloody hard, keeping in role and not letting anything slip."

"You were brilliant Sam! Especially the way you got into Ivanov. That was the turning point, when I knew we had Makarovich."

"I don't fancy Ivanov's chances much."

"Does that bother you Sam?"

He thought for a moment.

"I don't think he's any sort of innocent Mum, so no, not a bit."

46

Marsden had been busy since he'd landed back in Mallorca the following day. There was still no sign of North, but he'd seen Álvarez and Finn O'Neil and he'd put a plan together to sort things out, once and for all.

It was mid-morning and already baking hot. Parked a little way up the road from the Martínez villa, he was with Álvarez, in an unremarkable silver coloured saloon, rather than his stand out, *'look at me'*, bright yellow Porsche.

The phone tracker app on Lily's phone still showed she was there and hadn't moved throughout the previous day either.

He looked across at Álvarez.

'Were his hands shaking?' he thought.

"You alright Álvarez?"

"Yes, yes, I'm fine."

But Álvarez was a long way from being fine. He didn't like what was going on and he hadn't liked the way Marsden had spoken to him. He tried to ask him why they were going to grab Lily again, but all Marsden said was that they had a few more questions for her.

"Make sure you tell me if there's any movement during the rest of the day, otherwise, we go as planned, early this evening."

*****

"Well I think that all went rather well," said Carruthers.

It was 10am and he was sat with Greg, Anna and Sam in his office.

"I think you're the master of the understatement there Martin," said Greg.

"Yes, yes, it's an excellent outcome. Plus we've also got the data analysis of Makarovich's phone coming through now, and there's some very useful information on there as well."

"Well that's that side of things nicely positioned Martin, but we still need to iron things out with Groom and put this deal to him. So we'll make that approach sometime over the next few days."

"Good. Anna, will you be staying here just in case Makarovich wants to see you for any reason?"

"Yes, I'm hoping he won't, but Tommy and Sharon will keep watch over me. Sam, you're going back to Palma aren't you? You said you'd go and see the Greens for me?"

"Yes, of course, although I think Terri and Simon have things all in hand over there. But I know they're old friends, so I'll go and do some hand holding, at least until we get things sorted over here with Rawlings and his team."

"Do we know where Marsden is at the moment Martin?" said Greg.

"We know he left Nova Scotia on his own passport and we've seen him going into the GA offices, here in London, presumably to see Rawlings. He's back in his hotel room at the moment."

"Okay, let's get going. Anna, you and I have some planning to do about how we deal with Groom. Sam, we'll see you soon. I've got Lori coming across to the

353

island for a few days next week, so tapas with Miquel sound good to you?"

Miquel was Sam's oldest friend and he ran a couple of restaurants in Llucmajor, just outside Palma. They'd all eaten there a month or so before, when he'd first met Greg, his biological father and Terri, his half-sister.

"Great idea, I'll call him and book Contrabando."

*****

Sam got the early evening BA flight out to Mallorca. It had been hot in London, but even though it was now well after ten, he could still feel the heat bouncing back off the airport tarmac, as he went down the steps from the plane and across to the airport bus.

Although there had been a bit of a delay at LHR, Simon was there to meet him, when Sam appeared through the sliding doors, at the Arrivals Terminal of Son Sant Joan Airport.

"Good to see you mate," said Simon. "I hear you've been joining in on your mum's business, being a secret squirrel."

"Ha! Yes and I think I'll stick to the straight forward stuff from now on. Way too much pressure for me. All good back here though mate?"

"Yes, although Lily is getting very skittish at being, as she says, 'held prisoner'. She's a good kid, but I don't know how much longer we can keep her boxed in."

"Hopefully not too much longer. I'll call Terri and tell her I'm here."

He tried calling, but her phone was engaged, so he left a phone message.

'It's me, your half-brother Sis. Give me a call when you've finished running your multi-national corporation for the day.'

"She's a busy girl," said Simon.

"She surely is."

*****

354

Marsden and Álvarez were back in situ outside the Martínez villa. The sun had set and they could see lights on in some of the rooms. One person had left in a car about half an hour ago.

Was this the minder? The guy had looked to Marsden as though he might be handy enough, so it was useful that he wasn't there now. That left the blonde, plus Lily and her grandparents.

Marsden felt his excitement rising, at the prospect of what lay ahead for the night.

"Well get on with it then. We haven't got all night!"

"Okay," said Álvarez.

He sent the text.

'Lily, it's me.'

She saw the text and her heart started racing. Mateo! She so wanted to talk to him, to hold him.

'Mateo, I've sooooo missed you!'

'Me too. Where are you?'

'In my bedroom. Where are you?'

'I'm outside! Terri wanted me to surprise you with a late night visit, but she said don't wake everyone up.'

He added a smiley emoji and hearts.

Lily couldn't believe Terri had set this up. She was so kind and thoughtful, but she had been since she first met her.

She quickly pushed her shoes on and quietly slipped down the stairs. She could see a light on in the front room and had a quick look through the gap in the door. It was Terri. She was on her phone.

Lily pushed the door slightly open and smiled at Terri and mouthed the words *'thank you'.*

Terri nodded back and smiled, not really understanding what Lily was saying, as she had her father on the line.

"You okay Terri?" said Greg.

"Yes, sorry, it was just Lily, she was mouthing

something at me. She was saying something, but I didn't quite catch what it was. Anyway, sorry, what were you ringing for?"

"I've just finished a call with Martin Carruthers. They've lost Marsden."

"Bloody hell! How?"

"Apparently there was a bit of a commotion at the hotel he was in. The fire alarm seems to have gone off. Martin's team saw him come out. He went to the Fire Point, but then it seems that he managed to slip away in the melee."

"Jeez! When was this Dad?"

"That's why it was a difficult call. They lost him this morning. Don't ask why they left it till now to tell us. Maybe they thought they could find him again."

"So he's not left the country?"

"Not on his own passport," said Greg.

"You thinking false passport then?"

"We need to assume that's a real possibility."

"Okay, well Sam will be back soon. Simon's just gone to pick him up."

Terri suddenly felt a shiver down her back. She realised what Lily had said. It was *'thank you'*. But what was she thanking her for?

"Oh shit! Got to go and check something Dad!"

*****

Lily had opened the front door and ran outside. She couldn't see Mateo, so she rang him.

"Where are you?"

"At the front gate. Let me in."

She put her head back inside the front door and pushed the button to open the electronic gates, then she started running down the drive to the gate.

She saw him standing there, arms open with a massive grin on his face.

"I've so missed you!" she yelled.

She threw herself into his arms. He hugged her, but it was odd. It wasn't in his usual way. She pulled away and then saw him standing behind Mateo.

She knew it was him, even without any sort of mask or balaclava on. It was his eyes and then he spoke.

"Hello Lily, it's so nice to see you again."

She screamed, but Mateo had the chloroform-filled cloth on her nose in an instant and she slumped in to his arms.

Marsden was looking up at the villa. Had they heard anything? He almost wished they had as he fingered the trigger on the pistol in his hand.

"Get her in the van. Do it now!" snarled Marsden.

*****

Terri was hoping she was wrong. That Lily saying, or rather mouthing, *'thank you'* at her, was nothing untoward. Then she heard her voice. She sounded excited, but then she heard a scream.

'What's she doing outside?'

She saw the front door was slightly ajar. Terri went outside and started walking quickly down the driveway, before she broke into a run.

This didn't feel right. The front gates were open, but there was no sign of Lily. She got to the gates. She was calling out now.

"Lily, Lily! This isn't funny. I don't know what game you're playing, but come out now please."

She heard the voice behind her.

"Oh, but it is funny, especially as I've been so wanting to meet you again."

She recognised the voice before she saw him. She pulled back, going into a fighting position, on her toes, ready to spring forward.

"Yes, that's all very good, but if you want to see your friend Lily again, you'd better come with me and quietly," said Marsden.

He was standing there, holding a handgun, with a suppressor attached, a silencer. It was pointed at her waist.

Marsden was too far away for Terri to think about lunging at him. He'd get a shot off way before she got anywhere near him.

"I can see what you're thinking Terri. It is Terri isn't it? Well, in your shoes I'd be doing the same. Working through the rationale, but to be honest, I haven't really got the time for this now. So come with me and you can keep working on some sort of plan in your little head, where you think you can rescue Lily and all will be well. Or," he paused, "stay where you are and I'll shoot you where you stand."

She saw the look in his eyes. This wasn't an idle threat. Better to stay alive and see if she could do anything once she knew where they were going. She held her hands out in submission and he pointed to the gates.

She then saw the VW van ahead of her, the same one she'd seen in Puerto Pollensa. She was still thinking of something she could do, when Marsden stepped in behind her and smashed the butt of the gun against the side of her head and watched her drop to the ground.

"I've got another one. Put her in the van too. Now let's get going."

*****

"Sam, I think something's happened. Back at the villa. I was on the phone to Terri and she said she needed to check something and she rang off."

"We'll be there in ten. Call you back."

Simon got them there in seven. Seeing the electronic front gates open immediately put Sam on edge.

He looked across at Simon.

"Stop here."

Simon nodded and they were out of the vehicle and moving forward, covering the front grounds to the villa. One left, one right.

Nothing. No discarded items, like a phone, or even a shoe. Nothing that might have been lost in any sort of a struggle.

Simon watched Sam go in the front door and then slipped in after him and waited in the lobby, with a good view of all the doors.

Sam could hear the TV in the back room. The light was on, he could see it through the cracks in the door frame.

He gently opened the door and carefully looked in.

"Sam, how lovely to see you!"

It was Helen Green. She was sat on the sofa. Geoffrey also looked up and acknowledged him with a nod.

"Good trip Sam? Terri's about somewhere."

Then Helen saw the look on Sam's face.

"Sam, what's the matter?" She gripped her husband's hand.

"We don't know, but just stay here for a moment please."

They both nodded, but he could already see the worry creasing their faces. He stepped back into the lobby.

"They don't know what's happened. Let's check upstairs, then do the gardens, but Simon, I think they might have got them both!"

They searched the rest of the house and then the rear gardens, before going back inside to see Lily's grandparents.

"I thought you said we'd be safe here!"

Helen Green was crying, shouting and shaking with shock. Her husband was doing his best to console her, but Sam could see he was equally distressed.

He tried to think of the right words, but things like,

'Don't worry, we'll get her back,' just sounded like empty promises, especially as he wasn't sure they could.

"Should we call the police?"

Sam looked across at Simon, who shook his head.

Sam made a decision.

"Not just yet Helen. We will, I promise, but Simon and I have an idea that might help us get both Lily and Terri back.

He hoped he sounded convincing, because just at that moment, he didn't have any idea as to what they were going to do.

47

Next came the phone call to Greg. Sam heard the slight crack in Greg's voice, but otherwise he went straight in to professional mode.

"You've informed the police?"

"Not yet."

Sam waited.

"What are you thinking?"

"You're on speaker phone Greg. Simon's got an idea."

Greg listened, as Simon went through the basics of a plan.

"What do you think Greg?"

Before Greg could answer, Sam saw an incoming call from Mateo Álvarez. Why was he calling?

"It's Álvarez, I'll call you back Greg."

"Mateo, this isn't a good time."

"Sam Martínez. I thought we'd meet again."

Sam felt himself go cold.

"Marsden," he whispered.

Simon looked at him, his eyes seemed to be turning a cold grey colour as Sam looked back at him.

"If you…," started Sam.

"Yes, I think we've all heard that line before, haven't we Sam? Now, just listen. You're probably expecting this, but do not call the police. If I hear a sniff of them, either at your mother's house, or anywhere where I have eyes, I can promise you that you won't see either of these two lovelies again. Just back off and await my next call."

Marsden didn't wait for an answer.

*****

"So Álvarez is part of it then!" said Simon.

"We've got to think he is, at least for now," said Sam.

"It sort of fits, as he was the one who came up to the lighthouse at Formentor. He was the distraction to take the girls for a drink and I let that bastard get in and mess with Terri's brakes."

"I need to ring Greg."

As they went into the kitchen, Sam could hear Lily's grandmother crying. He closed the door behind them and rang Greg.

"What happened?"

"We're on speaker phone Greg."

Sam told Greg about the call from Marsden on Álvarez's phone.

"Thoughts Simon?" said Greg, "And make it quick because I don't think you've got much time."

"We need to look at what we've got and not try to second guess where Marsden has taken them."

"So a covert approach to get inside the GA Research Centre up at Pollensa?" said Greg.

"I think that's the best option, our only option in fact. Marsden will also think that's where he can best defend any attempt by us to get to him."

"What about the villa where Lily said she was held?"

"Problem is Greg," said Sam, "is that we don't know where the villa is. I also reckon Marsden will feel he's got more security with the fencing and cameras around the Research Centre."

"It sounds a bit light if I'm honest guys, but I don't think you've got any other option, but to at least check it out. Now if there's nothing there Sam, you must tell the police, okay?"

"Yes, of course," said Sam. "Can you make any inroads into Rawlings? To get him to back off if he knows we're on his case."

"I'll try, but I don't hold out much hope. This seems quite a move away from the intimidation they used against people like Roger Wall. That was just bully boy tactics."

Greg went quiet for a moment.

"Sam, before you go, a quick word."

Sam didn't know why he wanted it off speaker phone, but he switched it off.

"Yes?"

"Marsden murdered Simon's brother."

Sam's head started spinning, but he couldn't give this away. Not now. That was why Greg had wanted him to take it off speaker phone.

"I take it we're sure about that?"

"Yes, confirmed by Carruthers. He was in the army, then the police. He was Tom Harris then, followed by Tom Baker. The police suspected him, but they couldn't make it stick," said Greg.

"Okay Greg, we can talk about it when we get back."

"Something up?" said Simon.

"Just something about the Makarovich deal. Didn't want to clutter things up in your head as you're planning stuff out."

Sam didn't think Simon had heard anything of what Greg had said. He hoped he hadn't because he couldn't afford for him to be distracted in anyway.

*****

Sam didn't like the idea of leaving Lily's grandparents on their own, so he rang John MacDonald.

"Mr Mac, I can't explain, but can you send a car down

to mum's house for two house guests. They're friends of her's, so you might even know them. Quick as you can please."

"Of course. Sam, this sounds serious, whatever it is that's going on. Chris is here. He says he'll come. He'll be down in....ten, fifteen minutes max."

"Thanks, that's great. Tell him, it's Geoffrey and Helen Green."

"I know them. They'll be safe here, Sam. I hope you get done what you need to, but stay safe my boy, stay safe."

"I will and thank you."

Sam waited until Chris MacDonald had collected the Greens, whilst Simon went to Terri's apartment in Portixol to collect some equipment in the Hyundai hire car.

He was waiting outside the front gates when Simon got back.

"Second time we've needed Terri's arms cache."

Sam was trying to make conversation, but Simon was having none of it.

"You ready for this?" said Simon, a cold, steely grey look in his eyes.

"I'm ready."

Simon set off, ignoring all the speed limits as they made their way up the Ma13, before turning left at the end of the motorway and heading up the Ma2200.

They skirted around Pollensa old town and set out on the road to Puerto Pollensa, towards the Research Centre. When he spotted what looked like a secluded track off the main road, not far from the Centre, Simon pulled off and parked the Hyundai behind some olive trees.

It was dark now and Simon turned off the interior car lights, so as not to draw attention to themselves from anyone driving by.

"She's certainly got quite a stash of kit in that box area Tommy built for her," said Sam.

"It'll do," said Simon, who was clearly in no mood for small talk as he passed Sam a set of black combat gear, including a ballistic bullet proof vest and night vision goggles.

The two of them changed in silence.

As they prepared their weapons, two Glocks with two spare magazines, each with nineteen cartridges, Simon looked across at Sam.

"You sure you're okay buddy?"

"Yes, I'm good," said Sam.

"I'll lead Sam, if that's okay by you?" said Simon.

"Yes, no problem, let's crack on and Simon?"

"Yes, mate?"

"We'll get her back. We'll get them both back."

Simon gave a single slow nod of the head. He then reached into the back of the Hyundai and picked up a knife, a Fairbairn–Sykes double edged close combat fighting knife and tucked it into his leg sheath.

"Okay, text Greg and see if he's made any progress with Rawlings," said Simon.

A few moments later, Sam's phone flashed.

"No luck with Rawlings. He's getting *'unobtainable'* on the phone number Carruthers gave him."

"We tried. Right, let's get going."

48

Álvarez felt his body tighten as Marsden started to goad him again. He'd been winding him up all the way from the Martínez villa and hadn't let up, even when they'd got to the Research Centre and carried the two unconscious women from the van, into one of the basement rooms.

"Come on lover boy, let's go down and see if they've woken up yet?"

"Look Marsden, I've helped you all the way so far, but I'm warning you, don't push me."

Álvarez stood up tall. He was about two, or three, inches taller than Marsden and he made a point of looking down at him.

Marsden saw the look and didn't take his eyes off him, even as he pulled back his right fist and drove it hard into Álvarez's stomach.

Álvarez sucked his breath in hard and tried to steady himself, but he fell on one knee, before Marsden grabbed him by his hair and pushed the barrel of his gun hard up against his nose.

"Listen here lover boy," again the sneer in the voice. "Do not mess with me, or there'll be three, not two bodies in there by the time I'm finished."

"I thought…, I just thought you were going to frighten her again."

"Really? More like you convinced yourself that's what I was going to do. But you still don't mind getting your nice fat pay cheque from Rawlings do you? Not to mention your little side benefits from your girly. Now stop your whining and just get down there and open the bloody door."

Álvarez got up and Marsden motioned to him, with the gun, to move towards the stairs. The rest of the offices were empty, except for the late night security guard and the analyst, Finn O'Neil, who was in one of the offices somewhere, checking there were no remaining incriminating files on the Centre's stand-alone server.

As they got to the room down in the basement, Marsden cursed when he remembered there was no keyhole in the door. He'd have to open it blind. He took the silencer from his pocket and screwed it back onto the gun. He pushed Álvarez in front of him.

"Open it."

Álvarez unlocked it and slowly pushed the door in. Both women were on the floor where they'd left them, still out cold, or at least they looked like they were.

"Wakey, wakey you two," said Marsden. "Come on, I said, wake up!"

He lashed out at Terri, catching her on her thigh with a heavy kick. She grunted and slowly opened her eyes.

"Well, well, hello there Terri. It is Terri isn't it? Go and see to the other one lover boy."

Álvarez knelt down by Lily.

"Lily, wake up, you need to wake up," he said gently.

She stirred, hearing his soft voice, but when she looked up, she saw Marsden and flinched. She looked back at Álvarez.

"Mateo, how could you? How could you? I thought… I don't know what I thought. You bastard, you complete and utter bastard."

"Wow, you've got a mouth on you Lily," said Marsden. "Can't you see your lover boy actually started to feel something for you."

She saw the look on Álvarez's face.

"See, it's true! I knew it. I damn well knew it. You soft piece of shit. Well, I can't trust you now, can I?"

Marsden brought his gun up level and pointed it first at Álvarez, before moving it across to Lily.

"No, don't, you can't…" said Álvarez who started to move towards Marsden.

He never finished what he was going to say. Marsden fired two shots, one to the chest and one to the head.

Lily screamed and Terri grabbed her, to stop her rushing at Marsden.

"Now you two girls make yourself comfortable and I'll be back in a minute. And no tricks from you Aussie girl, otherwise I'll make it harder on Lily here and you wouldn't want that would you?"

Marsden slammed the door shut behind him and Terri felt Lily struggling with her. She let go of her and she dropped to her knees and cradled him in her arms.

"You stupid, stupid boy!"

Terri checked Álvarez, but didn't need to look any further after seeing the two gunshot wounds.

"He's gone babe," said Terri.

She could see the tears streaming down Lily's face and a look of resignation was flooding into her eyes.

"He's going to kill us isn't he? But first he's going to…" Her words tailed off.

Terri was gently feeling her head, where Marsden had pistol whipped her. She saw only a little blood on her fingers, so the gash wasn't too bad, but the pain was excruciating, but worse still, as Lily's words sunk in, she could feel her own body starting to shake.

'Hold it together girl!'

Fear. She recognised the feeling. When it gets into your body and you can't seem to stop it. It's like a drug rushing through your veins.

'Whoa now Theresa Jane Anderson. Let's just remember who we are shall we?'

They might have only been words in her head, but somehow, she felt them bring back memories of Iraq. Of going out on patrol and not knowing if you'd make it back.

'So, if we're not going to get out of this, we'll make bloody sure Marsden, or whoever he sends, doesn't get it easy.'

She needed to do something, to shake the fear. She needed to plan some sort of response, to give her and Lily something to do.

She gently shook Lily and waited for the explosion of emotion. But strangely, it didn't come. Lily came too gradually and slowly lifted herself up.

"What am I supposed to think of him Terri? I trusted him. I thought he loved me!"

She let Lily speak, whilst she kept looking around the room for something, anything that might give her some sort of edge to face Marsden.

"I mean, he's the reason I'm here isn't he? He set me up didn't he? The meeting in Tast, the kidnap? They knew where I'd be going. Then there was the lighthouse. You could have died Terri! He was just pretending that he..."

"I know, but...," started Terri, but she stopped, taken aback by the way Lily then reacted.

"Shit Terri, what the hell are we going to do?"

"Well, you've summed it up very nicely Lily. We are indeed in the shit, but it looks like you've still some fight inside you," said Terri with a smile.

Lily looked at her, her face taut and strained.

"Yes, I bloody have!" she said. "So what are we going to do?"

"We're going to see about sorting out this mess we're in, okay?" said Terri.

Lily nodded to her and then Terri started looking around the room again. Where were they for a start? It was cold in the room, so they must be well away from the heat from the daytime Mallorcan sun, possibly a basement? It all looked too modern to be a finca, so she guessed they were at the Research Centre.

"Is this the Research Centre?"

"I've never been down here, but by the general look of it, I think so," said Lily.

There wasn't much in there. Some storage shelves were screwed to wall with a few boxes on them and an empty water container, one of those 20 litre ones, the sort you have on top of water dispensers. There was a ceiling light, with some sort of thick plastic, or perspex cover, but nothing was jumping out at her as being anything near useful.

Terri tried not to show any sign of disappointment to Lily. If she was in some sort of film, then there would probably be something she could unscrew the storage shelves with, to make into a weapon, or she could fill the container with something and use it as a club to knock Marsden out with.

'Hell's teeth,' she thought, 'I'm rambling.'

"Stop," she said and realised she'd said it out aloud.

"There's nothing here to use, is there?" said Lily.

But she didn't say it in a defeatist way, which struck Terri as more than just a bit odd.

"Look, I'm not giving up Terri, but you need to know that since they took me, I've felt, well…, dead."

Terri started to say something.

"No, let me go on, please," said Lily.

"Marsden promised to cut my grandparents into pieces if I said anything about the UFDry30. What he, in fact none of them knew, was that I didn't really know anything about the damn file. I've been living in what seems like some sort of permanent nightmare with no end in sight. So, now I have a chance, even if it's just a small one to get out of this hell. And, if I don't, then.....well, I don't want to go back to a living nightmare. I just wanted you to know this."

Terri had listened and watched her as she spoke.

"Okay my girl. This guy has now got a fight on his hands and the good thing is that he thinks it will come from me. That's our advantage Lily, do you see where I'm coming from?"

Lily nodded.

"Marsden will expect me to attack and may well not even be looking at you. So if you're up for this Lily, then you need to be the one who is going to make the first strike to distract him," said Terri.

She saw Lily smile for the first time in some while.

49

Sam took one last look at where they'd left the Hyundai. It wasn't ideal cover from the road, but it was the best they could do.

He waited for his eyes to adjust to the light as he switched on his night vision goggles. He was now in a world of green. Terri had chosen well. This was good kit. Maybe not up to full military capability, but good enough for 200 metres of pretty clear vision. Sam had trained with this type of gear when he was a firearms officer in the Met Police, so it didn't take him long to get accustomed to how the world now looked before him.

Simon checked their comms and went over the map of the area one last time before they set off. They worked their way around to the right, keeping well out of the way of the huge Global Aggregates illuminated sign on top of the building. Straying too close to that would play havoc with their night vision googles.

The darkness of the night was their friend now and they made quick time in reaching the fence perimeter of the Research Centre.

"Any sign of any sort of electronics?" said Sam.

"Hard to tell. I can't see anything, but it doesn't mean it's not there. Let's take a look up and down the fence and see what we find."

They split up and Sam went left, back in the direction of the Pollensa road. This didn't look like it was a high-tech defensive type of fencing, but it was still worth taking a few minutes to make sure they weren't going to go activating any sort of alarm. He checked the next three fence posts, slowly working his way up and down the post, looking for any sign of alarm wiring, or infra-red beam transmitters.

"Nothing on the three I've checked Simon."

"Me neither," said Simon, as he started to cut the fence. "I wish we had Tommy here with his drone though, so he could take a look at our way in. There's a lot of open ground to cover Sam and we're sitting ducks when we go out there."

"I know, but we've got no other option. We could split up, but if they've got some sort of movement sensitive lighting, that will light it up like Wembley Stadium, then we'd be stuffed anyway."

"Good point," said Simon, who took one more look up towards the Research Centre. "Sod it. We're going in!"

*****

They went through the hole they'd made in the fencing and then crouched down once more. The night goggles were lighting up the ground in front of them. It was like a green haze, almost as light as day. Simon stepped forward, keeping a crouching position, but moving quickly across the open ground.

Sam picked up on Simon's direction of travel. They were heading towards a side door to the right hand side of the building, partly protected with cover from a large olive tree. That confirmed Sam's thinking that security wouldn't be too high here, because otherwise that tree would have been long gone. No Head of Security worth their salt would want any obstruction to the line of sight of a CCTV system.

As for any CCTV cameras? Well, they were committed now. Sam guessed it was around 180-200 metres to the building. Running, whilst trying to maintain some sort of crouching position was slowing them down. After thirty metres there had been no sudden explosion of security lighting and no apparent movement, from what they could see, from inside the building.

"Simon, let's just shift it," said Sam, as he stretched out and ran past Simon, who got the message and soon joined him at a full sprint.

They covered the remaining ground quickly, stopping at the olive tree.

"Okay, first part done. Maybe we've got away with it. What do you think?" said Simon.

"No point hanging around to see. Let's just get in and start looking for them," said Sam.

He checked the door. It was bound to be alarmed in some form or other and Marsden would probably be expecting them.

"Wait!" said Simon. "First sign that anyone knows we're here and Terri's going to be in real trouble, not to mention Lily, if she's still alive. Stay here and I'll go and check the back. If this place is just an office block like we think it is, then maybe someone has done the usual and left a back door open. It's a long shot, but hey, someone nearly always does it, to let some air in, or to go out for a smoke."

He went past the door and made his way around to the back of the building. The further he went, the more shadow he found. Another clear sign that there was nothing particularly precious being protected in the building.

He was almost at the back now. He stopped. He'd heard something, a noise, coming from not far away, just ahead of him. He edged forward to the corner of the building and quickly glanced around and immediately reeled back, blinded by white light in his eyes. He flipped the night goggles up and looked again.

"Bingo!"

A door was open! Light was spilling out into the night. The noise....it was music, some sort of Spanish pop song. Another voice, someone was joining in.

'Don't give up your day job amigo,' thought Simon.

"Sam, contact made. I've got a pub singer back here, but we've also got an open door."

"On my way."

50

Marsden was sitting in his office at the Research Centre. He was still annoyed that Álvarez had messed things up. He also knew Rawlings wouldn't be happy with losing Álvarez, but who could have foreseen the bloody idiot falling in love with the girl and then trying to save her.

Then there was the Aussie girl.

"Well she'll pay for that look she gave me outside Abaco, I'll make sure of that," he said out aloud.

Hmm, what to choose to help make her his party girl for the night? He went across and unlocked a filing cabinet. Inside was an array of drugs, mostly barbiturates of some sort. He picked up a phial of Rohypnol, one of the date-rape drugs. Whilst he sometimes also used GHB, Gamma-Hydroxybutyric acid, both worked well enough when he didn't want them to remember anything, although that wasn't something he needed to worry about tonight, because both women would be dead by morning.

But it was fast working, so he opened the syringe pouch and secured the phial and two syringes in the elasticated loops and zipped up the pouch. It would be time soon enough, to have some fun, but first, he needed to find Finn O'Neil.

"Okay Lily, let's go through this one last time," said Terri, after they'd worked through what they were going to do.

She saw Lily was standing tall. A calmness had come across her. But she knew she'd been subjected to a number of different drugs in the past week, so just hoped this wouldn't have any sort of impact on Lily's ability to think straight at the moment. She listened as Lily spoke.

"So we know Marsden's not stupid. He's not going to just stroll in. But we're going to have to make a judgement call that next time he comes in, he's now going to be on his own. He'll be thinking that the only threat will come from you, because...," she paused, "he's had a pretty good go at knocking all the fight out of me."

Terri nodded, "Go on."

"He'll be armed. With the gun which he used to ....." She looked down at Álvarez.

"In which hand?" said Terri. She didn't want Lily dwelling on what had happened to Mateo.

"I was coming to that," said Lily.

Terri detected a slight look of..., what? Was that disappointment, maybe frustration, because she'd interrupted her? *'Oh man, this girl's definitely still got some fight in her!'*

"This is good Lily," said Terri and she saw the slight smile again.

"His right. He had the gun in his right hand when he shot Mateo."

"Yes, he did," said Terri.

"I'll be standing here when he comes through the door."

Lily went and stood to the right of the door, facing it. They knew which way it opened – as they faced it, it swung back to their left.

"He'll come through the door and I'll be standing still, staring ahead, like a zombie. He'll see you lying on the floor and I'll tell him you've collapsed again and that I think it's your head injury."

She saw something in Lily's face. Uncertainty.

"Good girl. But what's up?"

"It's that last bit Terri, it's a pretty big ask for him to believe you've collapsed again because of being hit over the head a few hours ago," said Lily.

"Yes, you're right, but it can happen, I've seen it. Besides, I can't think of another way we can get any sort of element of surprise."

Terri got down on the floor.

"I'll be lying down like this, feet towards him and facing you. What I need you to do is to distract him somehow, scream or lunge at him, just enough to get him to turn forty-five degrees or so towards you."

"And bosh, you take his legs away with a lunging kick," added Lily. Again, Terri saw her smile.

"Well it's not great, but it's a damn site better than sitting here waiting for him to decide when and how he wants to kill us," said Terri. "Now, another unknown is when he's going to come down, so here's an idea."

Lily listened, nodded and took up her position. Then she started to scream. Terri heard and felt the emotion pouring out of Lily. This was no pretend scream and it made the hairs, on the back of her neck, stand on end.

'Oh my God,' Terri thought, 'this girl is really hurting.'

She blocked the noise from her head and focused on what was going to happen next. She lay in position. Lying still, 'set', like a sprinter on the blocks, but waiting for the noise of the door to get 'ready', before the explosive kick she would need to take his legs away and give her at least some sort of edge to get to disarm him.

Even if this initial attack went to plan, she knew Marsden would be no easy push over, not like the guy on the plane, that was for sure. If it came to it, she'd go down fighting. That was all she had in her mind. Better that than anything else that bastard might dream up for them. Again, she felt a slight shudder in her body.

"Breathe."

"I am," said Lily.

"Good, just checking," said Terri, forcing a grin. She hadn't realised she'd said it out aloud.

'Relax your body.' That's what Simon would say. Another half-smile. I bet he's worried sick about me.

'What? Why the hell am I thinking about Simon, and not my Dad, or Sam, or Tommy?'

She pushed her shoulders back and looked at Lily, who was standing stock still, but sobbing quietly before letting out another scream from deep inside.

'Focus. All that other stuff will have to wait,' she thought.

Terri closed her eyes, almost shut. She was breathing slowly, relying on her sniper training, box breathing they called it, four seconds to inhale, four to hold, four to exhale. She felt her body regain control. She was ready.

*****

O'Neil was still in his office at his keyboard when he looked up to see Marsden.

"Any issues?"

"No, it's all okay. I'll have it all sorted and cleaned up by the morning."

"Where's Álvarez? You left him down there?" said Finn.

"In a manner of speaking. He's dead."

"What?"

O'Neil couldn't believe what he'd just heard Marsden say.

"He changed sides and got in my way."

"What do you mean? Changed sides? Bloody hell Marsden! What the hell have you done? I know Rawlings told you to tidy things up, but we didn't need a blood bath," said Finn.

"Look, he was trying to protect the girl. Bloody idiot, he's really messed things up now," said Marsden.

"He! He! You're the one who has messed things up Marsden."

Finn O'Neil paused. He knew what Marsden was like. He was useful to Rawlings, but now it looked like he was becoming a liability.

"Rawlings is not going to like this," he said slowly.

"I don't suppose he will, but he's not here and we are," said Marsden.

"Where are you going now Tom?"

"I've going back to the basement. To check on the Green girl and her friend," said Marsden.

O'Neil knew Marsden was a sexual predator, so guessed what he might have in mind for the two women.

"What are you intending to do Tom?" he said slowly.

"Never you mind mate," said Marsden and patted his syringe case.

"Look Tom...," started Finn.

"Don't 'Look Tom' me. This has nothing to do with you. I've been given a job to do by Rawlings and I'll do it anyway I want. You stick with your data analysis and just stay out of my way and I'll stay out of yours," said Marsden.

Finn O'Neil thought for a moment. This was already one hell of a mess. He hadn't agreed with Rawlings giving Marsden the go-ahead for a permanent solution for the Green girl, let alone the other woman and now, Álvarez was dead too.

O'Neil wasn't so caring as to be worried about what

Marsden was planning to do with the women. But he was concerned about the overall situation and the impact of three more deaths on top of that of Kevin Cox.

He tried again.

"Tom, I'm just trying to look at what the best option might be here, you know, for us to get out of what seems to be an ever-worsening situation."

"Oh, stop with your officer management talk Finn…. *'an ever-worsening situation'*. I didn't intend to bloody kill him. Things just got out of hand and…."

"And? And what Tom?" shouted Finn. "I've got to call this in. Don't do anything except check they are both okay, do you understand me?"

Marsden shook his head. Typical sodding officer, trying to order me about, when he has no bloody authority over me.

"Tom? Did you hear me?" said Finn.

'Yes, I heard you. Yes, I understood you. Am I going to take any notice? No!' thought Marsden, but instead said, "Yes, absolutely, I'll see you soon."

Finn heard the tone in Marsden's voice. This was getting out of hand.

"I'm calling Rawlings," said O'Neil.

"Good for you, I'll be in the basement, doing the dirty work."

*****

Rawlings picked his phone straight away.

"Boss, we've got a problem here," said O'Neil.

"What's up Finn?" said Rawlings.

"Álvarez is dead," said Finn.

Rawlings sat up bolt upright.

"What the…?"

"It was Marsden, Boss. He said Mateo changed sides and tried to protect the Green girl."

Finn went to continue, when Rawlings interrupted.

"But why kill him?"

"I don't know, but he's got the other girl in there too."

"What other girl Finn!" bawled Rawlings.

"The Aussie, the one who's connected to that bloke you know from 3R."

As he waited for Rawlings to say something, he got up and walked across to the window. He could see a shaft of light shining out onto the pathway. *'That bloody security guard has got that damn door open again.'*

He was about to start for the stairs to go down and bawl the guy out again, when he saw a shadow outside. The shadow moved slightly.

'Was that the tree? It shouldn't be there in the first place.'

Again, a slight movement. Was it a shadow? Or maybe it was the tree? It was to the right side of the building, so it might even be that idiot, Gómez, coming back in after a smoke.

"Finn, I need you to sort out Marsden," said Rawlings. "Wait till he comes....."

Rawlings didn't get a chance to finish his sentence.

"Boss, I've got company," said Finn, as he saw a shape below, someone dressed in black, moving quickly from the corner of the building before stopping by the open door. A few seconds later a second shape, again in black, ran along the side of the building before stopping by the first shadow.

"Get out of there now Finn. Regroup outside and wait to see what happens. Answer me this, did those women see you?"

"No, they didn't, but they've seen Marsden."

"Well if he gets rid of those two women, then maybe, just maybe, he might get us out of the shit he's got us into," said Rawlings. "Now go!"

51

Marsden was still smarting from what Finn O'Neil had said to him. He was muttering to himself and he could feel the tension and stress building in his body.

But as he neared the door, he started to smile. He wanted that blonde, Terri. Yes, she'd try and fight, but she'd give in, just like all the others once the Rohypnol kicked in. He was going to have some fun with her, whether she liked it or not.

'What the hell was that noise?'

It sounded like some tortured animal. He took his pistol out from his waist band. It still had the silencer attached.

Lily was breathing slowly and evenly. On every release of breath, she uttered a deep wrenching scream that started at the bottom of her chest and grew in volume and intensity as it left her mouth.

Terri lay still on the ground, watching Lily's every move. She had seen the explosive noise erupt from her body as she started to scream, but she could see now that Lily's chest was moving in a slow rhythmical way.

'My God, she's got this under control,' thought Terri.

Then they both heard a noise at the door, the key being turned. This had to be him.

Marsden unlocked the door to Room B46 and pushed the door inwards and stood in the doorway.

He could see the Green girl was looking to one side, standing absolutely still and she was screaming at the top of her voice. He quickly glanced down at the blonde. She was flat out on the floor, head to one side.

'Why is she lying down there?'

But that noise! He turned to shut the Green girl up, bringing the gun with him as he turned.

It was enough!

Terri had been poised and ready to throw her body into a violent kick at the back of Marsden's legs. It worked and she almost lifted him off the floor, as she kicked his legs from under him.

He arched backwards as he lost his balance and started going to ground.

"Run Lily, run!" shouted Terri, as she tried to turn and attack Marsden.

But as he fell back, Marsden was able to flip his body to the right, to where Terri was trying to spin away. She saw too late, that he was still holding the gun.

He smiled at her as he pulled the trigger.

*****

Simon stepped out of the shadows and walked quickly towards the open door. There was no way to check for potential risks. He flipped his night goggles up, to avoid being blinded by the office lights, and went in with his Glock in hand, with Sam following immediately behind.

Gómez, the security guard, saw something move in his peripheral vision. It was to his right, but by the time he'd turned, Simon was on him and had him in a headlock.

"¿Hablas inglés amigo?" said Simon. "Do you speak English?"

"A little."

"Good, you won't need much. Where are the women?"

Gómez looked away.

"I don't know nothing about any women, Señor," said Gómez.

"Wrong answer amigo. My friend here, won't give you any more chances after this," said Sam.

At that, Simon rolled his shoulders slightly, enough to turn Gómez's neck and start to cut off his air supply.

"Now, last chance. Where are the women?" said Sam.

The guard started to wave his arms around, as though this would help him breathe. His face was contorting as he tried to force non-existent air into his lungs.

Simon just stood there, holding the man, who other than thrashing his arms around, was unable to move, despite his evermore desperate efforts.

"I think he may be trying to tell us something," said Sam.

Simon released the guard, who fell to the floor, gasping for air.

"I saw something on the CCTV. That's all. He took them from the carpark. They were in a van I think. He took them, with another man, into the basement. It was Marsden, the crazy one. That's all I know, I swear," at which point Gómez switched back into Spanish and started cursing Marsden and saying he should never have taken this job.

"Amigo!" said Simon. "Shut up!"

Gómez got the message and then as he saw Simon come towards him again, he cowered back down on the ground.

"I'm not going to kill you amigo, so get up and sit in your chair."

Gómez scrambled off the floor and into his chair. He sat passively as Sam applied plasti-cuffs to his wrists and ankles.

"Okay, one last question, this place looks like it's got a big basement. Where do you think he's keeping them?" said Simon.

"There's a room down there, where none of us are allowed to go. B46, that's the number, B46 Señor."

"Good, thank you. Got a gag of some sort mate?"

"No, can't find anything," said Sam.

"Not a problem," said Simon, drawing his Glock and hitting the guard across the side of the head, even before Gómez had a chance to react. "That should keep him out of it for a bit."

They found the stairwell to the basement and started to make their way down, just at the same time that Finn O'Neil was letting himself out of a side door on the ground floor, where he headed for one of the pool cars, a Hyundai Sante Fe. He took one last look at the building, before getting in and driving slowly away down the main driveway.

*****

Terri felt the pain erupt inside her, almost before the impact rocked her entire body. Marsden picked himself up and looked out the door, but Lily was gone.

"I'll get to her later, once I've finished with you," sneered Marsden.

Terri was trying to move, but couldn't get her body to engage and do what her brain was trying to tell it.

"You think you're so smart, but it didn't work, did it Terri? Your stupid little plan. All you have managed to do is make this so much harder for yourself. Okay, so this is how it's going to play out," he paused, as he took the syringe pouch out of his pocket and laid it out on one of the shelves.

"You've no doubt heard of Rohypnol?"

He didn't wait for an answer.

"Now whilst you're losing blood, the drug is going to make you start to lose all sense of what's going on. But don't worry, because by the time I've finished with you, you won't even remember what I've done and of course, then you'll be dead."

She could just about hear his matter of fact voice, but she was starting to lose consciousness too. The bullet had gone into her side, just under her chest, but this did not feel good. Not good at all.

'Don't give up Terri girl, fight this! The boys must be coming for you, please God they are.'

She could hear herself rambling.

"This is not good, not good, not good! Simon, where are you?"

"Now then, just relax and this will help," said Marsden, as he slipped the syringe into her arm.

His voice sounded caring, calming, she thought, but the drug was already starting to take effect.

'No, No, No! Do not go under. You need to fight this...'

She didn't know now if she was talking out aloud, or just thinking these words. The pain in the side of her chest was starting to feel better though.

'Oh God, that's not good either! Feel the pain, feel the pain!'

"There now, that probably feels a lot better doesn't it?" said Marsden.

She could hear him more clearly now, but she was pretty much defenceless now and she found herself just nodding. It even seemed like he was smiling at her. She felt his hands tugging at her. She knew what was happening, he was trying to get her clothes off. She tried to move her hands, to do something, but she couldn't seem to get her body to do anything to respond, to fight him.

Marsden put his gun down. The drug was working.

He could see she was now almost smiling and he was getting more and more excited as he took her clothes off, so he ignored Lily. The entire building was on an electronic lock, so she couldn't escape, so he'd find her later and deal with her then.

Lily had run along the corridor and up the first flight of stairs and straight into Simon and Sam. She was surprised at how calm she was, as she quickly told them what had happened and that Terri had told her to run.

Simon flew down the rest of the stairs and as he got to the open door of B46, he took a quick look inside. Marsden had his back to him and was standing over Terri.

Simon banged his fist against the side of the door and as Marsden spun around, Simon didn't hesitate and shot him in the right thigh. Marsden fell to the floor and looked down at his leg, seeing blood slowly seeping out around the wound.

He turned and forced a smile through the pain at Simon.

"Are you Simon then mate? She was asking after you. You two got a thing going have you?"

Sam had caught up by now and saw Marsden on the floor, holding his thigh.

"Cover him," said Simon.

Sam stood over Marsden, with his Glock pointed at his head, whilst Simon bent down to tend to Terri. He carefully picked away her clothing from around her wound. He could tell that it wasn't good. She was still losing a lot of blood. He took a field dressing from his leg pocket and applied it carefully and then held it firmly in place, trying to stem the flow.

"You need to come through this Terri," he whispered to her, as he pulled her to him and held her in his arms.

"Hmm, hello Simon, I knew you'd come. Knew you'd

rescue me, my hero. I love you," said Terri.

"Ah, such a lovely story," said Marsden, trying to taunt them.

Sam spoke, "It's right isn't it Marsden, that you've had a number of different names and careers? First the army, then the police? But you've always had to move on because you're always leaving some shit behind you."

"No law against changing your name Met Boy."

"No, and I suppose it helps when you can literally get away with murder."

Sam saw Simon was listening.

"So was it Tom Harris in the army and then Tom Baker for the police, or was it the other way around?"

"What does it matter to you?"

"One of the people you've hurt over the years was a PC Jim Barnes wasn't it?"

Sam saw Simon's mouth twitch, just a fraction.

"Listen, you're not a copper now Martínez, so cut all the crap. They couldn't pin anything on me about that shit Barnes and you can't start now."

"Sam, maybe best if you go and check on Lily?" said Simon.

"Sure?"

"Hundred percent mate. And Sam…, thank you."

Marsden eyes were flashing back and forth between the two of them now.

"What's going on? Martínez! Don't leave me. Why were you asking those questions?"

It hit him then. As Sam left the room, Marsden stared at the man left in the room with him.

"Simon Barnes?"

He ignored the question, but looked directly at Marsden.

"I've got a message from my brother's wife."

Marsden looked at him, concern spreading over his

face.

"Look, Barnes, I'm unarmed! Isn't this the bit, you know, where you put your gun down and we fight it out?"

"No," said Simon, as he shot him in the forehead. "That only happens in films."

Marsden was dead before he hit the floor.

52

At least the Rohypnol was keeping the pain away from her, but it was also releasing all her inhibitions.

"Simon, don't leave me, not ever. Just tell me you love me too."

He didn't know if she was delirious, or if she really meant all of this, but he knew he did.

"I love you too Terri, always have, always will do, but I've never had the balls to tell you."

"I'm glad you told me now," she said. She squirmed as her body was reacting to the gunshot wound. "Am I going to make it?"

"I hope so my love, I hope so."

"Don't flower it up then mate," said Terri.

He kissed her on the cheek, on the forehead and stroked her head and her hair.

"Try to stay with me, please stay with me," he said, as tears streamed down his face.

Simon hadn't seen Sam come back into the room behind him, so didn't know how long he'd been there.

"Simon, I've called 112 and an ambulance is on its way."

"Great. Be good if it gets here soon."

Sam just looked at him, trying to get a sense of how

she was doing.

Simon shook his head and mouthed, "Not great."

"What else can I do?" said Lily, who had come back down the stairs.

"Keep applying pressure and checking the field bandage," said Simon.

They all kept at it. Taking turns to hold Terri's hand and talk to her, but always applying steady pressure to the wound.

Lily went in search of anything she could find to help make Terri more comfortable. She found some seat cushions and sofa throws, but when she came back, she could feel Terri's body was starting to feel cold to touch, so she covered her with the throws.

"Come on Terri," she said soothingly. "We've got all those plans we talked about. You're going to come with me for a night out at Bar Bonys. We'll have great fun. You've got to try some of the cocktails. You'll love it."

Tears were in her eyes, but she kept her voice calm and soothing.

"Keep talking to her Lily. She'll be able to hear you and it will be helping," said Sam.

Lily spoke softly and gently, keeping up a constant one-way conversation about the things the two girls would get to do.

"Where's the ambulance Sam?" said Simon, his voice getting increasingly tense.

"It's coming mate…., but I've got an idea, but I need to check the rest of the building as well. Are you okay here?"

Simon looked up and nodded, his Glock by his side.

*****

Sam ran up the stairs to get to where he knew he'd have a far better signal. He flicked through his contacts. There!

He rang the number and prayed it would be

answered.

"Sam! ¿Qué tal amigo? What's up my friend?" said Johannes.

"I can't explain now, but are you still in the office? I remember you said you had a load of admin you were going to do this week?"

"You've got a good memory Sam and yes, I'm still here."

"Thank God, I've got an emergency on the go mate. Can you get up to Pollensa and quickly? I've got a friend with a bad gunshot wound and the ambo is going to take ages?"

Johannes started to run towards the door.

"Keep talking Sam."

He gave Johannes the location and suggested the carpark as a landing area.

"It's empty mate, so you shouldn't have a problem landing."

Sam hadn't known him long, but they'd met at an island business development event and had got on really well. Johannes was spreading the word about HeliXperiences, a helicopter tour business and they'd later had a drink in Bar 13%. Just in passing Johannes mentioned he had a load of admin work to do the following week, so he was going to be working late in the office at Aeródromo Son Bonet.

"Bloody good job I was here amigo. I'm on my way Sam, be as quick as I can. ETA is thirty five minutes, maybe thirty, but I'll call again once I get the go ahead from Air Traffic Control to take off."

"Man, you might just be a life saver," said Sam.

*****

Sam went and checked the guard. He was still out cold. The offices were open plan, with just a few individual offices each side of the room, so it didn't take long to see there was no one else there. He then went to the main entrance, to the carpark, to make sure there was space to land a helicopter.

He noticed a car had gone. He'd definitely seen two as they'd been covering the ground from the fence up to the building. They were both SUV types and there was just the one there now. He ran back inside and roused the guard. He needed a bit of persuasion, but he eventually started to come around.

"I don't know anymore, I told you."

"There's a car missing from out the front," said Sam. "Who else was here?"

The guard was still groggy, but after a moment, Sam saw he was obviously trying to get his thoughts together.

"That would have been Señor O'Neil. He's one of the specialists from London. His office is on the second floor."

"What number?"

"209, it's on this side of the building," said the guard.

Sam left him tied to the chair and ran up the stairs to the next floor. The lighting was movement sensitive, so as soon as he stepped into the main room, the lights came on and he saw the office directly in front of him.

The door was open and it was in darkness. A quick look confirmed O'Neil had gone.

'Where's he gone then?' he thought.

He parked those thoughts. He needed to ring Greg. He knew there was nothing Greg could do, but he'd want to know what had happened to Terri.

*****

Greg had gone to see Anna at The Savoy for a catch up over a drink in the Beaufort Bar. She'd seen him smile as he'd seen who was calling when his phone rang. But then his expression changed suddenly.

"Tell me Sam, will she make it?" said Greg softly, struggling to get the words out.

Anna didn't need to know anymore. She couldn't hear what Sam said, but Greg's response was enough to tell her that things were not good.

She heard Greg give a few non-committal grunts before he said, "Please look after her Sam. I'll be out just as soon as I can get a flight."

He looked at her as he put the phone down.

"What do we need to do?" said Anna, as she wrapped her arms around him.

He forced a smile. She was always calm in a crisis.

"I need to get out to be with her, but we need to finish this here with Makarovich...," his words trailed off.

She reached for her phone.

"I can do this. Now tell me what's happened as I find you a flight."

*****

"Okay, I've got a late night flight here. It leaves in a few hours, Luton direct to Palma. I'll call Tommy and then let's go and get your bag and get you to the airport," said Anna.

"It is the senior management who must bear total responsibility," muttered Greg.

"What's that?" said Anna.

"Just something John MacDonald said."

53

It was a good way past midnight when Anna hugged Greg and left him to walk through security at Luton Airport. He turned at the last moment and gave her a half smile. Anna could see how much he was hurting.

It didn't matter that his daughter was in her thirties and a trained and experienced combat soldier. She was still his little girl and he hadn't been there to look after her.

Anna understood what he was feeling, as illogical as it all was. She'd worried about Sam when he joined the police and she wasn't sure if it helped, or not, when he stopped telling her about what he was doing at work.

She walked back outside to where Tommy was waiting in the car.

"Is he okay Anna?"

"Pretty shaken up, but I think he feels better now he's on his way over there. Right we'd better get back too Tommy."

As he pulled away from the parking lane, she rang Sam.

"Hi Mum, how's Greg?"

"Worried sick, but putting a brave face on it. He's just gone through security. I'm with Tommy. We've just dropped him off at Luton, so he's coming in on Easyjet."

"Okay, so a quick update. She's on her way to hospital. Simon's gone with her. Hopefully she'll be there soon. The medics were going to take ages, so we're getting her heli-vac'd to the hospital at Inca. I rang Johannes and bless him, he was running out the door as I was telling him where to go. He landed the bloody chopper right outside the front of the building. Couldn't have been any closer. They're not supposed to fly at night, but they let him go when he said it was a gunshot wound and besides there were no ambulances. They're all committed on some massive smash on a motorway on the south of the island."

He went quiet. "I'm sorry Mum, I'm ranting on a bit here. Thing is...she's not great Mum. We could lose her."

She heard the pain in his voice.

"She's tough Sam, very tough, so let's pray she comes through this," said Anna quietly. "Now, one other thing I need to know, are you okay there? Are you safe?"

"Good question. I think so, is my best answer. We've got two dead, Marsden and Álvarez, but Lily is okay physically, but I think she's pretty fragile mentally."

"Did you, or Simon....," but Anna didn't finish.

"I'll tell you more when I've got Lily safe Mum."

"Understood," said Anna. "What's your plan now?"

"I need to get out of here somehow, but there's one more guy, Finn O'Neil?"

"Yes," said Anna.

"He got away before we saw him. He's taken a car, but I don't know, I just get this feeling that he's still out there."

"Are the police there?"

"Yes, I think they must have been despatched when I called the ambulance reporting a gunshot wound," said Sam. "I'd better ring Detective Delgado too."

"What will they 'think' has happened?" said Anna.

He smiled. He grasped how she was asking the questions.

"They will 'think' Álvarez and Marsden have had some sort of shoot out and killed each other. It will look like Álvarez tried to save Lily, which is in part true, as he seems to have had a change of heart and stepped in front of Lily when he and Marsden exchanged shots."

"Was Álvarez armed then?" said Anna.

"Well he was by the time the police arrived, let's leave it at that should we?"

"Understood."

He was beginning to recognise the words she used in times of crisis, when she seemed to instinctively return to her training, despite the fact that it was over thirty years ago.

"Always calm in a crisis."

"What's that my dear?"

"Nothing Mum," said Sam. "Right, I should go and see if we're needed anymore tonight. I'll get Lily home to her grandparents, they're staying with John MacDonald."

"Do you need any more help over there Sam? I could get Tommy, or young James to fly over."

Sam thought for a moment. He wasn't sure how much use Simon would be for the next day or so. But he also didn't want to leave his mother without back-up in London, especially with Rawlings still running loose, not to mention the silent Russian partners, who might wish to throw something their way for spoiling their money laundering scheme.

"I reckon I'm fine Mum, so best we keep some eyes on you, just in case," said Sam.

"What about your kit? Have you got that safely stashed?"

"Yes, I got it out before the police arrived and we

can pick it up later. We might still have some awkward questions from the police about the guard seeing us, but we can put it down to the slight bump on his head. I'm assuming we still aren't going to tell the police everything about this case?" said Sam.

"No, I suggest it's best they think it's some sort of crime of passion. Tell them you just happened to walk in on it when you went up there looking for your sister who had gone to find Lily."

"It's a bit thin Mum."

"True, but if you stick to it, it should hold. Besides, Her Majesty's Government's representatives still see a good ending to this, but only by keeping things under wraps as much as possible. That way, we won't bring down half the construction economy apparently."

"So it's a cover-up?" said Sam.

"Well, let's just say the waters aren't clear and Martin's bosses have no desire to see that situation change, so they would be grateful if we'd...."

"Do their dirty work for them?" said Sam.

"Quite," said Anna. "National interests stretch a long way Sam and the fish here are a lot bigger than Sir Charles Groom.

"Okay Mum, you're a better politician than me. I could have done with you at some of the sticky performance group meetings I used to have sit through in the Met," he laughed.

That seemed so long ago now.

*****

Sam found Lily in a chair on the ground floor, covered in a shiny first aid thermal blanket.

"How are you doing?"

She nodded her head.

"Surprisingly okay, if you think about what's happened," said Lily.

"Lily," he said quietly. "Are you okay with what I

asked you to tell the police?"

She looked at him.

"Yes Sam, I'm absolutely okay with doing the right thing for what happened."

He smiled at her. She'd watched as he'd taken Simon's gun from him and cleaned it of fingerprints. He'd asked her if Mateo was left or right handed, before putting the gun in his left hand and squeezing the trigger to discharge another round into a pile of boxes in the corner of the room, behind Marsden.

"You're doing all that to put gunshot residue on Mateo's hands?" said Lily.

"Yes, just in case. It'll help back up your story."

He was relying on the fact that Lily could give a convincing performance to the police investigators, as a distressed and disorientated witness. He wasn't sure she'd get this past a certain DI Lori Garcia, but fortunately, Lori wouldn't be investigating this case.

He decided not to spoon feed her a story. She needed to be believable, so better to go with a half-truth. *'Hadn't his mum told him about that recently?'* he thought to himself.

"Sam, it's okay. Mateo did try to save me, so there's not much I need to embellish to the story before you and Simon walked in to find them dead and Terri…."

It was only then that Lily let go.

"She was bleeding to death Sam, bleeding to death!"

"I know, but you helped her massively Lily. She'll be at the hospital soon and getting the help she needs," said Sam.

"Will she…?"

"I won't lie to you Lily. She's very badly injured, so at best, it's fifty-fifty as to her chances, but I need to also get you to safety. There's still a guy out there and I don't know what he might try to do."

"To tie up loose ends? With me being one of those

ends?" said Lily.

"Yes, so, come on. If the police have finished with us, let's see if we can get ourselves safely out of here."

She went to get up out of the chair, before stopping.

"One question Sam. Why haven't you told the police anything about what this is all about?"

He looked at her.

"To be honest Lily, I don't exactly know, but would they believe there's a Pollensa connection to a billion pound money laundering operation? I don't know."

"So that's what this is all about? Not the Witterings Shopping Centre collapse?"

"It's partly the deaths at the Witterings, yes, but it's mostly to do with the head of a global conglomerate, trying to protect his company's good name and reputation."

"But only in order to be able to continue as a money laundering facility?"

"Got in it one Lily and his Russian partners wouldn't take kindly to losing that sort of operation."

She smiled.

"When you put it like that, I can see why you haven't told the police."

*****

Simon tried to make her as comfortable as possible. The Robinson 44 wasn't intended to carry injured persons, but it was 'needs must', as time was now very much of the essence if Terri was going to survive.

"How's she doing?" shouted Johannes.

"She's fighting mate, she's fighting, but she's lost a lot of blood haven't you my love?" said Simon.

He knew enough about battle injuries and the sub-conscious to know that even when someone looked completely out of it, they can still often hear things, so he needed her to know she still had a chance.

"Well I've told you now Terri, of my undying love

for you," he tried to smile, but he could feel the tears coming again. "Anyway, I don't think you've got anything to worry about, as I don't suppose you'll remember any of this, what with the Rohypnol. That's going to block your memory of all of this soppy stuff."

He heard her make a noise. Like a grunt. She made it again. He moved closer to her mouth.

"Not soppy stuff," she literally forced the words out of her mouth and he saw a tear appear in her right eye.

"We'll be a right couple of losers if you don't pull through this my girl, so best you stay with me. Do you hear me?"

He saw her hand move, just a little. He held it gently.

"Johannes, we need to get there!"

"Two minutes amigo, two minutes. They're ready and waiting."

54

The sun was almost coming up as Sam pulled up outside the MacDonald's villa, just south of Palma. He'd seen nothing to worry him as they'd left the Research Centre, but that didn't mean O'Neil wasn't out there somewhere.

Lily's energy seemed to have left her as soon as they got into the car. It was understandable, she'd been through a hell of a lot and done well, really well, to hold it together when they were seeing to Terri.

Terri! God, he hoped she pulled through, but he caught himself going further. He needed to stay on his game, to keep Lily safe.

"Come on Lily, let's go and see your grandparents," he gently shook her.

She opened her eyes. He saw confusion to start with, followed by her shoulders relaxing as she recognised him.

"Where are we?"

"At a friend's place. Your grandparents are here too."

John MacDonald had barely got the door open when Helen Green pushed past him and hugged Lily.

"Are you alright my child? We've been so worried about you."

"I'm fine Gran," said Lily, smiling weakly.

Geoff Green came outside and looked at Sam.

"It's been quite a night, but it's over now and what she needs now is a good sleep," said Sam.

Lily went in with her grandmother, whilst Sam noticed Geoffrey Green stayed behind.

"What is it Sam, just tell me."

"Geoff, it's a long story and please forgive me if I ask you to just go with it for now, when I say it's almost over. You'll be safe here with Mr Mac for the time-being and I'll be back to check in with you later today."

John MacDonald looked at Sam and then at his friend.

"Come on Geoff, let's go inside. Trust me when I say Sam and the rest of the guys know what they're doing."

The last thing Sam heard was John MacDonald calling out.

"Consuela, please can we have some tea?"

*****

The doctor was still in her blood stained scrubs as she approached Simon.

"Hola Señor. ¿Estás con la Señorita Anderson? Are you are with Señorita Anderson?"

Simon nodded and stood up.

"Si, si, How is she Doctor?"

She spoke fluent English.

"She is very poorly Señor, let's sit down."

Simon was immediately worried. When a doctor sits you down to tell you something, then there was a good chance that it might not be good news.

"Just tell me Doc, is she going to make it? I'm ex-forces, so I know what a gunshot wound looks like and this wasn't a good one."

"Okay, no sugar coating soldier. She's fifty-fifty at best. We've put her into a medically induced coma. I know you probably want to sit by her, but honestly there's nothing you can do, at least for the next day or so, so best you go and get some rest. You look like you can use it."

He nodded at her and shook her hand.

"Thank you, but I have to stay with her and Doctor? I know you'll do all you can," said Simon.

"We will. And oh, you must be Simon? Yes?"

Simon looked at her.

She smiled back. "She's pretty out of it, with the Rohypnol and what we've given her for the pain, but she's been saying your name."

She saw the tears in his eyes and took hold of his hand again.

"We'll do our very best, I promise."

He nodded again and stepped back, forcing a smile as he turned and started walking. He had to get out of there, to get some fresh air. He was suffocating. He got to the doors and ran through them and found himself gasping, gulping in air. A nurse was walking by and stopped to see if she could help.

"I'm okay, I'm okay, gracias, gracias."

The nurse nodded and patted his shoulders. She'd seen enough of the impact of hurt and grief to recognise what this man was going through.

*****

"How much did you hear when we were at the Centre?" said Simon, as he picked up Sam's call.

"Enough," said Sam, who was at the airport waiting for Greg's flight to land. "But first things first, how is she?" said Sam.

Simon gave him an update on what had happened at the hospital.

"Your mate, the chopper pilot? He was brilliant, bloody brilliant. I need to thank him properly."

"He's a good guy and yes, we can get back to him at some stage. He rang me after he dropped you off. I'm at the airport waiting for Greg to arrive. He got a late,

late flight out, so is due to land about now. I've spoken to him and he knows what's happened and that things are," Sam hesitated, "pretty bad."

"Good, that's good. They've told me to go home, whatever that means, home I mean. But I'm staying here mate. I'm not leaving her," said Simon.

Sam waited a moment.

"That's okay mate, we don't want her there all on her own do we?"

"I keep thinking, if ..."

"There's no future in thinking *'if's'* Simon and I should know. I've told myself a thousand times, *'If only I'd not looked at the little girl, my mate wouldn't have got shot',* but shit happens and I'm starting to accept it, so no more *'if's'*, okay?"

"Okay, I'll park it. More important things to worry about."

Sam tried to change the subject.

"So what happened to your brother?" he said quietly.

"He died in a hit and run. The driver was never officially traced."

"But I take it you found out somehow that it was Marsden, or rather Harris or Baker, whatever he called himself then?" said Sam.

"Yes, but there was nothing evidentially that would ever secure a conviction in court," said Simon. "And then he went to ground, probably with another name change, but I lost him, then I got deployed overseas."

"So with regard to what happened up at the Research Centre....," Sam started to say.

"Sam, look, just do what you need to do okay? He's got the sort of justice he deserved as far as I'm concerned. I know it might not sit well with your values as a former police officer, so I don't have a problem if you tell them what I did."

"I've done that already, that was what I was starting

to tell you," said Sam.

"Right, so that's why you took my Glock...," said Simon.

"And put it in Álvarez's hand," said Sam.

It took a moment for this to register with Simon.

"But Lily? She knows what happened. I can't expect her to...."

"She's already given the police her statement. Mateo turned into a good guy and tried to protect her from Marsden. After one dodgy shot that missed completely, he managed to hit Marsden in the leg, before he got lucky and shot him in the forehead."

"A lucky shot then? That was handy," said Simon.

"Yes, so let's leave it there shall we?" said Sam.

55

S am wasn't sure what to say when he saw Greg
walk through the Arrivals gate. So he just held
out his arms and hugged him.

"Any more news?" Greg croaked the words out.

"There's no way of making this any easier Greg. The
doctor told that Simon that it's fifty-fifty at best, but
she did acknowledge that Terri is super-fit and a strong
young woman."

"Good, that's good. I'll go with fifty-fifty. At least
she's got a chance Sam."

Sam nodded. "Come on, let's get up there and see if
you can get in to see her."

As they got to the Hyundai in the carpark, Greg
looked at Sam.

"Where's the Beetle? Don't tell me it's given up
already?"

Sam grinned.

"No, it's back at Mum's. This is Simon's hire car."

Traffic was light and it took less than an hour to get
up to Inca. Simon had been back in to see the staff to
ask if Greg could see his daughter. He didn't know if it
was them being helpful, or because of the seriousness
of Terri's condition, but they let Greg in straight away
to see her.

Sam went in with him as well. She looked so pale and he could hear her laboured breathing through the ventilation machine.

"You're her father?"

It was the same doctor who had spoken to Simon.

"Yes, thank you for letting me see her, Doctor. I know she's in a critical state, but please let me know if she would benefit from any additional medical facilities, because we have very good medical cover."

"That's good to know Señor Chambers, should it be necessary. We currently have your daughter Terri in a medically induced coma. She's lost a lot of blood, that's why she's so pale, but the good news is that we found the bullet and removed it."

She saw Greg pick up a little. Getting the bullet had been so important to improving her chances.

"We'll have to wait and see how her body reacts to the surgery. There's a fair amount of damage inside, so we're looking at some time before we'll know anything."

"But you're not giving up?"

"No, not at all, especially because as I said, she's strong and otherwise healthy."

"What else can I do?" said Greg.

She recognised the look in his eyes of a parent with a child who is desperately ill.

"If you believe in God Señor, then maybe a prayer or two? I think your daughter may need every little bit of help she can get."

*****

"Sam," Simon whispered.

"Mate?"

"Don't tell Greg, you know, about what I said to Terri."

Sam looked at him.

"Why not? He'd want to know."

"Want to know what?" said Greg, stirring from an uncomfortable sleep on the hospital benches.

Sam looked at Simon and Greg looked at the both of them.

"Guys, my daughter is lying in the room across from us in a pretty shit state. This is not the time to be keeping secrets from me."

"If you don't tell him, I will," said Sam.

Simon looked panic stricken. Greg had never ever seen him like this.

"What the bloody hell is it Simon? Just tell me man!"

Simon took a deep breath and looked first at Sam, who nodded and then at Greg.

"I love your daughter and she told me she loved me too, but I don't know if it was the shock, or the drugs Marsden put in her, but…,"

Greg looked back at Simon.

"Was that it? The big reveal? Simon, I've known you long enough to know how much you dote on her you idiot. I just wondered why you'd never said anything to her."

Confusion ran across Simon's face and Sam couldn't resist a grin.

"You knew?" said Simon.

"Of course I bloody knew. What? Did you think I'd be disappointed that some squaddie had taken a shine to my precious daughter?"

Simon wasn't sure if Greg was kidding or not, until he saw he was smiling too. It had needed something like this to break the tension. He let out a huge sigh of relief.

"Can I go and sit with her?"

"Of course you can if they'll let you," said Greg. "Sam, let's go and find some coffee."

*****

As they walked into the main reception area Sam's

phone rang, it was Detective Sofia Delgado.

"Sam, I thought I'd see how you are?"

"Sofi, I was…"

"About to call me?"

He looked up. She'd caught him out again. She was sitting on one of the seats in the hospital lobby.

"And this is?" She looked at Greg.

"Detective Delgado? Encantado, a pleasure to meet you."

Sofi had to smile. He was just as she imagined he'd be from what she'd heard from the officers back at the station. But then the smile vanished.

"Sam! I told you to keep me informed, then the next thing I hear is you're not only back on the island, but you're involved in some sort of double murder in Pollensa."

"But we're not involved, we were just trying to find our friend, Lily."

The look was enough to show she didn't believe a word he had just said.

"You're damn lucky that the witness, your friend," and she emphasised the *'your'*, "is such a convincing witness."

She saw Sam's expression.

"Oh, so you're surprised she's such a good witness? What? Even after the briefing you presumably gave her?"

Sam put his hands up. He looked across at Greg, who nodded.

"Sofi, okay, here's a fuller version. Lily was kidnapped by the two dead men because of an issue that's going on in the UK. It was the collapse of a shopping centre in London, which could have indirectly affected a money laundering operation that runs into hundreds of millions of pounds. This is what initially led to the kidnap."

Sofi sat up a little straighter in her seat.

"I'm listening."

"They tried to silence her with threats and intimidation. We think there was no initial intent to kill her, but then things changed and the guy I went to see in Canada was killed in a road accident. However, it's highly likely that it may not have been an accident."

"This was Nova Scotia?"

"Yes."

"So the unknown guy in the hospital?"

"He was part of a team that tried to grab Terri, that's Greg's daughter, who's now..." and he turned his head towards the direction of the Intensive Care Unit.

"You want me to believe you and your friend? I think his name is Simon, were not involved?"

"Well I suppose you've checked the CCTV and we'd presumably be on there if we'd have been involved?"

She looked at him.

"I think you know only too well that somehow, perhaps for you miraculously, the Research Centre CCTV for the evening has been wiped, or in some way damaged."

He looked blankly back at her.

"Except for the section that shows the two dead men hauling Lily and Terri into the basement from a VW van."

He tried the blank look again, but was pretty sure she wasn't buying it.

"You know, I should have listened better to Inspectora Garcia when she said things may be difficult in getting to the truth with you!"

"So you won't be wanting to interview us at any stage then Sofi?"

"I have a double murder and a kidnap that has been solved in a faster time than my Boss can believe, so no one is minded to find out what the real truth behind all of this may be."

"Shall I take that as a *'no'* then?" said Sam.

Detective Sofia Delgado's look suggested he shouldn't push his luck any further.

56

Sir Charles Groom was yelling out of his office at his secretary.

"Find Stephen Rawlings!"

His Head of Communications had phoned him on his way into work. There had been an incident at the Pollensa Research Centre and two men were dead. One was one of Rawlings' Executive Team and the other was an unknown member of the public.

'So who was it and who was the other man and what was he doing there?'

Groom had tried calling Rawlings, but his phone was dead. *'It wasn't even ringing.'*

"What on earth is going on?"

His secretary could hear him shouting and swearing. He was like this only very occasionally, but this had been going on since he'd walked through the door first thing this morning.

She tried all the numbers she had for Rawlings and she was either getting number unobtainable, or it just kept ringing.

"I'm sorry Sir Charles, but I can't find him."

He'd known her long enough to know that if she couldn't find him, then it meant that Rawlings had gone to ground.

"Thank you Liz."

He sat down in his chair. He could usually tell when something was wrong. He just had a knack, a sixth sense that something had happened, or was about to happen.

He had that very feeling now.

57

Anna didn't recognise the number on her Stevens Bank phone when it rang two days later.

"Fiona Stevens."

"It's Penny Hastings, Mrs Stevens. Mr Makarovich would like to see you again, today if possible?"

"Do you know what it's about Penny?"

"I'm sorry I don't Mrs Stevens, but he mentioned something about lunch and he's asked me to book a table for one o'clock at The Ritz."

"Well that sounds very nice. Tell me, does he usually do this for business meetings?"

"No, Mrs Stevens and perhaps if I can prevent the need for a further question, no, he doesn't have any sort of female companion at the moment."

"I'm flattered, but do you really think it is just a lunch date Penny?"

"I don't know for sure, so I would suggest you make your usual support arrangements."

Anna smiled. She had been right. Penny Hastings was the source Martin Carruthers had spoken about and she clearly knew exactly who Fiona Stevens was.

"Thank you Penny. Do you have any messages for anyone else?"

Anna thought she should check if she could pass anything on to Carruthers.

"Not for the moment Mrs Stevens, but it was a pleasure to meet you, as I've heard a lot about you."

"Right, well tell Mr Makarovich I'd be delighted to have lunch with him and I'll see him there."

Makarovich had suggested he'd collect her from The Savoy, however, Penny was concerned that would put Fiona Stevens, or rather Anna Martínez, in a vehicle from where she could be taken anywhere.

"A wise move if I may say so Mrs Stevens."

"Thank you Penny. I hope to meet you again someday, perhaps soon."

"I would enjoy that as I feel my position here may well be coming to an end in the very near future. Goodbye for now."

Anna had been under cover for over a year once, but ten years! Penny Hastings, or whatever her name really was, had been under cover as Makarovich's secretary for a very long time indeed.

*****

Since Greg had gone to Mallorca to be with Terri, Anna had stayed laid up at The Savoy, waiting for the call she'd been expecting to come from Makarovich.

She was now on her way to Piccadilly, to The Ritz, with Tommy never more than fifteen steps behind, as she walked from The Savoy to her lunch appointment with Oleg Makarovich.

"I think a walk will do me good," she'd told Tommy before she'd set off. "It'll get some fresh air in my lungs and some sun on my face."

"So you think he just wants lunch? There's nothing else sinister about this?"

"That's what I'm thinking, but better to be safe than sorry and have you and Sharon's team as back up."

It had been an expensive option having Sharon

and her team on standby for the week, but Greg had insisted he wanted support in place for her whilst she remained in role as Fiona Stevens.

The doorman at The Ritz saw the elegant woman approaching and stepped forward to greet her.

"Good day Madam, welcome back to The Ritz and how can we help you today?"

She smiled. She liked the 'welcome back' reference, making the assumption she was a frequent visitor.

"I have a lunch appointment with Oleg Makarovich."

At the mention of the name, the doorman came slightly to attention.

"Mrs Stevens, please come this way."

'This man has so much power and influence,' thought Anna.

Tommy saw her go in and he took up a position where he had a view of the entrance. He then caught sight of another woman walking towards him from the Green Park Tube Station.

Very attractive, well dressed and he guessed she was in her early thirties. She had a pair of big sunglasses on, together with an equally big sun hat.

She seemed to notice him as she lowered her sunglasses a little and smiled. He smiled back as she turned and walked in through the hotel entrance, where he heard her receive a similar greeting from the doorman.

There was something about her.

'Had he seen her before?'

He heard Sharon's voice in his ear.

"What are you looking at Tommy? Looks like your tongue's hanging out your mouth?"

He grinned.

"She was pretty, that's all. I think I've seen her somewhere before."

"She looks way out of your pay league my boy," said Sharon with a laugh.

There were various other rumblings from other members of the support team who were all located in and around the nearby area.

Tommy laughed.

"Focus team, focus please."

'Back to the job in hand me thinks.'

*****

Oleg Makarovich had decided to invite her to lunch for no other reason than he enjoyed her company.

She was a very smart, intelligent and yes, still very attractive woman. Business was done and so why not take a moment to enjoy at a nice lunch.

"Fiona, thank you so much for coming at such short notice. I've ordered champagne."

She could get used to this life style. It wasn't hard to be enjoying this side of the role she was playing, but she knew she had to keep her wits about her.

"It's a pleasure Mr Makarovich."

"Oh, I think Oleg will do fine Fiona."

"Okay, thank you Oleg."

And it was just lunch. He didn't refer at all to the business they had worked on the previous evening, which in some ways made it harder for Anna, because she had to keep to her back story, which was at best, light.

But he enjoyed talking, so she focused on his background and his family, which fortunately, he was happy to talk in depth about. She also noticed the amount of champagne he was drinking. He wasn't drunk by any stretch of the imagination, but he might have lowered his guard.

"I know we weren't going to talk business Oleg, but something came in overnight about Global Aggregates that I thought might be of interest to you."

She might have underestimated his capacity for alcohol, because she saw his expression immediately change.

"What might that be Fiona?"

"They seem to be drawing some attention from the FCA."

"Why would the Financial Conduct Authority be showing any interest in GA?"

"Yes good question Oleg and at the moment, it's just speculation, but there's a rumour that the Health and Safety Executive are going to re-visit the Witterings Shopping Centre investigation. But perhaps a slightly more worrying concern may be the whisper that the Prudential Regulation Authority may be looking at the UK operations of your bank, the OBCR."

Anna had already spoken with Martin Carruthers about whether he could arrange for rumours to start circulating about the HSE and a possible approach by the UK banking regulators to the OBCR.

She saw a coldness appear in Makarovich's eyes and she felt the hairs on her neck start to flicker. He was right on the edge of controlling his emotions and she saw, really for the first time, a side of him that perhaps went some way to explaining, how he had gone from being a mid-ranking intelligence officer in the Russian Security Services, to acquiring a business portfolio worth billions.

"I'd like to know how you have access to such information Fiona."

She smiled back at him. This could go either way, so she glanced around to see who he may have close by. She could see his usual security detail, two men back in the lobby area.

"Oh Oleg, you know I can't go giving away my trade secrets."

She kept smiling at him and slowly she saw him

relax.

"Well, if you won't tell me who, then I'd at least grateful if you would keep me posted on those two issues."

"Yes, of course, now look at the time, forgive me Oleg, but I really must be going as I'm going to meet some old girlfriends. I hope that's okay?"

"Yes, yes, of course."

She left him, looking as though he was deep in thought, which with the two bombs she'd dropped on him, he most probably was.

58

Whilst Groom had been unable to track him down, Carruthers' team had eventually found Rawlings. He was spotted at one of the addresses they had for him. It had taken a couple of days and a lot of resources, which he was getting a lot of flak for from above. But Chambers had said it was important and Carruthers felt he owed him something, especially because of what had happened to his daughter.

Tommy and Sharon's team were now set up around a smart block of flats in Surbiton. They had people watching the entrances in OPs, observation points. One at the front and one for the back, ready to call up when they saw any movement.

It was 7.30 am and three days after Groom had last heard from Rawlings when he finally came to the surface again.

"OP1, I have a male, leaving the front door, wearing a baseball cap and dark coloured jacket. Pretty sure it's him, so definitely worth a look guys."

"Mobile 1 copied. Yes, we've got him in sight. He's walking, turned left and heading towards the town. Get the footman out and let's have a good look at him shall we?"

"Oscar 4, I'm on foot. Contact time in twenty seconds, just crossing the road. He's twenty yards away. Going silent."

They waited until the footman had passed the man. He wouldn't transmit anything until he was a good distance past to ensure he wasn't heard.

"Oscar 4, yes, a good likeness. He's got some facial hair, about a week's growth, but I'd say it's him."

"You're buying breakfast for a week if it's not him Jonny!" said Sharon, the team leader.

"Mobile 1," said Sharon. "Make your move."

The van pulled up alongside Rawlings. He thought later that it was a text book manoeuvre and as soon as he heard the door sliding back, he knew he had to fight, or give up as he was immediately boxed in.

He went for 'fight', but they were good. Especially the big black guy, Caribbean by the sound of his voice, as he heard him say, "Get down and stay down," as Tommy punched him hard in the kidneys from behind.

*****

They'd only driven to a house about a mile away. It wasn't overlooked and it had a secluded driveway.

Rawlings was now sat on a wooden chair, legs and wrists strapped to the chair, but with no eye, or mouth cover.

After they'd grabbed him, he'd been compliant. There were too many of them, so he thought it was now better to just wait and see who was going to come through the door.

It had to be one of two people. Either Greg Chambers, or Mikhail Makarovich.

It was something of a relief in some ways when he saw Chambers walk into the room.

"Feel familiar to you Rawlings? This was how you held Lily Green wasn't it?"

Rawlings looked at him.

"You had to screw things up, didn't you Chambers? You couldn't leave it alone could you? You had to keep digging, even though you knew it was me and yet, after all I did for you, you still wouldn't let go. Bugger all thanks for me dragging you out of that bloody hell hole in Bosnia. Fine bloody mate you are!"

"You know Rawlings, one thing you and I have never been and that's mates," said Greg. "I can go with colleagues, as we did very occasionally work together, but we were never in the same outfit, so mates? Oh, God no. Not then and not even after you admittedly saved my arse. But please, do not try and make this some sort of *we're mates, so let me off this like a good lad*' thing."

Rawlings looked at him. He was trying to buy time, to see where this was all going. He knew that Chambers realised that too, but he had to try something. He wasn't prepared to sit in some cell for ten years or maybe more, once the whole story was out.

"Look Greg, it was just business and I never told Marsden to hurt your daughter. He was a bloody loose cannon and I couldn't control him."

"You knew what he was like and you turned a blind eye to whatever he did, especially if he produced the goods."

"And what? You've never had to do stuff you didn't want to? It was something that had to be done. Think back to Bosnia my friend."

Greg tried to convince himself that things were different then. There was a war going on, but he'd had sleepless nights since then thinking of some of the things he'd had to do, supposedly in the name of *doing the right thing for Queen and Country*'.

"Yes, I can see what you're thinking Greg," said Rawlings. "You probably have the same nightmares I sometimes get too. There were things we had to do back then and we tell ourselves we were on the side of

Right. I know all that. So I swear to you Greg, I never meant for him to shoot your daughter, or even get her pushed off the cliff in Mallorca. Things just got..."

"Out of hand? I promise you Rawlings, if my daughter dies, it's you I'll come looking for."

Rawlings picked up on what he'd just said. A slow smile started to appear. They were going to make a play for him.

"What's going on here Greg? What do you want?"

When Carruthers told him that he'd locate Rawlings for him, it came with a proviso. Carruthers wanted information. Information on Groom that maybe only Rawlings would have. *'The bigger picture'* he'd called it. As much as Greg might want to inflict extreme pain on this bastard, the person he saw as having 'overall responsibility' for what happened to Terri, he'd given his word to Carruthers that he'd get the information from Rawlings.

Greg recalled the conversation. He'd been sat at Terri's bedside when Carruthers had phoned to tell him they'd located Rawlings.

"So he gets off Scot-free in exchange for giving up Groom?"

"Yes Greg, *'the bigger picture',*" said Carruthers.

Now, as he was saying it out aloud, Greg knew the *'bigger picture'* didn't matter anywhere near as much as the daughter he had lying back in a Mallorcan hospital on a life support machine. But he'd given his word.

"You have one chance to get out of this Rawlings. To get out without me putting a bullet in your head, or doing ten years in prison."

But Rawlings now knew he had a negotiating position. Chambers, or more likely someone else, wanted something badly enough that they were giving him a chance to walk away from this.

"Will I get this in writing?"

"Not a hope in hell."

He expected that, but it was worth asking. So he pondered who it might be who wanted the information.

"Is this HMG asking for the information?"

Chambers looked at him. He wasn't about to answer a question like that, but it was giving Rawlings time to think.

"Deniability," said Rawlings. That would explain why he wouldn't get anything in writing.

Chambers pretended not to hear him. He knew it wouldn't take long for Rawlings to figure out who was really asking the questions.

"I want to know what you have on Groom."

"And the Witterings Shopping Centre collapse?"

"Partly, but more to the point, his relationship with Oleg Makarovich."

So that's it, thought Rawlings. *They're going after Makarovich through Groom.*

"And for this, I get a free pass?"

Greg had been involved in many of these situations in his service career with MI6. He'd had to let people walk, in exchange for critical information. But they'd never harmed his daughter. The words were sticking in his throat as he forced them out.

"Yes, a free pass."

"Better untie me then and we'll make a start shall we?"

59

G reg was sat with Anna in Martin Carruthers' office. Carruthers had just said they could use the knighthood as leverage.

"But I must remind you that Groom is not the primary goal."

"So if he plays ball, he'll be allowed to quietly drift away to an island somewhere, knighthood intact?" said Greg.

"Yes, but before we go on, tell me, how is Terri? Any change?"

Carruthers could see the strain on Greg's face.

"No, she's just the same, or I should say, she's still stable. That's what they keep telling us. Stable is good apparently."

"Still in the medically induced coma?"

"Yes, it's been a couple of weeks now, so they're hoping her body is doing its own magic and helping the recovery process."

"It's a remarkable thing, the body, Greg. Let's hope we get some sign of improvement soon."

Greg nodded. He'd left Simon out in Mallorca. Simon had barely left her side since it had happened. Sam in turn was looking after Simon, keeping him fed and watered, although he looked a bit of a mess. Sam was also keeping tabs on Lily and her grandparents, who had now moved back home after Sam had a good quality alarm fitted.

Greg had felt he was going crazy, just thinking about Terri and it was Lori who had pushed him into having a break and going back to London.

"I think you need to get away for a bit my love. Go and sort out the thing you were doing before. Give yourself something else to think about, then come back refreshed and see how she is then. Simon's looking after her and she's still got a long way to go at the moment."

Lori had been right of course and Anna had told him the same, saying she'd wished she'd been able to focus on something else when Luis was slipping away, to give her mind a break from the sorrow of it all.

"Come back to London and we'll sort out Groom and Makarovich," Anna had said and now they were listening to Carruthers telling them that Groom was essentially being allowed to get away with it.

"It's a cover-up Martin. Those people killed in the Witterings collapse deserve better."

"And they will get justice Greg, I promise you. But don't let your anger, at what's happened to Terri, cloud your view here."

Anna changed the direction of the conversation.

"Martin, you say that John MacDonald is agreeable to Trent MacDonald fronting up a takeover of GA?"

"Yes, the Minister spoke to him yesterday."

"This really is being driven right from the top then?" said Greg.

"Yes Greg, it is. We'd all love to see Groom get his public come-uppance, but it won't actually help achieve the main aims of removing a major source of money laundering and get justice for all of those who died, and I include Kevin Cox's family in that."

Greg heard Martin use the word 'aims' – at least this wasn't all about business. The dead and injured, not to mention the families Marsden had intimidated, were all still important and so was his darling daughter.

*****

The plan was to see Groom and Makarovich at the same time. Anna would need a meeting scheduled with Makarovich, but Greg was going in unannounced, knowing where Groom would be, from the tracker they'd had on his car for a while now.

Anna had already phoned Penny Hastings, Makarovich's secretary, before they met Carruthers, to set up a meeting to coincide with Greg seeing Groom.

"Mrs Stevens, a pleasure once again. I haven't told Mr Makarovich yet, but I'll be leaving my position with him shortly," said Penny Hastings.

"Do you have anything else in the pipeline?" said Anna.

"Not yet, but I'm open to possibilities, including foreign travel."

Anna already had plans in mind to put to Penny once this was over, but for now, she needed the appointment with Makarovich.

"Can you make it for lunch time this coming Wednesday?"

"Yes, I can move things around and I'm sure he won't mind."

"I suspect he might do after we've met Penny, so be ready to move once he leaves to see me."

"Of course Mrs Stevens," she said, as Oleg Makarovich walked past her towards his office.

"That was Fiona Stevens sir, she has an update on your investments and another proposition to put to you. Shall I book lunch?"

"Please do Penny."

He'd seen some payments were filtering through

from Stevens bank already, of funds that had been flushed and were being returned to him as 'clean money'. This was working very well and he'd been able to update his associates with much better news than he had for some time.

*****

Greg had seen from the tracker data that Groom had gone to the GA Canary Wharf offices at his usual time the following Wednesday.

"Can I help you sir," said the young man on reception.

"I'm here to see Sir Charles Groom."

"Do you have an appointment sir?"

"No, and I don't think I'll need one. Please just phone his personal secretary and tell them Greg Chambers from 3R is here to see him."

A moment later, the receptionist directed Greg to a lift that had only three buttons. Basement, for the car park, Ground, for the reception and GAE, presumably for Groom's private executive office suite.

He pushed the GAE button, the doors closed and he felt the lift gliding smoothly up the thirty odd floors of the office block. As the doors moved apart, he stood slightly to one side of the lift. He wasn't expecting anyone to come at him firing all guns, but better to be safe than sorry.

He stepped out of the lift and saw a young woman across the hallway.

"Mr Chambers? Sir Charles will see you now."

He followed her into an office where he saw Groom standing by a full length window, looking out on to the City.

"Magnificent, isn't it? One of the major financial centres of the world's economy," said Groom.

"Or, one of the major centres of financial crooked and double dealing? Depends on your perspective as to

430

what's fair in the world of commerce, don't you think Charles?" said Greg.

"It's Sir Charles to you, you jumped up security guard."

"Oh, didn't you know Charles? Her Majesty hasn't yet decided whether to revoke the honour she previously bestowed on you."

He saw Groom flinch. His business was about to collapse and he was responsible for the death of innocent people, but all he was really worried about was his knighthood.

"Her Majesty? I think you mean those bureaucrats running scared in Whitehall, who jump at any chance, for a newspaper headline to boost their votes," said Groom.

"Well, you may have a point there Charles, but whichever way you look at it, you're back in the cheap seats with the rest of us," said Greg.

"Oh, I think you and I both know I'm a long way from that Chambers. I might lose my title, but I'll be able to slide away to the Caribbean and live pretty comfortably I should think."

"Well that's just it, isn't it Charles. I'm not so sure you will. Oh, you won't be destitute. I'm well aware you have far too much squirrelled away in off-shore accounts to not go too short. However, be aware that I bring a message from HMG that they intend to chase and hound you for 'every single penny' they can track down and as of now, you will find all of your UK assets, including your cash holdings, are all frozen."

Groom looked stunned.

"You can't do that. They can't do that."

Groom started walking towards him. Greg put a hand firmly up in front of him.

"Do not even think of doing anything Groom. Nothing would give me greater pleasure than to break something on your miserable body, so don't give me a reason."

Groom stopped in his tracks. He hadn't known what he was going to do. He wasn't that much older than Chambers, maybe five years, but he was in no way a physical match for him.

"Rawlings told us the complete story and we've now had a new HSE Report on the flawed Ultra-Fast-Dry30 concrete formula. It confirms the cover up regarding the new fast drying concrete you tried in the Witterings site. Plus, we've had the original owners of the other three developments, where UFD30 was used, come forward and make statements about the coercion and intimidation you used to enable you to buy up and demolish those sites."

"Look, can't we be reasonable Greg?" said Groom, trying a different tack. "There must be some sort of deal to be worked out here? I mean, even if you seize everything I have, Global Aggregates still belongs to Makarovich and the rest of the Board."

"A deal? What could you possibly negotiate with Charles? As you said, you only own five percent of GA and at the moment you're looking at corporate manslaughter, financial irregulation charges, not to mention coercion and of course, the even more serious charge of conspiracy to murder."

"That was all Rawlings! I never told him to murder Cox, or your daughter."

"My daughter's not dead," said Greg quietly.

"Quite, quite, and I sincerely hope she survives as well."

He couldn't stomach this man's bleating any more, especially when he mentioned Terri. He closed his fist and punched him in the stomach.

Groom was doubled over, gasping and his secretary came running to the glass door. But Groom waved her away, shaking his head at her. He didn't need the police down here as well.

"Makarovich. I could give you him, on a plate."

Greg waited for him to continue.

"But you must protect me. You know he'll come after me."

Just at that moment, Greg saw a red dot appear on Groom's immaculately starched white shirt. He motioned to Groom who looked down at the dot.

"What the...?"

Groom didn't get the words out before Greg threw himself at him, knocking Groom flying, before he grabbed him and pulled him behind a solid brick wall.

A quarter of a mile away, on top of an office block visitor viewing point, Tommy smiled and put the high powered laser pen back in his pocket and walked to the lift.

Groom was gabbling.

"I've got audio and video recordings and a copy of all the transactions that shows where the money went. It's all on file, but I need protection, I'll pay anything you want."

"How much are we looking at?"

"What? A bribe?" said Groom.

"No, you idiot, the money laundering. How much has been going through the company?"

"Hundreds of millions," said Groom, "and that's every year since we took GA back into private ownership."

"So that's why you needed to keep the real reason for the Witterings collapse under wraps, to protect the company reputation?"

"Yes, if we lost that, Makarovich would lose his money laundering operation and he'd made it quite clear what would happen to me."

"Nothing to do with protecting your own lifestyle

and your status then? Five people died Groom, plus thirty odd others were injured."

"Regrettable, but it was just business."

"The girl, Lily Green?"

"We needed to know if she'd found something out."

"Why ask her to look at it in the first place?"

"To be seen by the Health & Safety Exec to be trying to help. It was Paul Brooks' idea. She was just supposed to say that the concrete cover level was fine, but I never realised for one moment she'd find something about UFD30 in the damn files. It was just very unfortunate."

For a moment, he wished it had been a sniper's rifle out there trained on Groom. He wanted to hit him again, but what was the point?

"Give me the files on Makarovich, now."

Groom went to a wall safe. Opened it and took out a USB and went to hand it to Greg.

"I need your assurance that I'll be protected."

'Enough of your self-interest whinging,' he thought, and a right hook caught Groom square on the nose, dropping him to the floor.

He walked across to the door, where he saw Groom's secretary reaching for her phone.

"Don't! He's not worth it."

She gave him a slight nod and he saw her put the phone back on the cradle.

He turned back into the room.

"Okay Sir Charles, this is what you're going to do."

60

Penny Hastings had booked lunch at The Connaught in Mayfair. Once again, Anna met him there, rather than being collected by his car.

Sharon had already been into the restaurant and was satisfied with the cover she and her team could provide to Anna.

This wasn't a time to take any chances and so Tommy went with Anna in the black cab.

"How do you think he'll react?"

"Well, if I can sell the message, then I think he may actually end up thanking me for getting him out of a scrape, but I guess we'll soon know."

Tommy played the part of a security guy, jumping out of the cab and opening the door for her, before he followed her in at a discreet distance, but close enough for Makarovich to notice him.

The waiter came and they ordered lunch and he chose champagne again.

"Fiona, a pleasure, but tell me, why do you have a security guy with you today? Nothing I should be concerned with is it?"

She looked at him with a slight grimace.

"Sadly, yes. We've picked up something from a number of different sources that suggests all is not well with Global Aggregates."

He was immediately on his guard.

"Tell me more Fiona. It troubles me that you seem to find these things out before my own analysts."

"This isn't about who finds out first Oleg, but what I can tell you is that your GA investment is about to plummet. The HSE are all over Groom. They've reinvestigated the Witterings collapse as we thought they would and found Groom to be not only liable, but that he's conspired to hide the truth. He's ruined Oleg and GA is about to go down the tube."

She spoke quietly to reinforce the confidentiality of the discussion, so she wasn't prepared when he let out something in Russian, which by the sound of it, must have been an extreme profanity.

"I also have it under very good authority that the British Government are closing in on Groom. He could lose his knighthood, even go to prison and that means they'll be looking at you too."

"Let them come, I have British Residency."

"I would imagine they are already looking at that Oleg. Have you heard anything from the banking regulators? Have they made any approach to OBCR yet?"

She knew they hadn't, but by throwing in the word 'yet', she wanted him thinking they would be soon.

"No, nothing, as you say yet. I don't see how they can roll me into whatever it is Groom has been involved in. I'm just an investor."

"That may be so, but whatever your current holdings are with GA, well very soon they're going to be worthless."

He had something close to a billion pounds tied up in GA in either cash, that was being cleansed, or investment that provided a good source of return.

Losing a billion pounds would hurt his overall

wealth, but not significantly. However, it was more the impact on his position with his associates that was a concern.

She saw her moment.

"Unless," she waited to see if he'd bite.

"Unless what Fiona? What are you thinking?"

She waited until he had moved forward in his seat. Yes, he was ready to take the bait, he had to be.

"The British Government will not want GA to collapse if they can avoid it. It's a big British success story and it will severely impact on the London markets if it does go belly up. So maybe, just maybe there's a deal to be had."

"How, or rather, who with?"

"I might be able to pull something together, but I can't promise you will get anything like your billion pound investment back, but," she paused, "what if I could get you, say £300 million cash, plus you'll still have what I'm holding for you."

A thirty to forty percent write-off wasn't particularly appealing, however, it was better than losing everything and it gave him the opportunity to save some face with his associates.

"Okay, make the arrangements. I'll tell Groom this afternoon that I'm selling up and he's on his own from now on."

61

Two weeks later, Martin Carruthers was outside Henry Fielding's office, waiting to be called.

"Martin, sorry for keeping you."

"No problem Henry, I have the update you requested on Makarovich."

"Good, so where are we?"

"There will be an announcement in the business papers later this week concerning the takeover of Global Aggregates by Trent Macdonald, the engineering conglomerate."

"Run by John Macdonald isn't it?"

"Yes Henry, soon to be Sir John MacDonald by all accounts, for services to British industry."

"Well deserved too. How much?"

Fielding gave the impression of a slightly slow, old school type of chap, but he was razor sharp and little got past him.

"Just the fees and travel costs for Chambers' outfit, 3R, together with the bill for The Savoy, a string of pearls and some rather nice clothes we had to buy for Anna Martínez and her son."

"How did you manage that Martin? I remember seeing a good few hundred million quid swashing around one of our bank accounts at one stage?"

"Yes, that was Makarovich's money. We used that to pay him for his share of GA, although obviously he didn't realise that at the time. With the deal Anna Martínez put in play, we actually ended up with a hundred million spare."

"I bet the Treasury will be very happy to receive that," said Fielding.

"Yes, no doubt. We've heard that he's clearly not very happy and he's busy trying to track down the mysterious Fiona Stevens."

"Without any success I hope?"

"No, she's safely back in Mallorca, together with a new recruit for 3R."

"Ah yes, I heard about that as well Martin. She was a bloody fine agent, but I'm glad we've got her out in one piece. I think Penny, or rather Lara, will do very well with 3R."

"One thing, Henry."

"Rawlings?"

"Yes, we let him go, but suspect that should Chambers' daughter not pull through, then either Chambers, or Simon Barnes, will go looking for Rawlings. Do we need to intervene?"

Fielding considered the question for a moment.

"No, I don't think so Martin. What will be, will be."

*****

"John, or rather Sir John, it's so good to see you again," said Anna, as he greeted her at the door to his villa.

"Oh Anna, if only Sheila had been alive to see all of this. Lady Sheila! Ha! She'd have loved it, the pomp and circumstance. That was all her thing."

"I know, but she'll still be looking down and chuckling, proud as punch of you."

He grinned.

"Not bad for a boy from the East End."

"No, it certainly isn't. Now, I just wanted to say thank you for stepping in and looking after the Greens. I know things went on a little while longer than we expected, but it was very good of you to help keep them safe and out of harm's way."

"It was no problem at all. In fact it was nice having people here, now that the boys are back in London. So what about you? Are you back on the island for a while then? No more adventures lined up?"

"No, just a local book festival that Sam had started to arrange before all this happened, so I'm looking forward to that. What about you?"

"Well the GA takeover is keeping me busy. I'm back in London for two or three days a week working on that, but it's going well. I've got rid of Brooks, the Research Centre Director. He had far too many secrets tied in with Groom for me to trust him with anything going forward, but at least it's freed up some office space and I've bumped Lily's boss, Ian Parsons up to Temporary Director, to see how he gets on."

"A local office for you then," she grinned. "But make sure you don't overdo it John, let those boys of yours earn their money."

"Ha, yes I will, but in fairness to Groom, it's basically a very good outfit. They were running with such a high cash balance in their accounts that we've had plenty to use to sort out a compensation package for all the victims of the Witterings.

"We're flattening and rebuilding the entire Witterings site. It was in need of redevelopment anyway, so I've got Roger Wall back in as a consultant to oversee the project. And we've revisited the deals for Roger and the three other guys Groom forced into selling up."

They talked more over a pot of tea Consuela had brought in. Whilst he wanted to ask more about the 'hows and whys' of what had happened, he knew she wouldn't, or couldn't, share such things with him.

"Who'd have thought Anna? That you'd be back doing this sort of thing after Luis had passed?"

"Indeed John, who'd have thought it indeed?"

*****

The day after the announcement in the Business Press that Global Aggregates had been acquired by Trent MacDonald, the men who made up the group of Makarovich's business associates were sat at a table in the Board Room of a Moscow office block.

"So that's a unanimous decision gentlemen?"

There were nods around the table from the most powerful of people outside of the President's innermost circle.

"This is a difficult day for the Association, however, he's brought it on his own head and must face the consequences. What about his son?"

A short discussion followed, but there was little interest in pursuing any sort of retribution towards Mikhail Makarovich.

"Good, if that's everything? I shall make the arrangements. Meeting closed."

*****

The Russian received the message through one of her encrypted email accounts.

She called the number where the instructions and payment were confirmed and agreed.

She had carried out similar work for them before and as with some previous assignments, they sometimes indicated a preference as to how the task should be completed.

Occasionally a gunshot to the head was requested, to make a point. But often, as with this task, they asked for it to be done quietly, but to ensure the message was still very clear to all, as to who had arranged the hit.

Radio-active material, such as Novichok, is often the assassin's preferred choice of poison, but the Russian also used VX. The most dangerous known chemical nerve agent in existence, first discovered in the 1950's in British laboratories, she found it easy and safe to use, at least from her point of view, with a woman's perfume atomiser.

*****

Two days after the Press release about Global Aggregates, there was a message on Martin Carruthers' desk:

INTEL REPORT - UNCLASSIFIED

Oleg Makarovich collapsed and died at 23.00hrs yesterday, following a party on his luxury super yacht, currently moored in Monaco.

Initial police reports are inconclusive, however, the use of poison, possibly a nerve agent, through some sort of spray, is not being ruled out. The boat has been put into quarantine until tests are complete.

Party goers apparently noticed Makarovich with an East European woman, described as 'strikingly attractive,' before he seemed to collapse for no apparent reason. She has not been seen since.

Until recently, billionaire Makarovich was the majority investor in Global Aggregates before it was acquired by the Trent MacDonald group. The police are not linking the two events.

62

I t was eventually four weeks later when they finally got to get together at Contrabando. With Terri in hospital, it was a more restrained evening than the last time they'd all been together, but they still got the same warm welcome from Miquel and his team.

Sam had tried to get Simon to come out for the evening, saying it might do him good, as he was still spending every day at the hospital with Terri. But he decided against it, even when Sam had pressed him.

"I'll be rubbish company mate, so thanks, but I'd rather not."

Sam looked across at Greg. He looked like he was holding up okay, but he was quieter than usual, although he had relaxed a little when Lori had arrived on the island.

What had happened to Oleg Makarovich had been in the press and they talked about it at the table.

"Carruthers told me it was a nerve agent, a particularly toxic one. British made of course," said Greg.

"He wasn't the first of the business associates to disappear after what they called a *'performance issue'*," said Lara Cook, formerly Penny Hastings, the latest member of the 3R International team.

"Who are these mysterious assassins who wander the world, taking on contracts? Maybe it was the same person who took out Sonny?" said Sam.

"The news reports said it was a very attractive woman. But you guys never saw who shot Sonny did you?" said Sharon. "Or, maybe it was the same woman who distracted you, when we were at The Ritz Tommy?"

She looked at him and everyone else's eyes followed her.

"Listen, I was just checking my surroundings that's all. I was sure I'd seen her before, so yes, I was distracted, but just for a moment and for proper operational reasons."

"Sounds like you protesteth too much Tommy," said Sam, with a laugh.

"Was she like the one who *'distracted you'* in Barbados?" said Sharon with a grin.

Tommy's face stiffened.

"Bloody hell, you know what? I think it was. Do you think that's her? The assassin?"

"Who knows?" said Sam. "But Sharon's right, we never saw who it was in Goa did we? We just heard the shot."

Miquel joined them with another bottle of Ribas de Cabrera.

"Guys, come on, assassins, gunshots, you'll be scaring off my customers," he laughed.

Lori was holding Greg's hand. Together with Sam, she'd been trying to keep everyone's spirits up, but it was hard. Terri had been in the medically induced coma now for well over a month and the hospital had said they needed to talk to Greg. He knew they were going to ask him about trying to bring her out of the coma.

Lori spoke quietly to him.

"Have you had any more thoughts on what you're going to say?"

Greg looked down at his wine glass and then back into her eyes. He knew the risk was that Terri's body wouldn't be able to deal with it. Lori could see the tears were forming. As much as she knew Simon wasn't dealing with things well, Greg's brave face wasn't hiding his hurt either.

"You had to do it for Felipe didn't you?"

She'd told him when they first met. Her husband, also a police officer, had been gunned down fifteen years ago in an ambush by the criminal gang he was investigating.

"Yes my love, I did. He was on life support too, but there was no hope, no hope at all for Felipe, so I let him go. But this is different, There's at least a chance, that's what they've said isn't it? She has a chance, but they have to see if her body can stand it."

"I can't, and they won't, leave her like this, just existing. They've said her body has had enough time now to do its thing, to self-recover. So now we have to see what happens."

The table had gone quiet. Miquel, who had come back to refill the glasses, was standing quite still. Everyone was just taking in the seriousness of what Greg had been saying.

Greg looked around the table at his friends and family.

"This is possibly the hardest decision I have ever had to make in my life, but I think I need to see if my little girl can keep going on her own."

There were nods around the table and lots of tears before Anna spoke, "She's strong and tough Greg, so give her the chance you know she'd want you to give her."

He nodded.

"You're right, I know this is the right thing to do."

THE END

BOOK THREE

"**S**am, it's Tony Theakston."

"Tony, good to hear from you, but can I please call you back? This isn't a good time."

Sam was at the hospital in Inca with Greg, talking to the medical team about Terri, Greg's daughter.

"I just need you for two minutes. I promise, I wouldn't ask if this wasn't urgent."

Sam took a deep breath. Tony was his old boss and he'd been a great friend and mentor and now Head of Security for an international art gallery.

"Okay, of course. What's up?"

"I've got a ransom situation on the go."

"What's been stolen?"

"Nothing, at least not yet."

"Go on."

"Let me start by saying that we don't think it's a hoax. We've been told to pay £10 million by tomorrow, or lose a picture to that value from one of our galleries."

"If you don't think it's a hoax, then that suggests you have some other intel on this Tony?"

"This isn't the first time we've had this. It also happened twelve months ago. We didn't pay up then, or at least, not until a picture was stolen. We then paid the original ransom, plus a fifty percent mark-up, to get it back. We had to, it was on loan from another gallery."

"Why are you ringing me?"

"Our insurers suggested you, 3R International that is. We need this dealt with sensitively, because if galleries start finding out we're losing artwork, then we'll never get anyone to loan us a collection again."

It was the first of three things. All unrelated, or at least, that was how it seemed at the time, but all would have major consequences for the 3R team.

*****

THE POLLENSA
CONNECTION
LOCATION TOUR

I included this page in The Mallorcan Bookseller, after I had such a lot of interest from readers about the locations I used, so I've done the same here.

I wanted to highlight some of the great restaurants and cafes I have found in Mallorca over the years, so please go and find them. You may get to speak to the actual people in the book! I know they will all give you a very warm Mallorquin welcome.

As before, I have listed most of the specific sites from Mallorca and the other countries below, so you can see and experience the locations where the 3R team have been during this adventure and who knows, you may just see me there too!

Mallorca
Contrabando Tapas Restaurant, Llucmajor
Quina Brasa Restaurant, Llucmajor
(Contact: Miquel)

Bar Bonys, Puerto Pollensa
(Contact: José)

Coral Bar Restaurant, Puerto Pollensa
(Contact: Aina and all her family)

The Lighthouse Cafe, Cap de Formentor, Puerto Pollensa

Gustar Restaurant, Placa del Banc de l'Oli, Palma de Mallorca (Contact: Fidel)

HeliXperiences, Palma de Mallorca (Contact: Johannes)

London and Wokingham, UK
The Savoy, Strand, London
The Ritz, Piccadilly, London

Ruchetta, Wokingham
(Contact: Angelo)

Barbados
The Fairmont Royal Pavillion, St. James

India
Trèsind, Bandra Kurla Complex, Mumbai

Wolfville, Nova Scotia
Just Us Coffee Shop, Main Street, Wolfville

REVIEWS AND TYPOS

Book reviews are the life blood of all authors and so finding out what you thought about my book is really important to me.

Whether you have been given this as a gift, or purchased it new or from a charity shop, or perhaps you've borrowed it from your local library, please can I ask you to take a moment to submit a review on Amazon or goodreads.com

Finally, the book gets checked and treble checked by lots of people, but sometimes errors still slip through! Please email me with any typo errors you see and we'll get them quickly changed.

Please join The 3R International Series Facebook Group to find out more about me, my books and when the Book 3 is coming out!

Thanks again for reading my book.

Pete Davies
Email: petedavies01@hotmail.co.uk
PS. You can also follow me on Instagram
the_mallorcan_bookseller
and The Mallorcan Bookseller Facebook page

ACKNOWLEDGEMENT

My huge thanks once again to my growing army of helpers across the globe, be they proof readers, location hunters, early reviewers, or language advisors.

Special thanks to Deborah and Carolyn Shaffner for their help with the locations in Nova Scotia and the RMCP procedural detail and also to Johannes of HeliXperiences, Palma de Mallorca for all of his help and advice on the helicopter scene.

I also want to thank the restaurant and bar owners, who go along with my crazy requests to get them somehow involved in the storyline.

A few final words of thanks to two special people:

To my wife, Julie, for her love, support and not to mention her amazing patience in answering my constant stream of questions on grammar and choice of words.

To my cousin, Brian Tarr, for his massive support in trialling and producing images and backgrounds for Palma de Mallorca and Puerto Pollensa. I'm so pleased to be able to have Brian as part of this design process.

THE 3R INTERNATIONAL SERIES

An exciting action crime series set primarily on the beautiful island of Mallorca, featuring the 3R International team, where Greg, Anna, Sam and Terri find themselves drawn into complex crime adventures where danger is never very far away.

The Mallorcan Bookseller

"Is Anna in?"
It took just three words to change his life.

Sam Martínez, a London detective, is put on sick leave suffering with PTSD resulting from a firearms incident that went wrong and his best friend was shot.

Going home to Mallorca, where he grew up, he helps out in the family bookshop. But before long, he finds himself caught up with helping a family friend who has fallen prey to an IT scam.

When another scam victim is murdered, Sam finds he has to learn to play by a new set of rules and a different type of justice when he goes up against a ruthless boss of an Armenian organised crime gang.

ABOUT THE AUTHOR

Pete Davies

Retiring after a thirty year career in the British Police Service, Pete had held a wide variety of operational and training roles, including being a firearms commander.

In 2012 he started a new career as an executive coach, working with clients within the public, private and voluntary sectors before committing to writing full time in 2020.

Enjoying the beautiful island of Mallorca for many family holidays over the years led him to base his books on the island.

Pete lives with his wife and their Labrador in Berkshire, England.